BB BRADFORD

AND THE SANDS OF FATE

C. M. VOGELSANG

ISBN-13: 9798399268132
ISBN-10: 1477123456

Cover design by: Dave Hotstream
Library of Congress Control Number: 2018675309
Printed in the United States of America

EPIGRAPH

Few will have the greatness to bend history itself; but each of us can work to change a small portion of events, and in the total of all those acts will be written the history of this generation.

ROBERT KENNEDY

CHAPTER ONE

Fame's Enticement

"What do you think you're doing? Give me that knife!"

The eighth grade class turns to look at Parker standing next to a block of stone. His name is carved into the wall, the wall in the lobby of the Washington Monument.

"Shame on you! What possessed you to do a thing like that?"

"Don't get yourself all worked up, Mrs. Hardin. It's just a stone. It's not like I've killed someone!"

"Well you've certainly stabbed history in the back!"

A tall, strong man dressed in a National Park uniform strides toward the group. The teacher panics. This is only their first day in DC. The whole class could be kicked out of a national monument. Banned from the buildings and memorials. Fined for damages. And she has no reason not to take the blame. After all, he is her student, her responsibility. But she's not expecting the ranger's reaction:

"Now let's not get too upset. It's not like he's the first to come up with the idea."

He points to a Civil War soldier's carving in the same block. He steps in front of the teacher and turns to address Parker:

"Who knows? You might even be famous some day, just like this fellow David Hickey. People will see your name carved here for years to come. Let's think about this. George Washington has *his* name all over this city. For that matter, all over the country. You're part of the monument's legacy. You're now part of its history."

A confident smile breaks over Parker's face:

"I think you're right. My name *should* be here. After all, people will want to know that *I* was here. Today. In fact I'll just add a quick date, if you don't mind."

The ranger continues to support the boy's decision to deface the wall:

"Might as well finish it off right."

Shocked by the ranger's attitude, Mrs. Hardin stands helplessly by as Parker returns to his desecration and continues chatting with the ranger:

"I'd like your opinion on something our teacher wrote on the board this year: 'George Washington was *not* our greatest president.'"

The ranger immediately turns to Mrs. Hardin:

"That's ridiculous and certainly not true!"

"For goodness sake. I did that to stimulate a discussion. To encourage the students to discover facts and arguments against it. To show that it *wasn't* true."

Parker feigns innocence:

"Well, *I* took it as fact. I've been wondering about it ever since, waiting for the opportunity to ask a *real* expert on history."

He throws a sarcastic smirk at his teacher while the ranger berates her:

"As an educator you need to be more careful about what you're teaching our young citizens. You can't feed them lies!"

He returns to Parker:

"It's obvious you have a discerning mind. Good thing you're keeping an eye on your teacher. With your perceptions *you* could be an excellent teacher. Or maybe you might like my job. You could even run things there."

He points to the Capitol.

"Or even there!"

He points to the White House. With these grandiose ideas swimming in his head, Parker turns to address his class:

"Maybe I *will* be famous some day. I just have to figure out how to make it happen."

He looks to his close friends with their good looks and trendy clothes.

"What d'ya say, guys?"

The squad of sycophants is quick to pour on the flattery:

"You bet! But don't forget your pals when you strike it big."

The ranger takes Parker aside:

"You really know how to handle people. The city's yours, kid. We… uh *you* need a little more time. You're young now, but we can work with you to make it happen. When you're ready to really make your move, we'll be in touch."

The ranger hands Parker his card. It feels strangely prickly and cold in his fingers even on this hot, sticky DC day. The ranger smiles enticingly:

"Take a whiff."

Parker inhales deeply:

"What's that smell? It smells like leather and a new car and....

"That, my friend, is the smell of success!"

The vapor rising from the card takes control of Parker. Unknowingly he has come under the spell of The Abyss. Suddenly he's thrown off balance when his foot sinks slightly in sand beneath his shoe.

"Hey! What gives?"

But no one notices. He pulls his foot from the sand and continues walking. When he looks back he sees a solid block of marble where he'd been standing. He tucks the card into his wallet while the ranger calls after him:

"Keep it in a secure place. You don't want to lose it."

And under his breath:

"Actually you *can't* lose it."

The ranger congratulates himself:

"We've got another one."

He turns to two ravens perched on the white information building.

"You tell them I want credit for this one!"

The messengers take flight and disappear from sight. The ranger calls to Mrs. Hardin:

"Before you leave, I want to get a picture of you and your wonderful class in front of the Washington Monument."

Mrs. Hardin calls out names and arranges them in height order:

"Taller kids in the back. What are you doing Parker?"

"I want people to see *all* of me, not just my face."

His buddies cheer him on as he takes a muscle-flexing, one-knee stance in front of the group. The ranger snaps the photo, capturing Mrs. Hardin's annoyed face.

"What a great group of kids! Lots of leadership! I'm due for a break from my post. Why don't I take you down to the Lincoln Memorial."

His generosity takes Mrs. Hardin by surprise. Somewhat flustered she accepts his offer. As Parker stands up, his foot sinks into a pool of sand, this time farther up his ankle. He jerks forward as his foot releases.

"What's going on? There's a sand hole back there. I almost sank into it!"

But when his buddies go back to check, there's just the concrete sidewalk.

"Maybe all this *fame* is making you a little dizzy, Parker."

"Don't say that!"

"Just kidding. You've got this fame stuff figured out. Sure you do!"

CHAPTER TWO

Sinking into Sand

The class passes the World War II Monument and strolls along the reflecting pool to the Lincoln Memorial. The ranger actually wasn't being generous. He wants to be sure his recruit is firmly pointed in the right direction. He watches Parker carelessly drop a power bar wrapper on the walk next to the pond. A government worker nearby sighs and leans over to pick up the litter. Parker spots the back end of the man and "accidentally" shoves a smaller classmate into him. The man tumbles into the water with a yell and comes up drenched, water dripping from the bill of his cap. He stands there briefly and then slogs his way to the edge of the pond. Mrs. Hardin returns in time to see the innocent boy offering to help the man out of the pool.

"Lucas, I'm so disappointed in you."

"But I didn't do it. Parker pushed me into the guy. It wasn't my fault."

"Is that true, Parker?"

"Me? What? Oh come on, Mrs. Hardin. Just ask my friends. I was nowhere near him."

He turns to his trusted pals who immediately back up his story. But he's not finished:

"Hey! Check the sign: NO TRASH IN THE POND! There's MAJOR trash in the pond!"

He points to the dripping wet trash collector, still standing up to his knees in water. This gets the laugh he was looking for from his friends, especially from the girls in his group. Mrs. Hardin looks over to her students, the defeat evident in her slumped body, her downcast face. She grumbles to herself, mulling over these recent events:

"You don't know where you're headed! You're choosing the wrong path – what you only think *is important. I thought these kids were Rock Stars! How could I be so wrong? And now they've become my worst nightmare."*

Out loud she laments:

"This has to be my worst trip ever!"

Parker suddenly appears at her side:

"Actually, I think this worked out pretty well for me!"

She turns to the ranger:

"He was my best student. What have you done to him?"

"If truth be told, I just polished up some of his own qualities a bit."

His sinister chuckle sends a chill down her spine.

"Ma'am, I believe your bus is leaving."

Under his breath he congratulates himself:

"It's over! I've won again!"

Meanwhile Parker continues to stir up his friends, ridiculing the hapless trash collector. But his laughter stops short when he looks down at his right leg sinking up to his knee in sand. Frantically, he yanks it out and lurches forward, shaking off sand and the uneasy feeling in his stomach. He now realizes he alone is witnessing these events.

The disturbing scene pulls back until we see The Bond Council deep in the chambers of their headquarters viewing the previous events in a giant hourglass. The top portion shows the actual physical events taking place. The lower section reveals the spiritual reality of what is transpiring. The three Council members plus the Director grow more alarmed as they watch a foot... and then a leg... drop down into the lower half.

CHAPTER THREE

The Bond Confers

Sergeant Striker: "What did he expect? Typical obnoxious kid."

Agent Allen: "I don't understand it. All our data pointed to him. He was the perfect, obvious choice: smart, good looking, leadership qualities. What didn't we see?"

Lady Grace: "Oh this is too hard to watch. What's his future?"

Director: "It's clear what his choices will lead to."

The leg continues to drop down, and then a torso, until the boy's entire body is engulfed in sand. In the top part of the hourglass you can see him struggling to keep his head above the swirling particles. His hands desperately grab at the sides of the collapsing hole as his foot touches a descending stairway. On the steps various young figures look down at what lies ahead for their souls. Some regretfully search upward at missed opportunities. Words carved into the steps reveal their choices: Entitlement. Greed. Dishonesty. Vanity. Self-Indulgence. Disrespect. Cruelty. Pride. Arrogance. Cynicism. The scene fades. The Director quietly murmurs:

"We lost another. This isn't The Bond's plan. There's no joy in this latest downfall."

Striker: "What's wrong with these kids? How can they keep making these terrible decisions? Can't they see what's happening to them?"

Director: "Actually no. Even though their souls are dying, their lives continue the same. In fact many of them will prosper, according to the world's standards. Their physical bodies will continue for the usual life span. But they're really blank spirits in this world. Their existence will never matter in the course of history. The Abyss is working to make sure that this group, this generation, will never be remembered... for any reason... good or bad. It will be as if they'd never been born."

Lady Grace is in tears by now. She can't forget the harrowing scene. But then compassion overtakes her horror:

"Are they all lost? Is there no hope for them? Are they wiped out forever?"

The Director shakes his head: "I can't tell you that. Only The Bond knows."

Striker: "Things can't be as bad as you say. We're stronger! The Bond's on our side!"

Lady Grace: "Certainly there's hope!"

Agent Allen: "The data concerns me. Perhaps a margin of error we haven't assessed."

Director: "You need the vision I've been shown. The view into the future that has me so worried."

Personal holograms swirl from the agents' bodies and materialize in front of them. The Director sends these images to the top of the Washington Monument where they have a 360 view of the capital. His voice speaks from Headquarters:

"Look all around you. Keep turning. This is the spiritual reality of what's at stake."

The city is rimmed with ominous billows of churning steel grey clouds. The agents feel the dark foreboding pressing down on DC. Invisible to the ordinary eye, around the perimeter of the city a roiling bank of towering black pulses and steadily encroaches on the blue canopy overhead. Red glows within the darkness, and lightning flashes the message of impending doom. A counterforce strains to hold all of this in check. The agents fight against their rising panic, sensing the imminence of a final attack. The Director's voice continues:

"The Bond says our window of opportunity is closing. You see those clouds of The Abyss circling the city? The skies continue to appear blue for those who don't have our power to see. They have no clue what's really happening in our world. Until now we've been able to push the boundary back or at least prevent those clouds from advancing. But lately they've been gathering strength. It's like we're spitting into the wind! When those angry, boiling masses converge over the capital, our cause is lost."

The Director recalls the holograms to Headquarters with his dire warning:

"Without our next recruit, our mission will be set back for years, decades, perhaps even centuries. The soul of this generation and the generations it will give rise to will be corrupted not only here but around the world."

The three Council members grow increasingly alarmed and agitated.

Striker: "Those eighth grade classes are worse with each group. The Abyss agents are everywhere! And they're winning! This is war!"

Agent Allen: "The Abyss keeps taking them down, and the kids are oblivious!"

Lady Grace: "They always seem to know or guess which one we're after."

Striker: "Yeah. We need to be more careful. Not tip our hand so quickly."

Lady Grace: "I still think we're picking them too young. They're too impressionable."

Director: "It's The Bond's decision. They're perfect recruits because they *are* impressionable. We need those years to mold them into true believers before they turn 18 and come of age. Remember what happened when we waited too long to choose the last one. He'd already picked up traits we didn't identify until it was too late to turn him back."

Agent Allen: "I can't imagine what went wrong this time. What *keeps* going wrong! We've done everything humanly possible. All of the research and analytics have pointed to each one we've chosen. We have to trust the data!"

Lady Grace: "I feel we're missing something."

Director: "The other directors tell me they're in the same situation."

Agent Allen: "I've seen the other countries' assessments too. It's a pandemic!"

Director: "They're looking to us to stem the tide. Stop the spiritual slaughter of future generations. The battle begins here and now!"

Striker: "Right! We're the final line! If we break, all is lost!"

Director: "We have just one more new moon before the end of this school year. One more chance before we're too weak to push back against The Abyss. In the meanwhile we need to be thinking more carefully about our targets and why we keep squandering our opportunities. Why The Abyss keeps winning."

Striker: "We need a warrior! A winner!"

Director: "I hear you. And I agree with part of what you say. We *do* need a win! The enemy is laughing at us, waiting, as they say, to deal the final blow that ends it all."

Striker: "It's not our fault. We lose them before they move on from the Washington Monument! We're outmaneuvered, especially by that ranger. Who is he anyway?

Agent Allen: "I've been doing a little research on that particular park ranger. There was something not quite right about him."

Striker: "That's obvious."

Agent Allen: "No. I mean *really* not right. Check out this picture I took of him."

Striker: "Yeah. Sharp looking dude in uniform."

Agent Allen: "Look closer. At his badge. I'll put up another picture I got from the park service's website. Notice anything unusual?"

Striker: "Same old shaggy bison. Wait. What? Is that it?"

Agent Allen: "Exactly. The bison is facing the wrong way. He's not a real ranger."

Lady Grace: "Typical of The Abyss to be so close to the truth and yet full of lies."

Striker: "I wonder. Did it start with this guy or maybe earlier? Maybe the bus driver? We need to be more proactive. Get into the game!"

Director: "I didn't tell you this before. I didn't want you any more discouraged than you already are. The Bond has just received an ultimatum: Five more years, maybe even fewer. And then surrender! We cannot, I repeat, *cannot* let this happen!"

Lady Grace: "Well, I'm ready to give it my all. If this is our last hope, we can't sit back and watch The Abyss consume the soul of the human race."

Agent Allen: "The analytics indicate we're up for a girl next."

Lady Grace: "Which reminds me. What about our last recruit, the one who's still out there waiting for a new partner to replace the one who was turned. Thank goodness we didn't lose them both!"

Agent Allen: "That one's stuck in a geographic time chamber and can't get back to us. The two of them were in California when the breakdown occurred. That one's not aging and has to keep relocating to avoid detection."

Striker: "We have to at least attempt a rescue!"

Director: "Sorry. That's not The Bond's plan. We're too vulnerable when we expose our identities out there. We need to rely on the ones we send out, no matter how young they are. They're the best influencers. What's the status of that one?"

Agent Allen: "The last word we had, that one had time hopped to the spring of 1963 in order to escape detection. Our final communication said we could connect in hidden valley, or maybe it was *a* hidden valley."

Lady Grace: "California has so many valleys, I don't see how that's any help. But we *can't* give up, sir."

Director: “Time to focus. We have less than twenty-eight days to plan our strategy. We can’t afford a miss this time.”

Throughout this debate a light beats behind the far wall. What appears to be a plain white wall are actually interlocking blossoms of alabaster. The stone wall’s pattern and translucence are revealed whenever the light glows, manifesting The Bond’s strength and affirmation. When they are weak, that’s when The Bond is strong.

CHAPTER FOUR

Recruit Hopefuls

The sun's first rays cut through the mist like a blazing sword. A huge jet-black VIP tour bus races toward Ronald Reagan Airport, weaving in and out of the early morning traffic. Two soaring ravens shadow the vehicle far above. The wind current ruffles their wings' feathery fingers. Behind the wheel, a powerfully built man struggles to pull on his uniform jacket and adjust his cap. A brooding scowl dominates his features and warns the casual observer to beware. This is someone who doesn't suffer fools.

"You told me Dulles and then you switched it to Reagan! Can't anyone make a decision around here?"

In his ear bud a voice comes through loud and clear:

"Watch your opinions! The flight was diverted at the last minute and we just found out. You cannot, I repeat, *cannot* miss your pickup. You have to intersect and beat them. Their bus and driver are also on the move. If they were responsible for the terminal change, we can't win. If not, we have a chance."

The bus driver's chiseled body attests to his physical power. His massive muscles strain against the fabric of his shirt. As the bus careens around a corner, he spots a man pacing up and down the sidewalk, anxiously searching the incoming vehicles. The driver pulls up in front of the sharply dressed man and a group of kids waiting expectantly, their luggage lined up in a neat row. The ravens silently swoop down to perch on a light pole that arcs over the sidewalk. A voice continues in the driver's ear:

"This is the last eighth grade class to visit the capital this school year. The Bond has assured me it's one of these kids. Keep a close eye."

"With all due respect, how am I supposed to know which one it is?"

"Don't worry. You're on a 'need to know' basis."

The driver opens the bus door and steps down to the sidewalk where he's greeted by a flurry of accusations. He and the teacher have a terse back and forth:

"About time you got here. We're on a schedule you know."

"Sorry about that. Couldn't be avoided. Change of airports."

"I hope this isn't how our trip will continue. You *will* be on time from now on?"

"Absolutely!"

"Actually, I'm not sure if you're the company I hired. I was expecting a school bus."

The driver smiles uneasily, not used to being spoken to with such disdain:

"Uh, well... our school buses are all... uh... in the shop getting overhauled. The company had to lease this one special."

The teacher gives him a curious look, but regains control of the situation. He extends his hand and announces in a commanding voice:

"I'm Mr. Bateman. This *outstanding* class of eighth graders has come all the way from Escondido, California, to learn about and enjoy our great country's capital city."

He shakes the teacher's hand, at the same time measuring him up. This man could be either an asset or a liability, depending on how the days ahead play out.

"Pleased to meet you, sir. Name's Sam. I'm your driver in DC. I'll keep track of our time and scout out the best hours to visit each site on your list. Just leave it to me."

Sam lifts the luggage compartment doors on the side of the bus. Overhead the ravens let out a guttural crackling noise alerting him to their presence.

"By the way, warn your kids to watch their snacks. No telling what might swoop down and steal them."

As Sam begins to load the luggage, Mr. Bateman takes a count of his students.

"We're two short. Who's missing? I don't want to go through the whole class list."

Random voices call out:

"It's Jessica. And BB."

One kid snidely interjects:

"Ooooo... Jessica and BB!"

"Stop that, Nick! Don't you *dare* say that about my best friend! She's got better things on her mind. Don't mention the two of them in the same sentence ever again!"

"Oh, don't get all bent out of shape, Monica. I'm just teasing."

"Yah... well... just stop!"

Sam assures Mr. Bateman that he's got the situation in hand:

"Don't worry. I'll go find them. You just get the rest of the kids in their seats."

Sam hurries to the baggage area and speaks quietly into the cuff of his sleeve:

"So far so good. I'm ready to start the weeding out process. I've got our criteria memorized: intelligent, charismatic and attractive, with leadership skills. We want other kids to look to him or her for direction and confidence."

Meanwhile at the luggage carousel, the missing students, Jessica and BB, watch the few unclaimed pieces go round and round. Barely over five feet tall, BB is what you'd kindly call a late bloomer. From top to toe his outfit screams "Store Brand!" His general frame would earn him the wiry label. With the added metal braces on his teeth he is the epitome of awkward. Even worse is his unruly, sandy brown hair complete with a handful of cowlicks that refuse to be tamed.

BB can't believe his good luck. Here he is... alone... with Jessica, one of the most popular girls in his class, both searching for their bags. She desperately hopes each one that falls from the chute will be hers. But he's relishing the moment. He's just close enough to catch the scent of her freshly washed blonde hair. He closes his eyes and sighs. Suddenly Jessica blurts out:

"What if they've lost my luggage? I had everything perfectly planned for each day... my clothes... my shoes. This can't be happening! My life is ruined!"

Tears start to well up in her eyes. Her wails jolt BB from his reverie:

"I'm sure it'll show..."

"Oh shut up! I wasn't talking to you. As if I ever would."

At that moment her huge, flowered suitcase lands on the moving belt. BB rushes to help her with the heavy bag as it passes by. She grabs for the handle and BB lifts the other end. Together they set it on the floor.

"And if you think this is going to make me like you or even talk to you, you're mistaken. In your dreams, BB!"

"But I was just trying to... help."

His voice trails off as he watches Jessica roll her bag toward the exit, without so much as a glance back in his direction. BB grabs his bag that has finally appeared, pivots on his heels, and slams right into a brick of a body. His eyes slowly count the shirt buttons upward to stare into a pair of glowering eyes.

"You part of the group from California? Everyone's already loaded and ready to go."

BB scans the photo ID tag for a name. His voice squeaks out, straddling at least two octaves:

"Yes sir, Mr. Sam!"

The man barks back:

"It's just Sam!"

BB races to the bus, hoping he hasn't already got off on the wrong foot with Mr. Bateman. He watches Sam effortlessly swing Jessica's flowered suitcase into the last hold. He opens his mouth to comment, but Jessica steps in. Her voice drips with honey-coated admiration:

"Oh, my! You're so strong! Thank you *so* much for coming to rescue me in the terminal, mister bus driver."

She flashes him one of her best smiles. He tips his cap:

"That's Sam, Miss. At your service. I'm always ready to help when needed."

Hoping to make up for the trouble he's caused, BB starts to lift his bag.

"I'm really sorry I'm late. I didn't think my bag was ever coming."

After his exchange with Jessica, Sam's growl has softened to a gentler tone:

"No problem, son. Let me get that for you. That's my job, you know."

"Thank you, sir. You've got a cool bus! I thought we'd have just a regular school bus."

BB climbs the bus steps and is immediately greeted with a jeer from Nick:

"'Bout time you got here, Lame Brain!"

The other kids join in the laughter, calling out insults and jabs.

"What a loser."

"We shoulda left him back in California."

No one bothered to save him a seat. His two buddies, Josh and Mike, are in back, trying to fit in. They don't dare go against the ridicule he's facing. The only seat left is behind the bus driver. Mr. Bateman raises his voice above the hubbub with a firm reminder:

"Enjoy those phones and your other devices for the duration of this drive. Before you leave the bus, I will be collecting them all."

Groans erupt all around.

"Enough complaining. We will be looking *up*, not down at a screen! Remember the agreement you signed before we left. You know the rules. The seats you're in right now are yours for the next two and a half days while we're in DC. I don't want to waste time whenever we get back on the bus. Sam will be our driver for this part of the trip. Follow any further instructions he gives you."

A voice shouts from the back of the bus:

"Sam? As in *Uncle Sam*? Hey, Uncle Sam. We want YOU to be our bus driver!"

Two boys in the back dissolve into laughter at their own cleverness. Jessica steps in:

"Stop that, Nick! Show Sam some respect. After all, he's the one responsible for getting us to all of the sites in DC."

She calls to the front of the bus.

"I'll take care of these guys, Sam. They don't dare cross me! Right, boys?"

"Anything you say, Jessica."

The two boys obviously want to keep on her good side. She clearly knows how to use her social status. Mr. Bateman affirms his approval:

"Thanks, Jessica. I know I can always count on you,"

She looks up at him through the fringe of her long lashes and delivers her sweetest smile. Giving her hair a well-practiced fling, she walks toward the front of the bus and settles in next to her friend Monica, who congratulates her on her latest maneuver:

"Nice going, Jess. You've already got this bus driver figured out. Plus Mr. Bateman, one of your favorite teachers to manipulate. He's never going to catch on."

CHAPTER FIVE

Undercover Deceit

BB searches through the grey-tinted window for the first sign they're really in DC. He leans forward, his excitement bubbling over.

"Excuse me, Mr. Sam, I mean Sam. Where are we going right now?"

"After that red-eye flight from the West Coast... sure hope you got some sleep... I'm starting at the heart of the capital. The Washington Monument."

"Already? Did you know that nothing in DC is higher? It's five hundred and fifty-five feet tall and took forty years to complete!"

"Hmmm... Is that so? How do you know so much about it?"

Sam is only half paying attention. He's preoccupied with the scene that took place at the back of the bus and is focusing on Jessica as a possible candidate.

"Our teacher wanted to be sure we had some basic information on everything we'll be seeing. But I looked up lots more on my own."

BB proudly holds up his journal binder with color-coded tabs for each monument.

"We get graded on our participation plus the research we did before the trip. I got some great facts. I printed off the pages yesterday before we left. It's perfect!"

Sam isn't listening. He's pretty much dismissed this kid as a possible recruit. After all, just look at him. And with a name like BB, it's clear he isn't going anywhere.

(Actually BB's real name is Heybert B. Bradford III. Who names a baby that anyway? Well, if he's the "third" you know there were at least two other little boys who'd had to grow up dealing with that name. Most of the kids and teachers at school just call him BB. "Hey! Bert!" is an old joke by now. He tries not to react. It only makes things worse. He doesn't really mind his name. His dad and grandpa use "Bert" and so does his little brother. But when his mom calls him Heybert, it's a soft celebration in his heart.)

"Where'll we go after that?"

"After what?"

"The Washington Monument!"

"Ya know, you'll just have to wait and see. I need to concentrate on my driving."

BB settles back in his seat and sneaks a quick look at his classmates in the rear view mirror. Some of them used to be his friends ever since first grade. They were always together on the playground and after school playing all kinds of games and sports. But ever since middle school, no one's been interested in those things anymore, except for Mike and Josh. The rest of the guys hang out and talk about girls and the coolest clothes and shoes.

Now it's the "bad boys" who rule. They make fun of him when he gets excited about things they're learning, especially in history class. All of his ideas are "lame." They've changed and turned on him. He'd tried to fit in, sometimes even pulling off some stupid pranks at school that everyone thought were funny at the time. But it never got him far. Besides, he didn't want to get into serious trouble and lose the respect of his teachers. The kids all have their own groups now. And they never include him. Seems like he's always on the outside looking in.

BB sets his journal on the seat beside him. Every student has the same binder with pages to complete before and during the trip. BB followed all of the requirements exactly, even adding extra information. The only direction he's failed to follow is the same one he's always forgetting. He hasn't put his name on his work.

One row back on the opposite side of the bus, Jessica has been listening to the exchange between BB and the bus driver. She nudges Monica and then slides her journal out of her backpack. She waits until BB stares out his window and the bus driver is concentrating on not missing his exit. Then she quickly exchanges his journal for hers, which she hasn't bothered to put her name on either. Why should she? It's as blank as the day Mr. Bateman handed them out in class. She whispers to her friend:

"Give me your gel pen, Monica!"

Artfully she applies her name to the cover of BB's completed journal plus some hearts and flourishes for good measure. No boy would even think of claiming ownership of such an elaborately decorated binder. Meanwhile BB shakes away his melancholy thoughts and tucks the journal lying next to him into his backpack. There he finds an envelope with two notes inside, one from his dad:

Be respectful and helpful.
This is a time to learn.
You will remember this trip for the rest of your life.

His mom's has a gentler tone:

Keep your eyes and ears open.
Show your appreciation for what people do for you.
Please and Thank you!
But most of all... HAVE FUN!

His folks are right. With a determined grin, he turns his eyes to the passing scene.

"There it is!"

But no one hears him or sees the gleaming white obelisk that pierces the azure sky. The two ravens fly ahead of the bus, high enough to avoid detection. Sam brings his hand to his mouth, pretending to stifle a cough. Instead he murmurs into his sleeve:

"We have a solid candidate. I want the team's confirmation, but it looks promising."

CHAPTER SIX

Frustrated and Foiled

"First stop. Washington Monument. Everybody out!"

Sam hangs back in his seat to wait for the class to exit the bus. Mr. Bateman's voice rises above the clamor and the idling engine.

"Just a minute! Everyone stay in your seats! Sit down!

He strides to the front of the bus and turns to speak to the class.

"A few reminders before we leave. Keep in mind the hours we spent learning about the places we'll be visiting. Make the most of the time we have. I'm looking for excellent cooperation from you all. Stay with the group. Line up immediately when asked. Pay attention to whoever is speaking. Look up, not just around."

He pauses for their full attention. His voice rises to a higher purpose:

"I want you to understand how much it cost to get to where we are as a country. You have a responsibility for future generations. And as I constantly tell you..."

The whole class joins in with a loud singsong voice:

"History is people! We are history!"

"Remember. This is a time to learn. It is NOT a vacation!"

Groans slide out of several in the class as they stand and begin to move forward.

"Don't forget. All devices go in my bag as you leave the bus."

The groans are louder and longer. Mr. Bateman motions BB to follow him down the steps. With a quick thanks to Sam, BB hops to the pavement and walks toward the monument. Jessica is right behind, but when she steps down it's into a swirl of sand.

"What gives? Don't they ever sweep these streets?"

But the rest of the group steps to a solid pavement. She dismisses the anomaly as no big deal and sweetly calls to her teacher:

"Mr. Bateman, would you like me to get the group together for you?"

Her teacher dismisses the bus driver and turns to Jessica:

"That would be great. Get them lined up and I'll check in with the park ranger."

There are actually two rangers assigned to the class. Both offer to let the other take time off, and both insist on staying. One is Agent Allen. He recognizes the other as the ranger with the fake badge. He'll have to stay ahead of that one, especially if they're both after the same target. Mr. Bateman addresses the group:

"Class, we're getting a special treat today. We have not one, but *two* rangers who will share information about this monument."

The rangers begin the orientation with some basic facts and then move on to more obscure questions to test the class. Mr. Bateman proudly assures them his group is more than ready:

"Don't worry. I have students I know have done their homework."

BB gets out his binder for the first questions. But when he opens it, the pages are blank.

"Mr. Bateman, there's something really wrong here. All my work is missing!"

"What's the problem, BB? You're holding up the class."

"Look! Look at my binder!"

"It looks to me like you didn't spend any time on your research. I'm really disappointed in you, BB. I just hope the others won't let me down."

Jessica quickly steps up with her stolen portfolio:

"Don't worry, Mr. Bateman. I know how important history is to you."

She gestures to the class:

"As it should be to all of us. I did some extra work to be sure I could share some interesting facts with the class. Of course *you* will know all of them already."

"Jessica, I'm so proud of you. Look everyone. Everything neatly printed out and labeled. Good job!"

"But that's *my* binder, Mr. Bateman! I did all that work!"

"Seriously, BB? Since when do you decorate your binder with hearts?"

This gets a laugh from the class.

"Jessica's name is clearly on the binder. What name is on yours? Oh. None. Typical."

He turns to Jessica:

"I apologize for this accusation, Jessica. You deserve better than this."

Just then Mike and Josh rush up to BB.

"What happened to all that research we were doing? Mike said you were almost finished a couple of days ago."

Mike jerks the binder from him:

"What's going on? Where's all that work you showed me? You had lots more than either of us. How did Jessica end up with your binder?"

BB hangs his head in defeat:

"I don't understand any of this."

"Well, *we* know you did it. And you can still impress everyone with the facts you've crammed into your head. You can still beat her at her game."

At least he has the comfort of knowing his friends believe him. But BB knows they don't have any more credibility with Mr. Bateman than he does.

The scene at the monument continues. Each ranger competes to ask more and more challenging questions. Jessica completely dominates the answers, checking the notes in BB's binder and boldly proclaiming the facts. Her friends cheer her on with applause, and the rangers smile in amazement. Before long they invite her to stand next to them so the others can hear her better. Of course BB knows the answers too, but he's drowned out each time. Finally he's pushed to the back of the group, where he mumbles his responses to himself. At last the fake ranger holds up his hand to get everyone's attention:

"This has been one of my finest days. We often get intelligent eighth graders, but I don't believe I've ever witnessed knowledge like this from such a young person."

Agent Allen isn't to be outdone:

"Absolutely. This young lady certainly deserves some sort of recognition. I hope her teacher is planning to give her extra credit for this fine effort."

Mr. Bateman nods in agreement. Meanwhile the fake ranger returns from his office with a hardcover book, its leather binding slightly worn from years of use. Agent Allen is caught completely by surprise:

"Where did you get that? What is it?"

"You don't know about the book? I guess they didn't think you were important enough to recognize the future leaders who come our way. Jessica, I'm honored to ask you to sign your name in our special leadership book. Other names on these pages are famous people who've gone before you. They got their start as eighth graders right here at this monument. With me."

"This is *such* an honor!"

"In addition, as a reminder of this occasion, I have a special Presidential Certificate signed by the President himself. I'll write your name on the line and it's all yours."

As she finishes her signature, she turns to the others with a dazzling smile she'd often practiced in the mirror for just such an occasion:

"Fellow classmates. I humbly thank you for your support. And I encourage you as we continue this trip in our nation's capital to turn your attention to these experts..."

She gestures to the rangers.

"...who have so much to offer us as we begin our lifelong journey to become active citizens of this great country."

The others shower her with admiration and congratulations. She joins her good friend Monica and murmurs:

"How was that?"

"Maybe you laid it on a little thick, but Mr. Bateman was beaming the whole time. Looks like you added another one to your collection of adoring fans."

They smother their laughs behind their hands as their teacher joins them.

"Monica, you should be proud of your friend Jessica. She has given our school the recognition I always knew it deserved. We're off to a great start to our trip thanks to you, Jessica."

"You know, Mr. Bateman, without your inspiration this year, I never would have realized just how important all of this history actually is. I owe all of this to you!"

Just then BB calls out:

"Mr. Bateman, did you know you can see the Jefferson Memorial from here?"

"Yeah. I guess you can. We're heading over there our last morning. If we have time."

BB is intrigued by the classic structure. When the rest of the class moves on without him, Josh and Mike hurry back:

"BB! Snap out of it. You're not going to make points with Mr. Bateman if you keep getting lost in your daydreams and fall behind."

CHAPTER SEVEN

Flying Below the Radar

BB keeps a low profile for the next few days. His classmates dismiss him as just space filler anyway and ignore his finer attributes. Although he's no standout athlete, he likes sports, baseball and soccer especially. And he's a good runner. His eager smile and inquisitive nature have always made his face light up in a friendly sort of way. But lately, most of the guys in his class have been perfecting an indifferent, need-to-look-cool attitude that doesn't match up with his outlook on the world.

BB has a mind that can remember the oddest facts and statistics. But even that doesn't seem to be an asset on this trip. He's also the kind of kid who's always looking for what's coming around the next corner. Many of his teachers in grade school and some in middle school have appreciated his curiosity and courteous, helpful spirit. But it's obviously become a liability with his peers. Thank goodness for his two close friends who are just as socially clueless.

Meanwhile Agent Allen is rethinking his strategy. From all he's seen and heard, Jessica's qualities rise far above those of her classmates. She's a natural standout. But he's been outmaneuvered in his recruitment efforts. He's sure, based on what he's observed, that this girl is his target, but the fake ranger keeps stepping in. Agent Allen brings his wrist to his face and speaks quietly:

"I'm not making any headway. It's obvious we're after the same subject. The team's going to have to step it up. I can't follow the class everywhere."

Striker's voice breaks in:

"I'll touch base with the girl when she's on the bus and keep an eye on the opposition. Lady Grace, they'll be stopping at the Smithsonian on the last morning. I hope you've got something planned that will clinch our decision."

The rest of that first day includes a walk through the World War II Memorial area, along the Reflecting Pool, and up the steps of the Lincoln Memorial. Jessica continues to share her abundant, stolen knowledge, while BB resigns himself to anonymity. Mr. Bateman basks in the compliments on his star student's wide range of information. Coming down the stairs from the Lincoln statue, Jessica confides in her friend:

"I don't know how much longer I can keep this up. It's exhausting! I'm trying to cram as much as I can from this journal into my head before we visit each site. I can't believe how much BB found out about these places. It sure paid off for me, though."

As they reach the bottom of the steps, she twirls her sunglasses and suddenly loses her grip on the bow. The expensive, high fashion glasses go whirling through the air. To her horror, they land several feet out in the reflecting pool.

"Oh no! Those are my mom's! I promised not to lose them. She's going to kill me!"

BB steps up to offer his help:

"Here, Jessica. You can have mine. I'll be fine without..."

"You've got to be kidding me! Look at those things. I wouldn't be caught dead wearing them. Where'd you pick them up anyways? The dollar store?"

Jessica turns in a huff leaving BB standing there with his outstretched offer.

"I'll use the credit card my dad gave me for emergencies and buy a new pair at the next gift shop. I'll tell my mom it wasn't my fault. She'll believe me. I've had quite a few "emergencies" already. Dad's going to yell at me when I get home, but Mom'll back me up. She always does."

Just then Jessica almost trips. She pulls her foot out of a swirl of sand. This strange phenomenon has been happening more and more. Yet every time she turns around to look, her classmates walk over the same spot with no trouble.

CHAPTER EIGHT

Caught in the Act

The class grabs a quick lunch of hotdogs and ice cream from the street carts on their way to the White House. BB holds back on splurging so he can buy souvenirs to remember each stop. His growing collection includes giant coins, key chains, flip chart info packets, and even miniature models of some of the monuments.

The next day Jessica keeps the class and adults enthralled with her abundant knowledge of the sites they visit. Whenever she's in the company of her teacher, the bus driver, or one of the rangers or docents, she displays her apparent fine qualities. But out of their sight and hearing she reveals her true personality and character.

The class has crisscrossed the capital, sometimes by bus and often by foot, and it's now the final morning of their visit. Striker drops them off once more at the Washington Monument to walk down the Mall. The concrete heats up in the morning sun. There is no relief from the stifling hot air. The complaints are endless:

"Can't we take a break, Mr. Bateman?"

"How many more times are we going to walk this Mall?"

"My feet hurt!"

"Mr. Bateman, Ashley doesn't want to sit next to me on the bus anymore."

"I'm thirsty. And my sunburn is really starting to hurt! And I've got a headache."

"I left my sunglasses on the bus. Can we go back?"

Mr. Bateman knows he's been pushing the group for the past two days, but the end is in sight. Just the Smithsonian and then the Jefferson and they can check off the major sites and move on to Mount Vernon. He turns to Jessica:

"I could really use your help. We have a great tour of the Smithsonian this morning and I need a positive attitude from everyone. Our guide is the museum's curator, and I want to make a good impression."

Jessica is more than willing to help in order to get the attention of this important member of the government service sector. She calls the stragglers together:

"All right everyone. Listen up. It's really important to give this tour our best effort. Mr. Bateman's arranged a special guide. The person who runs this whole place!"

At that moment a fashionably dressed young woman approaches them:

"Good morning. This is the Smithsonian, also known as the country's attic. Or basement. Or garage. Or wherever your family stores their memories."

Jessica laughs at the attempt at humor. The curator nods with a smile in her direction.

"We don't have time for a full tour. It would take several hours and more than one day. We'll visit the highlights and items you might find interesting. Afterwards we'll go to the Mall lawn and try a new activity. My name is Grace. Welcome to my house!"

The tour takes longer than expected, mainly because of the information and questions Jessica adds. The "curator" makes a mental note to confirm her growing approval to headquarters at her next free moment. Finally the class files out to the lawn area where the nearby carousel revolves to a tune only BB seems to notice. Lady Grace is eager to get some hands-on activities started. She brings out sticks to roll hoops across the lawn and also a few ball-in-the-cup dexterity challenges. BB is impressed by the authenticity of all of the equipment:

"How did you get permission to use all of these things? They look really old."

Jessica jumps in with an explanation:

"Of *course* she can use them. She's the curator."

Lady Grace ignores BB and gives Jessica her full attention:

"That's right. What was your name again? Oh, that's right. Jessica. Actually the games aren't original, but they're true to the colonial period. There weren't many toys back then, and they all were made by hand."

The class takes turns rolling hoops and trying to master the deceptively easy ball-in-the-cup toy. Then Lady Grace introduces them to a game that includes the whole group.

"This is called the Game of Graces."

Jessica eagerly announces:

"My grandmother showed me how to play this!"

By this time Jessica has been telling so many lies that she's no longer believable. Monica quietly pulls her friend aside:

"Come on, Jess. Isn't that going a little too far?"

"No. She really did! I'm not making this up."

Lady Grace calls to Jessica:

"Well, young lady, why don't you help me pass out the sticks and rings. Then you and I can demonstrate to your classmates."

Several of the boys balk and complain:

"What a stupid looking game!"

But Jessica calls them out:

"Just because you don't tackle someone doesn't mean it isn't a fun game. And it's not as easy as it looks!"

She positions the ring on her two sticks and expertly slides them apart with a quick motion. The ring flies through the air to Lady Grace, who "gracefully" catches it on her sticks. She flings the ring back to Jessica who catches it with hers.

"Excellent! Well played and with such flourish! Why don't you help me teach your classmates the technique?"

The students pair off and give it their best try. BB catches on quickly and makes a good showing with his partner. Not willing to share the spotlight, Jessica saunters over and slyly trips him just as he's sending his hoop into the air. He lands flat on his face, spread-eagled on the lawn. Jessica adds a final jab:

"Remember BB. It's called the Game of Graces, not the Game for Klutzes."

Once again BB is the target of his classmates' ridicule and laughter. Two ravens watching from the tree near the carousel add their cackling jeers. Mr. Bateman checks his watch and realizes it's time to move on:

"Jessica, I'm putting you in charge of making sure all the games are accounted for and given back to the curator. I know I can count on you to do a thorough job."

"Absolutely, Mr. Bateman. Will we have time to visit the gift shop before we leave?"

Jessica gives Lady Grace an adoring smile and adds an incentive:

"I'm sure our curator has some excellent suggestions."

"Why yes! Books about colonial era games and even some small games to purchase."

The class continues to the gift shop while Lady Grace reports to the other Bond

Council members on her way to her office:

"I haven't noticed any more Abyss agents around, so we should be in the clear with our selection. The young lady is definitely a winner, covering all of our criteria and more! I'll rejoin the class before they get on the bus just to be sure. Agent Allen, with all of your hard work, you deserve to pass on our final report to the President."

As Lady Grace opens her office door, her assistant arrives with a worried look:

"You'd better come to the security room right away. There's been an incident."

The technician runs back the last ten minutes of the recorded surveillance in the gift shop. Lady Grace watches in horror as Jessica picks up one of the ball and cup games and slides it into her backpack. As they leave the store, she realizes the security guard is checking everyone's backpacks. With no time to lose, she takes it from her backpack, unzips the outside pocket of BB's, and slips it in. The guard discovers the shoplifted item and pulls BB aside. Lady Grace suppresses an urge to cry out:

"This can't be happening! I was certain she was the one. That sneaky little imposter!"

Outside the gift shop, Mr. Bateman is chewing out BB in front of the whole class:

"Of all the stupid things to pull. Here it's our last day in DC and you have to spoil it. Our class will now be remembered for a little thief like you!"

"But I didn't do it! I don't know how it got in my backpack. Really I don't!"

"It's a good thing you hadn't left the shop or you'd be facing prosecution for shoplifting. The security guard was more than generous not to press charges. See if you can stay out of trouble for the next few days. I'll be keeping my eye on you."

"But it wasn't me..."

BB's dejected voice trails off. Suddenly the humid day becomes even more oppressive as this undeserved shame weighs down on him. Even his two friends are wondering what's up with him. Behind him an accusing voice slices through the air. It's Jessica and her faithful shadow Monica:

"Nice going, BB. Too bad you're such a loser. I'm sure Mr. Bateman will remember this when it comes time for our final grade. A+ for trust and honesty, I'm sure!"

Jessica's laughter abruptly cuts off as her leg sinks past her knee into a swirl of sand.

"What the… This is getting creepy!"

But Monica and BB have already started up the sidewalk and miss it all. The two ravens at the carousel nod to each other and take flight with their report. The class is already a block away headed to the Jefferson Memorial by the time Lady Grace reaches the gift shop. She laments to the rest of the agents out in the field:

"I don't know how this happened. I was sure she was the one. This is a disaster. There's no time to recruit another kid. I wouldn't even know where to begin!"

Agent Allen: "You're kidding me! That whole scene at the Washington Monument was just an act? I thought we had a chance against that Abyss ranger this time for sure."

Striker: "She had me fooled too. I was watching her from the beginning and she seemed the perfect choice."

Lady Grace: "How will I ever explain this to the Director?"

Agent Allen: "The blame isn't on you alone. We're all in this together."

Back at Headquarters, the Director has been watching the past three days unfold in the hourglass. Because of the critical nature of this selection, The Bond gave him this unique view. He now knows why they have failed in the past. They've been using the wrong set of criteria. Their true targets have always "flown under the radar" with qualities not recognized and appreciated. The Bond assures him the recruit is one of these students. It has seen into the heart of this one and told the President to look with new eyes at what he's witnessed. He thinks he might have the right choice:

"I've got to be sure of this one. It's risky to expose myself to the enemy, especially at a critical time like this. But with the help of my favorite disguise, I think Ben Franklin and I can work a little magic."

CHAPTER NINE

The Hourglass

"I believe we have time for the Jefferson Memorial before we go to Mount Vernon."

The class raises a chorus of complaints:

"Aw, come on. No way I'm walking all that way just to see an old statue and some more columns. Mr. Bateman, please don't make us. Can't we skip it?"

"It's on our list, and I want to finish everything I planned. Go ahead and get started and I'll check in with our bus driver to be sure we have time."

BB calls out hopefully:

"Sure hope so!"

The rest of the class gives him accusing looks. Obviously he's the only one looking forward to another monument. BB shrugs in an attempted apology. He scuffs his shoe into the sidewalk, ambling along dejectedly. He falls farther and farther behind the rest of his class on the cherry tree path that no longer boasts its spring blossoms. BB stares across the water at the Jefferson.

Suddenly a white arrow streaks toward him. At the last minute it splits into two swirls of pink and white that encircle his body. Whirling around, he watches the arrow re-form and whoosh back across the Tidal Basin. BB grasps the top of his head with both hands and discovers five petals. Carefully holding his treasure, he breathes in their soft fragrance and then gently tucks them into his jeans pocket. Moments later he pokes in a finger to assure himself they really exist.

A momma duck and her fuzzy family glide closer to the walk looking for a friendly handout. As BB stoops down, a big rock cannonballs into the water, narrowly missing mother and babies. BB jumps to his feet and angrily faces his classmate:

"Hey! Don't do that, Nick!"

"Lighten up! They're fine. Mr. Bateman told me to be sure you stayed up with the rest of the class. Let's go, duck lover!"

As Nick turns to join his friends, an eagle skims the water and flies toward the Jefferson. BB shouts in disbelief:

"Did you see THAT?"

"*Now* what? I told you to hurry up! You're already in trouble."

But BB ignores Nick who's disappearing with his pals down the walkway.

"A bald eagle! I didn't know they were around *here*!"

Just then a perky little yellow bird swoops past his face and flies to a gift stand next to the path. Perched on the slanted roof, it chirps a welcome. BB draws closer where he discovers an older gentleman with long gray hair, a shiny domed forehead, a gentle smile, and eyes that crinkle behind round, wire-framed spectacles.

"I have lots of special items for sale here. Are you interested in creating a memory?"

"I love this kind of stuff. But I'm low on funds with all the other things I've bought."

"Take your time. I'm sure we can work something out."

Among the usual coins and miniature monuments, a small hourglass stands alone. BB carefully lifts it to eye level and reads the inscription on the base:

"Time and History and the Future are in Your Hands"

"Wow! I haven't seen anything like this in the other shops. It must cost a lot."

He turns the hourglass over, but there's no price sticker.

"This is the best thing I've seen on our trip. But I probably don't have enough money. I've spent almost all of it here in DC."

The old gentleman consults his ledger:

"Let's see. It's three dollars... and twenty-seven cents, including tax."

"Oh, I just have..."

BB checks his pockets for any extra bills.

"Oh! Four dollars! I *do* have enough!"

"Well, imagine that!"

The clerk offers a souvenir bag, but BB refuses his generosity:

"Thanks, but I'll just slip it into my backpack."

When the kindly clerk gives him back his change, BB realizes there's an extra quarter:

"You gave me too much. Here's your quarter back."

BB places the quarter on the counter. The man's hand cups over it in a prayerful gesture of gratitude that goes beyond the monetary value of the coin. Something so small is obviously a window into the boy's heart.

BB pops his purchase into his backpack. As he zips the bag shut, out of his view the hourglass begins to glow. The old gentleman smiles at him with a wink and a nod. Outside, the yellow bird flies around BB and chirps excitedly.

"Hey, little guy. What's got you so excited?"

BB's attention snaps back to his classmates and his teacher:

"Sorry about wandering off, Mr. Bateman. I just had to check out that gift stand over… there… Hey! Where did it go?"

"What are you talking about, BB? We've been here the whole time… with you."

BB appeals to his two loyal friends, but they just shake their heads and give him worried looks. He too is growing more concerned:

"What's happening? Why am I the only one experiencing these things?"

Mr. Bateman turns to the class:

"I've just heard from Sam that we don't have time for the Jefferson Memorial. We need get to Mt. Vernon before they close. And there's still Monticello, Jamestown, and Williamsburg to cover before we fly back home. But before we go… Jessica, come over here please."

She points to herself in a seemingly humble way as Mr. Bateman continues:

"Class. I'm making this announcement now hoping it will encourage others of you…"

He pointedly singles out BB with his glaring scowl.

"… to take our trip more seriously. Jessica received the top score for the DC portion because of her participation and also for the excellent research she did beforehand. She will receive extra credit for her end-of-the-year social studies grade."

Jessica works up a glistening tear in her eye for extra effect:

"Thank you so much, Mr. Bateman, for recognizing all of my hard work. I won't let you down for the rest of the trip. You have my word!"

"I know I can count on you. Now, time to get a move on! Sam had an emergency and is handing us off to another driver. He said there's an accident blocking our planned route across the Potomac, so we'll get a quick view of Arlington Cemetery after all.

As the bus crosses the Independence Avenue Bridge, BB looks over to the Jefferson Memorial one last time. He checks his pocket for the petals and then opens the zipper on his backpack. Sure enough the hourglass is there too. It glows ever so slightly. But he doesn't mention this to anyone.

CHAPTER TEN

The Revelation

At Bond Headquarters the Council faces the Director, his back a seated silhouette. They expect his disappointment, their faces displaying the defeat they all feel.

Agent Allen: "I'm sorry, sir. We've nothing to report except our failure. We've let The Bond down again. I still don't understand how the data could have been so wrong."

Lady Grace: "When someone can fake their actions and words so cleverly, it's easy to be deceived. We can't see into their minds or their hearts!"

Striker: "She even has her teacher fooled. What a bunch of suckers we all were! We wasted our time. And now it's too late. The Abyss has finally won!"

The Director allows them to vent their frustration and anger before he speaks:

"I was permitted to follow this last recruiting effort in the hourglass. I could see how you all focused on what seemed the obvious choice. But I also saw all of her actions and heard her comments when she thought no one was watching. At least three separate times I saw her foot and finally her entire leg dropping into The Abyss."

They all pause in sorrow at their miscalculation and this loss to the enemy.

Striker: "We know now she's not the one. So what? We're still stuck with no options."

Director: "Not so fast, Striker. Hear me out. I also was watching the other students, the ones you didn't notice. One young man was not only overlooked but also maligned in terrible ways. Yet he kept his cool and continued to do the right thing even when he wasn't believed. His feet were always on solid ground. And then the view ended."

When the Director recounts all of the incidents BB had faced, they stand guilty as charged. For in their minds they too had condemned this young boy unfairly.

Lady Grace: "But it's too late! They've left the city and our time is up!"

The Director calmly leans back in his chair. He brings his fingers together in an inverted V under his chin and smiles:

"Don't be so sure. I set up my own reconnaissance adventure to test my theory."

He shares his Ben Franklin scenario.

"And I was right! At least I think I'm right."

Agent Allen: "How can we be sure? This is vital. We can't make a mistake this time."

Director: "I totally agree! We need to hear from The Bond."

The Director looks past the group to the alabaster wall. It begins to glow, signaling The Bond's presence, and ultimately fills the room with its brilliance.

"The Bond confirms it. He's the one we've been waiting for. The search is over!"

Striker: "There could still be a mistake. We need to make sure."

He rushes to the darkened hourglass and tries to force it to turn over:

"Just one more look! Please!"

But despite his massive build and strength, the hourglass won't budge. Lady Grace gently pulls him away:

"It's okay. Don't strain yourself."

The Director knows it's pointless to try to force the giant timepiece. He reminds them of what lies ahead for them and for their recruit:

"His time isn't ready. His strengths haven't matured. He's too young now."

Lady Grace: "His heart is there, though!"

Agent Allen: "And that's what The Bond sees... and what I missed."

Striker: "We *all* missed it."

The Director brings them back to the task at hand:

"The next four years will be a crucible in developing his character. When he finishes high school... when he comes of age... he'll be ready. Meanwhile we must keep an eye on him. We can't lose this one. We need him!"

He points to the inscription at the bottom of the hourglass. It's the same as the one BB has on his: "Time and history and the future are in your hands."

"At some point The Bond will connect the boy's hourglass with ours. We don't know when. We must trust The Bond and be ready!"

Behind the alabaster wall, the mighty light affirms their commitment.

CHAPTER ELEVEN

Homecoming

"There he is!"

BB's mom spies him coming down the airport corridor. His little brother impatiently bounces around eager to give BB a hug. BB clears the security barrier and joins his family:

"Hi, Mom! Good to see you too, Johnathan!"

BB rumples his brother's hair and hands him his backpack to carry:

"Don't drop it! I've got some great stuff in there that I don't want broken. So how's fourth grade since I've been gone? Still talking about the California Gold Rush?"

"Nah. We finished that *and* the transcontinental railroad. There's just a couple more weeks of school, so we're talking about the wars and the 1950s and 60s."

"Yeah. I remember studying all of that. Movie stars and the neat cars."

BB gives his mom a big hug. She snuggles into his ear:

"Heybert, it's so good to have you home."

"Where's Dad?"

"He dropped us off and is circling around. We got here just as you landed, so he didn't want to waste the time parking. You know your father!"

BB breaks away to grab his bag off the luggage carousel. At the car, he gives his dad a quick hug, loads his suitcase, and climbs into the back seat with his brother. His dad immediately gets to the point:

"Did you have a good trip? Tell us all about it."

"It was the greatest. The last place was Williamsburg. It was like we were back in Revolutionary War times. Everyone had costumes on, and they acted like they were actually living back then. We saw two presidents' homes, Mount Vernon and Monticello. But the best was the beginning. Washington, DC!"

His mom and dad grin at each other, enjoying BB's outpouring of enthusiasm.

"We saw the Supreme Court, the White House, Ford's Theatre, the Capitol, Lincoln's Memorial, the Washington Monument. We didn't get inside all of them because of the long lines, but at least we saw them and learned something about each of them."

"What about the Jefferson Memorial? You didn't mention it."

"Yeah. That's because we ran out of time. I saw it across the tidal basin, but that's as close as I got. I was the only one who was bummed about not getting over there."

BB whispers to his brother:

"I've got something really neat to show you later. Promise not to tell Mom and Dad."

Johnathan nods, wide-eyed with wonder. Back home BB shows his family the mountain of brochures he collected plus the souvenirs he bought in DC. Except the hourglass. His folks are puzzled:

"Nothing from the other places you visited?"

"Well... I kinda got carried away with all of the cool stuff I saw and... well... I pretty much blew through my extra spending money in Washington."

BB's mom understands his love for memorabilia:

"All right. It was your money to spend, and I know you'll remember this trip for a long time. Time for bed for both of you now."

Upstairs, BB brings out the hourglass from his backpack to show his little brother:

"I got this at a shop that was there... and then it wasn't! It just disappeared! No one else saw it, and I think they thought I was crazy. But it was there. This is the proof."

He pauses to emphasize its importance.

"I'm putting it in the back of my shelf so Mom doesn't find it when she's in one of her 'Clean your room!' moods. It's really special, so don't touch it unless you ask me first. Okay?"

Johnathan solemnly nods and promises. Later BB lies in bed staring at the ceiling, too excited to sleep. All of a sudden he jumps out of bed and grabs his jeans hanging over the desk chair. The ones he's been wearing the whole trip. Sliding his hand into the right front pocket he gingerly extracts five perfect pink and white petals. Carefully he drops them into the special drawstring bag he's had forever and hides it far back in the bottom drawer of the old dresser. Back in bed, his head resting on his linked fingers, BB relives the best trip of his life.

"Goodbye eighth grade. Next stop... high school! It's going to be great. I just know it!"

The day's exhaustion finally wins out, and BB sighs himself to sleep. In the back of his shelf the hourglass glows briefly, faintly... and waits.

Over the next three years The Council will keep tabs on their protégé. They know there is no time to choose someone else. BB's hourglass, pushed to the back corner of his shelf, collects layers of dust. Yet it still sends out signals at pivotal moments in his life. Although The Council doesn't have a constant view, the hourglass at Bond Headquarters shows them updates on the progress he's making... or not.

CHAPTER TWELVE

A New Beginning

"See you later!"

BB gives his dad a quick wave and slams the car door. A new world opens before him. High school. A fresh start. He hopes. Unfortunately for BB and his friends, Josh and Mike, freshmen boys are first-day targets. Any scrawny, vulnerable young man is fair game for upperclassmen's taunts. Keep an eye out for a pack of muscular guys, or you'll find yourself upside down in a trashcan.

"So how's the weather down there, Shorty?"

The jeers and laughter from this heartless, cruel bunch of bullies rain down on their first victim. Legs flail upward from the open mouth of the trashcan. The hapless boy struggles to tip it over and finally emerges unscathed from physical injury. But his self-esteem is crushed. He picks off stray candy wrappers sticking to his shirt. The once well-groomed freshman no longer shines with hopefulness. He gathers up his scattered books and shoves them into his backpack. Josh whispers to BB and Mike:

"If we stick together, maybe we'll be safe."

As BB goes through this first day, his classes are a blur of assignments and teacher expectations, the usual get-to-know-you routine. But he's more interested in the swirl of activity taking place in the courtyard… the social scene.

"What is it about them? It's like they've moved on and left me in the dust. They've got game, and I don't even know what the game is!"

As he watches his classmates, BB realizes all of the posturing and social interaction he's witnessed the past two years in junior high were a preparation for just this moment, this easy-going interplay. And he's caught flat-footed. He decides, for the moment, to focus on his studies, which is his strength, and steer clear of any chance of being mocked.

The demanding days of avoidance stretch endlessly before him. He sits at the bottom of the social ladder and he knows it. His friendly open disposition turns into a vigilant wariness, ready to deflect any mean-spirited comment. To steer clear of intimidating upperclassmen, he spends his lunch period hiding in the locker room or in the back area of the school where the other social outsiders hang out. Studying in the library while munching on his sandwich becomes the norm. Clearly there are no girls, especially the popular ones, in his circle of friends. He keeps his good grades to himself.

Through it all, his parents maintain their support and encouragement. His complaints about "not winning" fall on deaf ears... or so it seems. They keep telling him to stay committed to doing the right thing. Have faith everything will work out. But he's not seeing it. After a few months of social stagnation he makes his appeal:

"I could use some new clothes."

"Didn't your mom take you shopping before school started? What's wrong with the clothes you've got?"

BB's dad carefully watches the bottom line in the family finances. No frivolous purchases are worth throwing off the balance he strives to maintain.

"It's just that they're not from the stores everyone else shops at. Kids notice."

"Since when did we teach you that labels are so important? You look just fine!"

BB looks to his mom for support:

"Mom, my shoes really are getting small. Could we look at some new ones? Please?"

"Oh Bert, there's no reason to not give in a little. Shoes are important. You remember what it was like."

She throws a placating smile toward her husband and turns to BB:

"We'll go to the mall on Saturday and see what we can find. Maybe even on sale."

His fashion statement isn't BB's only worry. Sports, the one thing he'd always been good at, suddenly is turning on him. His once fine-tuned body no longer cooperates. It's like his legs belong to someone else. His efforts on the track are laughable. Even his supportive coaches have trouble finding encouraging words when the boys' and girls' teams practice together.

"Hey, BB! Step it up! Monica's going to pass you up in a... There she goes!"

"Sorry, coach. This ankle's been acting up on me again."

Faking injury becomes a regular part of his stream of apologies. And according to the marks his dad makes on the wall in the garage, BB's body is stretching to new heights. Yet he keeps pushing himself. At night he crawls up the stairs to his bedroom. Growing pains are no joke. The pain is real! But the pain in his heart is what really hurts.

"What's wrong, Heybert?"

His mom's soothing welcome home catches him in a vulnerable moment.

"Something's bothering you. Can you tell me?"

"It's just not working!"

"What's not working? Is it your classes?"

"My life! I don't have any friends!"

"That's not true. What about Josh and Mike? They've always been there for you."

"They're not the right kind of friends. They don't matter anymore. Not at school."

BB throws down his backpack and trudges up the front stairs. His mom calls after him:

"Let's talk about it at dinner. When your dad gets home."

But BB knows his folks don't have an answer to this problem. He has to figure it out himself. He owns it. His bedroom is just an excuse to shut out the world. He needs a place that will open up his mind. A place where he can let his imagination soar. He walks down the hall to the front room, a catchall place that has no real purpose, just like his life, and decides to check out the roof. He slides up the heavy, wood-framed window and steps onto the tiny porch. Carefully climbing over the spindle railing, he settles down on the sloping shingles. Time for some serious thinking.

"I'm sure Mom and Dad wouldn't want me up here. I can already hear them: 'You'll fall off and break your neck.' But they'll never know if I wait until later… when it's dark… and I can't sleep."

CHAPTER THIRTEEN

The Struggle Continues

The remainder of BB's freshman year is uneventful and predictable. He doesn't get anywhere with his peers. And he never gets a second look from the girls whose attention he craves. Summer vacation stretches ahead with no social prospects. Since his birthday's in September, he won't turn sixteen until the beginning of his junior year. He has no access to a car or the summer jobs that might give a boost to his finances. He has a few lawn jobs and takes occasional trips to the beach with his family. He and his faithful sidekicks, Josh and Mike, spend countless hours playing his dad's pinball machine, perfecting their technique and developing their unique body moves to add style and panache to their game.

By the beginning of sophomore year, BB has definitely gained height, but his lack of bulk gives him an awkward, gangly appearance. He struggles to keep his changing voice under control, avoiding all conversations except with his most trusted friends. He dreads being called on in class and keeps a low profile, all the while maintaining an enviable grade point average. He knows he owes it to his parents and himself to keep his academic road to the future intact. But halfway through the year, BB starts to question himself, his friendships, his goals in life. The path he's been on isn't getting him anywhere. He becomes increasingly self-conscious of his appearance and appeals to his folks. Dinner conversations center more and more on him and his needs.

"Mom, can I get a couple of new shirts and a pair of pants?"

BB's dad isn't buying this end-around scheme:

"We've had this discussion before. I told you not to play your mother and me against each other. Be satisfied we're keeping you in clothes that fit you. After all, we have to keep up with your growth spurts, and Johnathan's too. Money stretches only so far!"

BB's little brother Johnathan has tried to keep from being drawn into the argument. Four years younger, he doesn't have the social pressures of his older brother. He gives BB a sympathetic, hopeful smile. But BB ignores his support:

"What's Johnathan got to do with anything? How about *my* life? You don't know what it's like at school! You don't even care if I fit in! You just don't care!"

BB leaves the table and stomps up the back stairs to his room. His mom calls after him with a plaintive pleading that he ignores.

By second semester, BB's body is starting to cooperate once more and his sports skills are returning. True he's no standout, but at least he isn't competing for last place anymore. He's not making any advances socially though. Back with his two buddies, BB mournfully points out a popular group:

"Look at those guys. All the girls go for them. They know how to stand. What to say. How to look cool. They're not even trying and the girls fall all over them."

Josh and Mike nod in agreement:

"Yeah. They sure make it look easy."

Later during lunch, BB sits alone in the mostly empty library, pretending to study, Through the window he can see the social crowd laughing and talking. It's like watching a show that he doesn't have a ticket to. He brushes tears from his cheeks.

That same night after the house is quiet and the streetlights are casting their luminous circles, BB climbs onto the roof, his preferred place for contemplation.

"I know I'm supposed to be thinking about college and my future. But where's it getting me?"

As he sorts through his hurt feelings, his resolve grows:

"I can do better than this! Be better than this! I just need to get my act together. I've wasted enough time!"

He thinks ahead to the consequences of his decision:

"This is going to cost me. But I need to make my own choices, my own decisions!"

But then comes the part that hits to his core. He's not sure he's ready for this break:

"If I keep hanging out with Josh and Mike I'm squandering any chances that might come my way. The other guys have made that pretty clear."

There's a pit in his stomach that he struggles to suppress. This transformation won't be easy, but he's got to give it a try for the rest of this school year. He has to find out if there's any hope at all of sending his life in a new direction. His plan starts to come together.

CHAPTER FOURTEEN

Break with the Past

The second half of the school year, BB begins to distance himself from Mike and Josh. No longer do they hang out at his house. The pinball tournaments are a thing of the past. At school he avoids meeting up with them between classes and at lunch, always having an excuse for leaving them out of his plans. He watches for opportunities to mingle with the popular guys but keeps himself on the edge of the circle for now. He joins in their laughter to appear he belongs. The ridicule they heap on his former friends is tough to take, but he adds his comments and snickers with them. Nick tags Mike and Josh with his latest derisive label:

"Hey, Pinheads! What's the latest game? Rocket ship to the moon?"

BB winces but then joins in:

"Yeah. 'Bout time you guys got a life."

His new buddies take off, and BB hurries away to class in the opposite direction. Josh and Mike run to catch up. Mike jumps in first:

"What's wrong with you, BB? I know you want to be accepted by these guys, but do you have to add your two cents when they're picking on us?"

Josh is even more to the point. He swings BB around and zeroes in:

"I thought we were friends, but I guess your loyalty only goes so far. As long as it doesn't wreck your chances at being popular."

BB knows he doesn't have a good answer. What they say is true, and it still bothers him. But he shoves those feelings down deep and dismisses their accusations:

"Aw leave me alone. Things are different now. We're not in junior high anymore. I've got to think about my future."

He opens the door to his class and lets it slam behind him.

By now Nick realizes BB is eager to be included in his group, and he works this desire to his benefit. That afternoon he suggests a way BB can be of real value:

"So BB, it looks like you've finally figured out that those two nerds aren't working out for you. I've got a proposition for you that I think the rest of the guys will be interested in. Something that shows you're solid with us."

"Anything, Nick! What can I do?"

"Everyone knows you've got some of the best grades in the class. Some of us just don't have the time to put into our studies, and we want to be sure our transcripts look good for the universities. Sooo... you could be a big help to us."

"You need me to tutor you? Help you study?"

"Not exactly. We don't want to actually put in all that time. We've got other priorities, you know."

BB is confused. Suddenly Nick's smooth talk is making him nervous.

"I'm thinking more of letting us use your homework. Maybe some helpful class notes we can sneak in during tests. You know... the usual. Later you could step it up and let us see some of your answers during tests. I'm sure you can figure out something. You know... stealth... just like the spies. You'd be good at that!"

BB isn't sure he wants to cross this line. But the more he thinks about it, he realizes this is his only advantage, the only thing he has to offer. He meekly agrees to the plan:

"Sure. We can work something out. Just let me know what you need and when."

"Now that's what I'm saying! You'll be a great asset to the group! See you around."

Nick gives him a slap on the back that knocks BB off balance. His foot slips in a circle of sand. But Nick and the others have already turned away and are sharing a joke he isn't part of.

BB replays what's just happened and stifles any indecision and worries about what he's just agreed to. If he's going to be anyone on this campus, there'll have to be some sacrifices.

Back at Bond Headquarters, things are getting tense. The Director calls a conference:

"I know it might look like he's slipping away from us, but we can't lose hope. The Bond is sending in as many Secret Legends as possible without tipping our hand to The Abyss. What's your take on this, Agent Allen?"

"I know what it's like to be on the outside at that age. It's not easy to resist the pull of wanting to belong. He's going to need a lot of encouragement."

Lady Grace is sympathetic, but Striker isn't buying it:

"He's gotta get some backbone! Stand up to those guys!"

Director: "This is out of our hands right now. The Bond is doing everything it can to strengthen him. Unfortunately those qualities we liked about him can become a liability if turned in the wrong direction. That's why this is so tricky."

The light behind the alabaster wall glows, encouraging them to stay the course.

CHAPTER FIFTEEN

Identity Dilemma

By the time summer rolls around, BB's popularity has grown, but it's just with the guys he's helping out. They rely on him not just for homework and test answers, but also for copies of his papers, as long as they have different teachers. He has quite the system going, and they're now dependent on him. Nick and his friends don't need summer jobs, and BB is still too young for any serious employment. By getting up at sunrise, he's able to get his lawn jobs done before the coastal marine layer burns off. Nick picks him up for the beach almost every day. He already has a license plus a hot car, courtesy of his folks. The beach becomes BB's second home. And that's where he connects with the girls he's been eager to get close to. They're still beyond his reach, but he's making headway. His parents have noticed a change in BB, though. His dad wonders about this transformation:

"Why don't we see Josh and Mike around anymore? I'm not sure who these new friends of yours are."

"Oh, they're guys I got closer to this year. You probably haven't heard much about them lately, but they've been in my class since grade school and junior high."

"But what's wrong with Mike and Josh? What's happened to *them*? You three haven't had a pinball tournament in months."

"Mom, they're not into things I'm interested in."

His dad gives him a stern warning:

"Well, I hope the *things* you're into now won't be a problem down the line. Remember to stay true to your commitments and the values we've taught you."

"Don't worry, Dad. I won't forget. I'm just having a good time. And I like hanging out with these guys."

By the end of summer, heading into his junior year, BB's relationship with his parents begins to deteriorate. The usual back and forth at the dinner table has turned into an outright battle. BB is more and more determined to carve out a new life for himself. He likes the excitement of his new friends and craves more.

"Heybert! Time for dinner!"

His mother's usual invitation gets no response.

"Heybert! Food's getting cold!"

BB flies down the stairs, flops into his chair and starts wolfing down his meal. He hunches over his plate, ignoring the family chatter. His dad tries to draw BB in:

"I thought we'd all take in a movie tonight. A last celebration before school starts."

"No thanks. Already got plans."

He hears the gentle plea in his mom's voice:

"No time for your family anymore, dear?"

"I told you. I've made plans already."

He avoids the questioning look from his brother and the resigned sigh from his parents.

"See you later."

BB bolts for the front door before there's any more discussion.

"But you haven't finished your..."

The door slams. His mom and dad exchange distressed looks.

Later that night, BB escapes to his spot up on the roof. From an open window below, the lyrics of a James Taylor ballad drift to where he's brooding. He knows his mom's a sucker for that sappy music, especially when she's in a thoughtful mood. And now those words speak to him, reminding him he can't let the world get him down.

"You've got that right, James! I don't need any more people telling me what to do."

The music draws out his deepest longings:

"I don't have a life! I don't even know what my life is supposed to be!"

He considers the new friends he's made and dismisses any worries about their true friendship. His parents' continued interference and concerns creep back into his thoughts:

"Enough worrying about what they think. I've got this figured out now. Just need to flesh out the rest of my plan."

The song continues to speak to his heart, telling him he can make his dreams a reality.

"No more dreams and wishes. Time to make it happen! Game on!"

CHAPTER SIXTEEN

No Looking Back

To begin with, BB needs a new look, especially now that he's free of his braces. It isn't going to be easy to convince his parents, but he's ready with his best arguments. The dinner table conversation is a test of wills. His mom offers her usual suggestion, which is really an assumption:

"It's time for back-to-school shopping. I thought I'd take you and Johnathan to the mall tomorrow."

"That's okay. I'm going with the guys this year. Just give me the money you'd be spending on me, and I'll pick out my own clothes and shoes."

His dad gives him a suspicious glance:

"Where did this come from?"

"Come on, Dad. None of my friends go shopping with their mom anymore. Besides, I've got my ideas already for what I want to get."

His dad smiles at the thought of another "Mom shopping day."

"Okay. But be sure you fit in a haircut before school starts on Monday."

His dad turns his attention again to his plate of food. BB offers an agreeable solution:

"One of the girls is giving me a haircut. She's really up on the latest styles."

"Just not too long. I can't stand the unkempt look some boys are wearing these days."

"Why do you have to be so critical all the time?"

Not rising to the bait, his dad evenly gives his final word:

"Time to end this discussion, Bert."

The exchange of words has had its usual dampening effect on the dinner conversation. No one has the energy to start a new topic, so the four of them finish their meal in silence. As his mom starts to clear the table, she once again offers to help him shop or at least drive him to the mall. BB's temper spills over, seething with resentment:

"Let me shop *for* myself... *by* myself. Just leave me alone!"

BB stalks off to his room to nurse a self-pitying justification for his own behavior.

At Bond Headquarters there is complete dismay. Frustrated, Sergeant Striker pounds his fist into the palm of his other hand. They've all been watching BB's decline and are growing more and more anxious.

Striker: "We can't just sit here and do nothing! Send me in! I'll straighten up the kid!"

Agent Allen and Lady Grace also offer to intervene.

Director: "We have to trust The Bond. Secret Legends are in place doing their best to advise and counsel him. The Bond is working on his heart, but the world has so many enticements. Plus his own desires are a strong force to contend with."

Lady Grace: "I know we have to trust the plan. But it's so hard to sit by and watch. Can't you send just one of us?"

Director: "No one can go in until he's anointed. We can't tip our hand. The Abyss can't know he's the one. They think we're still searching."

To assure them that they are heard and supported, The Bond sets off a slight earth tremor. Nothing serious, but a reminder that It is aware and in control.

CHAPTER SEVENTEEN

Tremors and Quakes

The school year begins with BB firmly planted in the group he's always longed to be part of. He continues to be a conduit of academic assistance and information, and their flattering gratitude strokes his ego. Their influence on his life, however, creates a whole new level of decisions. The pressure is on. Nick and the rest of the guys take him aside one day, seemingly concerned about BB's welfare:

"BB, we're worried about you. You know, you really aren't having fun. All you do is study. Don't get me wrong. We all appreciate your help in that department."

The others express their thanks and nod in agreement. Nick keeps working on BB:

"But... How can I put this? You have no life! What are you worried about? With your grades so far, you're guaranteed a spot at any of the state universities or even a junior college. Don't push yourself so hard."

"But my parents are counting on me going to the school they graduated from. I have to keep up my grades to get in. They want me to get a really good education."

"Aw come on! College isn't about *that*. It's about having fun and doing just enough to get a good paying job when you graduate. We've got this all figured out."

The warning voice in BB's head still nags him, but it's growing fainter and fainter. With his new look and strategies, the girls are starting to notice him more and more. Even though he's still a novice at this social scene, he talks the talk expected from a confident upperclassman. If he's going to become a solid member of Nick's pack, he's got to step it up though. But his folks question the motives and loyalty of these new friends. His dad starts dinner with the topic the family has been dreading:

"I'm getting concerned about this group you've been hanging out with lately, son. I know you've been around them since you were little, but I don't remember them ever being your true friends. Have they changed? Or have *you*?"

"I'm fine the way I am and so are my friends. Can't you see I'm finally having some fun?"

"That's another thing. Just what kind of fun are you into these days? You've been pushing that curfew more and more. I just don't like it."

"What is it with you? What's your problem? You never see my side of things!"

BB's voice is rising in pent up frustration with his parents. He looks around the table. Johnathan once again studies the food on his plate. His mom's strained look worries him, but only for a moment.

"I'm out of here."

His dad gives him a final warning:

"It's a school night!"

"Don't worry. I won't be late."

BB's tone is even and to the point:

"I need to spend time with people who understand me."

BB bolts from the table, down the hall, and through the front door. He spots the guys in Nick's car that's idling at the curb. Giving a quick wave, BB sprints down the wooden stairs. As he clears the last step, his foot catches in a pile of sand. In his eagerness to join his friends he doesn't give it a second thought.

The hourglass The Council has been watching back at Bond Headquarters starts to shake uncontrollably. The tremor extends to the foundation of the building and manifests as a small earthquake throughout the DC area. The Director orders the team into action:

"The engineers will be here within the hour checking for any structural damage. You know the drill. Everything moves behind that false panel. Let's go!"

Within minutes they clear the office. When the inspection team arrives, all that remains is a nondescript, solid white wall. Earthquakes are unusual for DC, but assured there's no damage, the engineers leave. The Council returns the room to its former arrangement. The Director motions them to sit down:

"We've known for some time that the lad's future was in trouble. The original plan was to wait until he was of age, until his 18th birthday. But obviously that will be too late. This wasn't a warning. It was an emphatic sign from The Bond. We need to be ready to intervene when the signal is given. Battle stations!"

The school year draws to a close. BB has put aside all concerns for his family and their aspirations for him. He's having the time of his life, though maintaining his new life and decent grades is pretty exhausting. But now the best summer of his life lies ahead. He imagines the endless days of sun and surf and hopefully growing closer to some of the girls. This first of many Friday nights is the springboard into his newfound future.

CHAPTER EIGHTEEN

The Final Straw

"I'm home! Just going to dump my stuff and grab a sandwich. I'm meeting up with the guys to celebrate."

As he runs up the front stairs his mom calls from the kitchen:

"Heybert! I planned a special dinner for you and your brother. Last day of school and all. Please don't disappoint me."

BB stops halfway up the steps, gives his shoulders a roll, and clumps back downstairs. He puts his arm around his mom and cajoles her with just a hint of a whine in his voice:

"But Mom! Everyone's going to be there. Nick, Justin. I can't go back on my promise."

He hopes this will soften her heart. But then his dad joins them from the front room.

"What's this about plans? Justin and Nick again? Not a good idea tonight, Bert. Remember I've arranged for that job interview at eight o'clock tomorrow morning. You'll be up early, son. I want you looking sharp, not like you just rolled out of bed."

"Come on, Dad. I can't let the guys down. I *have* to be there. I won't be out late."

"That's what you said the last time you were out with those two. I don't trust them as far as I can throw them, which isn't far at all! They're nothing but trouble."

"What do *you* know? They're *my* friends, not yours!"

BB's voice has lost all of its former polite tone. The negotiations aren't going well, and he's losing ground. His dad grows more and more irritated:

"Look. If you want that car you've been talking about for next school year, you'd better concentrate on making some cash this summer and not worrying about your social life. Insurance and gas money won't be coming from my wallet."

"My friends aren't driving around in second hand heaps. And their *parents* pay for their gas and insurance too. They'll be at the beach while I'm stuck bagging groceries at that crummy store."

"Son, it's time we had a talk. Upstairs. NOW!"

BB reluctantly follows his dad up the narrow back stairs, pounding each step in frustration. Just before he reaches the top, he stomps on a tread that dissolves into dry, loose granules covering his ankle. But BB is so angry that he shakes it off as a minor annoyance. He trudges after his father down the hall leaving a trail of sand in his wake. His parent's bedroom door closes behind them and the lecture begins:

"You should be grateful for any job at your age. Mr. Carlson is doing me a favor by taking you on for the whole summer."

"Favor? I don't need that kind of favor! Why can't I just enjoy my summer vacation? Isn't that what being a kid is all about? Why do you have to be so strict? It's MY life! Why can't I live it the way I want to?"

"We've had this discussion before. I'm not listening about the injustice of this family any more. Pull yourself together or don't bother coming down for dinner."

Unnoticed during all of this verbal combat, the hourglass in the back of BB's shelf begins to glow. As the battle continues, the glow brightens and pulses. Back at Bond Headquarters the huge hourglass connects to this signal. Light streams from every part of the gigantic timepiece. And then it begins to shudder. It's time! When BB's hourglass turns, it will too. And then the quest begins.

BB's dad joins the rest of the family at the table. He struggles to regain his composure in an attempt to reassure his wife and younger son that everything will be fine:

"He can just stay in his room 'til he cools off. I've had enough of his attitude. And we've got a whole summer of this to put up with. Just great!"

"Oh Bert. The food's getting cold, and the boy needs to eat something. Can't we just put this aside for a bit so we can at least have a meal together?"

"I'm not going to beg him to join us. He won't starve if he misses a meal."

Always the one to soothe the family's unrest, his mom gently calls up the back stairway:

"Heybert! Time for dinner."

No answer.

"I made your favorite. Chicken and dumplings to celebrate the end of school. Please come down and join us. Please?"

Finally BB comes stomping down the stairs. He slumps into his chair and leans over the old oak table. His unruly hair falls over his plate, covering his scowl and growing resentment. He picks at his food and finally shoves a huge piece of chicken into his mouth to avoid conversation. Johnathan stares wide-eyed at his big brother. Hoping this latest storm will pass, he pretends to search his plate for one last, cold bite. That old pit in his stomach starts up again. He hates these confrontations. Usually things blow over pretty quickly and the family moves on. But this is different. It's as if an earthquake is rumbling through his home. The family finishes their meal in silence. Suddenly BB throws down his fork:

"I'm sick of this town. I'm sick of this old house. It looks like it belongs in a museum! Why can't we live in a better neighborhood? And why don't I ever get a chance to do what I want? All I get is lectures and rules and speeches about how I should be proud to be part of this family. Well you know what? I'm sick of this family!"

BB hasn't noticed the impact his words are having on his mother. She's barely holding it together, her entire body rigid with fear, shaken to the core. The tears she'd been struggling to control begin to stream down her face. She looks down at her lap to hide her anguish. His father erupts:

"Don't you EVER make your mother cry! You're not going anywhere tonight. I don't care what you and your friends had planned. Go to your room! Now!"

As angry as he is, BB knows better than to continue pushing against his father. Bolting from the table he pounds up the stairs, slams the door, and throws himself onto his bed. He stares at the ceiling through hot, bitter tears. At the back of his shelf the hourglass glows brightly and begins to slowly turn over. On the other side of the country, the giant hourglass also rotates. He complains loudly even though his family can't hear:

"Why don't they understand? Why am I stuck in this family? Why can't I just get out of here and live the way I want? It's MY life!"

At that moment there is a frantic pecking at his bedroom window. BB looks over to see a fluttering yellow bird trying to get his attention. But for some reason he can't get out of bed. His body is pulled to a standing position. He finds his footing, but he isn't really standing on anything. How can he be suspended in air and at the same time feel like he's standing up? The pecking fades as BB realizes he has left not only his bed, but also his room... his house... his city. Nothing makes sense. He peers down a dark tunnel. Sparkling pinpricks form into arrows of light flying directly at him. He throws up his forearm to deflect the bright blades. But they streak past him... and through him. Should he close his eyes or just face whatever is his fate? He decides to force himself to keep alert... stay awake... or is he?

CHAPTER NINETEEN

Forward into the Past

The light arrows vanish and the blackness slowly peels back to reveal the dawn of what promises to be a clear day. Standing once again on solid ground, BB stares at a familiar sight: The Washington Monument.

"Well at least I'm not on some far off alien planet."

In the dim morning light he spots a few early morning joggers. He thinks one is calling to him from the monument but realizes it's really a park ranger:

"I'm talking to you! I need to show you something before the crowds build."

BB is thoroughly confused. Why would he be singled out? Then again, what's the point of any of this? Or is it all just a dream? He joins the ranger who begins his speech:

"You know there are 36,000 stones in the monument? It's the world's tallest freestanding structure. Those stones change color part way up. There was a big delay and they couldn't match up the blocks again when they started up construction again. It's held up totally by science and gravity! Imagine that!"

BB mumbles that he's known those things since eighth grade. The ranger continues:

"Are you also aware that you can see the Jefferson Memorial from here?"

BB had been scanning the area for a clue to his situation. At the mention of the monument he whips around and stares in wide-eyed panic at the face of this man he suddenly recognizes. The park ranger from the eighth grade trip! The ranger continues, looking deep into BB's eyes:

"You never know the importance of what you do or see or hear. What it means for you."

BB is really off balance now. The ranger takes him by the arm and leads him past the ticket area to the entrance where BB remembers waiting in line. This time they walk through an empty hall. The white gate spontaneously opens to let them pass and then closes behind. The ranger gets an urgent message in his ear bud. He drops BB's arm and gives him a firm warning:

"Wait here. I just need to confirm a few things."

He turns his back to BB:

"Go ahead. I'm listening."

BB glances around at the familiar first floor entryway and nonchalantly listens in to one side of a tense conversation.

"We can't let him leave now. I know he's the one but *they* don't know. The quest is too important! They think we're still searching. We've been lucky to throw them off with our decoys all these years. What do you mean they're coming? Who's coming? An early group of eighth graders? I've got to get moving!"

When BB hears the first few comments, his heart pounds in his ears.

"I'm the ONE? The one for what? What quest? They're not going to let me leave? I've got to get out of here! There's got to be another way out! Maybe I can get to the top and signal to someone… anyone!"

BB inches to the glass doors, slips through, and quietly pulls them closed. Keeping an eye on the ranger, he slowly backs up to the service elevator. He presses his palms against the cold metal doors, willing them to open. Above his head he hears a mocking hiss. BB rolls his eyes upward where two white stone cobras writhe toward his face:

"Ssssssee things assssss they are and not assssss you wish them to be."

He stifles a scream and lunges forward. But when he turns around, the relief profile of George Washington rotates from the wall forming a complete head that speaks to him:

"Do not think yourself equal to the task you are honored with."

"Actually, sir, I've never considered myself equal to any task."

"What am I doing? Getting into a conversation with a talking head?"

He glances over his shoulder at the ranger who's still deep in conversation.

"I've got to figure out how to get past this ranger or find another way out of here."

He hurries off to the left. There's a quick turn to the right down a short hall. Another right lands him between a full-length statue of Washington and, thankfully, the four brass panels of the public elevator door. Slowly Washington raises his walking stick and points it straight at BB. Suddenly shouts echo through the passageway:

"Hey… where'd you go? Wait!"

It's the ranger who has finally realized BB is missing. BB searches in vain for the elevator buttons. His pleas bounce off the brass door, mocking his efforts:

"Come on... come on... open up... please open up..."

His heart hammers his chest. His breaths come in the short gasps he remembers from when he'd run track, that last effort when he didn't think he could pull any more air into his lungs, his throat raw and tight. BB pounds on the doors, hoping and praying. And then they miraculously open! He rushes in and turns just in time to catch the ranger's frantic face through the sliver of the closing portal. It's over. The ranger's distress melts slowly into a smug, satisfied smile. He relays the news to Headquarters:

"We've got him!"

Although there's no logical direction but up, the elevator floor jerks downward. The sudden motion throws BB to his hands and knees. Through glass panels he sees the passing interior surface of the monument. But then the blocks of stone change to a newsreel alternating between color and black and white scenes. First is his majestic Victorian house. Following that are terrifying views of crumbling buildings and firestorms. The final frames show an iconic red-turreted hotel slowly collapsing into the sea. Through it all a commanding, booming voice speaks directly to him:

"Never was a cause more important or glorious
than that which you are engaged in."

"More human glory and happiness may depend upon your exertions
than ever yet depended upon any of the sons of men."

"No danger is to be considered when put in competition
with the magnitude of the cause."

"When all else falls away what do you have left?
Who you really are!"

The final frames flicker by, like the end of an old movie. Black and white letters and sprocket holes and then just glaring light. The elevator car gains greater and greater speed. BB is sure the end is near. He cries out what he's certain will be his last words:

"I'll go anywhere! Just get me outa here!"

Within his heart he hears a voice reassuring him:

"TRUST! HAVE FAITH!"

As if it has compressed a giant spring, the capsule shoots upward and explodes through the point of the great monument into the bright blue day. The elevator cubicle dissolves and BB finds himself once again standing on emptiness. The arrows of lights that brought him to DC reappear. But this time they move away, drawing him along out of his control. The arrows converge into two glowing balls on either side of the scene. Immediately there is a commotion in the middle. Tentacles of time twist and turn, creating a vertical line. White fibers from the two orbs stretch forward, attach themselves to the elongated temporal fingers, and pull them apart. As the fibers contract, a black opening appears, drawing BB into its depths. With nothing to grab hold of, he braces himself for the inescapable unknown.

CHAPTER TWENTY

Unfamiliar Familiar

BB lands with a jolt that buckles his knees. In front of him a tall, white, waffle-patterned building curves around the street corner. Between two trees shaped like giant torches he reads: **Escondido City Hall**

"That can't be true. The city hall is somewhere back over..."

BB turns around to stare down Grand Avenue, the four-lane street that stretches past familiar buildings. But the store signs are different. And the cars look like something out of an old movie.

"Where am I? This is supposed to be Escondido. But it isn't *my* city. Where are my friends? My mom and dad? I need to get home!"

Fear drops down and seizes him. Panic surges from his stomach to his brain:

"Is this my punishment? Cut off from everything I've ever known... forever?"

BB's hands shake and his mind spins uncontrollably:

"I always heard reminders about the importance of the past. But I never expected to actually BE in the past! I can't stay here! My family'll miss me... I think... I hope..."

His voice trails off remembering his last blowup at his parents, the heated words: "I wish I wasn't even part of this family!" BB forces down his fear, ignoring his cold sweat. Then once more a voice speaks to his heart:

"TRUST! HAVE FAITH!"

BB takes off down the street. His heartbeat settles down as his steps pick up the rhythm of music coming from the cars cruising up and down the center of town. He can't believe what he's seeing.

"Wow, a two-toned '57 Chevy! Just like the one my neighbor Mr. Cliffton restored. And a Thunderbird convertible! I wonder who worked on all of them?"

In every car teenagers swing and clap to the catchy tune, joining in the lyrics and basking in the brilliant sunny day. They stare at BB as they drive by. The guys point and the girls giggle behind carefully manicured fingertips. BB checks his reflection in a store window. No wonder! His clothes and hair are definitely out of place. From the car radios a voice breaks in:

"That was 'Maybe Baby' by Buddy Holly and the Crickets. An oh-oh-oh-so-oldie-but-still-goodie. Next up, a new release by The King. But first this word from..."

The voice fades away with the last passing car. BB finds himself in front of a music shop he doesn't recognize. Upbeat music drifts out through the open door. He joins a group of teenagers inside. The girls' hair is meticulously styled or pulled into sleek pony tails. The guys' hairstyles look like the ones in his dad's old yearbooks. Everyone is flipping through rows of 45s all along the counter. In glassed booths other kids listen to records and snap their fingers to beats only they hear. The shop owner's friendly voice rises above the chatter:

"Anything I can help you with? You got a special song in mind? Something by Frankie Valli or maybe Elvis?"

Well BB has certainly heard of Elvis, so he goes with something safe.

"Why don't you try this one? It's been a hit with all the kids this school year."

"I'm not sure. What's it like? Can I listen to it?"

"Hmm. All the listening booths are busy right now. I'll play it on the store speakers."

"Return to Sender" fills the store and spills out the open door onto the street. BB avoids the man's questions about his identity, giving him a general "I just got into town" comment. He thanks the man and apologizes for not buying anything. The music and words follow him as he continues down the street. Inside the music store the owner makes a quick phone call to the local radio station:

"Do me a favor, will ya? This new kid in town just discovered that song by Elvis: 'Return to Sender.' Why don't you put it out there to welcome him to our city? Play it a couple of times. Thanks, Jerry! I owe you one!"

Cars with their windows rolled down catch the summer breeze. They all blast out the popular tune from their radios. BB's body starts to roll with the rhythm. He quickly picks up the catchy refrain. And then he realizes how true the words are for his life right now. He has no address in the world surrounding him. And he may never return to what he knows. BB peers up Juniper Street, wondering if his house is there, wondering who might be living there. He shakes off the thought and continues to the next block. Suddenly in front of him a group of girls strolls through an open door. They're all trying on pink lipstick they've just purchased.

"I really like that shade! Don't you, Judy? Pinkie, let me try yours. Pleeeease!"

The owner of the lipstick offers it to her friend and then turns to give BB a quick lookover and smile. Even though he tries to look nonchalant, his heart takes a flip. She has a poised self-assurance that definitely stands out from the rest of the group. Her starched white cotton shirt compliments her cropped pink slacks. Her blonde side ponytail is pulled together with a jaunty scarf. The other girls intercept his stare and snicker at his appearance. BB feels his face flush a deep red. He quickly looks away to concentrate on a miniature carousel above a store across the street, pretending not to hear their comments.

"Still he's kinda cute. Hey! Why don't we stop at Ting's for a milkshake?"

BB's eyes follow the girls down the street. He couldn't have figured out anything clever to say anyway. Discouraged by this encounter, he jams his hands into the back pockets of his pants. To his surprise he pulls out a $20 bill in one hand and a nickel in the other. At least he's not broke! His confidence buoyed, he pops into Mel's Root Beer. Taking a swig of his favorite beverage, though he'd never admit it to his friends, he thinks about all that's happened. All the strange businesses and stores on both sides of the street. He should know them, but everything has changed. And he can't believe he got charged only five cents for his soda!

From the cars, teenagers start calling out to him and waving. He lifts his hand to wave back but realizes they're actually smiling and pointing at him. His hand self-consciously goes to his hair, his fingers sifting through the slightly shaggy mane. BB's mind races with real and imagined problems:

"Is it my hair? My clothes? What are they laughing about? Why can't I just go home? How long am I going to be here? What if I'm stuck here forever?"

No answers. No one's coming to his rescue. Resolved to his situation, BB takes on a matter-of-fact attitude. Just his luck, a barber shop is a couple of doors away. He settles into an empty chair for a haircut and unwelcome conversation.

"I don't remember seeing you around town. You new? Been here long?"

BB gives him an evasive answer as the white drape floats down around his slim frame.

"Just a regular cut today? Been pretty busy already and summer's just beginning. Exams are over and graduation's coming up next week. I'll be cutting a lot of heads."

BB isn't sure what to say so he just offers the first idea that comes to mind:

"Yeah. Bet they'll all be headed to the beach for the summer."

"Maybe this weekend. But most of the guys that come in here are getting ready for their summer jobs. Gotta look sharp!"

"Jobs? Doesn't anyone around here do anything for fun?"

"If you're looking for something tonight, a big group will be at the dance upstairs. I've heard they've got a great DJ lined up. You should check it out."

The barber brushes away the loose clippings, flings off the giant cover, and swings BB around for a look in the mirror. It's the shortest haircut he's had since middle school! He reaches into his pocket to pay, but the barber waves him off.

"No problem, kid. This one's on the house!"

BB nods his thanks and heads out the door. The barber calls after him:

"You might want to get some more up-to-date clothes. Why don't you check out The Wardrobe? It's across the street on the corner. Tell them Art sent you."

BB crosses over to the menswear store and past the mannequins in the windows. A helpful clerk shows him their latest shipment. The man suggests a pair of blue Levi's and a pale blue sport shirt. BB rolls up the sleeves and looks in the full-length mirror. He hardly recognizes himself! But suddenly he worries his $20 bill won't be enough. BB tentatively hands it to the clerk. He can't believe his response.

"Here's your change. That's eight, nine, ten and ten makes twenty."

The man recommends a shoe store across the street and farther down on the next block. On the way BB stops at a familiar building with a huge glass front. It's where his dance studio is supposed to be. He'd spent hours there studying tap and jazz. His mom knew from an early age he couldn't keep his feet still, so she signed him up. The rock and roll era was his favorite, and he and his partner won several competitions.

But now through the windows he sees only tools and lawn equipment. The door opens and a familiar group of guys pours out, congratulating one of their pals with encouraging slaps on the back.

"I can't believe I got the job! And seventy-five cents an hour!"

They stop their excited conversation when they notice BB. They pepper him with comments and questions that throw him off balance:

"Hey... didn't we see you coming out of Reese's up the street?"

"What's your name?"

"Good haircut, buddy!"

"You in town for long?"

"For the summer maybe?"

"If you need a job we can hook you up with something. Joe's boxing groceries over at Bud's Market. Dean worked weekends during school at Stan's gas station and they're keeping him on for the summer. They always need extra guys to help check the tires and wash windshields."

"The best money's at Joor Muffler. They pay a dollar and a quarter an hour! But it's really hard work."

"You coming to the dance tonight?"

"We might pick up some pizza at Lary's and maybe a burger and shake at George and Ann's later. Wanna come along?"

BB is overwhelmed by their stream of enthusiasm. Walking less than one block with them he's already included as one of the guys. They make it so easy.

"I'm not sure. I'm picking up some shoes, and then I'll see what's next."

The boys gave BB's running shoes a quizzical look.

"Yeah... you sure could use a new pair."

"Well I guess I'll see..."

BB stops mid-sentence when they pass the open door of a billiard parlor. He hears a familiar "Ping! Ping! Ping" and turns to go in. The other fellows hesitate:

"You don't want to go in there! Just old guys hang out in that place."

But BB is oblivious to their scoffs. He walks over to a pinball machine as if he's greeting an old friend. He approaches the middle-aged man who's testing his skills:

"Mind if I give it a try?"

"Sure, kid. I'm not having much luck with this one."

The other guys were holding back at the door, but now they're drawn into the magic of BB's artistry with this machine that mocks the amateur player. His body bends and leans as his fingers punch the two side buttons in rapid succession. The silver metal ball floats down the slope and then shoots to the top again and again. The flippers wave madly. The lights and sounds become a blur. The other patrons stop their pool games and come over to watch. Cheers punch the air with each achievement. The tally spins numbers reaching into the stratosphere. Finally, after one last desperate rescue attempt, the ball drops into the hole. Game over. BB casually comments:

"That was a nice warm up."

The other boys can't believe what they've just seen.

"Warm up? That was amazing! Where did you learn to do that?"

"My dad keeps an old pinball machine at our house. We've been holding family tournaments for years. This is a real classic you've got here."

The men in the game room aren't ready to see him go:

"How about another game?"

But BB's buddies break in.

"Sorry. We've got other plans for this kid. Big night ahead. Let's go!"

Back on the street, they spot a group of girls leaving a dress shop. And there she is again. The girl with the sideways ponytail, this time in a shirtwaist dress with a full skirt in that great shade of pink. The girls throw her heaps of compliments:

"I'm so glad you found that dress. And in your color! It fits perfectly! You always look good in your clothes. Lucky!"

With a quick glance back at BB, she and her girlfriends turn into Ting's Pharmacy.

"I love their milkshakes, especially strawberry. Hey, the gang's all here..."

The girls' voices blend with the chatter at the soda fountain. When the door closes behind them, BB wonders aloud who the girl in the ponytail is.

"She's been here since January. She calls herself Pinkie, but we're not sure what her real name is. Staying with her aunt and uncle up on Juniper Street. Her folks are out of the country. Something about an "assignment" or "appointment." Bob thinks they might even be spies."

Bob winks and adds a few more sketchy facts:

"Who knows? Anything's possible these days. She stays pretty much to herself. Lots of guys have asked her out, but no dice. Friendly enough and certainly pretty. Maybe you'll have a chance with her."

They give him an easygoing push and break out in good-natured laughter as they pull open the door to Ting's. BB really is enjoying their company, but he's on a mission.

"I don't know about that. Anyways, I've got to get those shoes. See you later."

In front of the store there's a rack of Times-Advocate *newspapers. His eyes zero in on the date: Friday, June 7, 1963*

"1963! What the...? This can't be real!"

He forces down a rising panic and bolts across the street to D'Agosta Shoes. A helpful saleswoman brings out a pair of leather loafers assuring him they are the latest style. They fit perfectly! And there's plenty from his $20 to cover his *purchase. What a deal! His outfit complete, his self assurance begins to grow. He turns back to Ting's, but his eye is drawn to the display of watches in a window on the corner. The open door lures him in where another friendly clerk greets him:*

"Looking for anything in particular, son?"

"I really like your watches, but I'm not sure I can afford anything you've got."

"I have a unique style that just arrived. I haven't even had time to unpack the shipment. I'll go in the back and get it."

He returns with a blue wristwatch, a one-of-a-kind piece that BB can't stop admiring.

"With tax, you can have it for $18.50. I know that's a lot, but it *is* a special edition."

Downcast, BB shoves his hand into his pants pocket to bring out his meager two dollars and change. Surprisingly there's another $20 dollar bill!

"Great! You'll have some left over for a good time tonight. Got any special plans?"

BB slips on the watch and adjusts the band.

"I haven't thought… Yeah! The dance! Thanks for your time!"

Back on the sidewalk, BB spots an aquamarine Chevy convertible waiting for the light to change. It's the guys he left at Ting's.

"BB! Jump in! We're headed to The Car Hop before the dance. The gals on roller skates are good friends of ours."

BB hops into the back seat of the '58 Impala. Cruising up Grand Avenue, he has a sense of belonging he's never felt before. Kids on the street wave back at him. He's part of the scene. It's been effortless. But then the car radio blasts out that Elvis song once more, the one that reminds him of his uncertain situation, his unknown future.

"Why was I sent here? Will I ever get back to my old life, my family? Why do I keep thinking about them? I've got everything I've ever wanted right here: acceptance, friends, people going out of their way for me. Maybe I'm meant to be here after all."

After a quick meal of burgers and fries, they set out for the dance hall. BB's pals introduce him to their friends as they weave through the crowd waiting on the sidewalk. Just beyond the arcade in another window display, BB's eyes laser in on a blue leather jacket with a large "B" on the front.

"Hey! Cool jacket!"

"*That* jacket? It's been in the window for months. All the athletes get their letterman jackets here. He's great about layaways until we can pay it off. But no one's interested in that one. Our school colors are orange and black. He said he's waiting for just the right person to walk through the door."

"Well, maybe I'm the one!"

The owner is locking up for the night. But when he spots BB he opens the door and welcomes them in. The others follow behind and introduce him to the owner:

"I think we have a buyer for that blue jacket in the front window. He's not from around here, and the color is just what he's looking for."

The shop owner brings the jacket from the store window. BB slides it on. A perfect fit!

"I usually don't let the boys take their jackets home until they're paid for, but I can let you have it on credit for $20 down."

BB's heart sinks. He knows he's spent almost all of both twenty dollars. He pulls out his money preparing his out-of-luck story. And then he sees another $20 bill!

"Great! I'll mark that down on your account. These boys tell me you're new in town."

"Oh, yeah... I'm just here visiting my... uh... my uncle. Right! My uncle! But when I got here, I found out he's left for a week. On a business trip!"

"Is that so? Did any of these friends of yours offer you a place to stay?"

The other boys suddenly are busy checking out the clothes on the racks.

"It's no big deal. I didn't want to bother them with my problem."

"You know, my wife and I have this big house with an extra bedroom. Why don't you spend the night with us, and you can figure out the rest in the morning."

He scribbles down a note and hands it to BB.

"Here's the address. We'll see you after the dance. You *are* going to the dance?"

"Sure he is!"

BB shoves the paper into his pocket. Back on the sidewalk, BB and his buddies hear the music from the windows above. A line of teenagers is crowding down the hallway and up the stairs to the second floor. BB congratulates himself:

"I was born in the wrong time! They LOVE me!"

CHAPTER TWENTY-ONE

Under the Spell

"What are we standing around here for? The girls are waiting! Let's go!"

Confidence in their prowess builds as they join the group and take the steps two at a time up to the hardwood dance floor. From the DJ's turntable, the lyrics and beat of Martha and the Vandellas' "Heat Wave" fill the dance hall.

In the center of the floor, as if a light were created just for her, Pinkie, the girl of his dreams, dances with a guy BB hasn't seen before. He's not about to get aced out of a chance to be with this girl. But first he needs to work his game, get her to want him. He brags to his new friends as he swaggers onto the dance floor:

"Watch and learn!"

The dance classes he's taken over the years serve him well. His feet move to the beat and he makes his move. He grabs the closest girl and shows off his steps. Before long the rest of the dancers fade to the sides to give him room to really cut loose. His partner adds her energy as their dance builds to the music. The rest of the crowd shouts out "Heat Wave" each time it repeats. As the song ends, the crowd cheers. BB looks around for Pinkie. She coolly surveys the room but finally gives him a riveting gaze that sends an exhilarating bolt right through him. His pals gather around.

"Where did you learn to dance like that?"

"That's nothing. You should see me when I really let go."

His eyes are still locked with Pinkie's as he pants slightly out of breath:

"I've always liked that song,"

"What do you mean *always*? That's a demo record. It hasn't been released yet."

BB's head snaps back to the group. He's caught without an explanation.

"Yeah, Frank's dad has a friend at Motown Records who sends him new songs to see if they'll catch on out here on the west coast. Frank brings them to our dances to test them out before they actually do a final recording session back in Detroit."

"Did I say that *song*? I meant I've always liked that *group*."

He suddenly takes an interest in Frank, someone he had dismissed as just a nobody. He puts his arm around Frank and draws him in confidentially.

"Does your dad really have connections to Motown? I'd like to hear more about that. You must be the first kid in town to hear about the hot groups. You're the kind of guy I'd like to get to know better."

Frank eats up this attention from BB, who has now distinguished himself as a man of many talents. BB once again turns his eyes to Pinkie.

"So, good buddy, d'you think she'll dance with me?"

"Who? Her? Are you kidding? You're going to have to wait in line. And she never dances with the same guy twice, so don't get your hopes up."

"I don't wait for anyone. I know how to get the prettiest girl in the room. Just need to know how to move in... work it. You gotta believe in yourself if you want to win!"

BB brushes off their concerns as they warn him he's heading into a no-win situation. His mind made up, his undaunted confidence carries him across the room. Pinkie greets him with a slow smile:

"Well, *hello* there."

He's already on firm footing with this girl, but her next comment is totally unexpected.

"I've had my eye on you. I was just waiting to see if you know how to get what you want. Looks like you do."

As BB and Pinkie take the dance floor, he watches the disbelieving reaction from the guys. The music seamlessly slips into the next number as the attractive, charismatic couple moves into a perfect combination of dance steps. It's as if they'd practiced them forever. The fast paced song ends and the music shifts to a slow dance. BB holds onto Pinkie's arm, wondering if she'll break the spell and walk away. But she stays and takes his other hand. They begin to sway to the haunting melody of "Soldier Boy." The lyrics, the emotions of young love, flow with the mesmerizing music. And he has this incredible vision in his arms.

"This can't be real. This isn't my life. I'm afraid if I pinch myself I'll wake up from a dream I could never imagine. Life can be so easy... so sweet... everything going my way. Nothing holding me back... weighing me down. Just look at her!"

BB soaks in Pinkie's beauty. His eyes search her face. Pinkie reaches her arms around his neck. He slips both of his arms around her waist, linking his fingers and resting his hands lightly on her back. The words continue, promising a future of never-ending love. BB breaks in with a compliment, his boldness growing with each passing moment:

"I really like your dress. You look great in that color."

Pinkie blushes and peers up at him through her lashes. BB is captivated by the curve of her mouth, the scent of her perfume, her voice as she draws him in:

"It's about time there was someone interesting in this town. You certainly are a step above those guys over there."

BB looks over at his new friends. They gape in disbelief at his good fortune with this unattainable prize. He gives them a quick, no-big-deal look. And then he turns back to her smile. He's lost in the moment... that musical invitation to romance. There's no turning back! He's gone!

The song ends and Pinkie excuses herself to join her girlfriends who are on their way to the restroom. BB walks over to his friends along the wall.

"Man, you've got all the right moves! None of us could even get a nod in our direction from her. She's in a league all her own. Nice going!"

"That's the way I always operate. Keep 'em off balance. Say all the things they're longing to hear. Works every time. Piece of cake!"

At that moment Pinkie returns to the dance floor and BB joins her. But she isn't interested in any more dancing:

"It's hot and crowded in here. Let's get some air."

BB is more than happy to oblige. He gives his incredulous buddies a final salute and heads down the steps with his conquest. However, Pinkie's the one who's still working her magic spell, and he's obviously smitten. She purrs close to his ear:

"I really wanted to spend some time... just with you."

Out on the street he makes a hopeful suggestion:

"Would you like to get a milk shake and maybe something to eat?"

"It's been a long day and it's getting late. I've got to pick up my car early in the morning as soon as the shop opens up. Maybe we can meet up tomorrow?"

Suddenly all of his swagger melts away. He doesn't want this evening to end. And he wants to be sure she won't forget him. He blurts out his concern:

"I don't want you to be by yourself. In the dark, that is. Let me walk you home."

As they stroll up Grand Avenue, Pinkie takes his hand. At her touch, his heart jumps to his throat. She turns to him:

"By the way, where are you staying?"

"I'm not sure where it is. This guy gave me a note with the address on it."

BB stops under the street lamp and unfolds the crumpled piece of paper.

"700 Juniper. OH!"

"Oh no! That's my *house! Or is it? What am I getting myself into?"*

"That's my aunt and uncle's house. I'm living with them while my parents are out of the country on an assignment for the university. My uncle is such a friendly helpful guy. Of course he'd invite you! Don't worry! There's lots of room."

Under his breath, BB quietly whispers:

"Yeah, I know."

Turning onto Juniper, they soon arrive at the huge Victorian house on the far left corner. It still has paint issues, always a problem to keep up with. But otherwise it has the same steep steps leading to the wide veranda and entrance. BB is welcomed as a guest in the house he's known his whole life. But now it's another family occupying the big, drafty rooms. The warmth of their concern for him quickly puts his mind at ease. Pinkie offers to show him to the guest room on the second floor. It's his room. But not quite. A few frills here and there plus a pink Princess phone on the bedside stand are a complete departure from his style.

There's one more surprise to add to this confusing yet strangely comforting day. Pinkie leads him by the hand down the hall to the front room. On a shelf sits a vintage box radio. She switches on one of the dials and adjusts the volume. Spinning the other knob past a distorted assortment of voices and sounds, she finally locates the local music station that's playing the Top Ten on the charts.

Her next move is something BB is very familiar with, something he often did late at night after his parents were asleep. Pinkie opens the window and steps out onto the tiny balcony. She reaches back to offer BB her hand. As he joins her, he hesitates briefly before releasing his grip. Carefully climbing over the low spindle railing, they settle down on the gently sloping roof. They pull up their knees and rest their chins, gazing out to the downtown lights. Through the open window the radio DJ's voice breaks in:

"This song came out last summer, but it's still a good one! It goes out to that new boy in town who's just here for the summer. Hope you're having a great time!"

The smooth, mellow tones of the Drifter's lead singer begins, the backup voices keeping a steady beat with "Up on the Roof." It's a different style but the familiar words haunt him. He remembers his moods that so recently drew him to this very spot.

BB starts thinking about this house, this town where everything feels and looks so different from his real life. It's the same place... but it isn't. He tries to sort things out in his head. He raps his knuckles on the roof shingle.

"I know I'm here on the roof of my *house. Still I feel more 'at home' here, more appreciated, more accepted. Can I say it? More loved. Is it real? Is* anything *real?"*

BB searches the night sky for the North Star, the one his dad taught him to locate when he was just a kid. The one star you can always count on. The one that never moves. He sneaks a peek at Pinkie. She's looking right at him! His face turns a deep crimson. He averts his eyes to the view over his knees. He hugs them tight, holding in his elation.

"This is the life I was meant to live. Time to leave it all behind and embrace this!"

The voices and music fade away, the final words leaving him with a hopeful promise. BB lets out a deep, shivering sigh. Pinkie assures him:

"Everything's going to be fine; I'll be right there with you."

CHAPTER TWENTY-TWO

Jarring Juxtaposition

BB's dream is interrupted by an annoying pecking on his window. He swims upward from the depths of sleep.

"Why is it always the best part that gets lost. Now I'll never know what happens."

He opens one eye and turns to see a fluttering yellow bird tapping its tiny beak against the pane. Once its mission is accomplished, it disappears into the trees. The inviting aroma of frying bacon and freshly baked cinnamon rolls sets his stomach rumbling.

"Mom is definitely outdoing herself this morning!"

He sighs and sinks back into his pillow.

"Wait! Oh no!"

He looks around and realizes it's the same room where he fell asleep the night before. Resigned to the fact his life is still in some sort of parallel time zone, BB pulls on his clothes and shoes, runs to the bathroom for a quick face wash, and tiptoes down the back stairs to the kitchen. He holds his breath, turns the last steps, and sees... Pinkie and her aunt. Her aunt gives him a cheerful greeting and smiles warmly:

"Sleep well?"

Between mouthfuls of the delicious breakfast Pinkie addresses him:

"We've got a big day ahead of us and we need to get going. Help yourself to the scrambled eggs and bacon. Don't miss out on my aunt's famous cinnamon rolls!"

BB is spared from conversation as Pinkie continues to fill him in on their schedule:

"Soon as you're finished, we'll walk down to pick up my car. It needed new brakes. They're also checking underneath while they have it up on the rack."

BB and Pinkie say their goodbyes to her aunt and stroll down the street past Grand Avenue. He wonders if Pinkie is thinking about the moments they shared last night. But she's on a mission. He hurries to keep up with her. On the far corner the familiar Joor Muffler Man looms over the street, twenty-two feet tall in his blue pants and white shirt, holding that huge muffler in front of him.

"Do you see your car?"

"They kept it locked up in the bay so no one messed with it overnight."

As they cross the street, Pinkie calls to the owner who's opening up for the day:

"Hey, Jerry! What's the news on my car?"

"Just the brakes. And I threw in an alignment to keep that beauty riding smooth. Your tires still look good though. I'll pull it out for you, and you can be on your way. Your uncle said to just charge it to him and he'd be by later to take care of it."

BB can't believe his eyes when Jerry backs out a blue Corvette convertible.

"Thanks, Jerry. Hop in, BB! We've got a big day ahead."

BB settles into the passenger seat and runs his hand over the rich black leather.

"Where'd you ever score this sweet ride?"

"It's really my dad's. I told you my parents are out of the country. He wanted to be sure his baby was kept in good running order. He trusts me."

Before long they're cruising down the highway to San Diego. They cross over the glistening water of a lake and begin the ascent to the mesa. BB is familiar with the drive, but it looks so different. No freeway and no houses and offices and malls. Just wide open space and blue skies above.

Pinkie turns on the car radio, flips the knob to a pop station, and cranks up the volume. The Chantays' masterful rendition of "Pipeline" booms from the speakers. BB slaps his knees to the driving rhythm from the electric bass. His "air guitar" follows the rapidly descending notes and then picks up the theme. Pinkie taps her fingers on the steering wheel. BB's feeling pretty confident about all that's happened so far, all that keeps going his way:

"I think I've got this. No. I know *I've got this! I'm just being myself and doing what I think is best and everything turns out great. Just look at where I am! This isn't so bad."*

He leans back, casually resting his elbow on the top of the car door. A cocky grin lights up his face. Pinkie glances over and shakes her head.

Within minutes they dip down to the river valley and back up through the eucalyptus tree-lined canyon. Pinkie expertly weaves the car around the turns and through the arches of the bridge spanning the canyon divide. She swerves onto a side street and up the hill to Balboa Park.

"I thought we'd start our day here. It's my favorite place to wander and just think."

Pinkie slides the Corvette into a parking spot and turns off the motor. BB looks around at the familiar park. A melancholy mood comes over him as he thinks about the picnics and concerts his family enjoyed here.

"What's wrong, BB?"

"Oh, nothing. Just remembering some... never mind."

He shakes off the memory and joins Pinkie on their expedition. Through the grove of trees the Spreckels Organ Pavilion comes into view. The massive edifice looks like a forlorn, rejected bride left waiting for years at the altar. As the road curves to the left, they arrive at a construction site. The picture of the proposed building is exactly the modern design BB remembers. The crumbled remains of the previous buildings are heaped to one side. Chimes from a carillon draw BB's eyes to the soaring California Tower to the left.

"I sure hope they're not thinking of destroying that one too."

BB gazes down the promenade to where the fountain should be. But it's gone! In its place is a structure he's never seen.

CHAPTER TWENTY-THREE

The Anointing

"It's open! I was hoping since it's Saturday they'd be running the carousel."

Joyful music calls to them as Pinkie pulls him along to the octagon-shaped shelter. Big wooden doors are flung wide to reveal a menagerie of wooden creatures bobbing up and down. He's not a huge fan of carousels, but he doesn't want to put a damper on Pinkie's excitement. While she buys their tickets, BB stirs up his enthusiasm:

"I've got the ostrich. You take that frog."

"No! We need outside animals so we can grab the rings! I want this horse with its beautiful tail."

"Okay, I'll be right behind you on my lion."

The band organ music puts them in a festive mood as the carousel begins to move and gradually picks up speed. Pinkie calls to BB:

"There it is! Grab one!"

The slotted chute is just out of reach of a little girl in front of Pinkie, and Pinkie has trouble timing her lean. But BB's long arms easily snatch a ring. The second time around he again plucks a ring. With each revolution, he manages to add to his growing collection. He calls out to Pinkie:

"So what do I get for these rings?"

"Are you kidding me? How'd you get so lucky?"

"It's not luck. It's skill!"

"Well, Mr. Humble, each of those rings is a free ride. And we can't stay here all day, as much as I'd like to."

"Well, then I've got some souvenirs!"

He shoves the brass rings into his pocket.

"Don't be such a Scrooge! Look at all these little kids who are too small to reach. This little girl in front of me's been struggling the whole ride."

Ignoring Pinkie's suggestion, BB concentrates on one last pass to add to his collection.

"Got it!"

But this one feels different, warm in his hand. When he looks down at the ring, the glint of gold catches the attention of two shadowy creatures perched high in a nearby palm tree. They've been waiting for just this moment, and their vigil has not been in vain. They consult with one another in an ominous crackle.

At the same moment, The Council is alerted in Bond Headquarters. They'll intervene when needed. The sand in the huge hourglass begins to flow ever so slightly and sends a link to the one in BB's room. Secret Legends are on full alert. Nature's special agents receive their orders. The hourglass now allows occasional views to Pinkie and BB. The light behind the wall pulses, ready to provide its strength to the young team.

Meanwhile, as BB stares into his hand, the gold ring dissolves into a swish of light and color that swirls around his head, threads through his hair, and then disappears with a splash of sparkles in the sunlight. He shakes off the vision. When the ride ends, Pinkie throws out a challenge:

"So are you going to give up those rings, Hot Shot?"

Eager to play the hero, BB holds up his handful of brass rings and calls out:

"Hey kids! Who wants a free ride? It's on me!"

"I do! I do!"

BB holds his prizes high above the children, enjoying the spotlight. Pinkie chides him:

"Don't be such a tease! Give them the rings!"

"Okay. Okay. Here you go. One each."

One of the fathers comes over to thank BB:

"You don't know how much this means to my two girls. This will be their last ride for a very long time."

Pinkie picks up on his downcast spirit:

"Why? Are you moving away?"

"No. My wife is losing her job. We won't have money for things like carousel rides."

"That's too bad. Can't she get another job?"

"Not as good as the one she has. She's the head housekeeper at the Hotel del Coronado. The current owner is tearing it down to develop the land so he can make more money. Everyone's getting laid off."

BB is less concerned about this family's plight than he is about the hotel's future:

"Tearing down the Del? No way! I've got to see it one more time before that happens. Come on, Pinkie. Let's go!"

"Absolutely not! We don't have time for this. I've got other things planned."

"Please, Pinkie. Have a heart! What will it take? An hour maybe?"

Pinkie mentally calculates the cost of this detour. They need to go downtown anyway to pick up Highway 101 and head up the coast. The trip over and back to the hotel for a quick look should take no more than forty-five minutes.

"I suppose we could. But no more suggestions! Come on. I'll race you to the car!"

Armed with this new information, the feathery spies hop into the air and row steadily to the west. Pinkie sets off at a quick pace, and BB lets her get a good lead. But then his years of track come into play as he effortlessly passes her. With a well-practiced final kick he sprints to the car. When she finally catches up, Pinkie gushes her admiration:

"I thought I was fast, but you're unbelievable!"

BB basks in her adulation. She starts the car, and the radio comes to life with "One Fine Day" by the Chiffons. It's not one BB's familiar with, but Pinkie obviously is:

"I love this song!"

As they pass the organ pavilion to the main drive, Pinkie joins the harmonies, singing the hopes of a young girl longing for love. Under the west park entrance and over the the arched bridge, BB nervously listens to the musical rendition of a romantic relationship. Thankfully Pinkie's keeping her eyes on the road and doesn't see his hopeful confusion. Does she really want this or is it just words of a song? His daydream abruptly ends as they roll down the hills to the city:

"What's going on? Where are all the tall buildings?"

This isn't the skyline BB is used to seeing. Pinkie ignores his questions as she concentrates on the route that takes them to the bay. Just past the tuna fleet a ferry is loading up. The booming boat whistle warns she'll soon cast off. Pinkie edges the car into the lineup.

"I hope there's room for us so we don't have to wait for the next one."

"Wait? What's going on? Why don't we just cross the..."

BB was about to say "bridge" but stops short when he doesn't see the graceful curve off to the left.

"Whatever you're thinking, forget it! Help me get my car lined up."

Pinkie slowly maneuvers the convertible onto the green-trimmed white ferry and turns off the engine:

"We're not sitting down here when there's a gorgeous day to enjoy up top. Follow me!"

Taking the stairs to the upper deck, they find a spot at the railing. As the ferry sets sail, the smell of the tar-coated pilings of the dock gives way to the salt air. Gulls soar and pelicans dive into the deep water.

"Pretty nice view for a quarter, don't you think?"

BB agrees with a nod of his head. He looks back at the polished teakwood benches and then turns to lean on the smooth varnished wood rail. He moves in closer, his right arm just inches from Pinkie's. But she's focused on the water.

"Look! A dolphin! What luck! We don't see them in the harbor that often."

The playful creature swims alongside the boat briefly and then turns away with a quick leap. The fifteen-minute ride doesn't last long enough to suit BB. The ferry approaches the dock and begins to slow down, the waves and wake slushing as the captain cuts the engine and they come to a stop. Pinkie grabs his hand:

"Come on! We've got to be ready to roll when they finish locking down."

Other passengers are revving up their engines as BB and Pinkie weave their way to their car. Moments later they disembark into a place where even time takes a vacation.

CHAPTER TWENTY-FOUR

The Lady by the Sea

"We've seen his organ pavilion. We even drove past a theatre and park on our way here. And now you're about to behold one more Spreckels gift to the city. Check it out!"

With a sweep of her arm, Pinkie draws his eyes to a one-of-a-kind Victorian structure. Its distinctive cone shaped red roof spreads its skirts over white exterior walls. Scarlet turrets stand sentinel. It's a familiar sight to BB but it still gives him a thrill. His heart sighs, remembering annual family visits to view the elaborate Christmas tree in the lobby.

They skip up the side steps and through white doors into a courtyard of tropical splendor. Following the path through the greenery and flowers, they finally arrive in the richly paneled lobby that soars more than two stories. Immediately a team of reporters and cameramen leap to their feet:

"Are you two starring in the movie Hollywood's been buzzing about? We heard you were coming to the Hotel Del. Let's get a picture of the two of you together and then we'll do some individual shots."

Pinkie assures them they've made a mistake, but BB is reveling in the attention. She grabs his arm and firmly steers him to a set of double doors on the left.

"Come on. Maybe we can peek in before someone catches us."

Through the open doors their eyes travel up to the finely crafted wood ceiling and the crown chandeliers. As they step onto the plush carpet, a deep, friendly voice greets them:

"You kids looking for something?"

"Sorry, sir. We just wanted to see if this room is still as beautiful as ever."

"It sure is, my dear. There's not one nail in that ceiling. Just wooden pegs and glue. Amazing, isn't it! I've worked at the Del for years. Seen lots of fancy, important people come and go. Served them their dinners and made sure everything was to their liking. Never thought those days would come to an end. But my job is gone or will be soon. And all the people who work here... busboys, maids, clerks, cooks... they're losing their jobs too."

"Isn't there anything anyone can do to stop it?"

"I appreciate your concern, young man. The new owner is tearing the whole place down. I thought for sure she'd live for years to come after the last owner spruced her up. She really looks fresh and beautiful again, don't you think? But this new guy couldn't wait for the ink to dry on the purchase agreement before he started talking about the end. He said the land is too valuable. He wants to get rid of her and build new fancy homes to sell."

"They can't do that. HE can't do that!"

"He can and he will."

He takes a yellowing, ragged-edged brochure from his breast pocket and reads:

"The Hotel del Coronado is one of the nation's most famous resort hotels. She's the unrivaled Queen of seaside resorts. This enchanting spot has no equal in America or the world. The Lady by the Sea is a truly iconic beach hotel, offering something special for everyone. She stands tall as a beacon of grandeur and refinement among vacation resort destinations.

How can he rip apart this beautiful lady? I don't know what's going to happen to some of these people who've depended on jobs here. Look at Mrs. Mendoza over there, our head housekeeper."

He points to a middle-aged woman in uniform standing not far from the reception desk, tears glistening in her deep brown eyes. They realize she's the mother of the two young girls from the carousel.

"She hasn't stopped crying since she heard the awful news. This was her first job after coming to this country, and she's worked her way up to a good paying position. Her family depends on her income."

He indicates a man reading a paper at a table near the far windows:

"There's the man responsible. Mr. Lawrence."

BB points to the timeworn pamphlet:

"Can I borrow that for a few minutes? I promise to take good care of it."

Reluctantly the older gentleman hands it over. Pinkie and BB resolutely walk over to the important man, their hearts pounding with determination coupled with trepidation. They take their positions, one on each side of his chair. BB starts his pitch:

"Excuse me. Mr. Lawrence?"

"What do you kids want? I'm a busy man."

"We heard about your plans to tear down this hotel and we'd like to talk with you."

"Nothing you say will change my mind. But go ahead. Knock yourselves out."

He continues to read his paper while Pinkie launches into their appeal:

"This beautiful hotel is an American treasure, a living legend."

And then BB reads from the pamphlet he's borrowed:

"Look at this brochure. It talks about the hotel being a Grand Dame, a Grand Lady:

> 'This Lady by the Sea is unparalleled in her glory, her uniqueness, workmanship, craftsmanship, and beauty. She is the Pearl of Paradise!'

How can you destroy something like that?"

Their words continue to fall on deaf ears. BB tries another tactic:

"Everyone else is tearing down these famous resorts, especially the ones on the beaches. This is the last one still standing. You own the last seaside resort hotel!"

Lawrence looks up at the mention of his uniqueness. BB pursues this line:

"No one will ever build something like this again. No one can afford the craftsmanship, the skill it took to create it."

Pinkie tries a new angle:

"Don't you care about the people who live here in Coronado? Your neighbors?"

Lawrence returns to his paper:

"Hmph! What did they ever do for me? Except give me headaches over my projects."

BB gestures to Pinkie to squelch this approach. He tries a personal appeal:

"You don't want to be remembered as the one who destroyed the Beautiful Lady by the Sea. You want to be remembered as her savior! Her hero!"

That catches Lawrence's attention, but only briefly. BB tries again:

"Just think of the stories she could tell if her walls could speak!"

Pinkie picks up on this thread:

"Like that movie they filmed here! They say Marilyn Monroe adored this place!"

Just within reach of the discussion sits a movie mogul who's spending the weekend at the hotel. Billy Wilder. He's finished his lunch and is scanning a script from a stack on the table. He's been half listening to the conversation only two tables away. But at the mention of Marilyn Monroe's name, Wilder neatly returns the script to the pile and stands up. By this time Lawrence has had enough of the young advocates and abruptly pushes back his chair. As he stalks away, Pinkie and BB hold back, realizing all of their efforts have been for nothing. But Lawrence isn't through with them yet:

"Get lost. I've got better things on my mind besides saving this sagging old lady. And I'd better not hear of you going to the newspaper about this. You'll regret it!"

BB and Pinkie retreat to return the borrowed pamphlet. Wilder isn't about to let this end, however. He strides over to Lawrence and puts an arm around his shoulder in a friendly but controlling way:

"What's this rumbling about tearing down the Del? You can't be serious, Larry."

Lawrence's tone abruptly changes. He loves being on first name basis with the right people. He chuckles nervously and wriggles out of Wilder's embrace.

"Oh, Billy, that's just rumors. You know you can't trust everything you hear,"

"Larry, we looked far and wide, but this was the only place we could find that hadn't changed in thirty years. People who've never seen this beautiful hotel will never believe we didn't make those scenes on a movie lot. It's like the past came to life!"

BB and Pinkie hover nearby to see how this plays out. Lawrence appears deeply concerned as he takes in Wilder's every word. They wonder if he's truly buying into this argument or if he'll dismiss Wilder as quickly as he waved off their concerns.

"You know, Larry, *Some Like It Hot* was one of Marilyn's best performances. This place inspired her! Now, the public is still grieving over her death. If you throw this bombshell at them it could stir up a huge backlash."

Hoping he's touched a soft spot in Lawrence's heart, he creates a romantic scenario:

"This place is more like a fairyland than a hotel. It fulfills the dreams of pleasures. Pleasures that awaken the senses. When you come here it's like passing through a door to enchantment, the possibility of living a rapturous dream at the seaside."

"I don't know about all of that, Billy. It's just a big heap of wood. A firetrap really."

It's obvious Wilder isn't making a dent in the hotel owner's determination to bring down the lovely structure. He decides to try a new tactic:

"This has been a relaxing getaway for the Hollywood set for years. Even back to the Golden Days of Hollywood. Just think of the rich and famous people who've stayed here: Charles Lindberg, Thomas Edison, Babe Ruth, Charlie Chaplin, princes and kings. You never know who you'll rub elbows with! People are going to be upset if you mess with their memories and their love for this place. When they find out you're tearing it down, they'll be devastated!"

Wilder still isn't getting through to him.

"Okay then. How about this? Keep her and really give her a great facelift. You'll have them clamoring for parties all year long. Hosted by you of course."

Wilder realizes he's hit the mark. He drapes his arm once again around Lawrence's shoulders and reverts to his movie director's charm. He paints a vivid scene with his sweeping gestures and stirring words:

"Picture it on New Year's Eve. Fireworks over the ocean right at your front door. People cheering and applauding... you, of course!"

Lawrence's whole demeanor transforms. During the conversation with Wilder he had warmed to the idea. But now he realizes the impact the story of "Saving the Del" will have for creating business. It will also burnish his image and, most importantly, cement his place in history. He summons the reporters and cameramen from the lobby for a press conference to announce his grand plans for the hotel's future. Combining all that he's heard in the past few minutes, especially the arguments from BB and Pinkie, he launches into a stirring narrative:

"First of all, I want to dispel any rumors you may have heard about tearing down the hotel. That has *never* been my intention. This place is one-of-a-kind. The beauty and craftsmanship! There's nothing like her in the world! She's the Pearl of Paradise! Be sure to write that down. I've been having a lovely chat with my good friend, Billy Wilder. He said no one else has my great vision. Everyone else is tearing down the old resort hotels left and right. They don't care about their communities like I care for the people of Coronado. I would *never* betray them. This hotel is an American treasure, a living legend, just like our dear Marilyn Monroe, God rest her soul."

He pauses for the desired solemn effect.

"While we can't bring Marilyn back, we can make sure the place she adored lives on! The Hotel del Coronado truly is the Lady by the Sea. You can quote me on that too. I'll be her savior against all who would even contemplate her demise!"

The newsmen are eating it up. What a story! Pencils fly across notebooks recording each sound bite flowing from his lips. Cameras close in to capture his emotions. Flashbulbs pop all around. Lawrence lifts the moment to new emotional heights:

"Let me get a little sentimental here. I sense there may be some doubt to my sincerity. I want to assure you I have a personal relationship with this place. It's like having a love affair with a beautiful woman. Sometimes late at night, after a hard day, I'll just roam through the halls. I feel like I'm having a date with my best girl!"

He pauses again to let this latest picture sink in and to give them time to quote him.

"When I thought of how important this place has been to everyone down through the years, all of the famous people who have called this their place of calm in the storm of life, I just knew I had to make an even greater commitment. So today I am opening my checkbook to give this lovely lady whatever she wants and needs to make her happy. You can count on it!"

The newsmen rush to send their stories back to their newspapers. Radio and TV crews set up remote locations for on-the-scene reporting. Even Billy Wilder has done his part to get the word out. Phone calls from Hollywood start flooding the hotel switchboard, congratulating Lawrence on his good judgment, his vision, and his wonderful generosity to save the Del. In the background, Mr. Wilder turns to a waiter:

"What do you think of Mr. Lawrence saving the Del *and* your job?"

"No, sir. Mr. Lawrence was determined to level her and develop this valuable property. People don't dare question him and his decisions. That kid over there was brave enough to confront him and try to get him thinking differently. He set the stage for you to step in to clinch the deal. If it hadn't been for him, you wouldn't have even known what was in the works. And I'd be looking for another job."

Wilder is fascinated with the possibility of turning this into a real story, the kind the industry loves. He wanders over to where BB and Pinkie are watching the action. BB can't believe the famous producer is walking toward him. When Wilder extends his hand, BB grabs it and pumps the man's arm up and down:

"It's a privilege to meet you, Mr. Wilder! You really know how to make great movies. I'm glad you changed Mr. Lawrence's mind."

"My pleasure, kid."

Wilder extracts his hand from BB's grip and continues:

"I've been hearing how you understand what's important to people, what they like. Wisdom beyond your years. Something we could use up in Hollywood."

"Thanks, sir. I try my best."

"Well your best is better than what I've seen from a lot of young people your age."

BB is eating up the praise, but he doesn't want to look too eager:

"That's nice of you to say."

"I'm having a party Monday evening at my home in Los Angeles. Anyone who matters in the business will be there. Why don't you and your friend stop by?"

BB looks over at Pinkie, wondering what her plans are going forward. Caught up in the excitement of meeting this famous man, she enthusiastically nods her head.

"Do you have a place to stay? No? I'll make a reservation at The Beverly Hills Hotel for you. Do you think you'll be in LA by tomorrow?"

In the back of her mind Pinkie's thinking they could be through LA and on their way north. She hesitates, but BB eagerly jumps in:

"This sounds great, Mr. Wilder. Thanks for the invitation!"

Wilder brings out a small business folder:

"Here's my card with the address on the back. Show it to the man at the door and he'll let you through. If you need anything, my number's there."

As Wilder walks away they congratulate themselves on their good luck.

"I can't believe this! Did you hear that, Pinkie? He thinks I've got possibilities!"

"I've always known there was something special about you, BB. It's about time someone else noticed too."

Mrs. Mendoza, the head housekeeper, has been waiting for them to finish. She wouldn't dream of interrupting an important man like Mr. Wilder. She eagerly waves them over:

"Everyone's heard the wonderful news about the hotel! They can't believe how everything changed so quickly. Come on. Come on. Come with me."

As she leads them through the doors to the kitchen, a joyous cry erupts:

"Hooray! Thank you! Thank you! You saved our jobs and our families!"

The kitchen staff, housekeeping maids and waiters are all gathered to cheer BB. One small action on his part has changed the lives of so many people. But Mrs. Mendoza isn't finished. She jingles a giant ring of keys and beckons them to follow her. Above the ballroom a door leads to an area that's off-limits to the public. She slowly pulls herself up the narrow circular staircase with Pinkie and BB close behind.

"I have the key to the tower. Not everyone gets the chance to see this view. Not even the famous people who stay here. Just us lucky nobodies!"

The tower door opens to a pathway circling the turret fifteen stories above the ground, Leaning on the railing, they get lost in the glorious vistas of San Diego, Mexico and the Pacific Ocean. Mrs. Mendoza, points to the peninsula on the right:

"There's an old lighthouse on top of the bluff that they've been trying to tear down for years. The light hasn't worked... Wait! There *is* a light!"

The revolving lamp suddenly stops and lasers in on BB and Pinkie. The intense glare penetrates their eyes and minds. Pinkie grabs BB's hand to pull him down the stairs:

"Come on. We've got to get out of here. NOW!"

Outside the hotel they race to the car. Tires squeal as they tear out of the parking lot and speed to the dock. The next ferry is just pulling in. Pinkie's clearly on edge while they wait to board. The trip back across the bay has none of the romance of the previous crossing. BB is afraid to ask why she's so agitated. Only when they're on Highway 101 heading up the coast does her breathing return to normal.

CHAPTER TWENTY-FIVE

Surf and Moonlight

"Can't we drive closer to the ocean, Pinkie? I want to see the beaches."

"We need to stay on the 101 and away from the coastline for a while."

"What do you mean? We're missing the ocean."

"We're also missing being seen! Trust me!"

"You keep saying 'Trust me!' But you won't tell me what's going on."

"You wouldn't understand."

"How do you know? Try me!"

"Forget it! I need to concentrate on my driving."

BB has had it with her secrecy, but at least she's no longer driving like a maniac. He stares off to the right, frustrated with her take-charge attitude. When the highway once again drops down and skirts the shoreline, BB spots a racetrack.

"Can we check out a race maybe? There might even be some famous people there."

"There aren't any races in June. We don't have time for horses anyway."

"What *do* we have time for? Are we just going to keep driving forever? Aren't we ever going to stop?"

"Just keep quiet! Please! I know what I'm doing!"

"Really? I'm not so sure about that. You don't seem to have any plan that I can see."

Passing through beach communities and skirting a lagoon, Pinkie finally spots the turnoff she's been looking for:

"Here we are. A safe little cove with a beautiful beach."

They park the car and make their way down to the water. A group of kids from the dance the night before have staked out a spot near one of the fire pits.

"Look! It's Pinkie! And BB's with her! We wondered what happened to you two."

A patchwork of beach towels covers the sand. Sunlight glints off the fins of the scattered surfboards. Pinkie retrieves her bathing suit from the car's trunk. One of the guys offers BB an extra suit from his car. A couple of the boys are just coming out of the water with their boards:

"You surf, BB?"

Actually he has surfed before but he's really terrible. He was hoping to work on his technique this summer. Back home. But he doesn't want to let on that he's a novice.

"Of course! Too bad I don't have my board with me or I'd show you."

"You can borrow mine! Give your jacket to Judy so someone doesn't walk off with it."

Pinkie joins BB with her borrowed board, and the two of them paddle out past the breakers. When she turns her board toward shore, she plays it safe and stays on her hands and knees. Eager to show he's more accomplished, BB hops to his feet and rides a gentle wave to shore where he's met with applause:

"Wow! You really have some moves there, BB! We're shutting down for the day now that the surf's smoothing out. Boy, you really know how to cut those waves! Here's your jacket."

BB casually slings his prized jacket over his shoulder. He and Pinkie stroll over to a two-man volleyball match that's just finishing up. BB's picked up the game at school in PE, but playing in the sand is a whole different skill. Maybe if he can pair up with Pinkie he won't look so bad. But one of the guys already beats him to it:

"Pinkie, you want to be on my team? Just one game. Come on!"

He tosses her the ball, and she awkwardly stands there holding it, totally unsure of what to do next. When she hesitates, BB lets his jacket fall to the sand:

"I'll show you how to serve. It's okay, guys. She can be my partner."

BB circles behind Pinkie and draws his arms close to hers, helping her balance the ball in her left hand. He firmly but gently grasps her right arm for an underhand serve. At that moment Pinkie gazes up at him adoringly:

"You're so wonderful to show me. You're about the most talented boy I've ever met."

BB's eyes lock with hers. His body slightly sways. A voice interrupts his daydream:

"Hey BB! Are we going to have a game or not?"

"Right. Sure. Just watch me, Pinkie, and do your best. I'll pick up the slack."

Surprisingly Pinkie is able to do just enough to keep them in the game. BB covers the court and manages some great saves. With a couple of well-placed spikes, he actually scores a win. He scores the admiration of Pinkie as well. She sighs as she takes his arm:

"Is there *anything* you can't do?"

BB isn't sure the shiver he feels is from her touch or from the ocean breeze that's suddenly turned colder. Pinkie moves in closer to avoid the wind, and BB slips his soft leather jacket around her shoulders. They wander over to where the rest of the gang is already gathering by the open picnic baskets.

"You two want to join us? We're roasting hotdogs. Some of the girls brought potato salad and dessert."

"Okay! BB and I'll be right back as soon as we change out of these suits."

"That's a yes from both of us. Save me a Dr. Pepper!"

When they return they are welcomed into the circle around the fire pit. Pinkie spreads her towel next to his. The sun dips to the horizon. By the time the meal is over, the glow from the fire matches the sunset over the Pacific. Everyone takes turns roasting marshmallows, some cindered in flames. They squeeze them between two graham cracker squares and half a Hershey's chocolate bar. Pinkie slides a perfectly toasted, golden brown sweet from her stick and offers it to BB. She playfully pushes it into his mouth, the gooey mess smearing his lips. Lost in this blissful moment, BB almost misses hearing the next question:

"So BB, are you and your girl staying the night? We've got blankets you can borrow."

"Did he just say 'your girl'? Is that what this looks like?"

BB checks for Pinkie's reaction. She gives him another one of her mysterious smiles that confirms his answer:

"I guess so. As long as you all are staying too."

"This is the most perfect day ever! Why can't my real life be this easy? I've got friends who appreciate me. And a girl who's really interested in me. I've actually got a girl!"

BB is only half listening to the ongoing banter. He stares into the fire, Pinkie so close he can breathe in her salty hair. The ocean gently laps the shore. Suddenly a girl cries out:

"There it is!"

They look up at a huge full moon rising above the bluff, casting its silver light onto the white sand. One of the boys speaks in hushed tones, bringing everyone closer to hear:

"Did you know the gangster Al Capone used this cove when he smuggled rum from Mexico? The boats could locate the beach when the moonlight hit the white sand. That's why it's called Moonlight Beach."

One of the girls anxiously peeks over her shoulder:

"Do you think there might still be smugglers that come here during the full moon?"

"You never know. You'd better stay close to me tonight just in case."

She throws a stick at him:

"Stop scaring me. You're just looking for an excuse to be a hero."

Pinkie picks up on this new topic:

"Actually we *do* have a *real* hero with us. If it weren't for him you'd be saying goodbye to the Hotel del Coronado. Tell them, BB."

BB feigns humility as he shares his tale. Everyone is riveted to his words, especially when BB embellishes his role in saving the hotel. Then he brings out Billy Wilder's card:

"Mr. Wilder. Billy that is. We're on a first name basis now. Anyway, he wants me to be his guest of honor at this big party he's throwing up in Hollywood. All the important people in the business will be there. I might even get a movie offer."

Everyone is duly impressed with his good fortune. Even Pinkie basks in the reflected glory of his popularity and accomplishments. She makes sure her blanket is next to his when the moon crosses above them and they settle down for the night.

CHAPTER TWENTY-SIX

Cruising up the Coast

"Hey, sleepyhead. Time to get going."

Pinkie's soft voice rouses BB from his dream of incredible fame and fortune. One by one the young crowd wakes and stretches in the early morning sun. BB groans:

"Isn't it awfully early?"

But Pinkie is eager to get the morning started:

"Come on! We've got a big day ahead of us."

She shakes the sand from her blanket and towel and begins to fold them. Seeing BB still avoiding her urgings, she pulls on his blanket and rolls him onto the sand.

"Hey! What gives?"

"Let's go! Help me fold these so we can give them back to Joe and get out of here. If you're good, I'll even let you drive."

BB's suddenly wide awake with the thought of driving that magical blue convertible:

"Well, what are you standing there for? I'm ready if you are!"

He grabs his precious jacket and heads to the car. One of the girls calls out to Pinkie:

"There's a couple of extra sandwiches from last night. Why don't you take them with you if you're not coming back to Escondido with us."

Back on the highway the ocean soon fills their view to the west. BB leans back, one hand on top of the steering wheel, his left arm resting on the door.

"Now this is the life. A beautiful girl by my side. An awesome ride. No worries. Just enjoying the good life. The guys back home should see me now!"

Gliding overhead just behind their vehicle, the two ravens have returned to their reconnaissance mission. The ominous pair is so intent on their target that they fail to notice a bald eagle that plunges from high in the sky to intercept them. With a sudden, bloodcurdling shriek it attacks. That warning sends the two ravens into opposing barrel rolls. The eagle swoops around to confront the interlopers. Outmaneuvered, the ravens retreat south to regroup.

Far below, Pinkie and BB are oblivious to the drama in the sky. They've left all traces of civilization behind and crossed into the desolate Pendleton Marine Base. Without warning, the high-powered engine begins to miss and sputter. BB moves the car to the shoulder where it chugs to a stop.

CHAPTER TWENTY-SEVEN

World Turned Upside Down

Pinkie turns on him, shouting accusations:

"What did you do, BB?"

"Nothing! I swear I didn't do anything!"

"Right! I just had the car checked over. Remember?"

BB turns the key. Nothing. He doesn't want to be blamed for ruining her dad's car!

"It's not my fault."

From out of nowhere a tough-looking Marine sergeant comes up behind them:

"What's the trouble, kid? Out for a joy ride with your dad's car? What'd you do?"

BB squints over his shoulder into the sun at the silhouette of a massive man in uniform. In a panic, he looks to Pinkie. She coolly stares at him, challenging him to attempt another excuse. The Marine strides to the driver's side of the car and confronts BB:

"You're on government property. You need to get moving before I take you in."

"I don't know what happened. It just stopped and I can't get it started again."

"Better step out of the car. NOW!"

BB hustles to obey this direct order and meekly stands to face the growling menace. Pinkie remains in her seat unfazed by the exchange she's witnessing.

"Pinkie, please tell this guy I wasn't doing anything wrong."

"Why should I? You haven't exactly been a stellar example of virtue."

BB is stunned by her sudden disloyalty. He was sure she was on his side.

"What do you mean? You've been with me the whole time."

"All I've seen is a self-centered, narcissistic boy who wouldn't help anyone unless he got something back, especially praise and adulation."

"That's not fair. You're the one who got me into those situations. I didn't choose where to go or what to do. What about all those jobs I saved at the hotel? As a matter of fact, there wouldn't *be* a hotel if it weren't for me."

With a knowing smirk, Pinkie just claps her hands slowly at this latest outburst.

"Exactly! Pause for the crowd's approval, especially if they're well connected!"

"So what? I did it! I saved it! It's done!"

"You're right about one thing. I *did* make sure you were where we wanted you to be. I even had that gold ring served up to you."

The Marine picks up on this bit of news:

"He got the ring?"

Full of bravado, BB turns to stare down the drill sergeant:

"What do *you* know about that?"

BB is becoming annoyed at this pair of conspirators who are ganging up on him. But as he looks into the Marine's eyes, he realizes he's seen him somewhere before. The sergeant's slow grin mocks BB's growing recognition.

"Wait a minute. I *do* know you. Back in Washington, D.C. On our eighth grade field trip. You were our bus driver!"

"So you recognize me after all. You certainly aren't the same kid I remember, though. You've changed. And I don't mean you've just gotten older. You've lost something since then. We're going to have to fix that. Knock some of that cockiness out of you."

"What's that supposed to mean? I like myself. I don't need your help."

"Shall we tell him, Sergeant Striker?"

BB swings around and faces Pinkie:

"You know this guy?"

"Of course. We're old friends."

Pinkie gets out of the car and runs around to give Striker a big hug.

"I'm so glad to see you! I've been on my own for such a long time that I almost forgot what it was like to have your support."

She then turns to BB:

"And now you've joined us."

Pinkie is all business now. No more games. No more manipulations.

"Once you clutched that gold ring in your greedy little hand, you became one of us."

"But it disappeared. I don't have it. So that's that. I'll just hitch a ride and head back."

The sergeant steps forward:

"And just where would you be heading back to? No one *really* knows you. You don't belong in this place or this time. You *have* no place to go."

"You know he's right, BB. Besides, once you held that ring and received the anointing, there was no turning back."

BB's heart pounds. His hands start shaking.

"What's going on here? What are you doing? Why me? What have I ever done to deserve this?"

Pinkie solemnly nods in agreement:

"Exactly! What *have* you done to deserve this? I guess we're about to find out."

Now BB's really in a panic. He scrambles for words to make sense of any of this:

"This has got to end! Right now! Just tell me what I have to do!"

But Pinkie and Striker are having their own discussion and completely ignore his frustration. Pinkie fills Striker in on their previous day:

"When we were diverted to the hotel, I wasn't sure if it was The Bond or The Abyss until it all fell into place. Except that lighthouse beam! That was a close call! And then I saw the full moon come up last night and knew the clock had started. The sand is starting to fall in the hourglasses and we're right on schedule."

Striker nods in agreement:

"Absolutely. According to my calculations you have exactly two weeks until the dark phase. The quest must be completed by then. There will be no more time."

BB doesn't know what all of this has to do with him. He demands some answers:

"Just tell me what I have to do!"

Striker turns to him and growls:

"You're here because you've been chosen. Don't ask me why. No one understands The Bond's reasons. But this is your boot camp, so listen carefully. I'll send you in the direction you need to go. *And* you'd better stay close to Pinkie if you know what's good for you."

This last comment from the Marine sergeant completely deflates any fight BB may have left in him. He limply leans against the beautiful car that has taken him into this wilderness of uncertainty:

"My folks must be really worried by now. I'll bet they've even gone to the police. I'm a missing person for sure. I just want to go home!"

"Home? HOME? There's no *home* for you."

CHAPTER TWENTY-EIGHT

The Quest Begins

BB is suddenly exhausted by all that's transpired over the past three days. But he doesn't receive one iota of sympathy. Sergeant Striker comes down hard on him:

"You have to work through your problems, not escape from them."

BB cowers under the intimidating man looming over him. Pinkie takes Striker's arm and pleads with her eyes to go easy. BB meekly argues his point:

"I don't understand. I saw the hotel crumbling in the video at the Washington Monument."

All at once BB becomes angry:

"And I saved it! It *won't* be torn down! That's it! It's time for me to leave! Now just make it happen!"

Pinkie shakes her head. Her even words are cool and unemotional:

"Sorry, BB. It's not in our power. We just follow directions."

BB's frustrations spill out:

"Directions from who? Who's running this show?"

Striker takes a deep breath and begins:

"You've been recruited by The Bond. Ever since that trip to DC three years ago, we've been watching you. We've sent Secret Legends to try to keep you on track so you wouldn't fall into the hands of The Abyss. You've done a pretty good job of ignoring the guidance we've tried to give you. And lately it became clear we needed to intervene."

Pinkie adds her story:

"I had another partner who was lost to The Abyss. I've been in limbo since then, waiting for someone to take his place. They sent me you."

BB's growing more nervous:

"I didn't ask for this. Can't I just quit?"

Striker smiles and shakes his head:

"That's why you're here in 1963. You don't know anyone. There's no place to escape to. You're simply going to have to trust The Bond and the help it sends you."

With this reality laid before him, BB's resolve to flee disappears:

"So I'm going to get help?"

Pinkie jumps in:

"Sure! Don't you remember all of those people back in your town? You don't think that just happened by coincidence, did you?"

Striker continues:

"You will continue to meet up with Secret Legends. But be careful! The Abyss is also going to send people who might seem safe to trust, but the only help they'll give you is 'over the cliff' and into the arms of The Abyss! If necessary, you'll also get assistance from two other members of The Bond's Council. We can't intervene unless we're allowed, and then only one time. Pinkie will recognize the others, so you won't have to worry."

Pinkie has one more piece of information:

"Nature also can work for or against us. That's an ongoing battle between The Bond and The Abyss. But nature will intervene *for* us at critical times."

Striker is puzzled:

"Speaking of nature, where's your little feathery friend, Pinkie?"

"He's around here somewhere. I told him to keep a low profile around BB until we secured him."

Striker is ready to deliver orders:

"Let's put this assignment into gear. Prepare yourselves for any number of challenges and attacks. That hotel thing was just a warm up. The easy road is behind you. Anything can happen now. Be ready!"

"But I *am* ready. I've already got the look I need, and Pinkie's filled in the rest with this great car. Plus I know how to handle people."

He turns to Pinkie for support:

"You saw how I worked around that hotel owner 'til he came to his senses."

"I was watching you all right. Quite the impressive moves."

BB can tell she's mocking him. Striker is back in his face, his finger jabbing BB's chest:

"It'll take more than a 'coat of paint' to deal with what lies ahead. You've got to be tough! On the inside!"

Striker brings out the backpack Agent Allen sent with him. He takes out a blue wallet and a fine leather pouch.

"These will see you through the quest. You'll need food and other things along the way. This wallet will have the funds you need, no more, no less. Remember your pockets back in Escondido? Same deal."

Striker directs this next comment to Pinkie:

"You'll also find that Agent Allen has included his usual item. Use it wisely!"

Striker isn't sure BB is absorbing the seriousness of the moment:

"Now pay attention! It's vital that you don't lose this."

He opens the leather pouch and takes out a handful of small white alabaster chips. He hands one to BB:

"Go ahead. Put it in the gas tank."

BB unscrews the gas cap and drops in the tiny shard. He jumps back as the car springs to life and the engine begins to purr once more. Astonished, he stares first at the car, then Pinkie, and finally Striker, who is proud to explain this latest asset:

"Don't worry about stopping for gas or repairs. You have the ultimate power source that won't let you down. Just be careful you don't let it fall into the wrong hands!"

BB still isn't sure what he's getting into. Pinkie's serene attitude really bothers him. It's like she's been expecting this to happen all along. But he doesn't want to show he's worried. He pulls himself up to his full height and strikes a confident, indifferent pose:

"I've handled things pretty well so far. Whatever you or *they* have planned, it can't be much more than what I've faced already."

At this, Striker loses his temper:

"You have NO IDEA what lies ahead. You think you've had challenges before this? Wait 'til you hit LA!"

Pinkie gives Striker a worried look and shakes her head. She doesn't want him to completely deflate BB's spirit. Striker regains his self control, but he can't keep from wishing he had more time to shape this kid into a real warrior. Through clenched teeth he continues in a barely audible voice just inches from BB's face:

"Here are the orders I was given. You'll receive three artifacts from three different sources. They are your ticket home."

He looks at Pinkie, his voice full of unexpected tenderness:

"And Pinkie can get her release."

He turns to BB again:

"Without these items you cannot complete your quest."

"What do these 'artifacts' look like? Where will I find them? Who will I meet?"

"Here are the descriptions I've been given:

'What fills the smallest space?'
'What can give yet never grows smaller?'
'What is worthless to life, yet is sought by millions?'"

"What's that supposed to mean? Where will I find them? Who'll give them to me?"

"Don't worry. They'll find *you.* Once they're in your possession, your final destination is San Francisco. The Bond will take it from there. The Council hasn't been given any more information. You need to trust each other, something you both definitely need to work on. Stay together! The Bond will always be there for you, so you're never completely alone. The members of The Bond Council will be keeping an eye on you from time to time in our hourglass back at headquarters."

BB's head is spinning with all of these new revelations. His anger boils over:

"This is crazy! I don't want any part of this! Who *is* The Bond? Where's headquarters?"

Striker has come to the end of his patience with this raw recruit:

"No more questions! Stay on Highway 101 and keep heading north. I can't tell you anything more! Now get outa here!"

Pinkie steps between the combative pair and confronts BB. Placing both hands firmly on his chest, she pushes him back from Striker, turns him around, and shoves him to the other side of the car.

"You obviously are in no condition to be driving. The last thing we need is a hothead behind the wheel. I'll take it from here. And I'll take that backpack too."

"Why should *you* get the backpack? He was going to give it to me!"

"Do you think I'm going to trust you with something that important to our quest? We'll talk about this later. For now, I'm in charge."

BB yanks the passenger door open, takes his seat, and slams the door. Pinkie throws the backpack into the trunk. She gives Striker a quick hug and slides in behind the wheel. Brushing a tear from her cheek, she drives away, but not before catching a final glimpse of her friend in the rearview mirror standing proudly at ease in a cloud of dust.

BB is still steaming from his confrontation with Striker. He hates taking orders. And now he's lost out on driving too. Tight lipped he scowls at the wilderness scenery that climbs the coastal hills. Pinkie decides to let him simmer down before she attempts any further discussion. But BB is having his own conversation… with himself!

CHAPTER TWENTY-NINE

Reality Check

"What've I gotten myself into? Wait a minute. I didn't ask for this. I get dragged out of my bed... my life... for what? Who are these people anyway?"

He takes a furtive glance at Pinkie and then stares straight down the highway.

"What does she really think of me? I thought I was getting somewhere with her, but looks like it was all an act. Maybe she doesn't even like me. And what about all those kids I met back in Escondido and at the beach? What's their part in all of this?"

At the same time Pinkie is wondering about this new recruit:

"The Bond must know what it's doing. This one is just as cocky as the last one I got paired with. But he seems to have a different spirit that could be an asset. I'll have to be firm. Still there's something about him I can't quite put my finger on."

BB wants some answers:

"So has everything up 'til now been fake?"

"Oh, it's real all right."

"Well, you don't act like it. You sure aren't treating me very nice."

"What do you mean? I'm treating you just fine."

"You seemed to think I was pretty special before. Why did you keep telling me things about how great I was and how much you admired me?"

"Because that's what *you* wanted to hear. Admit it. You were eating it up!"

"Yeah, but the other kids were joining in. Was that all fake too?"

"Oh, BB! You're so full of yourself. They were just being nice. They're sweet kids. You were a new guy and they wanted you to feel part of the group. It's not like you were actually some standout."

"Oh."

BB isn't dealing with the truth of his ordinary status very well. He'd just as soon end this topic and move on. Pinkie takes pity on him:

"Don't take it so hard. We've got our orders. It's time we started focusing on them."

At the mention of "orders" BB's irritation immediately flares up again:

"What's with that guy back there? He's so mean. Such a jerk!"

"He is not! He saved my life! He got me on the right path!"

"I don't know how you can stand him. All he cares about is ordering people around."

"He just wants what's best for you."

"How would HE know what's best for me?"

"Trust me. He's the best thing you've got going for you."

"And what's with the hourglasses? What's that all about?"

Pinkie fixes him with one of her cool stares:

"That's our push to keep going. Remember your little hourglass back home? There's also a larger version at Bond Headquarters. Both of them have sand that's steadily trickling downward with no way to stop it. We have to finish before it runs out."

This latest information has BB worried, but he doesn't want to let on:

"Where's Headquarters?"

"I don't know. It's where The Council meets, and I'm not part of the inner circle. Don't worry about it. We're getting close to LA, and the roads can be confusing. I only get up here once in a while for surfing competitions."

"Surfing competitions? You aren't that great. I saw you!"

"Right... that was part of The Bond's plan. Keep you focused on yourself. So you wouldn't notice. So you'd be set up for Sergeant Striker."

BB stares straight ahead:

"You're really good then. You were just laughing at me."

She sees his glum face and decides to give him a task to take his mind off his woes:

"My dad sometimes keeps maps in the glove compartment. See if you can find a Los Angeles one in there."

BB punches the button and the door drops down. To his amazement a bird flies out and perches on the dashboard. He chirps furiously and preens his feathers. Pinkie laughs:

"Hunnybird! So *that's* where you've been."

The tiny creature twitters back at her, obviously perturbed.

"Well you needn't blame me! How was I to know you were in there? I thought maybe you were hiding under the seat waiting for your grand entrance."

Pinkie switches her comments to BB:

"He's got to be thirsty and hungry too. There's some water in my thermos on the floor. Give him a piece of the bread from that leftover sandwich too."

BB stares in disbelief at this interplay. The little yellow critter continues his accusations fluffing up his white feathered chest. Pinkie warns him:

"Watch yourself! Don't get so worked up or you'll lose your footing,"

Sure enough, Hunnybird flaps his wings a little too vigorously and slides into BB's lap. Not sure what to do, BB freezes as the bird decides his next move.

"BB, it's going to be a long adventure and we're stuck with each other. Hunnybird will try to keep you pointed in the right direction. Not necessarily a geographical compass. More like a reminder when you stray off course."

Hunnybird cocks his head and blinks up at BB. He lifts his tiny shoulders and heaves a little sigh. Pinkie encourages him to join in:

"You can't stay in his lap if you want to see what's going on."

Not waiting for an invitation, Hunnybird flutters up to BB's shoulder and then drops into his shirt pocket. Poking his little head out, he has a perfect view of the road ahead. BB stiffens at the bird's sudden proximity.

"Relax! Hunnybird's not going to hurt you. He truly is your friend and will look out for you. You can trust him."

BB releases some of the tension he's felt since they met Sergeant Striker. He looks down at the little fellow and offers him a corner of the bread.

CHAPTER THIRTY

Detour

All at once the car is swarmed by a flock of swallows. BB figures they're after the sandwich and quickly hides it in the glove compartment. But they keep coming. He covers his head with his arms and closes his eyes anticipating an attack. But it doesn't come. Hunnybird flutters onto BB's shoulder and listens intently to the birds' chatter. He hops to the top of the steering wheel to address Pinkie. His animated monologue of chirps alarms her, and she pulls over to the shoulder.

"Are they absolutely sure about this, Hunnybird?"

The little bird frantically nods his head again and again. The swallows reassemble their flock and wing their way back north. Pinkie turns to BB:

"Change of plans. The scouts for The Abyss, two ravens who've been tracking us, had to take a wide path out to sea to avoid Camp Pendleton. They know we've been following the 101 so they picked Capistrano as their next rendezvous. They figured no one would suspect them of hiding out at a mission. The swallows saw them coming in from the ocean. They know every bird in the area and immediately set out to warn us."

"Seriously? We're worried about a couple of big black birds?"

"Those birds are nothing to fool with. They're intelligent and crafty, and worst of all they report our moves to The Abyss. They'll even try to throw us off our quest. Who do you think I've been hiding from? Running from?"

They pore intently over the Los Angeles area map BB finds in the glove compartment. BB is good at maps and quickly sees an opportunity:

"Here we are."

He points to a location just south of the Orange County border. His finger travels up the red line where it splits into two roads:

"Just below Capistrano, there's an alternate 101 route that follows the coastline. By the time the ravens figure out we're not coming their way, we'll be long gone. It'll take them forever to find us again."

"I don't know about *forever*, but at least it could buy us some time. Keep that map handy in case we need another detour."

Pinkie's on high alert as they pass through the inland orange groves. Once they turn off to the coast, BB scans the bright sky for any sign of the ravens. Soon they're cruising through beach communities with their endless surf and sand. The highway curves inland and then returns to more coastal towns. Just beyond the turnoff to the Los Angeles airport, BB thinks he sees two planes off course heading their way. But he's mistaken.

"Pinkie! It's those ravens! What are we going to do? I know they've spotted us!"

"Just watch and learn. Remember what I said. We need to trust The Bond!"

The two spies are gaining on them. Suddenly a huge flock of gulls flies in from the ocean straight toward the ravens. They catch the two huge birds by surprise with their flank attack. There's a flurry of feathers, wings, and beaks as the aerial foes clash. The gulls swirl around the huge black birds, their numbers overwhelming the ravens' usual advantage. The battle recedes from view as BB and Pinkie race north ever closer to the coast. Pinkie remembers a place where they can hide out for the time being. She takes the next left to the sights and sounds of Pacific Ocean Park and the Santa Monica Pier.

CHAPTER THIRTY-ONE

LA Draws Them In

"There's no time for diversions, but we have no other choice. We can't have those birds following us. Who knows what orders The Abyss has given them."

Pinkie pulls into a "No Parking" zone. BB's looks around in a panic:

"We can't park here! Look at the signs!"

"Don't worry. We have an advantage, courtesy of Agent Allen."

She pulls the backpack from the trunk and takes out a small folded square. Holding one corner, she shakes out a full-sized shroud.

"Don't just stand there. Grab the other end!"

As the cover floats down over the car, BB watches them both disappear. There are faint waves of light where the vehicle had stood just moments before.

"We had to hide it from the ravens. If I parked it in a regular spot, someone would've run into it. We can see the remnants of its atoms, but no one else can."

BB stands there, trying to grasp it all. But Pinkie knows they have to take cover in hopes the ravens fly by and up the highway. She slings the backpack over her shoulder and pulls BB by the hand over the bridge onto the wide wooden pier. The late morning Sunday crowd queues up for the food and carnival games. To the left, music from the carousel blends with shouts and screams of the roller coaster thrill seekers.

"The best place to hide for now is the bathrooms. Yours is over there. I'll meet you back here in ten minutes. That should be enough time for the ravens to realize there's nothing here and move on up the road."

When BB returns to the spot a few minutes later, he hears a familiar pinging sound calling to him from the arcade building. Pinball machines line the walls, their flashing lights enticing him to try his luck. He checks his pocket and finds some spare change. Before long he becomes lost in the challenge of the game, throwing his body into each push of the buttons. The flurry of pings draws a crowd. As the silver ball flies to the top again and again, the onlookers mirror his moves, adding victory shouts as the points pile up.

Pinkie panics when she returns and BB isn't there. However, she figures he's the source of the commotion coming from the arcade. She weaves her way through his adoring fans and speaks intently into his ear:

"I hate to break up your big moment, but it's time we started back to the car."

BB spreads his arms to the surrounding spectators, warming to their adulation:

"What do you mean? I just got started. They want to see a show. I can't disappoint them! We've got time for at least one more game."

"What are you talking about? Have you forgotten we're on a time limit?"

BB turns his back on Pinkie and prepares for another round. He flips the ball again and again to the top of the slope, collecting points and basking in the cheers of his admirers. But Pinkie doesn't back down. She jerks his arm away from the side button. Groans from the ring of fans accompany the steel ball that slides to the bottom. BB is furious:

"What are you doing?"

The "GAME OVER" flashes on the screen.

"I've never had this rotten of a score!"

But the screen has a new message: **"PINK'S! NOW!"** *Pinkie's eyes widen with alarm:*

"No time to argue. Let's get out of here!"

She steers him away from the game, ignoring the crowd's jeers. BB waves and smiles back at them. Disappointed voices attempt to lure him back.

"Sorry. I'm needed elsewhere."

"Forget your adoring fans! Didn't you see that message? We've got to get out of here. The ravens must be onto us."

Pinkie neatly folds the shroud and drops it into the backpack. She picks up the LA map from the floor and lays it on the hood, desperately searching the tangle of streets.

"I think Pink's is in Hollywood. But we need an address or directions."

At that moment Hunnybird flies down to her shoulder.

"So where have you been all this time? Hanging with your beach bird friends?"

Hunnybird begins to sing excitedly about his adventure, but Pinkie stops him mid chirp:

"Okay. Great! But right now we need to get to Pink's. Message from The Bond. And I don't know how to get there."

Hunnybird flies off and returns with a new gull friend who often flies over to Pink's to pick up stray food. The gull takes off down Santa Monica Boulevard.

"Hey! Tell your buddy to wait for us! Your turn to drive, BB."

BB edges the car into traffic. Pinkie slips the backpack to the floor and scans the map.

"This is perfect! The Bond comes through again. We're at the beginning of Route 66. If we follow it east after we stop at Pink's, it reconnects to the 101, and we'll be back on track. This detour should keep those ravens off our trail for now."

Pinkie settles back into the comfortable leather seat, keeping her eye out for their feathered guide. Hunnybird keeps tabs on his friend from the dashboard. As they cruise closer to Hollywood, they're surrounded by some very expensive cars: Mercedes Benz, Rolls Royce, Bentley. The luxury isn't lost on BB:

"Check out the cool rides. When I'm famous *and* rich, I'm going to get me one of those. Complete with a chauffeur of course."

"So, Mr. Rich and Famous, what's your plan? The only skill I've noticed is pinball. It's a fun game. But where's that going to get you if that's what you spend your time on? You're so self-absorbed! The only people you notice are the ones stroking your ego. Why don't you have some concern for others in this world, people you probably walk by without so much as a glance their way?"

"I care about other people! How do *you* know how I feel? Who made *you* the judge?"

At that moment Hunnybird interrupts their argument with an agitated chirp. Pinkie points to the gull careening to the right onto La Brea Avenue. Turning the corner, they spot an iconic sign: a hot dog in a bun with Pink's *underneath in bright pink letters. BB's rumbling stomach reminds him they haven't eaten for a while:*

"You didn't tell me we were stopping for food! I thought we were going someplace because it sounds like your name."

"We're here because we were sent. My LA friends say it's the best hotdog stand on the west coast. Lots of famous people come here."

With the thought of meeting a celebrity, BB eagerly searches out a parking spot. But he's not so sure Pinkie is giving him the straight story:

"They come *here*? It looks like some hole-in-the-wall joint."

"Well, the huge line should tell you the food's great."

BB and Pinkie join the line that trails up the sidewalk. There are families and grandparents with grandkids. Construction workers rub elbows with businessmen. A chauffeur orders for his client who's behind the dark windows of a limo. When they finally get to the counter, Pinkie orders a chili dog and fries. BB scans the menu board:

"What's a Brando Dog?"

The friendly order clerk fills him in:

"It's an extra long hotdog with onions, mustard, chili and cheese."

"But why's it called a Brando Dog?"

"We name some of our specialties after the famous people who've ordered them. Marlon Brando came here when he was just starting out, and he keeps coming back. We've got his picture up on the Celebrity Wall in the back room. Signed too!"

BB orders the Brando Dog plus fries and grabs a couple of Dr. Brown's Root Beers. While they wait, he gets lost in a daydream of fame:

"Maybe some day I'll have my own picture on the wall and a hotdog named after me!"

Pinkie snaps him out of his reverie:

"Here's our food. Find a seat before they're all gone. Hurry up BB!"

They take their trays to the back and settle under the gaze of celebrities captured in black and white glossies. Halfway through their meal the table begins to vibrate. They grab their soda bottles to keep them from tipping over. Pinkie holds the backpack securely on her lap. When the entire building starts to shake, the customers and employees all rush outside fearing the roof might cave in. In a few seconds the tremors stop and they all return to finish their meals and talk about the latest rumbling. Just then a man rushes in:

"The cop in his patrol car outside got a flash on his scanner. The earthquake hit in the mountains past Santa Barbara. The tunnel on the north 101 is partially collapsed and the southbound lane is covered in a giant rockslide. There's damage to that bridge that crosses the Santa Inez River on Highway 154. No one will get through on the 101 or even go around it for days."

BB and Pinkie exchange panicked looks. They've been instructed to stay on the 101. Now what? Other concerned voices in the crowd chime in:

"But I *have* to get to Lompoc for an important meeting tomorrow. Guess I'll leave early and circle north over the mountains."

"Didn't you hear about the fires in the national forest? They closed Highways 99 and 33 until they're contained. They think an arsonist set one or both of them."

"It looks like LA is the place to be for the next few days. Thank goodness there's plenty to keep us entertained."

"Yeah. And plenty of hotdogs too!"

Everyone joins in the good-natured banter that steers the conversation away from the disasters to the north and west. But BB and Pinkie aren't laughing. Pinkie is furious:

"I'll bet anything The Abyss is behind this. They're always creating chaos."

"An earthquake? They can start an earthquake? Come on Pinkie! That's ridiculous!"

"Okay. Maybe not the earthquake. But the arson fires sound just like them."

"So what now?"

"Just finish your fries and let me think."

As BB scoops up his last morsel, he notices lettering on the bottom of the paper container. In a hushed voice he reads to Pinkie:

"**Go to the Y in the middle of Hollywood.** What's that supposed to mean? And who put that there?"

Pinkie lifts the backpack to her shoulder, grabs her tray, and deposits her garbage in the nearby waste bin.

"We don't question. We just act! Get rid of your trash and let's get going."

BB shoves his papers into the trashcan. Neither he nor Pinkie notice a young man slouched in the corner, watching from under a lowered cap. As soon as they leave, he rummages through the papers to find BB's paper container. He smiles at the message and shoves it back into the waste can. He casually walks to his car just as BB and Pinkie reach their convertible. He's in no hurry. He'll just wait for them at their next destination. There's only one way in and out, so he can't miss them.

Pinkie has the LA map out again. She keeps mumbling to herself:

"The 'Y' in the middle of Hollywood."

"So where are we going? Where's the 'Y' we're supposed to find?"

"Be quiet! Let me think! Maybe we're supposed to go to the center of Hollywood."

Suddenly she jabs her finger to the map:

"Here's Hollywood Boulevard. It goes through the middle of Hollywood."

Keeping her eye on the map, she points to the next intersection:

"Take a left there and another left when we get to Highland Avenue."

Just then Hunnybird flutters into the front seat and lands on the console. A stray piece of French fry comically dangles from his beak. BB is grateful for a break in the tension:

"Looks like you enjoyed Pink's too, little fella."

Arriving at the corner of Highland and Hollywood, they scan the area, waiting for the light to change. Pinkie repeats the words:

"A 'Y' in the middle of Hollywood."

Hunnybird spots the answer and flutters in front of their faces to get their attention. BB swats his hands at the flapping wings, but then his eyes focus on the distant hills:

"There it is! The sign! The 'Y' in the middle of Hollywood!"

CHAPTER THIRTY-TWO

Losing Control

"You're right! It *has* to be it!"

BB congratulates himself with this win:

"Now that I figured out the clue, maybe she'll give me a little more credit from now on."

Using the map, Pinkie directs BB through steep hills past gorgeous homes nestled in the canyons. At the end of Mulholland Drive a chained gate blocks a rough road. BB stops the car, figuring their luck has run out. However, when Pinkie pulls on the metal rail, the chain falls to the ground. Swinging the gate wide for BB to drive through, she closes it behind and carefully rearranges the chain so it appears secure once more. They follow the narrow road and stop behind the giant letters. Carefully they make their way down through the tangled underbrush. On the ground propped against the "Y" is an ancient Greek theatre mask. Inside is another message:

"Beware of hidden followers. No need to shout in this place!"

BB is suddenly on his guard:

"Did you see that black car parked by the side of the road near the end of the street? There was a guy inside hunched down with a cap hiding his face."

Pinkie doesn't want to alarm BB, but she knows The Abyss would recognize their car:

"Maybe he's just taking a nap. We probably shouldn't go back the way we came. But there's only this dirt maintenance trail, and I can't mess up my dad's car."

"Then let's do the hidden car trick again and hike down. It can't be that far."

"We still have to solve this clue so we know where to go. And what's with the mask?"

"Maybe we need to connect the message with the mask. We studied the Romans and Greeks in one of my history classes. They used these masks in their theater productions. There's a built-in megaphone. See! Like this one has!"

"Well that's great. But I don't think I could hear you through that mask if you were even fifty feet away. Unless you shouted, that is."

"Yeah. But it says we don't *have* to shout in this place. It can't be here. Wait a minute! My folks came to LA for an outdoor concert last year. They said it was like sitting in a Greek theatre. Someone even demonstrated how you could hear a person on the stage from the top row without a microphone. Maybe that's the place. Check the map and see if there's anything around here that sounds like that."

Pinkie's finger moves across the map, first finding their location and then circling out:

"Here's Grauman's Chinese Theatre. That could be it."

"That doesn't sound right. Anything else?"

"Nothing but Dodger Stadium. Wait. The Hollywood Bowl?"

"That's it! So, as my dad would say, what's the shortest route as the crow flies?"

Hunnybird chirps from the top of the "Y". Pinkie laughs:

"Well we don't have a crow, but I think Hunnybird will do just fine!"

They scramble up the slope to the convertible. BB grabs the backpack from the front seat, and Pinkie hides the car. Picking their way around the prickly vegetation, they start down the hill. An hour later, the mysterious black car creeps to the sign from the street below. The driver gets out, looks around, and consults a voice in his earpiece:

"Where'd they go? They had to come back my way. They disappeared and so did their car. At least we know they can't leave the city. Boy, that earthquake sure saved us a lot of extra work."

Far below BB and Pinkie face a major highway in their path. It's the busy 101 again. Hunnybird calls to them from across the way and flies to a nearby overhead crossing. Once on the other side, they walk up the long entry drive to the huge amphitheater. Before Pinkie can stop him, BB sprints up the steps:

"Come on! I'll race you to the top!"

After that long hike down the canyon, she isn't in any mood for another climb. But she trudges partway up to get a better perspective. When BB reaches the highest seats he hears a firm but kind voice coming from the stage:

"Are you kids looking for someone in particular?"

They didn't realize they were being watched. They climb down to meet an unassuming man dressed in slacks and an open-collared white shirt with rolled up sleeves. The man extends his hand to shake theirs:

"I'm Mr. Stanley. What's your name, son?"

"It's Heybert. People usually call me BB. My folks were right. You *can* hear someone talking even from the top. This is Pinkie. It's our first time here."

"Well, there's not much to see that's not right out in the open."

He gestures with a sweep of his arm. Pinkie is curious who this man could be.

"Are you the caretaker of this place?"

"Oh, no. I *am* a caretaker of sorts, you might say. I teach at the Otis Art School."

BB hopes this man is a celebrity:

"So you're an artist? Are you famous?"

"I've done a few pieces you can see around Hollywood and LA. That is, if you know what you're looking for. But I prefer spending time teaching, helping kids discover their talents and encouraging them to devote themselves to their art."

"It seems Hollywood is the place *everyone* wants to be discovered."

"Ah yes, Pinkie. The place where magic is possible and dreams come true. But all people care about these days is the glitz and glamour instead of art. That's why I keep teaching at the school. They're the future artists who love their work."

BB wants to find out if this guy has any useful connections:

"Our plans have changed so we're spending a few days in the area. Maybe you can help us out. Billy Wilder invited me to his party tomorrow night. I'm hoping he'll discover some of my talents while I'm there. Any suggestions on how to play this?"

"So you've met Mr. Wilder. Fine man. He's helped out a lot of young stars. We connect with each other every so often when the occasion arises."

Then his eyes soften with sadness:

"Lots of people are chasing their dreams of fame in this town. One of my sculptures is their biggest desire. Whoever possesses it finds doors will open to all kinds of possibilities. But it also carries a burden. Many people can't handle its magic."

"So where *is* it? This sculpture?"

"The one *I* have is even more powerful because it's the prototype. It creates opportunities unlike anything you've ever seen. I don't have a use for it anymore, and you look like you could use some help. But are you sure you can handle it?"

"I can handle just about anything, Mr. Stanley."

BB's ego has reached a whole new level. Pinkie pulls him aside and whispers sternly:

"What are you getting us into? You heard what he said about its power."

"We were sent here, right? We're also stuck in LA until we can figure a way to get back to the quest. For all we know, this is part *of* the quest. You heard the man. Magic! Power! We might need this sculpture!"

Pinkie reluctantly agrees to his plan. He turns back to Mr. Stanley:

"So how big is it? Is it heavy? Can it fit in my backpack? Do you have it with you or do we need to go someplace to get it?"

Stanley has seen this eagerness before, the headlong rush into uncharted territory:

"One question at a time, young man. It's about a foot tall and not too heavy. You can easily hold it in one hand. It isn't far from here, but I can't show you where. I keep it hidden for a reason. But if you're determined to find it, you will. **My statue is in my statue.** That's all."

The mysterious man turns away, walks to the recesses of the stage, and disappears through the back wall. BB calls to him, but there's no answer. They stare dumbfounded at this strange exit. BB shakes it off and turns his attention to solving this new clue:

"Look around, Pinkie. See any statues?"

"There was something near the entrance. I don't remember what, but it was huge."

"Let's go! Maybe there'll be another clue there."

At the Highland Avenue entrance, they look up at a modern looking white sculpture. Fountain steps lead to the figure of a woman. Overgrown brush and untrimmed bushes threaten to overtake the monumental structure.

"BB, how do we know this is it?"

"He said '**My statue is in my statue**' so now we have to figure out if this is his. Come on. Help me look for a name or maybe another clue."

Hunnybird watches as they begin to clear away some of the overgrowth. He tunnels into the tangle and discovers some letters. Hearing his chirp, BB and Pinkie attack the vines and leaves. First there's a G, then the name George, and finally Stanley. BB's confused:

"Now what? There's another statue inside this? It's solid concrete and granite!"

"Maybe not. Let's look around."

They scramble up through the vines and begin searching. BB is first to call out:

"Here's a round cover. Maybe we can lift it."

Sure enough the lid raises up. A metal pipe ladder reaches down into a dark pit.

"Go ahead, BB. It's your idea."

At the bottom of the ladder, BB feels around the stifling chamber and discovers a small form. Hoping it's the statue they're seeking, he makes the awkward climb, careful not to drop his treasure. As he reaches the top rung, he hands it up to Pinkie who gasps:

"BB! Do you know what this is?"

BB steps out of the hole into the bright California sunshine. He closes the hatch and turns to Pinkie. Although it's missing its gold coating, he recognizes the smooth lines of the face and body and the distinctive sword. The most famous piece of artwork in the world: The Motion Picture Academy Award! The Oscar! He can't believe it!

"He said '**My statue is in my statue**,' which means Mr. Stanley created this!"

BB grabs hold of the figure with Pinkie. They gaze at this icon of Hollywood, mesmerized by its classic design. But then they feel a magnetism emanating from its core. Pinkie is the first to pry her hands from the slate gray figure. But BB can't seem to release it. And he doesn't really want to.

CHAPTER THIRTY-THREE

Doors Begin to Open

"Let go, BB! Maybe we shouldn't take it. It's kinda creepy, like it's got control of us."

"Mr. Stanley said it has power. I'm ready to see what it'll do for me."

"Well we can't just walk around with you holding it. People will think you're weird."

BB reluctantly slips the figure into the backpack, and they climb down. Hunnybird finds a safe spot in BB's pocket.

Back at headquarters, the Council is in a heated debate.

Striker: "Well he failed the first test. Completely ignored the warnings about the statue."

Agent Allen: "No wonder Stanley kept it hidden. Wouldn't want *that* to fall into the wrong hands."

Lady Grace: "I'm surprised at Pinkie. She should know better than to let him keep it. The power seems to be affecting her judgement."

Director: "You're right about Pinkie, but I can't say I'm all that surprised at BB. His head isn't in the quest. That's for sure. And his desire for money and fame has a firm grip on his heart. The Bond has a few more Legends to intervene in this city. But if that doesn't steer him in a new direction, we won't have any other option except a personal appearance from one of you two."

He gestures to Lady Grace and Agent Allen.

"If Pinkie pays attention to the moon, she should realize they can't stay in LA for much longer. I'm not sure what The Bond has in mind to get them back on course. All I know is we can't let those two keep wandering around Hollywood. They're an easy target for the Abyss."

Without a car, BB and Pinkie are undecided about their next move. There's been no other message, no direction. As they reach the sidewalk, a sleek black limousine pulls up to the curb. Unsure of what to do, they stand their ground. A uniformed driver comes around to open the door.

"Mr. Wilder wants to offer you comfortable transportation while you're in his city."

Realizing they don't have an alternative, they hesitate briefly and then climb into the beautiful car to settle back into luxury. Hunnybird peeks from BB's pocket and then snuggles down out of sight.

"There's soda in the refrigerator if you're thirsty. It's not far to the hotel, but the traffic is building up. It might take us awhile."

The limo joins the stream of cars on Sunset Boulevard. They grin in disbelief at their good fortune. BB, though, is quick to recognize what's behind it all:

"Looks like the statue's already working for me. I can't wait to see what's next!"

Soon the luxurious car floats past a line of tall palms and up a long, curving driveway with lush green vegetation on either side. Pinkie is relieved to see the huge letters of The Beverly Hills, the very hotel Wilder had mentioned. At the entrance an attendant opens the car door. He offers his white-gloved hand to Pinkie, who steps onto a rich, red carpet leading to the lobby. The bold green and white striped canopy draws them into the brightly lit interior. They stroll past huge pillars and giant potted banana palms that brush the ceiling. As they approach the reception desk, elegantly dressed guests give a slightly alarmed appraisal of their disheveled clothes. But the desk clerk greets them warmly:

"We've been expecting you. A short while ago we received word that Mr. Wilder's guests were on their way. We didn't have any names besides BB and Pinkie to put on your room keys. But Mr. Wilder assured us you were among his select group of friends and would expect only the finest from our staff. He said you were traveling light, so we will provide *anything* you need. I emphasize the word anything."

He hands two gold engraved keys to the bellman, who collects BB's backpack. He looks surprised at its heaviness, but turns to a different topic as he leads them away:

"I noticed you had a pink registration card, the one for our elite VIP guests. Most people have a white card or a blue one if you're one of our regulars. You must be *very* special guests of Mr. Wilder."

They pass a sparkling pool rimmed with green and white striped cushioned lounge chairs and elegant cabanas. The late afternoon sun has left shadows over the abandoned scene. A young man in white shorts and shirt heads their way.

They take notice of his tanned, muscular physique and his well-groomed, thick blonde hair.

"That's Svend, the pool manager. He's a really nice guy. Came over from Denmark. Been here just a few years, but he knows how to make all of these rich and famous people relax and enjoy themselves."

Svend approaches them with a wide grin. His excellent English has a slight Nordic accent:

"I'm so glad to welcome you to our beautiful hotel. I hope you will enjoy your stay with us. Tomorrow this place will be filled with guests basking in our California gold sunlight. You might see some famous people here, but please don't disturb them. No autographs or photos. We guard their privacy completely."

They continue on with their guide down a winding, flower and palm lined walkway that circles lazily to secluded bungalows. Hunnybird pokes his head out of BB's pocket and quickly escapes into the lush foliage, all the while keeping a close watch. The bellman smiles back at Pinkie:

"When I saw your name on your bungalow key, I knew you were our perfect guest."

He gestures to the towers overhead, a Mediterranean fantasy clothed in pink gold dust with staircases that seem to appear out of nowhere.

"After all, this beautiful lady is also known as the Pink Palace."

BB is eager to learn more:

"I heard there are lots of movie stars that stay here."

"Too many stories to share. And I wouldn't want to spoil the reputation of such a glorious place. Plus I could lose my job! Pinkie, you'll be staying in number 7, one of Marilyn Monroe's favorites. Since her death, a great sadness has descended on this hotel. They've decided to name this bungalow the Norma Jean in honor of her humble beginnings. BB, you're in number 17 on Bachelor's Row. When you've finished freshening up, Mr. Wilder has arranged for dinner in the Polo Lounge. Don't worry about tipping the staff. Mr. Wilder is more than generous in taking care of us."

Pinkie and BB are grateful for a chance to shower off the remnants of their beach sleepover plus the strenuous trek down the canyon. BB has bought into this life of luxury without question. But as she lets the hot shower drain away the day's endless complications, Pinkie can't help but wonder:

"Is this part of The Bond's plan? Or are we being manipulated by The Abyss? Everyone seems so nice, though. Mr. Stanley was wonderful, but a bit melancholy. I can't quite figure out what that statue is all about. Is it something

The Bond wants us to collect?"

She shakes off her conflicting thoughts and concentrates on the promise of a relaxing evening. At her feet Hunnybird fluffs up his feathers and ducks in and out of the falling drops. She laughs at his fluttering antics as he too sheds the dust from the day's adventure. His cheerful chirps boost her spirits.

When they rendezvous once more, Pinkie is wearing a casual pink frock and sandals, the perfect resort wear. BB stares in disbelief:

"Where did you get those clothes? And I'm stuck with these?"

"I forgot to mention another perk of The Bond. Check your watch. The small button on the left is the same as mine. Press it and see what happens."

BB looks down at the blue watch he bought back at the jewelry store. With a gentle push on the tiny button, BB suddenly is fashionably dressed in a clean pair of pants and shirt with deck shoes to round out his outfit. Pinkie smiles at his bewilderment:

"Whenever we need a clean set of clothes or a more suitable outfit, The Bond provides it. Our watches are completely waterproof too. No worries wherever we are. I can't believe how big my place is. No wonder Marilyn loved it. It's three times the size of most people's houses. And they call it a bungalow!"

"Mine's huge too. And did you see that gold button on the wall. It says, 'Push for Champagne.' Maybe I'll try it later and see what happens."

"Don't you dare, BB! You need to keep your head clear."

Hunnybird adds his stern warning chirps to stay focused. He knows he isn't welcome inside the main hotel and gives BB a quick peck on his head as a reminder before he takes his watch in a nearby hibiscus bush.

The maître d' welcomes them into the Polo Lounge with its peachy pink walls.

"Good evening. We've been looking forward to your arrival. May I provide you with a jacket, sir? We're a resort, but there are certain guidelines for our dinner guests."

BB slips on the proffered coat. They cross the deep carpets to one of the dark green leather booths. The soft spoken gentleman gestures to the phone nearby:

"If you need to make a call, the hotel operator will connect you to your party. Mr. Wilder took the liberty of ordering your dinner. I'm sure you will be pleased."

The kind man bows and leaves them to their newfound luxury. BB eyes the phone and is tempted to pick up the receiver to see what happens. But who would he call? A wave of homesickness overcomes him but quickly disappears as suddenly as it came. He looks around at the richly dressed diners. He's one of them! He's living the good life!

Finishing up a truly magnificent meal of lobster and filet mignon, BB and Pinkie feel the day's events beginning to take their toll. They return to their bungalows to find complimentary pajamas and robes laid out and their beds turned down to welcome them into luxurious sheets. Hunnybird keeps close to BB, snuggling under a fold of silk, just inches from BB's face. If anything happens during the night, Hunnybird will immediately waken and raise the alarm.

Before long the two young adventurers are lost in fanciful, grandiose dreams, their exhausted bodies yielding to the comforts of a good night's sleep. Little do they know how much they will need this fortification for the day ahead.

CHAPTER THIRTY-FOUR

The Hollywood Hook

After a leisurely breakfast in bed, BB and Pinkie slip on bathing suits and robes, provided as a courtesy, and saunter to the pool area hoping to rub elbows with the rich and famous clientele. The sounds of laughter and splashes are interrupted by an official-sounding voice rising above the hubbub:

"Paging Elizabeth Taylor! Paging Miss Taylor!"

BB and Pinkie exchange excited looks. Svend comes over to greet them like family:

"I hope you had a restful night and are ready to enjoy the parade around the pool."

He points out several good looking, swimsuit-clad individuals showing off their sleek figures and fine-tuned physiques.

"Those young men and women are hoping some movie mogul will discover them."

The public address interrupts again:

"Paging Cary Grant! Paging Mr. Grant. Please pick up the nearest phone."

BB bursts out eagerly:

"Is he really here?"

"Maybe... and maybe not. Sometimes they just announce famous people to add to the excitement. This place is Hollywood's playground. There's even a movie being filmed here right now. If you see some stars on break, remember to be discreet."

Pinkie and BB take a quick dip in the pool and stretch out on the comfy lounges. Hunnybird stays out of sight in the shadow under Pinkie's chair. The warm sun seeps into their bodies draining away all the stress and anxiety of the previous day. Svend returns with the offer of one of his private upper cabanas. He also orders them a light lunch with drinks.

"Don't get too fond of this intense sun. It can quickly sap your energy. Let me know if there is *anything* else I can do to add to your stay with us. I understand you have an open reservation, so I expect to see you around for quite some time."

From Sven's cabana above the pool, BB and Pinkie have a perfect view of the famous stars and wealthy guests. The lure of the good life tantalizes them, and they embrace it. Even Pinkie's guard is down:

"What's the harm of a few days of R & R? The roads are all closed. We might as well enjoy this place. Maybe The Bond is rewarding us with a break."

Totally relaxed, the hours slipping by, they are oblivious to the sand that is quickly filling up the bottom of the two hourglasses. Halfway through their delicious lunch, a dark silhouette blocks their view to the pool. It's the chauffeur.

"Mr. Wilder sends his regards and hopes you are enjoying your stay. He has a surprise for you this afternoon. He's arranged a behind-the-scenes tour of a movie studio he sometimes uses. That is, if it's to your liking."

BB gushes his enthusiasm:

"Are you kidding? This is great! A movie set! Can I meet some stars and a director?"

Pinkie gives him a "Calm down!" look and answers for them both:

"How kind of Mr. Wilder! We'd love to! It will take me a few minutes to shower and change. Shall we meet you in the lobby?"

A short time later BB and Pinkie emerge from their bungalows freshly groomed, Pinkie in a stylish shirt and skirt outfit. BB has on his usual shirt and jacket and blue pants.

"Oh no, BB! Don't you have anything else to wear?"

"I like these pants. And apparently The Bond approves. So there!"

With Hunnybird following from above, they take a short drive to a nearby Hollywood studio. It looks like any other building from the outside. But once they are past the gate, the scurrying people and commotion create a vibrant scene of frenzied activity. An electric cart swerves around them carrying costumed actors to a sound stage. BB's head is spinning. He can't believe he's really living this fantasy.

And then he spots her... a pretty young girl about his age, dressed in bright green pedal pushers and a crisp white sleeveless blouse, its collar casually unbuttoned. Her carefully coifed, raven black hair glistens in the sunlight. Artfully applied makeup highlights her liquid brown eyes and shining lips that curve into a welcoming smile. BB is lost in this lovely vision:

"I can't believe she's coming this way! She's so beautiful!"

The young woman drives her studio cart straight toward them and stops just inches away. Her voice is as soft as a satin pillow:

"Hello, Handsome! I'm finished for the day. The director told me to head home, but when I saw you I thought you might want someone to show you around."

BB swallows and gives her an adoring smile:

"That'd be great. Are you one of the stars?"

Pinkie pokes him in his ribs and whispers:

"Of course not! She's just a starlet who's trying to make it big. She's a nobody."

BB whispers back, grinning foolishly at their new acquaintance:

"Well *I* think she's something."

Pinkie can't believe how easily he's impressed and wonders at his obvious fawning:

"Good grief, BB! You aren't being very subtle! Stop looking so eager!"

The lovely girl giggles at his discomfort and flashes her bright smile:

"I'm Betty Jo. Around here they call me Jodie. They said it looks better on the marquee. That is, when I finally *do* get my name up in lights. Hop in and I'll give you a quick tour. If we see an open door, I'll get you into a set where they're filming."

Jodie checks with their driver:

"I'll be sure to have them back to you in an hour or so, if that's okay."

This isn't the plan, but he agrees and leans on the limo to wait. Pinkie isn't keen on this new arrangement but decides this Jodie is harmless enough:

"She does seem to know her way around. Everyone we pass is waving and smiling back at her. I guess I can put up with her for an hour."

Jodie is in no hurry however. One hour stretches into three as she points out the movie sets and adds a tour of the back lot. They even spot a couple of well-known stars, but Jodie keeps her distance. She says it isn't a good idea to look too eager when you're just starting out. The sun is setting as they begin their return to the limo. Three rough looking fellows emerge from one of the huge sound stage buildings and block their path. Jodie slams on the brakes. She's anxious and obviously on edge. One of the men steps forward, a cigarette hanging from the corner of his crooked grin:

"Whatcha up to, Sugar?"

"Nothing much, Frankie. Just showing some friends around."

Frankie and his two pals slowly circle the cart, eyeing BB and especially Pinkie. Pinkie does her best to look calm and under control, but their disturbing stares start to unnerve her. BB eagerly jumps out of the cart to speak to Frankie:

"Jodie's been really helpful, but I was hoping to meet someone who could set me up. Mr. Wilder says he might use my story for a movie script."

Frankie gives him the same sly smile. He puts his arm around BB's shoulders and pulls him in close for a confidential chat:

"Wilder. Billy Wilder, eh? Why don't you come with me? I've got someone you should meet. The boys here will keep tabs on the ladies while we do some business."

Pinkie calls out to BB, but he pays no attention. He's already mesmerized by the possibilities for his future. Jodie reassures her:

"I wouldn't worry too much about Frankie. He's a jerk but basically harmless. Anyways, what can go wrong here on the lot? People watch out for each other like family. We'll just wait in the cart 'til he comes back. I'll go get some sodas."

Resenting this change in plans, Pinkie drops the backpack to the floor between her feet and covers it with her skirt. She watches Jodie stroll away, her jealousy simmering just below the surface:

"There's no way I can compete with this girl's glamour. Looks like I'm just the "extra" around here."

Hunnybird swoops in and lands in her lap. He cocks his head and chirps his encouragement, reminding Pinkie she gets "top billing" in his heart.

"Thanks, Hunnybird. But you're not the one who counts right now. This Jodie can't distract BB from our mission. I'm going to have to run interference the best I can."

Hunnybird flits away when he spots Jodie returning. He too is worried about this current detour and finds a good spot to observe what happens next.

Meanwhile in an executive trailer near the back lot, BB meets a producer who knows how to appeal to the egos of eager young talent. BB shares the story of the Hotel del Coronado and then reveals some of the more astonishing events of the past two days, including how his fortunes changed once they found the statue. The producer leans forward, arms crossed on his desk, cigar clenched between his teeth. BB continues to regale them with details that sound more and more fantastical to everyone, but not to a tall, good-looking young man standing in the background. The producer breaks in:

"This has the makings of a great Hollywood story. You got what it takes, and I want to work with you. We can make you a star. I'll hook you up with my best agent. Just give your information to my assistant, Reggie."

He jerks his thumb back at the young man who winces visibly at the casual nickname. He addresses BB formally as he confidently extends his hand:

"Actually my name is Reginald."

The producer comes from behind his desk and circles his arm around BB's slim frame:

"Stick with me, kid. You're going places! Have you seen much of LA? No? Things really pick up after dark. Why doesn't Frankie give you the grand tour?"

BB is barely able to contain his elation. He shares his full name with Reggie who shakes his hand to seal the deal. BB skips down the trailer steps and slides sideways on a patch of sand. Quickly catching his balance, BB turns to wave. A knowing smile flickers across the assistant's face.

Meanwhile the producer consults with Frankie and the others:

"I don't know what all of that other stuff was about. But I do know that statue is something we need to get ahold of. If it's really magic, and it sure sounds like it is, it'll save me money and time moving my projects to the top and me into that mansion I've had my eye on. Billy Wilder won't be the only big name in this town. In fact I intend to knock him right off his pedestal. And into the gutter!"

The others join in with the producer's sinister laugh.

"Frankie, keep a close eye on this kid. In fact I want you to stick to him like he's your long lost rich relative. Find out where that statue is and get it. Don't come back to me with any more of your lame excuses. Understood?"

"Yes, sir!"

Frankie knows this assignment will move him up in the organization. That statue's his one-way ticket to having his own crew. Back at the cart, he sends his two buddies away and takes the wheel. Pinkie turns sideways in the front seat to keep an eye on BB and Jodie. She's glad they'll soon part ways with this girl. Suddenly Jodie leans forward:

"Where are you going, Frankie? This isn't the way to the front gate."

"I'm supposed to show these two around town in the boss's car. I sent Whitey to tell their limo driver the change in plans."

Pinkie gives BB a worried look, but unconcerned he turns to Jodie:

"Want to come along?"

Jodie nods, her enthusiasm bubbling over. Pinkie's resentment continues to build. Totally disgusted with the whole situation, she turns to the front in a huff and stares straight ahead. Under her breath she mutters:

"Why does *she* have to come?"

Frankie leans over and breathes in her ear:

"Don't worry, Sweetheart. Starlets like her are a dime a dozen. They never last. Your boyfriend'll get tired of her and be back with you before you know it."

She recoils at his voice, the words oozing from his fleshy mouth. She starts to protest against the "boyfriend" remark. Her queasy stomach warns her not to get too cozy with this unsavory character.

At the back gate Frankie spots Wilder's limo and driver. The appearance of this muscular man rattles him, but he puts on a good show of bravado. He hops off the cart and directs the others to a big Lincoln Continental, calling to the other driver:

"I've got it from here. The boss wants me to give them the royal tour of LA."

"Wait just a minute, pal. Mr. Wilder wouldn't be too happy if his guests didn't show up to his party at a decent hour. If you don't mind..."

He pauses to emphasize he's not really asking permission. Frankie quickly agrees:

"Sure. Anything you say."

Jodie squeals out:

"Mr. Wilder? Mr. Billy Wilder? You're going to one of *his* parties? Only really important people get invited to those. You suppose I could join you? I keep a skirt tucked in my bag for emergencies like these!"

This latest comment is too much for Pinkie:

"Sure you do. A skirt. For emergencies."

But BB doesn't see the harm in including her:

"Why not? It'll be fun! Maybe you'll even meet someone who can help your career."

Pinkie gives him an "I don't believe you're doing this!" look that he ignores. Jodie slips on her "emergency" skirt and slides her slacks from underneath.

"All set!"

She laughs at the others who stare at her quick-change maneuver. Their driver dismisses Frankie and settles the three of them in his limo. Hunnybird decides to keep following from a distance. The driver rolls down the window behind the front seat:

"I know you've been promised a tour of LA after dark, so I thought we could drive around for awhile to see some of the nightlife before going to the party."

BB and Jodie quickly agree, but Pinkie is tight lipped. Between the two girls in the comfy back seat, BB ignores Pinkie's lack of enthusiasm. He lays the backpack with its precious contents safely on the floor against his shins. Meanwhile Frankie is fuming at being outmaneuvered. He picks up the car phone:

"Sorry boss. They're headed to Wilder's party. They'll never let me in after what happened last week. I'm sure you can smooth talk your way past the front door. They've been watching over that backpack like it's some royal treasure. That must be where the statue is."

CHAPTER THIRTY-FIVE

Caught in the Limelight

"Look over there!"

Jodie's been enjoying the views of Los Angeles and spots beams of searchlights just ahead:

"That's got to be Grauman's Chinese Theater. They just had Paul Newman's handprint ceremony there last week. Can we stop? Please?"

BB leans forward to talk the driver into a quick detour. A few minutes later they're all staring up at the giant red Chinese pagoda. They approach the main entrance guarded by two Ming Dynasty lions. Hunnybird perches on the huge dragon overhead, hoping for a break to catch his breath. Fanning out on the pavement are variously colored celebrity tributes. Jodie runs from square to square, standing in footprints and testing handprints. At one site a few scattered flowers have been left in tribute by adoring fans.

"Here's Marilyn! Look! My hand is the same size as hers!"

Even their driver gets into the mood:

"My fist's as big as John Wayne's! Must be all the extra stress I put on mine."

He pounds his fist into the palm of his left hand. Alarmed at this show of force, Pinkie has a less trusting opinion of this massive man.

"Are you finding everyone you're looking for? I know where they all are. Just ask."

The strong, even-toned voice startles them. He introduces himself as John Tartaglia, the man who sets up and supervises the hand and footprint ceremonies. Jodie bursts out:

"Did you do Marilyn Monroe?"

"No, I started right after. This fame… it's not always a good thing. It comes with a price. Lots of people regret the limelight thing later on. Too many sad stories. You feel sorry for them. But here's a happier tale! Newman and Woodward."

He takes them to the spot completed just a few days before: May 25, 1963.

"Nicest people. Great couple. I can tell this one's going to stick. They asked me a lot of questions about my work. Made me feel real special."

BB wonders about the searchlights that make lazy circles in the night sky:

"Do they always have these lights going?"

"That *is* strange. Usually they're just for premiers. But sometimes they turn them on for the tourists. Folks kind of expect these big waving lights when they come to Hollywood. I was getting ready to mark off the spot for our next ceremony at the end of the month. One of my favorite actors. Jack Lemmon. They say he's a regular sort of fellow, always good to ordinary people like you and me."

BB strikes a dramatic pose:

"The way things are going right now, in a couple of years you might be seeing *me* putting my own hands and feet in this place."

Immediately the lights halt their aimless search and converge on BB. The brightness is overwhelming, even painful. Pinkie instantly feels the presence of The Abyss. She pulls BB to the sidewalk out of range of the searing lights:

"We've got to get out of here! Where's Jodie? And our driver? Let's go!"

On the way to the party, Hunnybird races to keep pace with the limousine. Meanwhile Pinkie's mind sifts through the events of the past two days:

"How much of this has been coincidence? And how much is it the work of The Abyss? Who's calling the shots? Where's The Bond? Who's really *in control? And just who can we trust?"*

She cuts a suspicious look to Jodie and kicks herself at how vulnerable they've become. Deep down she senses danger lurking.

"I've got to be more careful. We've *got to be more careful."*

She can't seem to shake off this feeling of dread. Maybe this party is just what she needs to soothe her nerves.

Back at Bond headquarters The Council has been watching the hourglass. Their view has been limited, but they've seen everything unfold since BB emerged from the trailer.

Director: "The Abyss is tightening its grip on him with the lure of wealth and fame! He keeps ignoring the warning signs. And none of our interventions have stopped his desire to join this life. We've got to get him out of this town before we lose him. Time's running out!"

Striker slams his fist on the desk: "Give me another shot at the kid. I'll shape him up!"

Director: "Sorry, Striker. You've had your chance. We appreciate the way you started him on his quest. But now it's up to the others. Those kids will need all the help they can get at this party."

Agent Allen: "I don't think I'm going to blend into this social scene very well. Besides, you might need me later for my tech expertise."

Lady Grace smooths her hair and steps forward: "Time to put on my party dress for my entrance. I should be able to sort out the good guys from the crooks easily enough."

Director: "We're counting on you, Lady Grace. If you don't turn him around now, we're running out of options. It's a make or break moment. We'll be out of time and The Abyss will have won."

CHAPTER THIRTY-SIX

The Party

The big limo crosses over the 101 and into the mountains bordering Griffith Park. The twisting maze of streets crawls up the canyon to the top of the ridgeline. A gate opens to a beautifully lit landscape and a driveway leading to the front door. Hunnybird flies to the back yard pool area to keep an eye on the party scene through the huge windows.

The doorman offers to check his jacket and the backpack, but BB claims he has personal items he needs to have with him at all times. They cross a marble paved entryway into an opulent living room with modern sculptures on display. Every wall from floor to ceiling is covered with beautifully framed Renoir and Picasso paintings. BB and Pinkie hold back from the swirl of guests, but Jodie joins right in, waving across the room to a group near the lavish buffet of seafood and tempting dishes. Several nod in her direction. Just then their host breaks away from a conversation to greet them:

"Welcome to my home! I hope my driver has taken good care of you. I'm so very glad you could take the time to join me."

BB vigorously shakes Wilder's hand:

"Thanks for inviting us, Mr. Wilder. You remember my friend Pinkie."

"Of course. I'm pleased you both could come. And who else do we have here?"

"This is our new friend Jodie. She's in the movie business too."

"Well, any friend of BB and Pinkie is always welcome."

Jodie is beside herself with excitement. This could be her chance to make a lasting impression on this titan of the industry:

"Oh my goodness! Mr. Wilder! You don't know how much I admire your work!"

Wilder is used to hollow expressions of adulation, but he senses her sincerity and warmly takes her hand in both of his:

"You just enjoy the rest of the evening. Perhaps we'll have a chance to meet again."

Pinkie comments on the art that surrounds them, and Wilder chuckles:

"You know I've worked every day of my life. I never owned horses or yachts. But I do love art. And I like my friends to enjoy it too. Actually I have more fun collecting art than I do making movies!"

A voice breaks in behind BB and Pinkie:

"Even *Some Like It Hot*? I thought you loved making that one!"

"Jack Lemmon! You old son of a gun! Who let *you* in?"

"Well, you know, I try to sneak my way into any party I can find."

Wilder invites his jovial friend into their small group:

"Jack, I want you to meet the young man I told you about. The one at the Hotel del Coronado. This is BB and his friends, Pinkie and Jodie."

Lemmon leans in to enthusiastically shake hands all around. They quickly warm to his engaging smile and energy.

"Billy told me all about how you alerted him to the plans to destroy that beautiful place. And if Marilyn were here, she'd be thanking you too!"

Jack puts his arm around Wilder's shoulders and draws him close like a best friend. A gregarious, talkative fellow, he continues in genuine admiration for Wilder:

"This guy here is probably the *finest* human being in the business. He looks out for the little guy, especially newcomers who are still learning English and have to work low paying jobs. He was an immigrant himself and never forgets it."

Jack points out the staff who are serving the party:

"Look how much these waiters are smiling and enjoying themselves, rubbing elbows with all of these rich, famous people. Billy always has a kind word for them."

"Come on, Jack. This isn't necessary."

"Oh yes it is! These kids need to know that being famous doesn't mean you don't have principles. The great thing about Billy is he works *with* people. Man, you shoulda seen the way he coaxed that magnificent performance out of Marilyn. It was the best thing she ever did, as far as I'm concerned."

Pinkie breaks in:

"Did she get an Oscar for it?"

"Nah. But she should have! Billy and I got nominated but no wins."

BB wants to know more:

"How many Oscars *do* you have, Mr. Wilder?"

"That's not something we need to talk about."

Billy is in his usual humble mood, but Jack is eager to fill in:

"He's got SIX of those babies. He keeps them in his back office."

He turns to Wilder:

"Say, I was over at Grauman's the other day setting things up with Tartaglia for my handprint ceremony the end of the month. Heck of a nice guy! Maybe you'd like to join the celebration with me and Shirley."

Wilder needs to move on to mingle with his other guests. He excuses himself with a promise to attend if he's able. Jack watches him go:

"He knows everyone. Actors trust him. They feel safe. Famous people, and I guess you'd include me too, we have an obligation just like everyone else who does well in life. We need to send the elevator back down to people starting on the ground floor."

He turns to the three young people and draws them into his intimate circle with his serious tone. He looks directly at Pinkie, and then Jodie, and finally BB:

"Any one of you could be that next star, that next one on the way up. Don't lose sight of how you got there. Don't step on others to get to the top. And be sure to reach back to the ones behind you."

The three friends watch as Lemmon cuts through the crowded room, greeting everyone with his congenial laugh and smile. His good-natured high energy leaves a trail of joy. They wander over to the buffet near the back of the spacious room. A tall, slightly overweight man with round, black-framed glasses breaks away from his group and walks toward them. His distinctive white pompadour and smartly tailored chalk-striped suit signal his wealth. He sidles up to introduce himself:

"Wintergreen's the name, Janus Wintergreen. I've been noticing your familiarity with some of the best of Hollywood... Wilder and Lemmon. If you *really* want to see how a person can move up in this world, though, you need to set your sights higher. I was the personal assistant to Mr. Hearst for years. I watched and learned from him."

BB suddenly makes the connection:

"Are you talking about the guy who built the castle on the coast?"

"Exactly! Only important people were invited to the castle. Movie stars of course, but also politicians and history makers. He surrounded himself with the best. Best people. Best things."

Pinkie is confused:

"You keep speaking in the past tense. Is Mr. Hearst dead?"

"Yes, of course. But I carry on the castle's traditions."

The trio is still not sure who this man is and what he's suggesting he can offer them. Janus leans into the group and gives them a wily wink:

"Everyone here knows I can still make things happen. After all, it's *who* you know that counts. The castle is crowded with day visitors now that it's a state park. But I have keys to the entire complex, so we can wander the castle and gardens after hours."

BB gulps hopefully:

"Did you say *we*?"

"But of course!"

He drops his voice confidentially. They hang on his every word:

"I don't deal in losers. My people are winners, just like my friend Mr. Hearst. Come see me at the castle. I'll take care of you personally! It's a big, beautiful place. Nothing like it in the world!"

In her excitement Jodie blurts out:

"Do you think there'll be any famous people there when *we* come?"

"You never know. We'll have to see what happens."

He draws out a business card from his wallet:

"Meanwhile, here's my card. Don't lose it. If you need my help, you know where to find me. We'll have a beautiful time!"

Janus tucks the card into BB's shirt pocket and pats it for assurance.

"Thanks, sir."

"No need to be so formal. Call me Janus."

He flashes them a smile of even, white teeth and disappears into the crowd. BB takes out the classic business card and admires the rich design. He runs his finger across the engraved lettering and slides the card into the back pocket of his pants. Meanwhile Janus mutters to an unseen source:

"This one's mine. He'll come to me soon enough. Trust me. I know what I'm doing. Remember, I honed my skills on the best! He won't get far from us anymore, now that the signal's in operation."

CHAPTER THIRTY-SEVEN

Neal Weasels In

Behind them a commotion at the front door breaks the pleasant party mood. It's the producer from the movie set and his shadowy assistant. Wilder steps in to calm things down. The doorman is standing his ground:

"These fellas don't have an invitation, Mr. Wilder. I didn't think you would want any party crashers ruining your big night."

"That's okay. I'll take it from here."

Wilder moves the intruders to the side for a personal chat:

"What's this all about, Neal? I thought you preferred your own crowd."

"True. Usually I'm not interested in your stuffy parties. But I got a chance to meet your special guest today. I'm thinking I could use him in a picture I'm working on."

Wilder barely contains his disdain for this overbearing man:

"You're welcome to stay. Just be sure you don't cause any trouble."

"Me? You know I'm *always* the perfect gentleman!"

Neal struts away, straightening his lapels and puffing out his chest. He barges through a small group in his path and strides to the pool area, his assistant Reggie in tow. BB and Pinkie hadn't witnessed the previous scene, but Jodie recognizes the odious producer from his departing silhouette. Pinkie feels a sudden chill when she glimpses the back of his assistant. She shakes her head to clear the thought and returns to their conversation. Jodie drops her voice to a whisper:

"I'm glad he didn't see us. He has a creepy way of sucking the air out of a room."

She takes two glasses of champagne from a tray held by a circulating server. She hands them to BB and Pinkie and then grabs one for herself.

"You don't have to actually drink it. In fact it's usually better *not* to drink any alcohol at these parties, even the safe ones like this one. Watch and learn."

Jodie puts the glass to her lips as if to take a sip. She casually walks to a nearby potted palm and surreptitiously pours half of it into the dirt. She then mingles with the guests who are none the wiser. Pinkie and BB quickly pick up the technique. In less than an hour most people would think they had each downed at least two or three glasses of the sparkling wine. Pinkie and Jodie excuse themselves to find a bathroom, leaving BB on his own. A voice comes from behind him:

"Let me get you another glass."

It's Neal. He's surmised BB and his friends are well on their way to inebriation and figures it's a good time to make his move:

"Come with me. I've got some people I'd like you to meet."

It doesn't take the fog of alcohol to work on BB's ego. He willingly joins Neal and some Hollywood hangers-on by the poolside. Reggie keeps a watchful eye as his boss gets BB to recount the events at the Hotel del Coronado. As Neal enhances his importance to its salvation, BB basks in the admiration of the group. He decides to step up his game and slips the backpack from his shoulder. He's willing to reveal its hidden treasures if it will give him face with this group. Neal has been waiting for just this moment, and even Reggie is on heightened alert.

"Inside this backpack are things you only dream of. There's a statue that's magical. Ever since I got it, the most amazing things have happened to me. Doors open. People want to be around me."

Neal's hand creeps to the zipper of the backpack, hoping to get a view to the contents. But BB grabs it away from him:

"Hey! If you want a look, just ask. I'll even let you touch it and experience its power."

BB holds the bag open for them to gaze in and stroke the figure inside. Neal can already feel the energy surge. He's determined to own this statue no matter what. Reggie is less impressed. He knows they've got BB locked into LA. All he has to do is make sure the moon disappears and his job is finished. But then BB reveals another secret:

"I've also got a bag of custom white stone chips that will power anything. I don't even have to stop for gas."

As BB brings out his bag of fuel fragments, Jodie and Pinkie appear behind him. Pinkie realizes what's going on. She snatches the fuel bag from him, stuffs it in the backpack, and pulls BB to the side. Turning from the group of men, she catches a glimpse of Reggie's profile as he ducks out of sight. It's as if she's seen a ghost!

"Van Detta? No, that's foolish. Wishful thinking on my part. There's no way."

Pinkie shakes off the thought and addresses BB through gritted teeth:

"What are you thinking? Why are you giving away our secrets? At what price? Your ego is going to be the end of us yet!"

Meanwhile Reggie ducks behind a pillar to confer remotely with his higher-ups:

"We have one more reason to get to this kid. The Bond has supplied them with tiny fuel stones. He keeps them in a bag in his backpack. Apparently they're a kind of power source. If we get our hands on them, there's no limit to what we can accomplish. I want this in *my* report! I want the credit."

Just then Jodie wanders by. Reggie pulls her behind the pillar. He suggests a deal if she can get BB to split from Pinkie and deliver him to Neal:

"Name your price. I'll be sure Neal pays close attention to your career."

He slides his arm around her shoulder and draws her in close. Jodie struggles out of his grasp and turns to face him:

"That's not the way I work, Reggie."

He bristles at this name and draws himself to his full height:

"My name is Reginald. I'm not in the same lowly league as my boss and his friends."

"Well, *Reginald*, you don't seem all that different from your disgusting pals. I don't *do* anything to get ahead. And I *don't* sell out my friends."

"Have it your way. But Neal isn't going to like it."

The threat is real and Jodie backs away, keeping her eye on him. Behind another column, Reggie speaks privately into his sleeve:

"I'm going to back off before I'm recognized. I've cut it close too many times. This guy Neal will serve our purposes. He can have the statue. It's that power source that will move our agenda forward. That backpack is the key. Neal will do anything to get ahold of it, but it's not going to happen here. I'll slip out front and catch them when they leave. Neal's crew can do the dirty work. We'll get rid of those guys later."

Jodie rejoins BB and Pinkie and shares the offer she's just turned down. Realizing she's misjudged Jodie's motives all along, Pinkie views her with a newfound understanding. At that moment there's a stir of excitement at the front door. A stunning woman in a satin gown wearing long white gloves and a dazzling necklace of pearls enters the party. Immediately the mood changes. No one has seen her before, and everyone is hoping to make her acquaintance. Pinkie just stares in disbelief at the exquisite vision:

"Lady Grace! I can't believe you're really here! I can't wait to catch up with you..."

Her excited thoughts come to a sudden halt:

"She knows something. Oh, no! What have we done? What have I done?"

The beautiful woman glides through the parting crowd and zeroes in on BB. Now Neal is convinced of that statue's magical power! She smiles at BB:

"I'd like a word with you, young man."

Her smooth, confident gaze locks into BB's eyes. He gulps, gives her a weak grin, and follows her into a nearby room with Pinkie close behind. Pinkie is hoping for a friendly reunion. But Lady Grace has her orders and shoves down any sympathetic feelings she has toward this young pair. As the door closes, she turns to BB and begins her lecture:

"I don't know what kind of game you're playing here, but it's all about to change."

Her tone briefly softens in disappointment:

"Pinkie, I'm surprised at you. It's like you've lost your bearings. This Hollywood thing is infecting you too! The Bond is so saddened by what's been happening."

Pinkie's self-assurance melts in the face of truth. Lady Grace continues with BB:

"And as for *you*. You have no idea what kind of fire you're playing with. You're so mesmerized by these promises of your name in lights that you forgot that you're committed to us. To our goals. Goals more important than your self-absorbed life."

"But I'm just following my dreams. How can that be so awful?"

"Dreams? *Your* dreams? How selfish can you get? It's not all about you. This isn't some Hollywood movie you're starring in."

BB's resentment turns to confusion and finally the beginnings of recognition:

"Wait! I know you! You're the lady from Washington, DC. The woman at the Smithsonian when I was there in eighth grade. How did you get *here*? I mean, that was three years ago. And this is 1963! And you don't look any different!"

He sinks into a nearby couch and stares at the floor. He's either lost his mind or is dreaming. But this sure looks and feels real. Pinkie offers a feeble defense:

"Lady Grace, I'm so sorry! It's not as bad as it looks. We've got this... I think. We just have to figure a way out of the city and back onto the 101 and our quest. There's still time... I think."

Lady Grace isn't having any excuses. Even so she has a soft spot when it comes to Pinkie. Her voice pleads with Pinkie to understand the gravity of the situation:

"You *think?* This isn't like you! You haven't been doing *any* thinking lately. You don't have *anything* under control. You've been living the life of leisure while the moon disappears and the sand keeps falling."

She turns again to BB, who withers under her gaze. Her exasperation pours out:

"And *you!* I don't know how we're going to get you out of this. With all of your bragging and big talk, you've got some of the sleaziest gangsters panting over your backpack, willing to do anything to get it."

BB mumbles dejectedly:

"Yes, ma'am."

He knows he's messed up big time. All his dreams of fame and fortune are turning into a dangerous nightmare. Lady Grace senses his contrition and gentles her tone:

"Oh don't get so down. I'm not usually the one to lay down the law. I leave that to Sergeant Striker. He's better at this than I am. He says I'm too much of a pushover. But he's used up his intervention so you're going to have to listen to me."

Pinkie is happy to see Lady Grace hasn't completely changed. She's always looked up to this confident, gentle member of the Council and leaned on her when feeling unsure or lost. In spite of Pinkie's mistakes and wrong turns, Lady Grace has always been there for her, ready to forgive even when Pinkie didn't deserve her devotion. Lady Grace continues, her voice sympathetic to their plight:

"The Bond will figure out your next step as soon as I find a way to get you out of this place. It's time to get back to the party. Stay alert and be careful who you trust!"

The three of them exit the room and rejoin the other guests. Neal is making a nuisance of himself ordering the staff to get more of his favorite hors d'oeuvres. Wilder steps in:

"Neal, I'll ask you just this once. Do *not* be rude to my staff. You've obviously had enough to drink. Maybe it's time you take your leave."

"What's the deal, Billy? These people are just nobodies. They probably don't even understand half of what I'm saying."

Wilder gives him a look of disgust mixed with pity:

"Neal, you really don't get it, do you? You've sold out your friends in the past. You think you can gain success by stepping *on* and *over* people."

He pauses to let his words take on weight:

"You're basically a weak, little man."

As Wilder walks away, Neal fumes at this verbal takedown. But he isn't about to miss his chance with the new guest or *his shot at getting that backpack. He brushes off Wilder's words and checks the crowd. The elegant woman has just reentered the room. He approaches Lady Grace as if he already owns her:*

"Well hello, Doll!"

She recoils inwardly from this lecherous man but maintains an air of gracious calm. Neal moves in to establish his dominance and puts his arm around her slender waist. As his hand begins to drift downward, Lady Grace, in one quick motion, spins away, grabs a glass of champagne and tosses the drink in his face. Neal isn't used to being rebuffed, especially in such a public setting. He grabs her wrist and pulls her to him, breathing hot words into her face:

"No one messes with Neal, Sweetheart!"

Lady Grace doesn't lose her poise. Angered by her indifference, Neal clutches her strand of pearls, drawing her ever closer. She smiles serenely as the small white orbs glow hot red. Neal cries out and backs away to sooth his singed fingers. He scowls back at her, making a note to serve up some retribution later. Billy Wilder signals his doorman and one of the waiters:

"See that our 'friend' finds his way to the front door... and out!"

The two men, one on each side, roughly grab Neal's arms and hustle him to the door. Incensed, Wilder calls after him:

"You've earned your nickname tonight. 'Neal the Weasel' had better keep a wide berth from me and anything associated with me from now on."

Wilder regains his cordial attitude for his guests, but his soul has taken a beating:

"I don't know why I even have these parties. I like bringing people together other than at work, but some of them just want to use it to make their moves, get ahead. It's all so tiresome... this Hollywood glamour and gluttony. It takes all the enjoyment out of it. It's as if we're trapped in our own desires."

Neal is summarily tossed from the house. He walks a short distance before spotting his waiting limo. Reggie is there, leaning against the car. Neal is steaming. He's got to get that statue! Nothing will stop him from finally showing up Wilder:

"This is personal. He's going down! Then he'll look up at *me*... standing at the top."

Reggie wishes it were time to part company with this repulsive but valuable asset. But he can't leave just yet. He has to make sure these gangsters wrap this up tonight. Even so, he plans to hold back so he doesn't get his hands dirty unnecessarily. And he needs to be careful around Pinkie or he'll lose his advantage. If she gets a good look at him, she'll alert The Bond. The Abyss won't be happy if these two escape this perfect trap they've so carefully crafted.

Neal consults with his bodyguard and Reggie about their next move once they spot their prey. His driver lights a cigarette. This could be a long wait.

CHAPTER THIRTY-EIGHT

Escape to the Chase

"I'm so glad you stood up for yourself! Neal can be so... so..."

Jodie searches for the right word, which Lady Grace is quick to provide:

"Predatory?"

Jodie's eyes widen. She's called it for what it is. She nods slowly to the self-assured woman. Lady Grace gathers the young people together and steers them out to the back yard where Greek style columns and fountains surround the pool. Hunnybird flies down to chatter to Lady Grace. She nods in response:

"I know it's not your fault. You're not responsible for their decisions. We appreciate all you're doing to keep them on track."

Jodie stares in disbelief at this conversation. Lady Grace continues to admonish BB and Pinkie, pointing to the dark fringe beginning to eat away the moon's glow:

"Look up and let this sink in. Chasing this Hollywood fantasy has got to end. Now! It's time for you to leave. But obviously you can't go out the front door."

When BB and Pinkie disclose the location of their car, Lady Grace is stumped for an idea. However, Jodie has a possible solution:

"If we can find the back gate to this place I know another way. There's a trail not far from here. I've hiked to the sign many times."

Confident she's now restored their attention to the quest, Lady Grace excuses herself:

"I'm only allowed this brief visit with you. You're on your own now."

She gives Pinkie a tender hug and then a second, longer embrace. She draws back to regard them both with concern and trepidation, pondering what dangers they might face. She steps to the edge of the pool and executes a perfect dive. As her silk clad body hits the water, she disappears from sight. Jodie stares at the tiny ripple on the pool's smooth surface and the floating bubbles of pearls that burst into flashes of starlight:

"Wow! She sure knows how to make an exit!"

Jodie leads the way down a path to the back fence. There a latched gate swings outward into the wilderness beyond. Pinkie hesitates as the gate shuts behind them:

"I'm not sure you're going to hike very well in that skirt and sandals, Jodie."

"No problem! I'll just slip my pants back on and change my shoes. I keep an extra pair for emergencies."

"Yeah, we've got a little something for emergencies too."

She and BB press the buttons on their watches. Their shoes become a more sturdy style. Pinkie's outfit switches to pants, shirt and a comfortable jacket. Jodie just stares:

"Wow! I thought I was the queen of the quick change! How'd you *do* that?"

Realizing they might reveal too much, Pinkie offhandedly explains:

"We have certain advantages with the company we work for."

Jodie finds the trail in the moonlight and Hunnybird flies just ahead. Pinkie quickly changes the subject as they start off up the hillside:

"So how do you know so much about this area?"

"I'm really an outdoor girl at heart. I love to hike. When I discovered this beautiful area right here in the middle of the city, I followed the trail up to the sign. I come here to sit and think... and dream. Another girl came up here long ago. Her story is really sad. She'd been trying to make it in Hollywood and finally gave up. One night she was really depressed. She came up to the Hollywood sign and killed herself."

BB can't believe he's hearing this:

"That's awful! Didn't she have anyone to stop her? Being famous can't be *that* important that you'd give up your *life!*"

"Oh, it's true! Lot's of people would *give* anything, *do* anything for the chance to make it big. Sad thing is, the morning after she died, one of the studios delivered a notice to her apartment that she'd actually landed a role in a really good movie. She could have been a star after all!"

This story weighs on BB's mind. Suddenly the statue in his backpack seems heavier. The trio continues up the trail and finally ends at the road above the sign. Jodie is astonished when they flip the invisible cover and the blue Corvette appears:

"What *are* you guys? Spies or something?"

BB isn't really sure what he's involved in, but Pinkie just laughs it off:

"Thanks, Jodie, for getting us back to our car. We'd give you a ride, but as you can see, there really isn't any room."

Jodie suddenly panics. Will they actually leave her out here at the mercy of the elements and those shady characters back at the party? Tears well up in her eyes. Hunnybird chirps and flutters his dismay. Pinkie realizes how heartless her comment is. After all, Jodie's been nothing but helpful, even if she's dominated BB's attention.

"I'm just kidding. We can make it work somehow. Right, BB?"

BB pulls his eyes away from the lights of the city far below, the lights that have been calling to him. The lights he's craved. He's not ready to say goodbye to this sweet girl:

"Sure we can. Maybe you can sit on Pinkie's lap and I'll drive. Or you can sit on *my* lap and Pinkie can drive."

"How about I ride in the trunk? It's pretty big, and I can fold myself right in!"

Jodie snugs into the trunk. Hunnybird pops into BB's pocket, ready for the next leg of their adventure. BB makes a U turn and heads down the mountain. Back on the street in front of Wilder's home, the last of the guests leave the party. Neal sends his driver to the front door to find out what's happened to their targets.

"They're gone! Nobody's seen them for a couple of hours. How'd they get past us?"

Neal thinks he's figured it out:

"They must have gone out the back and circled around behind us. They're probably walking down the road now. Let's go!"

Reggie sends out the word. A searchlight from the observatory scans the hillsides looking for the fugitives. Within seconds it zeroes in on the convertible crossing the ridgeline and winding down the mountain. Reggie reports their movements:

"They're driving a blue Corvette down to Mulholland Drive on the other side of the reservoir. If we hurry we can catch them when they reach the 101."

Neal shouts to his driver:

"Do what he says, and put some speed on this thing!"

As soon as the blinding light spots them, Pinkie knows who's tracking them. They race down the residential streets, hidden under a canopy of trees. The light gives up its search. As they wind their way through the canyon neighborhood, Hunnybird chirps along, glad for another round of excitement. Poor Jodie is tossed about in the trunk. They blindly take left turns continuing their descent.

But then the road begins to climb.

"BB! It's that statue! I know it is! You think it's bringing you good luck and opening great doors. Well I don't agree. I think those doors are opening to your downfall."

"Yeah, but look at all the super people we've met up with. They've been great to me! They want me to succeed! They want me to be famous!"

"Is fame really all that important? Is it really worth it?"

"Forget it! I'm taking this right turn. It looks like it's going back down the canyon."

The new street finally straightens out and leads them directly south. At the next light a sign for the 101 points to the left. Just as BB is making his turn, Pinkie spots the limo:

"There they are! Step on it!"

They fly down the street and take the first entrance onto the 101. In their panic, they don't notice it's taking them south, back to where they came from. Ignoring the red light, Neal's driver shoves the pedal to the floor:

"It's them, Boss! We've got 'em now!"

The car lurches forward, hurling the bodyguard into Reggie and his furious boss:

"Get off me, you muscle bound oaf!"

The limo is no match for the speed of the sleek Corvette. Watching the taillights gradually pulling away from them down the freeway, Neal is beside himself:

"We're losing them! Reggie, you got anymore ideas?"

"We won't lose them. They'll be slowing down soon. Just relax. I've got this."

Back in the Corvette, Pinkie spots red and orange flashing lights ahead:

"Oh no, BB! A detour! We're somewhere in the middle of LA, and those guys are still after the backpack. How can we ever shake them?"

Sure enough the detour sends them north into a new neighborhood. BB turns down a side street that ends in a **T**. *He nudges the car to the curb. Undetected, two ravens fly away to report their location.*

"Get Jodie out of the trunk, BB! Let's get this thing covered before we're spotted!"

CHAPTER THIRTY-NINE

Echoes of Death

Jodie emerges disheveled but in good shape. She straightens her blouse and flips her hair out of her face:

"I know this place. It's Echo Lake! Isn't it beautiful?"

Pinkie shouts at her:

"Forget the lake! We've got to hide. Neal's gang is after us!"

"Oh, that's why BB was driving so crazy. I thought I'd never survive!"

From out of the darkness a voice responds: "Survive... survive... survive..."

BB is on guard for anything threatening:

"Who was that?"

"Silly boy. Why do you think they call it Echo Lake? Come on. I want to introduce you to a friend."

BB is concerned about their own little friend:

"Hunnybird, we have to move fast. I don't want to take the chance we'll get separated. Hide in the glove compartment for now."

Hunnybird chirps in protest, but Pinkie reassures him:

"Don't worry! We won't forget you!"

After Pinkie and BB conceal the car, Jodie leads them to a nearby point overlooking the lake. In the moonlight a figure raises her arms in a blessing. Jodie stares up at her face.

"This is my friend. The Lady of the Lake. She's blessing the city, but I always imagine she's blessing me too."

Jodie breathes out a deep, wishful sigh. Behind the statue, three fountains come to life, their plumes reaching into the moonlight. Jodie stares in disbelief:

"That must be a sign! I've never seen them at night before."

Pinkie's urgent voice brings Jodie back to their predicament:

"Jodie, we really don't have time for this. They'll see us out in the open."

Jodie points to a gently arching bridge that leads to an island:

"Over there! They'll never suspect we're there. Come on!"

Jodie leads BB and Pinkie on the path that skirts the lake. Meanwhile the limo arrives where the Corvette is parked. But there's no car. Neal lays into Reggie for his faulty information, but he defends himself:

"My source is never wrong. They've got to be here someplace. I know it!"

The ravens call from the direction of the lake.

"I told you! Let's go!"

The gangsters arrive at the stone statue and scan the lake with their flashlights. One of the beams catches the three young people in midstride crossing the bridge. Realizing their island hiding spot is now a trap, they pivot to return to shore. Neal calls out:

"There they are! And Jodie's with them. Well, she'll be sorry she hitched up with those two. This will cost her. Big time!"

Reggie is pleased with this turn of events:

"We've got them!"

But Neal wants to be sure. He calls to his two henchmen:

"Take them out!"

His loud command reaches the three friends. Jodie's plea pierces the night:

"NO!"

Reggie shouts his own resounding NO! He can't lose BB and Pinkie now! How would he ever explain this? Two candidates he's been working on so carefully. It would throw his plans off completely. He grabs the gun closest to him and wrenches it to the sky.

Jodie steps in front of BB and Pinkie just as the gunshots ring out. She collapses into BB's arms, and the three sink to the floor of the bridge. Across the lake the fountains go still. The Lady of the Lake gives a silent benediction as a solitary tear flows down her cheek. Back at Bond Headquarters the alabaster wall glows brightly. The light sends forth its strength. BB gently lowers Jodie's lifeless body. The reality of the true cost of his search for fame finally grips him as he stares into the mask of death:

"Oh Jodie! You had a deeper wisdom of right and wrong when it came to this city. Never compromising even if it meant you wouldn't win. I'm going to miss your

joy for everything, your bright spot of hope."

Her breath trembling, Pinkie tearfully brushes Jodie's hair back from the beautiful face. Her thoughts collide in an admission of guilt:

"I'm so sorry! I really am! You didn't deserve this. Please forgive me for the way I treated you."

But it's too late for regrets. Pinkie sobs her sorrow for Jodie and her own failings. BB takes the statue from the backpack and turns away. Alone in his grief, he reaches through the railing and lets the statue slip from his hand into the water. As it sinks to the murky bottom, he feels the vise grip loosen from his heart, his soul. Hidden from view, they crawl away from the deadly scene. Once on shore they race down an alternate path back to the car, throw off the shroud, and zoom away.

When Neal and his men arrive at the bridge all they find is Jodie's lifeless body. Reggie turns away, realizing how close he came to an even greater loss. Neal callously growls about the fate of this young life:

"I told that stupid girl she didn't know how to play the game. Grab some of those rocks over there to weight her down. Then toss her over the side. She'll sink to the bottom. Just another body in the lake. Hope you've got some good ideas, Reggie old boy. They've still got the backpack, and they're on the run again."

Shaking off this grim episode, Reggie confidently reassures him:

"No problem. My surveillance spotted them on their way back to the 101. Those two always return to what they know. But I've got one more way to slow them down that will lead them to a dead end."

Neal adds his own twisted comment:

"You could say it's the *ultimate* dead end!"

Meanwhile the Corvette races toward the freeway. In desperation BB takes the closest entrance to the 101. South once again! Before long, BB spots a familiar set of headlights in the rearview mirror and embraces the challenge:

"Let's see how fast this thing can go!"

The sports car outpaces the limo. But with virtually no traffic, Reggie can occasionally make out their distinctive taillights. With the ravens overhead, they'll know exactly where those two stop. He relishes the chase, his adrenalin pumping through his body. The Abyss will never question his loyalty again if he brings them in. Meanwhile in the speeding convertible, BB and Pinkie are screaming at each other:

"BB, we're going the wrong direction! This is heading south!"

"I can't drive *and* navigate! Oh no! More construction. Another detour!"

This final obstacle from The Abyss sends them to Long Beach and the harbor. When they run out of road, it'll all be over. Pinkie is desperate:

"I know they're still back there. What'll we do, BB?"

The road ends at a pier where several boats are tied. The two ravens circle around and fly back up the highway for their final report. Pinkie and BB have no other options. They park the car and grab the backpack. A muffled chirp calls out in desperation.

"BB! Let Hunnybird out!"

Safely liberated, the little fellow dives into BB's pocket. Near the docks BB and Pinkie find several steel drums to hide behind. They secure themselves under the shroud just as the limo pulls up. Neal is furious:

"Here's their car. Check the trunk. No backpack. Figures! Well they can't be far. And if they don't have a car, they'll be easy to spot on foot."

Reggie is puzzled that the tracking signal isn't working. Neal calls to his two henchmen:

"Grab the gas can in the back of the limo. The one I keep for emergencies like this."

At Neal's urging, the two thugs splash gasoline over the blue convertible. Neal lights a celebration cigar and tosses the match. Reggie shields his face from the impending blast. Horrified, BB and Pinkie watch the beautiful Corvette burst into flames.

Just then a boat's engine sputters to life. BB and Pinkie feel a surge of movement and realize their hiding place is a barge tethered to a tugboat. They clear the harbor and head out to sea. The torched Corvette lights up the dark sky, a red orange pillar reflected on the barge's wake and on letters stamped on the steel containers: DDT

"Pinkie! DDT? It's been illegal for decades! Nobody even makes it anymore!"

"Remember it's 1963. It's perfectly legal."

They sway with the slow steady motion of the barge cutting through the ocean swells. Far out to sea, the tugboat engines shut off. BB and Pinkie lift the covering and watch several tough looking men climb aboard the barge. As they maneuver the barrels to the sides, the foreman shouts out his orders:

"Make sure they reach the bottom and don't float away."

Pinkie and BB inch farther to the back of the barge as one by one the men grab

the steel drums. Using heavy axes they chop deep slices into the metal barrels and heave them overboard. The toxic liquids flow from the gashes as they sink to the ocean floor.

"That's the last of them, Captain!"

The men congratulate themselves on another job well done. The tugboat and empty barge begin a wide turn to the coast. BB and Pinkie are heading back into danger! And now they don't have a car!

CHAPTER FORTY

Catalina Connection

Just then a violent storm swirls in from the northwest. The captain struggles to maintain course, but it's pointless. He lets the current and winds take them south in hopes of finding shelter at one of the Channel Islands. In the dim light of dawn the outline of Catalina Island appears. Following the sheltered eastern shore, the captain turns to the cove at Avalon. While they wait out the storm, the crew decides to take advantage of this unexpected bonus. From their hiding place BB and Pinkie watch the the men disappear into the picturesque village.

"Now what, Pinkie?"

"How should I know?"

"Well, I'm beat. Let's catch some sleep and figure it out later."

Pinkie is totally dejected:

"I'm tired of having to work things out on the fly. How will we ever get back on track now? Has The Bond deserted us?"

She keeps her fears and trepidation to herself. No sense sharing with BB her lack of confidence, adding to his doubts and uncertainties.

Safe beneath the shroud, the stowaways lean back against the hull of the barge and give in to their bone-weariness. As the sun reaches a point overhead, the raucous voices of the returning crewmen rouse them.

"We can't stay here, Pinkie. If they go back to the mainland, we're toast!"

They throw off the mantle and secure it in the backpack. Immediately the business card in BB's pocket sends out a signal. When they step from the barge onto the dock, one of the crew catches a glimpse of them from the tugboat:

"Hey! What're you kids doing? Get away from here!"

"We're just admiring your... your... *fine* craft, mister!"

"You're a couple of those environment jerks poking around where you don't belong. Scram! I'd better not see you hanging around here again!"

BB and Pinkie run to the shore and down the road that hugs the shoreline, being careful to avoid any late returning crew members. Around a curve they see an old woman coming their way. Her melodious, mesmerizing voice stops them in their tracks:

"You planning a hike along this road? You'd better have some water."

BB realizes it's been hours since they've had anything to eat or drink:

"Actually we're pretty thirsty. We forgot to bring any water with us."

"Let me give you some from my canteen."

As they gratefully gulp down the cool liquid, the old woman sizes them up:

"You two don't look familiar. You come over on a tourist boat?"

"Uh, sort of."

Pinkie nudges BB in the ribs and he blurts out:

"Yeah, sure did!"

She eyes them warily as they struggle with their story. But then she spots a tough looking character coming up behind them. The old woman grabs her canteen and makes a futile effort to conceal it in her loose dress.

"Hey! Is that the canteen I've been missing? You dirty old thief!"

The churlish fellow grabs it from her gnarled hands and pretends to examine it:

"Naw! Just your old, worn out flask. You filling these kids up with your wild stories? Everyone else is tired of hearing 'em, so I guess you need a new audience."

BB and Pinkie unconsciously back away from this belligerent man. But the woman silently stands her ground while he addresses the two of them:

"She's been here for years. Even when I was here during the war. After it ended I decided to stick around. Who wouldn't want to live on this island paradise? By the way, you know what they call this place? Lovers Cove."

He winks at BB, and Pinkie blushes. BB gives him a nervous laugh. The man turns again to mock the woman:

"But this old hag thinks she's special. A princess even! Full of fairy tales about her 'magic' water. 'Drink it and you'll be smart!' Well let's see."

He takes a swig from the canteen.

"Yup! I'm a genius!"

He laughs uproariously and pours out the remaining water. He hurls the canteen as far as he can. It disappears in the brush up the nearby canyon.

"Ha, ha, ha... Go fetch! Stupid Indian dog!"

BB and Pinkie watch the man disappear down the road, still laughing at his own foul humor. The woman quietly pronounces her judgment:

"He will never benefit. He doesn't believe in anything but himself."

BB and Pinkie offer to help search for her flask. She trails after them up the arroyo through the coastal scrub where they discover the empty canteen. She motions them to follow her farther up the canyon. Hunnybird squirms out of BB's pocket to join the free-spirited wildlife. An island fox stops to bow its head to the old woman. He barks sharply and bounds away. Farther on, she abruptly halts. A rattlesnake slithers from under the shadow of a rock and coils to attack. She calls out in a strange language. The serpent drops its aggressive pose and slides deeper into the underbrush. Pinkie and BB are astonished at the effect she has over nature.

A little more than halfway up the ravine, the old woman pauses and carefully scans the area behind them and then above to the top of the canyon. Assured they're alone, she pulls aside a mass of chaparral to reveal an underground cave. BB and Pinkie follow her down over one hundred steps past strange pictographs on the narrow walls. At the bottom BB nervously squints up at the circle of light from the entrance far above, their only way out.

"No one knows we're here. We're at the mercy of this lady. She could do anything she wants to us! Who knows what's down here?"

He peers through the dim light at Pinkie. But she seems more curious than concerned with their fate. And then the old woman speaks:

"This island is surrounded by water. But you will die if you drink it."

She takes them into the shadows where a spring bubbles from the ground. She urges them to sip the cool, clear liquid:

"My people drank freely from this. Even in times of no rain this water nourished us. This is special water. It generates life. It kept my people alive. They thrived on it. This water will make you wise. You just need to believe."

They don't feel any different after drinking the water. Maybe it's just a hoax like the man said. The old woman stoops down, fills the canteen, and hands it to BB:

"My days are soon ending. I pass this on to you. You may need it."

BB accepts the gift and secures it in the backpack. Slowly they climb to the top of the shaft where the woman carefully replaces the brush. They hurry to keep up as she nimbly clambers over rocks and around bushes. Abruptly she stops and pushes aside a branch to reveal a large nest with cracked and broken shells. Flies cover dead baby birds too young to survive. A tear trickles down the woman's weathered cheek:

"The body of the mother bird crushed the fragile shells. Something is hurting the eggs."

BB knows what that something is. They had just watched a chemical company throw DDT into the ocean. Their boat had followed the same current that carried the poison to the island. Reaching the top of the canyon, they stop to catch their breath.

"This is private property!"

CHAPTER FORTY-ONE

Truth or Dare

The owner of the voice strides toward them, holding his hand against the blinding afternoon sun. His dusty clothes hang loosely on his frame. A wide-brimmed hat shields his face. BB guesses he might be around his grandfather's age, early 70s maybe.

Pinkie has learned that bold self assurance in such a situation goes a long way. She greets him with her winning smile and confidently offers her hand:

"Hello, sir. Our friend here has been showing us some of the natural beauty of your island. I hope it's okay if we do some exploring."

"Just as long as you don't leave any trash behind or start any campfires. We've been in a drought. One spark could set this whole hillside on fire."

Just then the old woman speaks up:

"Now P.K. Don't worry about these two. They seem like good kids."

Immediately there is a change in his attitude:

"Sorry. I didn't realize it was you, little Toovit."

She laughs at this pet Gabrielino name from her childhood:

"I'm not much of a rabbit with these old bones. And you aren't up for a race either!"

P.K. addresses the young people:

"When my father arrived, there was no water source that lasted through the dry years. She shared her hidden spring, so he gave her permission to live on this land."

"Yes, P.K. Good, clean water is more precious than all the gold in the world."

The woman takes her leave. P.K. watches her trudge up the road:

"When she was young, she paddled a canoe over twenty miles to this island to experience its natural beauty. You know, she's a Tongva princess."

BB blurts out his skepticism:

"*She's* a princess? She sure doesn't look like one."

"Don't be fooled by her simple attire. Royalty goes much deeper."

He leads them to an overlook to view the village of Avalon and the distant mainland:

"If you look carefully you can just make out Long Beach."

This jolts BB and Pinkie back to the reality of how vulnerable they are on this small island. P.K. continues good-naturedly:

"Want a stick of gum?"

His offer calms their anxiety. They accept two pieces of spearmint. P.K. takes one for himself and then gives them an unopened pack. BB slips it into his backpack for later. The three of them gaze out onto the ocean, silently chewing away. Pinkie tentatively approaches a subject that's been bothering her:

"Did you know they're dumping chemicals into the ocean just north of here?"

P.K. swings his gaze to stare at her. BB adds his two cents:

"They're putting barrels and barrels of DDT right into the water! We saw an eagle's nest today with broken eggs that never had a chance to hatch. It could be the DDT!"

P.K. looks thoughtfully out on the beauty of their natural surroundings.

"I always thought this island could be a magnificent, world-class resort. But maybe it should become something else. I'll talk this over with my son."

Just then a loud voice calls out from behind:

"P.K.! I've been looking for you."

A lanky fellow ambles down a stairway on the hillside. He's dressed in jeans and a sweat-stained work shirt with rolled up sleeves. A slouch hat is pulled low over his brow, but they can still see their partial reflection in his aviator sunglasses.

"Harry, meet these young people who are visiting the island."

They shake the fellow's hand as P.K. continues:

"Harry's my new hired hand. Just came over from the mainland. Good worker and smart too! Hope he sticks around for awhile."

At that moment a bright beam of light zeroes in on their little group. P.K. assumes it's a reflection of the setting sun off a building below. But Pinkie and

BB can see it's coming from the mainland and duck behind some brush. Harry suddenly expresses an interest in their plans. He suggests a tour of the island.

"Great idea, Harry! Take the jeep and show them the viewpoints on the back roads. These kids got me thinking about taking care of our island. I need to meet with some people down in the village about an idea I have. Catch you later!"

Harry urges them up the long flight of stairs. Part way up, Pinkie and BB look back to the mainland and spot a fleet of speedboats headed straight for Catalina. At the top of the steps, Harry hurries them to a jeep parked in front of a huge colonial-style mansion. Pinkie joins Harry in the front seat. BB climbs in the back, and they're off. Harry skids to the right onto the main road. Before long he turns onto a dirt road that rolls up and over canyon ridges and down into ravines. This is hardly a sightseeing tour! Pinkie grabs the dashboard to steady herself and her nerves and glances over to Harry:

"Which side is this guy on? He looks okay, but you can never be sure."

Harry wrestles the wheel straight after hitting a deep rut in the road. Pinkie looks back at BB with growing alarm.

"I hope BB's up for a fight. This guy could be taking us to some secluded place to hand us off to the Abyss or something worse!"

Harry keeps his eyes forward as he shouts over the engine:

"So you got yourself connected with Mr. Wrigley. Nice move! You know he owns most of this island. Or used to. Passed it on to his son."

He can tell this is news to them.

"He didn't tell you? I'm not surprised. The big house has been closed up since his mom died. He's been urging his son to sell off everything."

BB is stunned by this revelation:

"But he didn't seem like anyone important. We thought he was the caretaker."

"Don't be fooled by his humble ways. He's pretty quiet. People around here think he's arrogant. But he's really a good guy. Did he give you some of his gum?"

"Sure did. *And* a fresh pack too!"

"Hang onto that gum. Don't give any of it away."

The jeep lurches over a deep rut. Harry grabs the wheel more firmly to keep them from sliding off into the canyon below. The deserted road switches back and forth, occasionally revealing panoramic ocean views. Each time they glance to the mainland the boats are drawing closer. Pinkie is certain of the danger facing them, but knows their options are limited. BB mutters to himself:

"She's a target. And so am I. And there's no one to help us except a tiny yellow bird. Why did we ever agree to this stupid ride?"

The road descends to the shore, out of the searchlight's sightline. Harry parks the jeep in a dusty turnoff just above the beach.

"We're on foot now. Watch your step."

Pinkie nervously whispers to BB:

"If this guy lets down his guard, be ready to run!"

They half walk, half slide down an old path that follows the cliff erosion. Carefully they drop down the final few feet to the deserted rocky shoreline. BB and Pinkie panic! They're trapped! But then Harry points to the right:

"There's your new vehicle."

About a hundred yards down the way a single prop amphibious plane is moored just off shore. BB and Pinkie stare in disbelief, first at the plane and then back at Harry. He raises his arms in a questioning gesture:

"What's the matter? What did you think this was? A smuggling operation?"

He takes off his hat and sunglasses. Pinkie shouts out her relief:

"Agent Allen!"

She rushes to give "Harry" an all-embracing hug, the comforting assurance she's needed for so long.

"It's going to be okay, Pinkie. I'm sorry you've been left on your own for so long. Things'll be different now."

He brushes away Pinkie's tears of joy. She's so grateful to know this man of many talents is by their side. Hunnybird has been keeping a cautious distance, but now he flies around Agent Allen's head chirping uncontrollably.

"It's good to see you too, little fellow. I hear you've been having quite the adventure."

BB is still confused by this whole scene:

"You know this guy?"

Pinkie breaks away and gives Agent Allen a friendly shove:

"Well I do now! I should have seen through that thin disguise of yours. But I wasn't expecting to see *you*. I was sure we were... oh never mind. I'm so relieved it's you!"

BB searches the man's face and then remembers:

"You again! I thought I'd left you back in D.C. at the Washington Monument. Back when all of this started."

"Focus, BB! Striker and Lady Grace have helped you. And you have the backpack I prepared. I'm your final in-person support from The Council. From now on use your experience and gut instincts. Be careful who you trust! Stick together. Come on. I have a few special features to show you on this little beauty."

BB isn't so sure this is the answer to their dilemma:

"But we don't know how to fly a plane."

He looks straight at Pinkie:

"Unless you have *another* hidden talent."

Pinkie gives him a tight-lipped glare. They scurry down the beach around smooth, wave-washed rocks and wade out to the plane. They take their seats and Agent Allen leans in:

"She's equipped with dual controls in case of an emergency. An automatic switch turns the controls over if your hands lose their grip on the wheel. As long as you're the pilot, though, the other person can't override you."

BB looks at the unfamiliar gauges and dials. He has no idea what any of them mean. He gives a sideways glance to Pinkie, who's staring blankly at the controls. Oblivious to their growing alarm, Agent Allen gives a complete rundown of the various components:

"It's a typical control panel. The ignition has an automatic starter. There's an off and start position. This refers to the magneto, or electrical generator within the engine."

Agent Allen points to the various gauges, obviously engrossed in the technical details:

"Here you have your basics: the ASI, that's the airspeed indicator, the altimeter, and the VSI which uses the pitot-static system. This provides the ram air pressure from the pitot tube and ambient pressure from the static port."

Pinkie and BB give him terrified looks. Neither wants to touch anything for fear of breaking something or setting off a disastrous chain of events. Agent Allen is coming dangerously close to completely shattering their confidence. He laughs off their concern and switches to a casual, non-technical tone:

"Don't worry about any of those. They're just for show in case someone gets nosey. I wanted this little gem to look as much like a regular plane as possible. Just turn the key and the engine will start. The steering wheel acts just like a car. Use the pedals on the floor to accelerate and brake. Turn the wheel to go left or right. Pull back on the wheel to go up. Push it away to go down. No new skills are really needed since you both obviously know how to drive."

Agent Allen pauses for a moment before describing the final detail:

"There may come a time when you have no good choices, when everything makes no sense and you aren't sure which way to go. There's an override system built in for just that moment. You may be tempted to wrestle back the controls. But if you allow it to proceed, if you *trust* it, you will get an answer you never expected."

BB's fears are somewhat alleviated. They should be able to actually fly the plane. But this last mysterious comment renews his frustration and irritation:

"Why didn't you show up before? We could have used you!"

BB looks to Pinkie for support that doesn't come. And then he turns to Agent Allen again, his resentment boiling over:

"Why does everything have to be so complicated? Why doesn't The Bond just pave the way and solve all our problems?"

Agent Allen doesn't waver:

"This isn't just about reaching a goal. You'll be surprised what you'll find out about the world… and yourself on this journey."

BB still isn't buying into this "learning process." He slams his hand onto the steering wheel, startling Hunnybird, who hovers just over his shoulder.

"I know plenty about me. And I know what works in this world. I don't need your lessons. I'm tired of lessons. Just give me what I need."

Pinkie grabs his arm to restrain him:

"There's no use arguing. They won't give in. Get your head back in the game."

BB calms down and regains his focus. Hunnybird decides it's safe again to pop back into his shirt pocket. BB starts the engine, ready to take off. He hopes this plane will be as easy to fly as promised. Agent Allen has a last minute question:

"Pinkie, I forgot to ask. Did you get the water flask from the Indian princess?"

Pinkie unzips the backpack to show him the canteen.

"Good. It's the first item Striker said you needed to collect."

Pinkie speaks the riddle out loud:

"What fills the smallest space?"

BB is confused:

"An old canteen?"

Pinkie rolls her eyes and sighs:

"The *water*!"

"Right. I knew that!"

Agent Allen gives the two youngsters a concerned look:

"My time is over. The Council is counting on you. Wait! I almost forgot!"

He takes a paper sack from a leather sling pouch:

"Sandwiches. It's probably been a while since you ate."

Agent Allen steps down from the plane and wades back to the shore. He returns with the mooring line and throws it into the back of the plane. At that moment his eye catches movement to the left. Around the bend a broken line of boats bears down on them.

"They're coming! Go! Head north along the coast. That's the route the 101 follows. And don't forget to keep an eye on the moon!"

Pinkie desperately calls to him:

"But we can't leave you to them!"

Agent Allen sloshes a few feet away through the shallow surf. BB guns the motor, and the plane skims across the smooth surface of the water:

"Hang on! Here goes nothing!"

He pulls back on the wheel, and the plane rises effortlessly. They can see the boats closing in on Agent Allen. With a final wave of his hat he melts into the water. The boats circle around to no avail. He's gone for good. The plane disappears into the coastal fog that rolls toward the island. The Abyss is thwarted once more!

CHAPTER FORTY-TWO

In and Out of Danger

"What now?"

BB looks over to Pinkie. No response. She leans back and relaxes in her seat, relieved this latest encounter is behind them. Annoyed, he presses her:

"We can't just keep heading out to sea! What's our plan?"

Pinkie sits up straight and turns her whole body toward him:

"*Our* plan? Your recent plunge into the Hollywood scene cost us more than we'll ever know. I hope you now realize what we're up against."

Hunnybird gives them both a stern chirp and disappears down in BB's pocket for a nap.

"Okay, okay! Let's move on! We have to keep going north along the 101. We should be able to follow it from the air. I'm going to drop down to see where we are."

Just below the cloud cover the northernmost Channel Islands come into view. BB skims the gentle wave swells where a pod of dolphins greets them with their playful leaps and twists. The plane rises over the coastal mountains where Highway 101 swings inland, but BB takes the route that follows closer to the shore:

"Close to the coastline we'll avoid detection. If they're still out there."

"What do you mean *if?* Of course there are scouts out looking for us!"

"Look, Pinkie!"

BB points below to a kaleidoscope of colors stretching over massive flower fields. The colors merge into a magical carpet of orange poppies that directs the little plane northward. Before long it lifts in an upward slope pointed directly into the blue sky.

"BB! Pull up!"

"I am! I just don't want to stall the engine!"

The carpet breaks into gold and orange confetti that flows over, under, and around them. As BB levels the plane, Pinkie grips her seat and stares ahead:

"What's happening? Are we going in the right direction?"

Pinkie's alarm dissolves into surprised laughter as a cloud of Monarch butterflies engulfs the plane and disappears into sparkles of tangerine and black.

"Pinkie, check out the dunes and the wide beach! We're still heading north."

"Good! Get back into the cloud bank and keep our altitude up."

BB guides the plane into the relative safety of the cloud cover. But the lure of possible sights below is too much for him. As he drops down for a look, a huge stone mountain blocks their path. Pinkie screams. BB instinctively pulls the plane hard to the left barely clearing the massive rock. Pinkie swallows her fear and gasps:

"What was THAT?"

BB calms his ragged breathing:

"That was Morro Bay. My dad brought us here one summer. Highway 1 starts climbing up the coast from here. We'd better get farther out to sea for awhile."

Back in the fog cover, the plane noses farther and farther north. When the clouds finally give way they spot a waterfall ribbon spilling into a sandy beach cove. BB takes a winding path up the rugged, rocky coastline. And then he spots a real challenge. Turning inland, BB swoops down into a tree-covered canyon that leads to the ocean. Ahead a huge, arching bridge spans the gorge.

"Stop, BB! We're going to crash!"

But BB is focused on this test of his skill. Faster and faster they race down the ravine. Pinkie covers her eyes, expecting the end.

"You're going to miss it, Pinkie! Watch!"

Pinkie first peeks between her fingers and then embraces the sight full on. With just enough room on either side and above, the little plane flies under the arch and straight out over the rocks toward the bright sun. Pinkie settles into her seat to catch her breath and calm her beating heart:

"That was incredible. But incredibly risky and stupid! We could have been killed!"

"Oh, don't be so dramatic. There was plenty of clearance."

Just then another gray marine layer engulfs the plane.

"I can't tell where we are, Pinkie. I think we're getting close to San Francisco.

But I'm afraid to drop down again. Who knows what we might run into."

"Let's just keep going north then and hope for a break."

Far below, San Francisco slips by. No sunset to enjoy. Just more grey mist.

"Over there, BB! The fog's drifting apart! I can see trees!"

"That won't help. Look for a place to land."

Pinkie squints through the dissipating mist:

"There's a dirt road. Near that clearing. It looks long enough to land on."

"Pray it is. We don't have any other options. We're running low on fuel. Hang on!"

BB turns the plane around and straightens it out for the approach. They narrowly clear the trees surrounding the improvised landing strip. The branches grate on the windows and sides of the plane setting their nerves on edge. Every muscle tenses as they try to see the ribbon of road. At the last possible moment BB pushes the wheel forward, and they angle sharply down. A quick pull back and they're on the ground. The wheels bounce along under the pontoons, rocking the fuselage from side to side. BB slams on the brakes. They jolt to a stop and share a huge sigh of relief. The rough landing wakes Hunnybird. He stretches and yawns unaware of the excitement he's slept through. Pinkie flashes BB a wide grin:

"That was really great!"

"No criticism?"

"Not this time. Good job, BB!"

CHAPTER FORTY-THREE

Redwood Renewal

BB guides the plane to a small clearing and parks it under the cover of the trees:

"We've got to be near the coast with all of these redwoods."

Hunnybird flies off to explore this new forest. A gray fox skitters across the road. The fog crawls in, closing down on them. Pinkie shivers:

"We need to find a place to sleep. Let's follow this road while there's still light. I hope we don't meet up with any snakes. Or bears."

Descending into the grove of majestic redwoods, they notice blackened and scarred trunks. Yet the massive trees have flourished in spite of fires. BB spots a trail marker:

"There's a sign by that tree! 'Colonel Armstrong Height 308 feet Diameter 14.6 feet Approximate age 1400 years' Wow! That's a really old tree!"

BB and Pinkie peer up to where the tree stretches through the mist to the canopy above. Unnoticed by either of them, a figure emerges from the shadows:

"Colonel Armstrong's daughter Lizzie made the first sign to mark this tree. She wanted to honor her father who'd just died."

BB and Pinkie whirl around to the husky, no-nonsense voice. A short, stocky, thick-necked ranger wearing khaki pants and a long-sleeved, sun-bleached canvas shirt marches up to them. Pinkie offers her sympathies:

"I'm so sorry to hear that. Was his death sudden?"

The ranger squints up at them from under a wide-brimmed hat and remarks dryly:

"I wouldn't know. He's been dead over sixty years."

When BB chuckles, the ranger tilts back the hat brim:

"What are you laughing at, young man? The Colonel was one of our most honored citizens around here!"

BB squeaks out an apology. Taking a good look at the ranger's face and close-cropped, salt and pepper hair, he realizes they have encountered a formidable woman.

"Where'd you two come from anyway? I saw you walking down the road from up above. Didn't know anyone was camping up there."

"Uh, we just dropped in for the night."

Pinkie whispers to him through a frozen smile:

"Watch what you say. We don't know who we're dealing with."

"Name's Carole."

She gives them a firm and decisive handshake. BB hazards a guess:

"Is this Muir Woods? It looks like the spot my folks took us to a few years ago."

"No. Armstrong wasn't as famous as John Muir, but he's just as important. He set aside these beautiful trees so you and your grandchildren could see what California was like before most of the old trees were cut down."

"So he saved them from the lumber barons?"

"Actually he was a lumberman himself. Owned most of the acres around here. It was the main industry for many years. People depended on it. My grandfather worked for him. He was one of the Colonel's foremen."

"Why didn't he cut *these* trees down?"

"They had just taken down a huge tower of a tree that had been scarred by fire. The Colonel picked up a piece of the blackened wood and showed it to my grandfather. A shadow of sorrow crossed Armstrong's face. He suddenly felt an overwhelming responsibility for ending the life of these great trees forever. That's when he decided to preserve some of them for future generations. Come on. I want to show you a special place."

They follow her to a clearing where rows of benches line up like pews in a church. Soaring redwoods create a ceiling worthy of a cathedral. The mystical fog threads its tendrils through the branches. Pinkie and BB sit to pause and reflect. The cool, moist evening air is the perfect climate for these giants of the earth. It's also the perfect respite for their weary souls. After several minutes of silence, Carole's voice breaks in:

"Time to go. Night comes early. Do you have your camp set up?"

Pinkie and BB sense they can trust this woman who is humble in appearance, but more importantly, humble in her nature.

"Actually Pinkie and I were hoping to find some lodging nearby. We have money."

He reaches for his wallet, but Carole puts up her hand to stop him:

"Nonsense! My cabin's not far from here. You can stay with me if you don't mind roughing it a bit. Follow me. Watch your step. Don't want you to trip in the dark."

Before long Carole opens the rough-hewn door to a rustic, one room log cabin. Inside are a couple of narrow beds, a table with two chairs, and a basic kitchen. She carries a big pot of stew to the table, sets out plates and forks, and invites them to sit down:

"At one time the whole west coast of Oregon and northern California was covered with redwoods. Not too many left now. Lizzie caused a ruckus with her campaign to create this state park. It worked! But I'm worried now."

BB swallows his last bite:

"What's there to worry about? Aren't the trees safe?"

"There's been some talk about letting a few loggers in the back areas where the public doesn't go. I know the lumber is valuable and people need jobs, but we can't let shortsighted people like that win! We need a better way to protect these old trees. Maybe a natural reserve. The legislature needs to act!"

Pinkie wipes her mouth and grins:

"Well, if the Armstrong clan isn't around to do it, then it's up to you!"

"Me?"

"Pinkie's right! You're the perfect one to speak for the grove! You can make a difference. You can be another Lizzie Armstrong!"

Carole is flattered by their confidence, but she knows the road ahead will be long and difficult if she decides to take on this battle.

"It's getting late. You two take the beds. I'll grab my sleeping bag and stretch out on the floor. And no arguments from either of you!"

Before long BB and Pinkie are deep in a dreamless sleep that spreads its restorative power through their bodies. Meanwhile Carole lies awake, formulating a plan. A smile spreads across her weathered face.

CHAPTER FORTY-FOUR

Trust or Doubt?

The distinctive whiff of bacon and eggs pulls BB and Pinkie up from their fog of sleep. They scramble to put the bed coverings back in order before sitting down to the hearty breakfast. Carole greets them with a surprise:

"Look at this friendly little guy I found pecking at my window this morning."

She steps aside to reveal Hunnybird, happily enjoying a bird-sized meal on her counter. BB and Pinkie act amazed. But when Carole turns her back, Pinkie wags her finger at the little fellow and smiles. Between mouthfuls they thank Carole for her wonderful hospitality. It's time to go, though they hate to leave this interlude of relative safety.

"By the way, you never answered me last night. How *did* you get here?"

By now they're quite sure they can trust Carole. They've been cared for by someone they never expected would help them. They did nothing to deserve this kindness. Yet they were blessed with hands that held them up. BB takes the plunge of faith:

"Actually, Carole, we're on a quest. We've been following Highway 101 and the coast to San Francisco, but the fog was so heavy yesterday we missed the city. When we spotted this opening in the fog layer, I took the chance and landed our plane on the road up there."

"The road? That was some lucky landing! Take me to it, and I'll see how we can get you out of here and on your way. Let me grab my backpack."

After a short hike, they spot the plane. Carole holds them back:

"You're about forty or fifty miles north of San Francisco. Keep the sun on your left and you can't miss it. Before you go, I've got something for you. While you were sleeping this morning, I put together a few sandwiches and some fruit. Just in case you were moving on."

She brings out a large paper sack and hands it to Pinkie. She then pulls out a small blanket that looks as old as the nearby trees:

"You don't seem to have much gear. This should help you out."

Finally she brings out a smooth, blackened piece of redwood and holds it out to BB:

"Before he died, the Colonel gave this to my grandfather. It's the wood he picked up those many years ago. Go ahead. Take it. The Colonel said it has the power to regenerate. I'm not sure what all that means, and I've never seen it. But somehow I feel you'll need it on your journey. So it's yours."

BB hesitates, not wanting to accept such a treasure, but Carole insists:

"And I'm going to talk with some of my friends in town. The ones I need to convince that this whole area is worth saving. They've got grandkids that come here all the time. The tourists really boost the economy too!"

Arriving at the plane they spot two huge black birds perched on the wings. BB and Pinkie look directly at each another, visibly alarmed. Carole calmly continues:

"You've got company keeping an eye on your plane. They'll be easy to get rid of."

With a nod of their shaggy heads the birds take flight.

"See? No problem. Just a couple of nosy ravens. Help me push this thing down the road. You'll need plenty of takeoff room if you're going to get up over these trees."

At the farthest point, they swing the aircraft around. Just out of Carole's view, BB drops some alabaster shards into the fuel tank. Hunnybird flutters into the cabin and out of sight. As BB and Pinkie jump on board, Carole calls out over the roar of the motor:

"Vayan con Dios!"

BB presses the accelerator to the floor. At the last possible moment he pulls back on the controls, and the light plane cuts through the morning fog. Pinkie fears the worst:

"How long before those spies tip them off to our location?"

"We should have at least a little time to figure out our next move."

To their left BB spots another plane bearing down on them:

"Or not!"

BB guns the motor and the chase is on. Hunnybird hides under Pinkie's seat, unsure of how to help. Pinkie shouts above the engine:

"Where are we going? Which direction are we heading?"

"Just let me think! Oh shoot! Look at the sun! We're going north! Check down there for some way we can escape."

The morning glare blinds Pinkie for a moment, but then she spots another grove:

"Look, BB! Cars are driving right through that tree!"

Suddenly the wheel takes on a life of its own. An unseen force sends the plane into a sharp dive toward the opening in the giant tree. Cars veer off the road. Pinkie screams:

"BB! What's happening? Do something before we crash into that tree!"

BB tries to wrestle the controls back, but then a voice calls out just to him. Words he's heard from his parents and recently from Sergeant Striker:

"You have to work *through* your problems, not escape from them."

And then the voice continues:

"We'll always be there to help you. Trust us. Have faith. Go *through* it!"

BB is resolute:

"Hang on! We've got this! Here we go!"

Pinkie can't believe this suicide mission. But BB calmly stays the course. She sees with her eyes, but BB goes with his heart. He guns the motor and flies into and through the tree! Intent on its prey, the pursuing plane explodes into pieces that mysteriously vaporize. BB and Pinkie burst through a fog screen into a vision of trees, lakes, and rivers. Sparkling waterfalls plunge hundreds of feet. Sheer cliffs and steep mountains hug the valley, one peak distinctly missing half its dome.

CHAPTER FORTY-FIVE

Gold Fever

Everywhere they look there are more spectacular vistas that BB instantly recognizes from a family camping trip. Hunnybird figures it's safe enough to pop back into BB's pocket for the view. The small plane snakes up the gorge and begins its climb to the summits bathed in a golden glow. Pinkie gushes with delight:

"Are these mountains made of gold?"

"Of course not! Gold isn't *that* easy to find. But that's a great idea! If we follow this mountain range, we should reach real gold country."

BB veers to the north along the rim. Pinkie soaks in the beauty below and then turns to speak to him. She draws back, startled at his appearance. The same golden glow they'd seen on the mountain peaks is radiating from his face. The wild and hungry look in his eyes makes her uneasy. His voice and words have a metallic, brittle tone:

"Check out the snow in these mountains. It's melting now, bringing gold down into the rivers. Just waiting for us to scoop it up!"

Pinkie nervously nods and returns to the wilderness scene below. She jumps at BB's shout:

"Sutter's Mill! By the river! Same as fourth grade when I was here!"

BB circles and drops down, skimming the water. He parks the plane in a clearing across from the mill and throws his shoes and jacket in the back. Hungry to get started, BB calls out:

"Come on, Pinkie! Here's an old rusty pan we can use. I'll show you how it's done."

Avoiding a possible cold dunking, Hunnybird escapes from the shirt pocket to watch BB rush headlong into the icy mountain stream. BB coaxes Pinkie into the river and gives her the shallow metal dish. Leaning over her shoulders he guides her hands and the pan down into the river bottom to scoop up rocks and dirt. Slowly he swirls the pan until the water washes away the dirt and debris. Pinkie can feel his breathing growing more and more frenzied. His heart pounds through his chest against her back.

"Look! A couple of flakes!"

Pinkie can't believe he's getting worked up over such a skimpy find. She smiles up at him all the same but recoils at his wild-eyed face with its strange gold glow. She wriggles out of his grasp and rushes away, shivering from the cold and his appearance:

"My feet are numb. I'll watch from the bank. Go ahead. I know you're enjoying this."

"Suit yourself."

Pinkie sits at the water's edge, Hunnybird perched on her shoulder. They both stare in growing concern as BB feverishly pans for the elusive treasure. Finding no luck, he finally stands up to stretch his stiff back and spots a scruffy old gentleman sitting on the opposite shore. The man raises his slouch hat in a friendly greeting. BB studies him for a moment and cautiously returns his wave.

"Hey, young feller! You've got quite the technique going for you. Couldn't do a better job myself. Any luck?"

BB shakes his head. The aged man's gravelly voice continues:

"No? Why don't you try over to your left a piece?"

BB has already worked that area, but he humors the man. He gives a healthy dip into the riverbed, bringing up a huge pan full of rocks and sediment. The miner's reassuring words catch the rhythm of BB's swirls:

"Work it slow now. That's it."

The water and dirt slide over the sides of the pan. BB focuses on the diminishing residue at the bottom. Through the muddy water the sunlight catches a brief reflection. Eagerly BB reaches toward the brilliance, his fingers closing around an irregular chunk twice the size of a golf ball. When he opens his fist, there in his palm is the biggest hunk of gold he's ever seen! Even bigger than the ones in the museums!

"Pinkie! Look! I did it! I struck gold!"

Hunnybird chirps wildly at the sight of this gleaming treasure. Pinkie jumps to her feet. They look over to the miner slapping his thigh with his hat. He whoops with glee:

"I knew you'd find it. Just needed the right touch."

BB can't believe his luck. He offers to give a sliver of the nugget to the old man. After all he's the one who guided him to the spot. But the miner refuses:

"Naw! You did all the work. Besides, you might be needing it. Put it in that backpack of yours for safekeeping. Don't go advertising where you found it either. We don't need another gold stampede!"

Pinkie has captured the excitement of the discovery. She's back in the river, greedy for more nuggets. But the old man waves her off:

"You won't find any more."

But Pinkie isn't about to give up. She brushes off Hunnybird's warning chirps as he flutters around her head. She scoops and swirls and scoops and swirls, her voice becoming more and more agitated:

"Just a little longer, BB! I just know there's more!"

The old miner just shakes his head:

"Trust me. There's no more to be found. You'd better get going before daylight's over. I'm sure your journey doesn't end here."

BB drags a reluctant, protesting Pinkie out of the river to the plane. They speed down the river, lift into the cloudless blue sky, and turn west back to the 101. On the horizon, an ominous darkness is building. Flashes of white draw closer and closer. Less than a minute later they're surrounded by an enormous flock of gulls swirling around the small plane and calling to them. Hunnybird is beside himself chirping frantically, finally diving deep into BB's pocket for safety.

"Turn around, BB! Don't chance it! You don't know what we'll hit! Hunnybird says they're trying to warn us! Turn! NOW!"

BB banks sharply to the right, the little plane responding with all the power its engine can muster. The flock of white and gray birds escorts them away from the dark danger pursuing them, pushing them farther and farther to the east. They climb the forest-covered foothills and cross the snow-clad peaks of the great Sierra Nevada mountain range. The blackness finally halts, its mission accomplished. The gulls peel off and head to their ocean home just as a cerulean gem bursts into view, the bluest lake either of them has ever seen. BB scans the skies for any further threats. With the mountain barrier shielding them from danger, all is peaceful. For now.

CHAPTER FORTY-SIX

Tahoe Terrors

As they circle the lake, BB leans out to peer into the depths of the water:

"I think we're at Lake Tahoe. It's really cold and super deep. There's rumors and spooky myths and legends about this place, but no one's been able to prove them."

Skirting the western shore, BB dips the plane down for a closer look. Pinkie is fascinated by what she's seeing in the clear waters below:

"Look at those dead trees way down there. I wonder what else is hiding at the bottom. What do you think? BB? BB!"

BB stares straight ahead, ignoring her completely. Mysterious singing only he can hear draws him to a cove. Pinkie tries to shake him, with no success. BB noses the plane downward, his hands locked onto the steering wheel. Pinkie spots jagged rocks just below the surface. They're certain to break up in a terrible crash. She grabs the second wheel, but BB's oblivious to the danger and continues their descent.

"BB! You're going to kill us both! Let go!"

Her screams drown out the music. BB relaxes his grip on the controls. In a flash she wrestles control of the plane. At the last second she pulls up and clears the evergreens that ring the bay. BB falls back in his seat, completely wrung out from the ordeal:

"What just happened? It's like you weren't here. There was this music. All I could think of was getting to that beautiful sound."

"I'm going to find a sheltered place for us to set down. We don't have enough fuel to get us out of here and back on track."

Pinkie stares at him, realizing just how close they'd come to death. Even Hunnybird gives him a wary look and takes a cautious perch on Pinkie's shoulder. Flying south she spots a bay with an island. She sets the little plane down on the water and nudges it against the island shore. Leaving their shoes behind, they slide down onto one of the pontoons. Pinkie tentatively dips a foot into the clear water and quickly draws it back:

"Whoa! You're not kidding! It's icy cold!"

BB opens Carole's bag of sandwiches. He passes one to Pinkie and breaks off a corner for Hunnybird. The pristine view calms their spirits. Munching a crisp apple, Pinkie leans back against a strut, her face turned to the warm June sun:

"This is just what I need. I'm going to sit here for a while and soak in this sun."

BB pulls out Mr. Wrigley's packet of gum and offers a piece to Pinkie. They quietly chew away, lost in thoughts of the past few days. BB looks over at Pinkie holding her knees and remembers this silhouette on a porch roof not long ago. Suddenly feeling playful, he tumbles her headfirst into the icy water where she disappears from view. Knowing what a good swimmer she is, BB waits for her to reappear. But as the splash clears, BB squints down far below to see her suspended, motionless body.

"Oh no! The water's too cold! Pinkie!"

BB dives straight down, expecting to find a lifeless floating figure. Instead, Pinkie is nonchalantly chewing her gum. She points to her mouth, encouraging BB to keep chewing. BB realizes he not only is generating warmth in his body, but also is able to breathe under water. Meanwhile Hunnybird hovers over the spot where the two disappeared. He grows more and more frantic as the time passes. Assuming the worst he keeps watch over their watery grave.

Far below, Pinkie and BB swim out to the main lake where they begin the search for what lies beneath. Unexpectedly they meet up with a host of little human-like creatures with smiling baby faces. Their long blonde hair streams behind like golden silk. They beckon BB and Pinkie to join them, spinning and tumbling around in a game of tag that takes them all far out to the deepest parts of the lake.

All at once the water babies' joyful squeals turn to alarm. In the dark recesses of the lake, BB and Pinkie spot a prehistoric creature that resembles a snake-like fish. Swimming straight toward them, its long, beaklike mouth opens to reveal rows and rows of sharp needle teeth. Clearly this monster has lunch on its mind. And they're on the menu! The screeching water babies grab BB and Pinkie's hands and propel them through the water, racing at top speed toward the safety of the cove. Holding tight to the little creatures, frantic at the thought of those razor filled jaws, they pass through the neck of the bay. The monster turns aside and undulates back to its deep-water lair. Safe on shore, BB and Pinkie scramble onto the sun-warmed rocks. The little creatures join them, stretching out to absorb the heat and spreading their long hair to dry.

"Pinkie, did we almost die? What was that thing anyway? And how does this all fit into the quest? We're so far away from the coast."

"I don't know. Nothing makes sense. Are we just supposed to relax and enjoy this beautiful lake?"

As if in answer, a piercing screech fills the air. High above a giant bird hovers, eyeing its prey. It swoops lower, its huge wings beating the air and bending the trees. Pinkie and BB look once again to the little creatures, hoping for another deliverance. But when the water babies turn, they transform into ghoulish, bloodthirsty hunters. Baby blue eyes mutate into reddish yellow orbs. Fangs emerge from hungry grins. Slowly they creep toward their victims.

"BB, I think it's time to go. Like NOW!"

BB and Pinkie plunge back into the water, frantically swimming to the island and the plane, their only hope. The water babies and the frightening bird close in on them.

Just then another war cry pierces the air. From the top of a tall pine a huge bald eagle takes flight from its sentry post. Extending its claws toward the water babies it skims the surface, daring them to continue their pursuit. They quickly retreat to the safety of the shore, cowering behind the rocks from the onslaught of the mighty champion. But the eagle isn't through. It aims its fury at the giant bird, timing its attack to zero in on the vulnerable throat of the vicious bird. Again and again the sharp beak rips feathers and flesh until the giant bird flies off, screeching its disappointment. Victorious, the great eagle returns to its perch, ready for another intervention if needed.

BB and Pinkie drag their weary bodies onto the island beach, their hearts still pounding. The water babies return to their sweet innocence. BB and Pinkie ignore their mewling cries from the shore and grab the last of the sunlight to dry their clothes. This recent brush with death tugs at BB's heart. He's not sure what his relationship with Pinkie is, but he senses their futures are inextricably linked.

"I'm really hungry, BB. Wish we hadn't been so greedy finishing off those sandwiches Carole sent along. The sun's setting and I can't keep chewing this gum forever to keep warm. We need to find some shelter."

"While you were landing earlier, I saw some stones at the top that looked like a little house."

"My clothes are almost dry. Let's check it out."

"First we need to be sure the plane is secure."

When they reach the plane, Hunnybird overwhelms Pinkie with chatters and flutters.

"Oh, Hunnybird! Of course you were worried. I'm so sorry! Everything's fine now. We're back together safe and sound."

They collect their gear and circle back to a path they'd spotted. They scramble around boulders and climb the remnants of a stone stairway to the top.

"There it is! The house I saw! Over there!"

In the light of the setting sun BB leads Pinkie over the rough, rocky ground to a small cabin. Unfortunately there's no roof.

"Let's hope there isn't any rain tonight."

"This is a great find, BB! We can scrunch down over in that corner next to the fireplace. There must be some matches in the emergency kit to light a fire."

BB and Pinkie scour the area for firewood and return with a small bundle of sticks and a few dead branches. Pinkie is discouraged by their meager find:

"This won't last even an hour. Your jacket and that small blanket aren't enough to cover us. And we can't stay up all night chewing gum to keep warm."

BB pulls out the piece of wood from Carole:

"Maybe this will help. Might as well give it a try."

"I don't think we should use the whole thing. Carole said it has the power to regenerate, whatever that means."

Together they stack the kindling and few branches in the fireplace and light the fire. Using a small pocketknife from the kit, BB shaves off a sliver of the blackened wood and tosses it into the small blaze. Immediately flames flare up filling the fireplace. Weary from the long day, BB and Pinkie hunker down against the stone wall nearby. He drapes his jacket over their shoulders and covers their hunched up knees with the blanket. Hunnybird snugs into BB's pocket, relieved he doesn't have to keep a look out. Soon the warmth of the flames closes off their drowsy conversation. Their eyelids grow heavy. Pinkie's head droops toward BB's shoulder where it finds a comfortable spot. Too tired to notice, BB mumbles agreeably as his cheek rests on her hair. The fire glows through the night as the stars above make their journey across the sky.

CHAPTER FORTY-SEVEN

Who Do You Trust?

In the shadows of the dim morning light BB and Pinkie carefully make their way back down the rocky path. They're eager to get going, especially after seeing the disappearing edge of the moon the night before. But when they reach the shore, the plane is gone! Through the morning mist they spot it drifting about 100 yards away.

"BB! What don't you understand about securing?"

"Don't look at me! I had my side tight."

"Well so did I!"

Hunnybird scolds them both for bickering. They realize that other hands might have loosened the mooring ties. BB is willing to let it go:

"There's no sense arguing about it. Help me look for a piece of driftwood to put the backpack and emergency kit on to keep dry."

Before long they locate a sizable log and toss their shoes and jacket on top of the backpack and kit. BB takes out two fresh pieces of the magical gum. They chew in earnest, waiting for the flow of warmth to saturate their bodies. As they wade into the frigid water, pushing the log ahead, the lake bottom suddenly gives way. Kicking furiously toward the plane, BB reminds Pinkie of their previous swim:

"Last time we were in the water we were swimming with those water babies."

"Sure hope they're far away from here."

At that moment something flowing and soft brushes against BB's legs. The sensation is so familiar that he lashes out with a strong kick and a wild cry. His gum flies out of his mouth and disappears into the depths of the cove. Immediately his body turns cold. He gasps at the shock. Terrified at the possible consequences, Pinkie shouts out:

"BB! Don't let go! Keep kicking!"

But his efforts are futile. The cold quickly overtakes his strength. Hunnybird hovers helplessly, frantically calling out. Pinkie keeps encouraging him:

"We're almost there! Just hang on!"

Back at Bond headquarters The Council looks helplessly at the scene in the hourglass. However, the light behind the wall grows stronger with each passing moment.

Despite the drag of BB's body, Pinkie strains to push the log the final few feet. At last she grabs the pontoon. She hauls her weary body out of the water and throws their belongings safely into the cockpit. Behind her, hypothermia is overtaking BB. As she turns to help him, his grip on the log opens and he slips farther into the water.

"BB! No!"

Grabbing his arms and pulling with all her might, her muscles scream with exhaustion. Finally he's clear of the water and stretched out on the pontoon. But he's not responding. Pinkie refuses to give up. She wraps her arms around him, holding him close to warm his body, desperately chewing her gum.

"Come on BB! Wake up! Don't leave me now!"

Pinkie's sobs fill the air. She looks to heaven and pleads:

"Please don't let him die!"

"What are you...?"

BB mumbles incoherently. The combination of her body temperature and the warming rays of the morning sun slowly revive him. He peers through half closed eyes at Pinkie's distressed face. He stiffens at her embrace and struggles to get loose:

"Whoa! What's going on? What are you doing?"

"What do you mean, 'What am I doing?'"

Hunnybird is completely confused by his reaction and gives out a small scornful chirp. Perturbed at BB's lack of appreciation for what she's done, Pinkie lets him drop onto the pontoon with a clunk.

"Hey! You don't have to be so rough!"

Pinkie doesn't want to reveal how much his brush with death affected her:

"I really didn't have much of a choice. What was I supposed to do? Let you die?"

BB chews the last piece of gum, rubbing away the numbness in his arms and legs. Unsure how to show his gratitude for her courage and concern, he changes the subject:

"We'd better fuel up. No telling when or where we'll have another chance to land somewhere safe."

Pinkie's thoughts trail off as she contemplates how close she came to continuing on alone. But she doesn't want to let on how much she's hurt by his attitude. She matter-of-factly turns to the next phase of their journey:

"We need to head west over the mountains to get back to the 101. When we see the coastline we can figure out our next move."

"And maybe there'll be a place where we can set down and find some food."

Clearing the mountains they face a sea of white and the coastal range beyond. An unseasonal Tule fog blankets the entire Central Valley. Pinkie searches for a break:

"BB! There's two gulls flying right below us! Slow down a little."

BB spots the silhouettes, the grey mist obscuring their color and details. As they escort the plane, BB is heartened by their presence:

"They were a great help back in LA. Getting rid of those ravens and finding Pink's."

Pinkie closes her eyes and savors the memory:

"That was the best hotdog I've ever eaten."

They begin to review the entire meal until BB can't stand it:

"Stop! This isn't helping. We've got to stop thinking about our stomachs."

"These birds can't be just a coincidence. Keep following them!"

The two shadows lead on, creating a subtle zigzag route that BB carefully matches. One of the pair drops lower into the white shroud. Once out of sight, it flies up through the fog layer and heads south to the coast to announce their arrival. Its fluttery wing extensions and black body glisten in the bright sunlight.

"It's taking forever to cross this valley. Maybe we shouldn't trust this bird after all."

"Don't worry, Pinkie. Once we clear these mountains, we're back on the coast."

As they begin their climb, the bird that Pinkie's been tracking peals off and disappears.

"So much for our guide. Looks like we're on our own again."

Just over the mountain range they soar above the marine layer lingering late into the day. Below them fog swirls up the mountainsides.

"BB! Turn around! There's a break back there. I think I saw a house. Or maybe it was a palace."

BB banks the plane in a tight circle, hoping to land and locate some food.

"There's even a landing strip, BB! Look over there! Oh my goodness! Where are we?"

"I know this place! I've seen pictures of it. It's Hearst Castle. That really rich guy built it."

"Hearst? The guy at the party told us about him. He gave you his card."

BB reaches to his back pocket and pulls out the crumpled business card, the name partially rubbed away. He shoves it back in his pocket. Their oasis of hopefulness rises out of the fog. Its siren call beckons.

CHAPTER FORTY-EIGHT

Back in the Lap of Luxury

The little aircraft sets down on the surprisingly smooth runway and rolls into a field. Pinkie takes out the small fabric square from the backpack:

"Help me cover the plane with the tarp."

"Why? It's safe enough here. Besides that thing isn't big enough to cover a whole plane!"

"Don't be so naïve! We don't know what we're facing. Give me a hand!"

Surprisingly the tarp unfolds again and again, expanding to a giant sheet that conceals the plane. Pinkie looks around for a marker. But BB's moved on. On the horizon two spires float above the mist. He wanders off in their direction as if in a dream. Hunnybird keeps close, swooping and diving in the cool ocean breeze. Pinkie shoves a large stick into the ground where the last of the plane's tail has disappeared and runs to catch up. As they climb down and up the gently sloping hills, they encounter a strange sight.

"BB! Is that a zebra? What's a zebra doing with a bunch of cattle and horses?"

"Beats me! Must be some ranch and safari combo. Come on! I want to see the castle."

The two of them trudge up the last hillside and weave their way through a lush garden. Pinkie hears distant voices and worries what will happen if they're discovered:

"Hunnybird, I'm not sure what we're getting into. We might get separated. Stay out of sight in the backpack while we look around. Just in case."

Hunnybird isn't thrilled about this idea, but he knows Pinkie's instincts are usually right. As he slips into the backpack, a loud, authoritative voice nearby startles them:

"George Hearst brought his family here to camp in the summer. Later he built a lovely Victorian home just beyond that grove of trees. It's sort of an 'elegant rustic' place. But when his son, William Randolph, inherited the property, he wanted a more elaborate venue to display his extensive art collection."

When the docent turns her head to lead the group forward, Pinkie urges BB to join in:

"Just pretend you belong. Act natural!"

The guide continues her narration as the visitors take in the incredible beauty of the grounds, the marble columns, and the valuable vases and paintings:

"When George died, his wife Phoebe worried her son would squander his father's fortune. She refused to turn over any of the wealth to him. Instead she used much of it to found universities, schools, and other worthwhile entities. But when she died in the 1918 flu epidemic, William Randolph was free to use the money any way he pleased. And it *pleased* him to collect iconic pieces of art and architecture and artifacts. But he needed a place to display them to impress his friends and the public. And so began the never-quite-finished castle project! It was about this time that his longtime associate, Janus Wintergreen, became his close confidant."

The name jolts BB to attention:

"That's it! Of course! No wonder we're here. It's all part of the plan. I'm sure of it!"

He looks to Pinkie, but she's mesmerized by a painting and missed the name reference.

"After that there was no controlling him. He accumulated compulsively and indiscriminately. His frenzied purchases accelerated over the years: Medieval armor, tapestries, sculptures, paintings, furniture. He kept his faithful architect, Julia Morgan, frantically producing one magnificent structure after another. Now, look up! This is a European church ceiling dismantled piece by piece and reconfigured to fit this huge room. His art collection fills this place, his five other homes, plus several warehouses. His life was an endless quest for the most beautiful and grandiose."

By this time, the docent is beginning to lose her audience's attention so she brings them back with a tantalizing suggestion of scandal:

"He also collected people. The *most* beautiful, the *most* influential, the *most* famous. and also whoever captured his eye."

She gives the group a suggestive wink, which is quickly picked up by one of the women:

"I heard that he kept a mistress here in one of the bungalows."

"Oh yes! He was quite open about it. She was his hostess for gatherings of famous movie stars, sports figures, and even presidents. Once his wife Millicent found out what was going on, she refused to come to the castle.

But now that he's dead, she often entertains guests here."

The tourist is hoping for some juicy insider gossip:

"What were those women like? Millicent and..."

"His mistress? The movie star Marion Davies? Actually they were more like his mother, generously donating to many worthwhile projects. Quite different from the man whose only interest was accumulating wealth."

As the docent continues her endless storehouse of Hearst minutiae, BB and Pinkie drop back. BB pulls Pinkie behind a large piece of overstuffed furniture:

"Let's get out of here before someone realizes we haven't paid! Remember what she said about the other house. It's got to be back near where we landed. Come on!"

Careful to avoid another tour group, they retrace their path through the gardens and back to the grassy area. BB lets Hunnybird out of his cramped quarters. They hurry toward a grove of trees where they discover a lovely white Victorian-style home with an expansive porch. They fail to notice two ravens taking flight and disappearing into the branches of the surrounding foliage. BB is ready to knock on the front screen door, but Pinkie holds him back:

"We've got to think this through. There could be a back door close to a kitchen. Maybe we'll find something to snack on while we plan our next move."

Circling around to the left, they discover the entrance to a typical farmhouse kitchen, not at all like the castle they just left. BB opens the refrigerator:

"Wow! Fried chicken, apples, milk! It's like they were expecting us!"

Suddenly leery of this turn of events, Pinkie slowly repeats his words:

"Yeah... Like they were expecting us."

"Come on. I was just kidding. Don't be so suspicious of everything."

BB pulls out the plate of chicken and grabs a couple of apples. Pinkie finds glasses in the cupboard and pours the milk. She offers a few tidbits to Hunnybird. As they finish their last bites and lean back in their chairs, a voice bellows:

"What are you kids doing here?"

Hunnybird quickly drops to the floor and peers around a chair leg. Pinkie and BB jump to their feet and turn to face their accuser. Despite his more casual outfit, they immediately recognize his white, combed-back hair and round, black-framed glasses.

"Mr. Janus! I mean Mr. Wintergreen! When I heard your name on the tour

I hoped we'd meet up. Sorry about the food, but we haven't eaten since yesterday."

Although he's been fully aware of their presence on the castle grounds, Janus pretends to be surprised at their appearance in his kitchen.

"Of course! It's BB, isn't it? And your friend, Pinkie? So glad you decided to join us! I mean join *me!* We, that is, *I* was hoping you'd find the time to stop by."

Pinkie studies Janus, not sure she's ready to accept this chummy attitude. But BB is visibly relieved and eager to secure this valuable connection:

"I still have your card!"

From the back pocket of his pants BB pulls out the bent and mangled business card. Now, in the presence of Wintergreen, it gives off a strange prickly chill. But BB is too engrossed in their conversation to notice. Janus continues with his familiarity, feigning ignorance:

"How did you kids get here anyway?"

BB starts to fill Janus in on their amazing journey, but Pinkie quickly breaks in:

"We just dropped in. Nice place you've got here!"

Janus interjects one more topic to keep them off balance:

"So where's the other girl? Your friend?"

Their faces droop remembering Jodie's traumatic end. Pinkie offers an evasive answer:

"Oh, she couldn't make it."

Janus draws them in with his smarmy smile:

"No problem. While you're here you can help yourself to anything. You can have your choice of any of the bedrooms upstairs."

He pauses with a sly wink:

"There are adjoining rooms too."

BB blushes at this suggestion of intimacy, but Pinkie coolly puts the matter to rest:

"Separate rooms would be best, thank you."

"No matter. I'll show you where you can freshen up and leave your belongings."

Janus tries to be nonchalant with this last comment, but he can't keep from zeroing in on the backpack sitting on one of the kitchen chairs. When Janus turns to exit the room, Pinkie opens the zipper wide enough to sneak Hunnybird in. She hands it to BB who slings it over his shoulder. They smile agreeably at Janus' next suggestion:

"Why don't you take a short rest before dinner and our tour of the castle? Once the tourists and park employees leave, we'll have the place to ourselves."

BB and Pinkie climb the richly carpeted steps, their fingers lightly skimming the wide, polished wooden banister. Pinkie reminds BB to keep the backpack always in sight and hide it under his pillow when he sleeps. Hunnybird's muffled chirp warns him to be careful where he lays his head. After long, leisurely showers they wrap themselves in plush white robes and lie down for the renewing rest their bodies have been craving.

CHAPTER FORTY-NINE

La Cuesta Encantada

"Leave me alone. Just a few more minutes. I was just getting to the good part."

BB groans and rolls over, wrapping his body in a cocoon of blankets and sheets. Pinkie, dressed and eager to get moving, has no patience for his sluggish complaints:

"Come on! We've been promised a tour I don't want to miss. Wake up!"

She lets Hunnybird out of the backpack so he can stretch his wings. Impatiently he chirps loudly in BB's ear. BB wills himself awake with a promise to join Pinkie downstairs. Hunnybird snugs into the backpack once more. Descending the stairway, BB overhears Janus' voice, puffed up with pride:

"Hearst was nothing 'til he met me. He had the newspaper and this property. But he needed someone to bring out his best qualities and potential. He was just going to settle for this old frame house. But I set his sights on something much grander."

When BB enters the front room, Janus gives him a hearty welcome:

"Glad you could join us, BB. I was just filling in your friend here on how much I admired my good pal Hearst."

Janus has been working his charm with his stories of fame. Pinkie gives BB an encouraging nod:

"Did you know famous people have stayed in this house as guests, just like us?"

Janus chimes in:

"The ones from Hollywood were more exciting than some of those stuffy political people. I told Hearst he had to mix it up a bit. You know. Add some color!"

BB and Pinkie are growing more comfortable in their own importance. This obviously well-connected man is putting them on equal footing with these celebrities. And then Janus eyes the backpack slung over BB's shoulder:

"There's no need to lug that old thing around. Put it in this closet for safekeeping."

"That's okay. It's not that heavy."

"Well, then... follow me!"

He dangles a huge ring of keys, assuring them there will be no locked doors to block their path. Janus keeps up a steady commentary as they wind through the gardens and past the private bungalows. He tosses in his opinions of previous guests plus stories of people falling in and out of favor with Mr. Hearst. When they arrive at the main dining room a sumptuous feast is already laid out. The elegant European décor resembles an English manor house. The night air is calm, yet mysteriously the banners hanging above them ripple ever so slightly.

"Guests always knew how they rated with Hearst by their seating at dinner. Those who dared cross him were relegated to the ends while those in close favor sat across from or next to him here in the middle. That's of course where we'll be sitting since *you* are my special guests."

With an ingratiating smile Janus gestures to the overwhelming variety of succulent meats and tasty dishes. And then he offers a special treat:

"Even during Prohibition, Hearst kept a magnificent collection of the finest wines money could buy. Several bottles are still locked away in cellar vaults. Here's one from a particularly good year."

Pinkie is quick to refuse:

"None for me. But thank you!"

When BB leans forward to grab his glass, Pinkie kicks him under the table, a reminder they need to keep a clear head. He smiles at Wintergreen and shakes his head.

Throughout the lavish dinner, Janus answers their inquiries and offers more tidbits of insider information:

"Hearst wanted a unique name for his property. I suggested 'La Cuesta Encantada'— 'The Enchanted Hill.' It perfectly captured his dream."

BB breaks in, his mouth half full:

"It's not really enchanted, is it?"

"Only rumors from visitors who swear they've spotted figures lurking around the pool or peeking from empty rooms. I wouldn't put much stock in that."

Pinkie offers a more plausible explanation:

"Maybe it's just some neighbor kids trying to be funny."

Janus dismisses this suggestion with a snort:

"There *are* no neighbors. We have 250,000 acres and fourteen miles of shoreline halfway between Los Angeles and San Francisco. Visitors can *hardly* arrive unnoticed either by plane or car. Hearst liked it that way. He wanted control."

"But there are certainly lots of visitors now."

"Uninvited guests, actually. Hearst would be aghast at the riff raff that tramps through his personal palace these days. But he'd be happy to know he's forever immortal because of this castle, just like I said he would. His name is forever linked with art, beauty, and wealth!"

"The lady on the tour we were... uh... following..."

Pinkie gives BB another kick under the table.

"Uh, she mentioned famous visitors: Winston Churchill and Charles Lindbergh."

"Ah, yes! They were *very* impressed by his remarkable achievement... the castle. Anyone who was *anybody* wanted to see it. He only invited those deemed most interesting and valuable to him. Of course they all became *my* friends too. Like you."

Janus rises from the table and neatly places his napkin next to his wine glass. Pinkie quickly grabs a partially eaten roll from her plate and sneaks it into the backpack for Hunnybird. They join Janus as he resumes their tour:

"There are over 100 rooms just in this building, the 'Casa Grande.' Hearst needed a place to display his treasures so his friends could admire them and, of course, admire *him* as well! Many would normally be found in museums."

"Didn't we see some of his things at the house? Wasn't there a big vase?"

"Good eye, Pinkie! You mean that *priceless* 2,000-year-old Grecian urn in the entrance hall? That was Hearst's pride and joy. He worried some careless guest might damage it, so he kept it there. Of course he often mentioned it in his conversations to be sure people knew just how brilliant a collector he was."

As the trio winds its way through the many elaborate rooms, BB lingers behind, absorbing the opulence. Passing the Billiard Room, he glances in and stops. The billiard balls are moving on their own, quietly clicking as they hit each other and bank off the sides into the pockets. Invisible players with their cues are engaged in an actual game. BB calls to Janus and Pinkie to hurry back. But when they look in again, there's just a rack of balls in the center of the pool table.

"Wait! There was a game going on just now. I swear it!"

Pinkie gives him a concerned look, but Janus just laughs it off:

"It's probably just the 'ghosts' people are convinced haunt this place. Supposedly former guests who fell out of favor with Hearst and didn't want to leave."

BB shivers at the thought. Pinkie is really concerned:

"Pull yourself together, BB!"

"But I really *did* see something. Someone's messing with me."

"Just forget it and try to enjoy this lovely evening."

BB resumes his admiration for the castle and their good fortune. He whispers to Pinkie:

"This guy's great! I can't believe we met him at that party and that he remembered us. What a life! Money to buy and do anything you want."

"I know. It's hard to imagine being this wealthy."

"Maybe he'll let us hang out for a few days. I'm tired of roughing it."

Pinkie too is drawn again to the life of the rich and famous. But a nagging thought pricks her conscience. Janus breaks into their chat:

"And now for the centerpiece of his creation: The Neptune Pool!"

Outside is a panoramic vista of mountains, the ocean, and the main house. It's as if they've stepped into a temple of ancient Rome.

"Hearst had this thing built and torn down three times before he was satisfied. He must have been paying Julia a bundle to put up with all of his demands."

Pinkie pulls BB off to the side:

"Just pretend we're enjoying the view. Maybe it's only the fog coming in, but I think I saw a woman in a wispy white gown behind that pillar over there."

"I *told* you something freaky's going on. But *no*! You thought I was imagining things."

Their eyes catch a gossamer skirt floating in the gentle breeze… or is it a trail of mist?

CHAPTER FIFTY

In the Grip of the Abyss

"So what do you think? Like to spend a few days here in the lap of luxury soaking in the sun and cooling off in the pool?"

BB is more than ready to accept Wintergreen's offer. But the press of time ebbing away tightens its grip on Pinkie. She stares at the moon's reflection in the still water, a large section obscured by the earth's shadow. Hundreds of miles away on BB's shelf, almost half of the sand has slipped to the bottom of the hourglass.

Back at Headquarters, The Council grows alarmed at this passage of time in their own hourglass.

Lady Grace: "Think, Pinkie! This is the same trap you were entangled in the last time I saw you."

Agent Allen: "I thought that encounter at Tahoe was enough to scare them into realizing the dangers from the Abyss. Can't they see through this guy?"

Striker: "I'd like to give that Janus what he deserves and wipe that smirk off his face!"

Director: "You know what to do, Pinkie. Listen to The Bond."

"That's a great offer, Mr. Wintergreen, but we really need to move on."

He comes closer to lean into Pinkie, touching her arm intimately:

"Please call me Janus, my dear."

His fawning smile and husky delivery of this desire for closeness stiffens Pinkie's resolve to put distance between them:

"Whatever you say... *Janus.* But right now BB and I need to get some shuteye. It's been a long day. A *wonderful* day, of course! But tomorrow comes early. Right BB?"

She gives BB a pointed look, hoping he'll pick up on the urgency to get going.

"Uh, right. You're absolutely right, Pinkie! Sorry Janus. Got to get our beauty sleep."

BB laughs lightly at his own poor attempt at sophistication. Janus realizes he's not going to win and guides them with a gallant sweep of his arm to the path back to the house. They follow him at a discreet distance. BB whispers his protests to Pinkie:

"I still don't know why we can't take Janus up on his offer. This is the life! No worries. Comfort at our fingertips."

"Are you crazy? Snap out of it! Didn't you see the moon? It's disappearing inch by inch. We don't have much time left!"

Back at the house, Janus closes and locks the door behind them.

"We don't have issues with intruders, but one can never be too careful."

He notes their quick exchange of concerned looks.

"I'm kidding! You don't have to worry about security around here. If anyone gets past the perimeter, I'm handy enough to stop them."

He opens the hall closet and retrieves an ancient looking firearm.

"This beauty is a 6.5 Mannlicher Austrian military rifle. Hearst loved this old family keepsake. Sometimes he'd loan it to his hunting guests."

Janus brings the rifle to his shoulder and aims his sight down the barrel right at Pinkie. She scrambles backwards onto a nearby chair, pulling her legs up to peer over her knees. Janus chuckles condescendingly at her alarm:

"Don't worry, little lady! The safety's on."

He lowers the gun and points it to the floorboards. But Pinkie is slow to recover. The memory of looking down the black hole of the gun barrel has unnerved her. They thank him for the evening and head up the stairs, drained from their day's adventures. Eager to finally have some uninterrupted sleep, BB hastily drops the backpack onto a nearby chair and flops facedown on his bed. He buries his head into the soft, goose down pillow. Before the lapse of even a minute, his gentle snores drift into the quiet night.

As darkness wraps itself around the old house, someone lurks outside BB's room. The knob turns. The door silently swings open. Janus is thrilled to see the backpack carelessly tossed aside. He was hoping BB would be less vigilant under the weight of exhaustion. Tiptoeing over the old boards, he reaches for his prize. But the shift of his weight triggers a loud creak. BB lifts his head and sees a dim figure. A dream? A ghost? And then fully awake, he realizes it's Janus:

"Hey! What's going on? What are you doing in my room?"

"No problem. You can go back to sleep. I thought one of the old farm cats slipped inside and found its way to your room. Didn't want it to bother your rest. Doesn't seem to be here, though. Sorry to wake you."

Janus puts a finger to his lips to quiet any further protests from BB. He silently retraces his steps to the door and closes it behind him. BB glances over to where he'd discovered Janus. The backpack! He jumps from the bed and zips it open, carefully feeling for their precious collection. He accidentally pokes Hunnybird, who is miffed at being disturbed from his sleep. He slides the backpack under his pillow and cradles both in his arms.

It isn't long before the early morning sun slants through the narrow curtain opening. BB wakes with a start to a determined knock on his door and Pinkie's insistent voice:

"Let's go sleepyhead! Time to get out of here. Let's move it!"

BB slips on his shoes and gathers up the backpack. He yanks open the door just as Pinkie is ready with another rap:

"Janus was in my room last night with some story about looking for a cat. But I think what he was *really* looking for was the backpack. Don't worry! He didn't have a chance to open it or even pick it up."

"Thank goodness!"

"Just watch him carefully and don't trust anything he says."

"Oh, sure! *Now* you're worried. Didn't believe me last night, did you?"

"Never mind. We don't have time to argue. Just be careful."

Janus invites them to a quick breakfast of biscuits, cheese and fruit. BB slips some morsels to Hunnybird in the backpack on the floor between his feet. Janus is eager to restore their favorable relationship, especially after his encounter in BB's room the night before. He joins them at the table, his chair blocking the backdoor exit. Maintaining a friendly, casual manner, he munches on an apple:

"So what's today's plan? Hang out at the pool? There's some great hiking trails. The rangers and tourists won't be arriving for at least another couple of hours."

Pinkie is equally nonchalant:

"Actually we're planning to take off soon. We're meeting friends north of here."

"Friends? How far north? San Francisco?"

It's BB's turn to be evasive:

"I'm not sure. We're just following the coast."

Pinkie and BB get up from the table and make their move down the front hallway. Janus rushes to cut in front and turns to face them. The mask of friendship disappears:

"Enough games! I know you've got some valuable things in that backpack, and I'm not going to let you leave with it. It's going to be mine, one way or another."

BB protectively hugs the backpack to his chest. He and Pinkie plant their feet, ready to make a stand. Janus isn't backing down:

"Look you two. I could easily take you out. *Both* of you! But I have my orders. Anyway, I don't want to get my hands dirty, so I'll let someone else handle it."

Janus reaches over to the house phone on the hallway credenza and lifts the receiver:

"Yes, operator. Get me the San Simeon sheriff. Yes, it's an emergency. Officer, this is Janus Wintergreen at the Hearst Castle. Actually I'm at the house out back right now. I want to report two armed and dangerous criminals who have just robbed the castle of some very valuable objects. They have them in a backpack and are still somewhere on the grounds. Yes, I'm perfectly safe. But I hope you can be here soon. Now? Perfect! I've just spotted them, a male and a female, sneaking away from the castle. If I catch up with them, I'll wait for you to arrest them."

He returns the receiver to its cradle and smugly regards the dumbfounded pair:

"So... Shall we just wait calmly for them here? Or do you want to choose a more foolish option?"

BB is ready to embrace any plausible plan, however desperate it might be. He spots an item in a nearby alcove. Calmly he hands Pinkie the backpack and springs into action. He grabs the priceless Grecian urn that Wintergreen had raved about the night before and holds it high above his head. With a sly grin he lasers a look at Janus:

"Oh, let's be foolish! I think I might just *accidentally* drop this beauty. What do you think, Janus? Want to play catch?"

Janus is visibly shaken. He's responsible for protecting everything in the house, but especially this extremely valuable vase. BB exploits Wintergreen's moment of terror:

"Take the backpack and run, Pinkie! Run!"

He waits for her to get a good head start and then launches the vase high into the air. Janus is so relieved to save the precious artifact that he stands for several moments, cradling his prize, swaying back and forth, thankful he's avoided a costly tragedy. But then his eyes snap open to catch sight of BB quickly disappearing over the meadow and up a hill. A bank of fog folds over him and curls toward the house.

"Pinkie! Where are you?"

"Over here! Keep walking toward my voice. The fog isn't as thick here. In fact it seems to be circling the area right where we left the plane."

BB follows her voice, finally breaking through the white wall.

"Hurry up, BB! It's got to be here somewhere."

"I can't see those tiny waves against all this grass. We'll just have to wander around until we bump into it."

"No we won't. I shoved a big stick into the ground right next to the plane."

BB scans the area:

"Over there! Is that it?"

They race to the stick that Pinkie confirms is her marker:

"The tail of the plane should be close. Here it is!"

Just then they hear Janus leading the search party:

"Those kids have to be around here. What's with this crazy fog? Circle around to the other side and start climbing. We'll tighten the noose and have those two thieves in our grasp!"

BB doesn't wait to hear more:

"Quick! Slide under the cover!"

They work their way to the front and climb into the cockpit. BB hesitates:

"How can I start it up with the cover still on?"

As if on cue, a breeze lifts the tarp just enough to clear the propeller. Over the roar of the engine they hear Janus' angry shouts:

"Those kids couldn't have slipped through our dragnet. Listen! A plane engine!"

Back on the runway, BB accelerates for takeoff. Amazingly the tarp clings to the plane until they're clear. They lean out to watch the cover float away in the blue sky. Far below Janus fires his ancient gun, but they're out of range. The tarp, their salvation from so many dangers, disappears into a burst of feathers that floats over the hilltop and transforms into a thick cloud covering the castle and the entire "Cuesta Encantada." No longer able to see the plane, Wintergreen dismisses the search party with an offhand comment that really explains nothing. He's furious those two gave him the slip. He stomps back to the house where he hears the insistent ring of the phone. He acknowledges the angry, accusing shouts on the other end of the line:

"All right. I hear you. But the vase! That lovely ancient vase! Okay! I know! I was frustrated. Don't worry. They were too far off to hit them with that old rifle. Well it's not my problem now. They should arrive shortly in San Francisco. Good luck to the rest of the force! I'm through with this!"

His tone changes to one of self pity:

"I have enough to do here. Feeding the public with stories of fame and fortune. Keeping their eyes on things they can only dream of. That's *my* forte."

Avoiding any more demands, he slams down the receiver:

"I was never good with kids anyway."

The fog parts before the little plane, creating a path along the coast. The Abyss wastes no time regrouping. They gather their strength and numbers for what could be the final showdown.

CHAPTER FIFTY-ONE

The City by the Bay

"Is this fog ever going to lift?"

BB is weary of following the narrow channel through the misty clouds. He hates missing the beautiful views of Big Sur. Pinkie too is on edge, not sure what lies ahead. Freed once again from the backpack, Hunnybird peers ahead from BB's pocket. Suddenly they burst through a thick cloud into the bright sky. BB drops lower to get a better view of the rocky outcrops along the rugged coastline. As they clear the end of the land, Pinkie cries out with delight:

"It's the Golden Gate Bridge! San Francisco! Finally!"

She points to the pale white moon in the late morning sky:

"It's the last quarter. The hourglass must be getting close too. We have just enough time to finish what we started and get you back home."

At the word "home" thoughts of his family tug at his heart. To break his melancholy mood, BB banks to the right and flies straight at the bridge. Hunnybird senses danger and dives deep into BB's pocket.

"BB! What are you doing? No more tricks!"

BB ignores her pleas and dips the nose lower. Hunnybird can't resist a peek. Checking for any large ships, BB skims the choppy waves and neatly slides under the bridge span. The tourists gathered at the observation point wave and clap their delight at his daring move. The plane glides to the water. Hunnybird bobs his head and chatters his approval. Dismissing his needless risk taking, Pinkie focuses on their next move:

"Beach this thing, BB. These rolling waves are making me woozy."

During their final approach they failed to notice a searching beam coming from the Alcatraz lighthouse. As they step foot on the sand, it catches them full force.

"Let's get out of here, BB! The Abyss is onto us already! We need to find someplace where they can't spot us."

BB grabs his jacket, the emergency kit, and the backpack and gives their little plane a wistful last look. They race along Mason Street toward a tan and brown domed building. Hoping to find shelter from the prying beam, they discover a lovely lagoon and a palatial open-air structure.

Hunnybird dips to the shoreline for a quick sip, avoiding the ducks who motor lazily around the perimeter. BB is following a few steps behind Pinkie when he encounters a city employee tacking up a public notice:

Be advised! This property is scheduled for
demolition beginning January 1964.
Any persons with business connected with this
site are urged to contact City Hall.

"Pinkie! Over here! Check this out! They're tearing this place down!"

The worker urges them to relax:

"Take it easy. No need to get excited. Look at those crumbling cornices. This place is going to fall in on itself before long."

"But what are they putting up in its place?"

"Thanks to Mrs. Hearst's influence and another donation of a couple of million dollars, the city's going to restore it to its original glory."

Pinkie breathes a sigh of relief:

"I'm so glad. This place seems so romantic."

"You should be here after the sun goes down. There's lots of young couples like you strolling around the lagoon, especially when there's a full moon."

His mention of the moon reminds them it's time to move on.

"Pinkie and I were hoping to get something to eat. Maybe at Fisherman's Wharf?"

"Sure. But you can't just follow the shore. Fort Mason's in the way."

His directions include various turns onto unfamiliar streets. BB and Pinkie nod agreeably though they are thoroughly confused. Hunnybird chirps confidently, certain he can find the way. Eager to move on, Pinkie thanks the gentleman:

"We really appreciate this. Any suggestions for food?"

"You bet! Look for the Alioto's sign. They should be opening up about now for lunch. If you see Nunzio, tell him Fred sent you."

With Hunnybird flying from one lamp post to another, they take a slightly inland route using the buildings between them and the water to avoid the searchlight. With a last turn onto Beach Street, they're in the heart of Fisherman's Wharf. BB and Pinkie realize they're more vulnerable nearer the water. They duck into a nearby fish market.

CHAPTER FIFTY-TWO

A Legend of Generosity

"I hope you have enough money in that wallet, BB. I couldn't eat much at breakfast with Janus staring at us. I'm starved!"

They move closer to the stalls where the workers are cracking fresh crabs.

"Won't find any fresher than right here at Alioto's!"

A kind looking, middle-aged man warms them with his smile. His eyes sparkle behind large black frame glasses. His work apron covers a white shirt and tie, hardly the uniform of someone who cleans crabs. Pinkie returns his smile:

"Hello! We were hoping to get some lunch. Any chance we can get a sandwich?"

The gentle-spoken man finishes his last crab, washes his hands and removes his apron:

"I think I can fix you up with something. Just a minute."

He goes into the restaurant and returns with a loaf of bread:

"My friend Steve has the best sourdough around here. That's his picture on the bag."

He takes out four big slices and lays them out on waxed paper. Grabbing two hefty portions of crab, he creates two sandwiches and hands them to BB and Pinkie:

"See what you think."

They struggle to handle the huge sandwiches but finally manage a bite. Pinkie closes her eyes to savor the flavors. BB bursts out his approval:

"Wow! That's fantastic! But I forgot to ask. What do we owe you?"

"Forget it! They're on the house. Courtesy to our first customers of the day."

BB and Pinkie finish their scrumptious sandwiches, dropping bits of bread to Hunnybird. They call out a thank you to the kind gentleman who disappears into the restaurant. One of the workers waves them off:

"He doesn't want your thanks. Nunzio's really quiet about his generosity, all his gifts to the community. Kids around here get to go to summer camps because of him."

Another worker chimes in:

"Don't let that tie fool you. He's here every morning before the sun's up, lighting crab pots for the fishermen. Then he helps us crack all these crabs before greeting customers in his restaurant."

This catches BB by surprise:

"*His* restaurant?"

"Sure. That's Mr. Alioto himself. Best boss around!"

Just then a bright light scans the waterfront between the piers. BB and Pinkie jump behind a stall as the puzzled workers gaze out to the harbor:

"What's with the searchlight? Can't be a prison escape. That place closed down in March. Must be some prank. Probably some college kids."

But Pinkie and BB know it's searching for them. They sneak away, keeping close to the buildings that block the view to Alcatraz. Hunnybird hurries to catch up as BB and Pinkie turn toward the hills to get farther from the bay and the searchlight. And then Pinkie spots a white cylinder rising into the sky.

CHAPTER FIFTY-THREE

Discovery and Escape

"What's that, BB?"

"Coit Tower. I was there before. With my family. Come on! There's a great view if you take the elevator to the top."

The way up the hill seems easy enough until they keep hitting dead ends. Hunnybird makes a reconnaissance flight and circles back to find them. A few twists and turns and they're on a street that wraps around the hill to the tower. Leaving Hunnybird outside in a nearby tree, they climb the steps to the entrance.

Inside, the main floor is packed with a large group of middle schoolers. Their teacher stands guard at the elevator, giving small groups time to ascend to the top and return.

"BB, we don't have time for this. It's going to take forever. Let's just forget it."

"I can show you a different way to the top."

They turn to the voice and discover a woman with a smile that crinkles her eyes. She puts a finger to her mouth for them to keep quiet and beckons them to follow. When BB and Pinkie hesitate, she holds up a key.

"Come on. It's okay. You're with me."

They slide behind ropes and poles guarding a set of brass double doors. Her key opens to a narrow flight of stairs that spirals upward along the outer wall of the tower. As they climb the stairway their steps mirror the people in the murals ascending and descending the steep hills of the city. The woman stops to look at two little girls with green hair bows.

"There they are. My two little cuties. I gave them matching outfits and dolls. The bows were my idea too!"

"*You* painted them?"

"Yup. Back during the Depression when work was hard to get, especially for artists. That's why I have a key. So I can revisit these murals whenever I want."

Round and round the stairwell winds up the tall monument. Finally a door opens to a spectacular 360-degree view of San Francisco and the bay. BB is overjoyed:

"Wow! This is great! I never thought we'd be at the very top."

"BB! Look at the crooked street on the hill over there."

Their guide joins them at the arched opening:

"That's Lombard Street. You should see the beautiful flowers all along that stretch."

But BB is concentrating on the view back to the bay. A light flashes from the lighthouse.

"Uh... Pinkie... Are we okay up here?"

The beam of light hits him full frontal. Pinkie drags him back through the arch and against the inside of the wall. Adding to their alarm, the elevator door opens on the floor below them. It could be just more students. On the other hand, they might be trapped! The woman peers at them curiously:

"Are you two all right?"

"Actually Pinkie just remembered we're supposed to meet someone. And we're late! Thanks for the great tour. Gotta go!"

In a panic they bolt down the stairs. Clearing the last step, they burst through the doors and knock over ropes and poles. They squeeze past the startled students waiting for the elevator, dash through the exit door, and run headlong down the steps. Hunnybird hurries to catch up as they race through the trees and down Lombard Street where tall buildings once again shield them from the bay.

Pinkie urges BB to wait so they can catch their breath:

"What's our plan? We can't just keep running up and down these hills. It's exhausting!"

"I don't know! Here we are finally in San Francisco, but now what are we supposed to do? We've collected everything we need. Why are we here?"

"I've always had clear instructions before, BB, but this is different. The moon is disappearing fast. We don't have much time to figure this out!"

"We're out of sight of The Abyss for now. We just need to find a place to sit down and decide what to do next. Maybe The Bond will send us more help."

Hunnybird chirps for them to keep moving. He flies ahead and disappears around a corner.

"Wait a minute! This is Powell Street. I remember now! It's one of the trolley lines. Come on!"

"But there aren't any tracks."

"It links up with another line a few blocks from here. I'm sure of it."

It's not long before they both feel the strain of the long blocks and the steep climbs. Pinkie's had enough:

"So where *is* this trolley? We're at the top of another hill, and I don't see anything."

"I can't understand it. We haven't even heard the trolley bells. They're supposed to be all over this area."

"What now?"

"Okay, okay. Let me think."

Hunnybird chirps around their heads. He flies ahead, encouraging them down the hill.

"Well, it looks like the little fellow is more confident than we are. He must know something."

"I'll feel better when we get some help, BB. I don't trust The Abyss."

"Have you seen any sign of their agents? No. Nothing except the searchlight. Nothing but wonderful people since we got here. I'm ready to just let The Bond take charge."

"I know. But The Abyss is clever and sneaky. This isn't over yet."

Hunnybird flies ahead and circles back to urge the weary pair to keep going. A few blocks later, a huge park beautifully designed with flowers, trees, and manicured lawns greets them. In the center on top of a tall granite shaft a bronze figure gleams in the sun.

"It's Union Square! Come on, Pinkie. Let's get some popcorn and relax. No more hills to climb!"

CHAPTER FIFTY-FOUR

High Class Rescue

While others lounge about on the grass, they choose a park bench. Munching on their snack, they lean back to enjoy the bright afternoon sun. What they didn't expect was a flock of unwelcome visitors. Pigeons! Eager to snatch a kernel or two, the pesky birds descend on the helpless pair, crowding their feet, landing on their shoulders and heads, and pecking at their hands and necks. Hunnybird, powerless against this onslaught, flies to a safe palm tree. Pinkie desperately flails her arms:

"Stop it! Shoo! BB! What are we going to do?"

"Don't look at me! I've got enough birds to deal with!"

"Be gone, you persistent, pesky beggars!"

A commanding voice addresses the flock. A tall young man rapidly opens and closes his black umbrella as he wades into the sea of birds. In a moment's time he's cleared the area. BB stands up to thank him:

"That was amazing! You sure know how to work that thing."

The young man deftly secures his umbrella, which becomes a walking stick. He casually leans forward on the curved handle:

"Not at all. I'm glad I arrived in time to rescue the two of you. You're obviously new to San Francisco. If you feed those annoying birds, they'll overwhelm you in a flash."

Pinkie is impressed by the fine manners and sophisticated ways of their deliverer. She takes the hand he offers and stands to join them.

"Let me get rid of the rest of that popcorn."

The young man deposits their bags in the nearest trash bin. Pinkie smiles up at him:

"I'm not really hungry anyway after that experience."

"I hope you're okay. No scratches or bites?"

BB assures him they're fine:

"Just a little overwhelmed. That's all. Good thing you had *that* with you."

The young man swings his umbrella in a circle by the handle and flips it into the air. He artfully catches it and slides it under his arm:

"I always keep my umbrella with me. You never know when it might rain. Plus the sharp point is a great help in emergencies. You two look like you could use a break. Let's pop into the St. Francis for a bit where you can collect yourselves and get away from this riff raff."

He indicates the birds and people lounging on the grass. Hunnybird is insulted. He pouts on a palm branch watching them dodge traffic on their way to the imposing hotel.

"By the way, I'm Aeron."

"I'm Pinkie. And this is my good friend BB."

The doorman tips his hat as they enter the elegant lobby. Aeron leads them to the front desk where a stately gentleman greets them:

"Good afternoon, Master Abaddon. I see you've brought some friends with you. Shall I phone your mother to let her know you've arrived? She went up to your apartment just an hour ago after her lunch with the other ladies in the Mural Room."

"Don't bother. I'll check in with her later."

The desk clerk eyes BB's backpack:

"Young man, may I keep that for you behind the desk? I'll be sure to watch it carefully."

Immediately BB is on his guard:

"Thanks, but I like to keep it handy."

The clerk hands Aeron a note:

"I'm so sorry. I almost forgot to give you this."

Aeron glances at the distinctive handwriting:

"It's from my sister, Zilla. She says she'll meet me at the clock."

Aeron points to a huge grandfather clock nearby that's twice his height.

"Everyone who's *anyone* knows this is the place to meet up. That clock's been here since just after the big earthquake."

He calls back to the desk clerk:

“Isn’t that right Stanley?”

“Absolutely, Master Abaddon. One of my duties is to wind it each Sunday morning. I’ve become quite attached to it over the years. I remember...”

“Right. I’m sure you do.”

Aeron cuts him off abruptly and turns back to his two friends:

“She should be coming any minute now... There she is! Zilla! Over here!"

CHAPTER FIFTY-FIVE

California China

Zilla breezes in and takes Aeron's arm, completely ignoring BB and Pinkie:

"Be a dear, won't you, and pay the taxi for me. I left my car in the parking garage across the street last night and couldn't reach Mother's driver to come get me. I hate dealing with cab drivers and money. It's so... well, you know... *common!*"

BB is immediately entranced by this vision of loveliness. Her smartly belted, high-profile black slacks accentuate her tiny waist. The upturned starched collar of her sleeveless blouse frames her perfect, heart-shaped face. BB is lost in the pools of her deep black-brown eyes.

Next to this stylish young woman with her perfectly manicured nails, Pinky feels awkward in her slightly rumpled clothes. But Zilla doesn't seem to notice. When Aeron returns she puts her hand on Pinkie's arm, immediately connecting with her in a familiar way:

"I hope Aeron hasn't bored you with tales of this old hotel. He can be so annoying!"

She gives Aeron a teasing poke and then smiles at Pinkie:

"This place is so stuffy. Let's take a walk and look for some excitement."

Now Pinkie's the one who's wary:

"We really have to get going. It's been nice meeting you both."

BB doesn't want to be rude, especially after Aeron's rescue. He offers a suggestion:

"This is Pinkie's first time in the city. Maybe we could ride the cable cars for a while."

Zilla gives him a puzzled look:

"Cable cars? What cable cars? What's he talking about, Aeron?"

"They got rid of those old things back in the 40s. The city didn't want to keep them up, and the private lines went out of business too. Buses are much more modern and convenient. The cable car building is going to be demolished so they can sell the machinery for scrap."

BB's in shock. No cable cars in San Francisco? He can't believe what he's hearing. But Zilla is eager to get going:

"Besides, we're going just a few blocks down the street to Chinatown."

"Great idea, Zilla! You kids been there yet? No? Let's go!"

BB is still thinking about the loss of his beloved cable cars as he slings the backpack onto his shoulder and follows the others out the front entrance. Pinkie is outnumbered but still cautious:

"They seem nice enough. The Bond has been generous lately with its help. Let's give it a little more time and see if this gets us to our final goal."

Hunnybird wants to voice his concerns to Pinkie, but he doesn't have an opportunity to get her alone. As they cross Union Square, Zilla raises an objection:

"I don't like the tunnel. Let's take Grant Avenue instead."

BB snaps out of his depressed mood as they enter mysterious Chinatown where signs turn into artistic confusion. Zilla's right at home admiring a rack of beautiful silk dresses with traditional Mandarin collars. Pinkie picks up a fan that opens to an ancient Chinese garden scene. They pass shops with baskets of unfamiliar vegetables. Savory cooked ducks hang by their necks in a window. Hunnybird flits from stall to stall enjoying the aroma of new foods and exotic spices. Aeron is curious about their plans:

"So where are you staying while you're in San Francisco?"

They admit they don't have accommodations for the night yet.

"Then stay with us! We'll have a grand time."

Pinkie hesitates to accept their offer, but then reluctantly accedes, thinking the St. Francis should be safe enough:

"I suppose it's okay. But are you sure there's enough room at the hotel? We wouldn't want to be a burden to your mother."

Aeron laughs at the thought as Zilla explains:

"We weren't thinking of the hotel. It's luxurious, but that place cramps my style."

"Zilla and I prefer entertaining at Mother's country place. It's only an hour's drive from here, just south of the city."

Immediately BB and Pinkie are ready to reject this plan that only heightens their vigilance. BB casually puts them off:

"What we really meant to say was we hadn't *checked into* our hotel yet. But we'll think about your offer."

Zilla is perfectly happy to change the subject:

"Aeron, let's go over to Waverly Place. I want them to see the beautiful balconies."

Cantonese tones fill the late afternoon with a musical lilt. Wives call to husbands and mothers shout to their children. No need to translate. It's time for dinner. Figuring they're safe in these public surroundings, Pinkie lets down her guard. She breathes in deeply as the sights, sounds, and aromas mingle together and saturate her senses:

"I really *do* feel like I'm in Hong Kong. Or what I imagine it must be like."

BB, however, is focused on satisfying his hunger pangs:

"With all of these restaurants, how do you decide where to eat?"

Aeron picks up on this hint:

"That's easy. We just passed the place."

Zilla moans:

"Oh Aeron! Not there!"

"Why not? Great food. Cheap too! Come on, Zilla. Be a good sport."

Zilla gives him an unenthusiastic okay. They arrive at a narrow building with a sign overhead: Sam Wo Restaurant. Hunnybird is sure he won't be welcome here. He hunkers down on a nearby window ledge hoping for a handout later from Pinkie and BB. That is, if they remember their little friend. Aeron opens the door and sends the others ahead up a narrow flight of stairs to the second floor. At the top, BB bumps into an imposing waiter sporting a crew cut. The man turns to their group with a scowling face. BB blurts out a quick apology, but the response he gets stuns him into silence.

"Sit down and shut up!"

CHAPTER FIFTY-SIX

Rudeness on the Menu

"Come on, Fung. These are my friends. Give us a good table."

"Ah... Mr. Abaddon! I didn't know you *had* any friends."

"Real funny, Fung. Yeah... Funny Fung! That's got a ring to it!"

Aeron obviously knows this impertinent waiter very well. They continue their banter, which takes an even ruder path:

"So these are your friends? Now *these* gals I heartily approve of."

He leans into Zilla and Pinkie with a leering eye. They visibly recoil from his advances. To ease her urge to retch, Pinkie focuses on his furry eyebrows that look like black caterpillars doing pushups. He turns to sneer at BB:

"But what's with the scrawny kid? Doesn't your mama ever feed you?"

BB doesn't know how to respond, and Fung doesn't wait for him either:

"I thought I told you to sit down. THERE!"

He points to a corner table. As they take their seats, he slams the menus down and struts off. BB slips the backpack to the floor between his feet. Another diner waves Fung over requesting a fork.

"Read the sign, you moron. NO FORKS!"

The diner jumps back in fright and stammers:

"Then could I get a cup of coffee?"

"Check the sign: 'NO COFFEE, MILK, OR SOFT DRINKS" Only tea! Got it?"

BB and Pinkie peer over their menus at the mayhem Fung creates in his wake. Returning from the kitchen he spills soup on a customer without so much as an apology. Another table complains he got their order completely wrong. But Fung justifies his "mistake on purpose":

"You made some stupid choices, so I changed things up a bit. You wouldn't like the other anyways. Shut up and eat your dinner!"

Aeron thinks this is all hilarious. Zilla pretends not to notice. Fung returns to their table and shouts his demand:

"So what's your decision?"

BB is thoroughly confused by the listings in Chinese:

"Do you suppose I could get a menu in English?"

"English? What kind of restaurant does this look like to you? Speak up!"

"Chinese?"

Fung applauds BB's timid answer. His comments drip with sarcasm:

"Very good! Aeron, you've got a real genius for a friend here. So if I go to an American food joint can I ask for a *Chinese* menu? Think about it!"

There are no menu pictures, so BB and Pinkie ask Aeron to order for them. On his way to the kitchen, Fung confronts a couple who are just leaving:

"Hey, Cheapskate! What's with the measly tip? Next time I'll let you wash the dishes! Get outa here!"

He grabs a half eaten plate of noodles and pork from another table:

"Come back here! I wasn't finished with that!"

Fung ignores the protests and disappears through the kitchen door, plate in hand. By now Pinkie isn't hiding her loathing of this boorish man, especially when she hears him insulting the other patrons:

"He's got to be the rudest waiter I've ever seen."

But BB thinks the whole thing is hilarious:

"Oh, come on, Pinkie! Lighten up won't you?"

Zilla rolls her eyes in disgust. Aeron laughs and explains:

"You can't take old Edsel Fung seriously. He's the entertainment around here. People come just to see what new insults he's dreamed up. It's all part of the fun!"

BB is now eager to join in. When Fung returns with their food, he's ready:

"So Fung-the-funny-man. My friend Aeron says you're in charge of writing all the fortune cookie sayings."

Aeron gives BB a startled look and quickly shakes his head to stop him. Fung leans in, just inches from Aeron's face:

"Oh he did, did he?"

Aeron braces himself for a verbal lashing. But Fung just laughs:

"Chinese fortune cookies! Ha! They're as much Chinese as you are."

He jabs his forefinger into Aeron's chest and turns to leave. Aeron compliments BB on his quick wit:

"Nice one, BB. But you had me worried. I wasn't sure how old Fung would take it. He *hates* it when people ask for fortune cookies."

BB immediately apologizes, but Aeron doesn't seem to mind at all:

"Don't give it another thought. But I owe you one!"

The four of them dive into their meals. BB and Pinkie manage to get most of their food to their mouths with their chopsticks. Fung comes back for one more round of insults and hazing. BB laughs along to gain Aeron's approval. The two of them bond over this preposterous experience. That old need to belong that BB felt in high school comes flooding back. Pinkie is appalled at BB's behavior and would just as soon ditch him for a couple of hours. Zilla's had enough of this scene too:

"Aeron, take care of the bill. And don't forget to give a generous tip. I don't want to hear any more out of that awful man tonight. We'll meet you downstairs out front."

Back on the sidewalk, Zilla drills into her brother:

"I don't know why you have to egg that guy on every time we come here. Actually I don't know why I even agree to come to this place."

Pinkie angrily addresses BB with her scorn:

"You embarrassed yourself joining in with that crude behavior. I don't even want to be seen with you!"

BB's had enough of Pinkie's lecturing. They exchange glares and stalk off in opposite directions with their new friends. All of The Bond's admonitions to stick together are a dim memory. They ignore the alarms going off in their heads. All thoughts of the quest give way to their anger and personal hurts. Neither hears Hunnybird's warning chirps. Suddenly BB's foot slips sideways in a small circle of sand. Aeron quickly jumps in to distract him:

"We'll catch up with them later. Don't worry. Zilla knows the way to Mother's place. Looks like you're stuck with me for now."

Arm in arm with Zilla, Pinkie briefly looks back over her shoulder. But BB seems to have completely dismissed her from his thoughts. Hunnybird doesn't have instructions who to follow if there's a split up. He heaves a sigh and chooses Pinkie.

Striker: "This can't be happening! Can't they see these two aren't to be trusted?"

Agent Allen: "Isn't there some way to get through to them? Hunnybird's doing his best, but this split is dangerous!"

Lady Grace: "Pinkie's so angry at BB she's letting her emotions color her actions again. Aeron is obviously up to no good. Zilla is more subtle, but she's manipulative. Who knows what Pinkie will agree to?"

Director: "It looks like this is going downhill fast. I wish we knew what the endgame was. But we can't lose hope. The quest isn't over yet. Remember The Bond has a way of working things out, even when it looks like all is lost. I just hope they keep an eye on the moon!"

They look to the alabaster wall for assurance. The glow increases in anticipation of the strength BB and Pinkie will need in the coming hours.

CHAPTER FIFTY-SEVEN

Under the Spell

"Come on Pinkie. Don't give those two another thought."

"I know. But I'm still mad at BB for acting so rude and ugly. It's like he lost all his manners."

"When guys get together, they just feed off each other and the worst comes out. They'll catch up with us later. Or meet us at Mother's estate."

On the way back to Union Square they pass window displays of double-sided embroidered pictures. Red paper globes and silk brocade ornaments hang from the doorways tickling Hunnybird as he flies under their fringes.

Just ahead, the sidewalk is blocked by a group of older gentlemen engrossed in a serious game of tiles. A crowd spills into the street, craning their necks as one man is obviously close to victory. The tension grows.

Suddenly a large ball bounces into the middle of the table and scatters the tiles and onlookers. Pinkie and Zilla are pushed in opposite directions as the men leap up to confront the culprit. A small girl hurries to retrieve her ball, but quickly draws back from their scolding. She hides behind Pinkie and grabs hold of her legs. Inching toward the door of a teashop, she uses Pinkie as a shield from the angry shouts. At last she grabs Pinkie's hand and pulls her into the shop. Behind the counter a lovely Chinese woman smiles and shakes her head:

"What have you done now, Shasha, to make your grandfather so upset?"

"It wasn't my fault, Mama! The ball got away from me and bounced into their game. It was possessed by a spirit! I'm sure of it!"

The mother laughs and looks hopelessly at an elderly woman seated nearby. She explains to the old woman in an unfamiliar language. The child protests:

"It's true, Grandmother!"

The two women shake their heads and smile. Shasha pulls Pinkie forward:

"This is my new friend. She rescued me!"

Pinkie assures the mother that there was no such dramatic intervention. But Shasha insists they reward Pinkie, and her mother quickly agrees:

"Don't worry about her grandfather. He never stays angry for long with his favorite granddaughter. Can I offer you something to eat?"

"My friends and I were just at Sam Wo's restaurant, so I'm really not that hungry."

The mother's face falls at the mention of this place:

"I suppose Fung was causing his usual chaos. He's the most insulting man I know. He gives all of us Chinese a bad name. I wish he would just leave the community. Or better yet, leave the city completely! He thinks he's so funny. But I don't think so."

"I totally agree! He was a nightmare!"

Immediately Pinkie is drawn to this woman. Perhaps she's been sent by The Bond? Or maybe this is part of the quest. Suddenly Pinkie panics knowing she's separated from BB and the backpack.

"You should have some real Chinese hospitality after that experience. Have a little dim sum and tea. Here are two sweet ones to take that bad taste out of your mouth."

The little girl nods encouragement. Just then Zilla enters the shop:

"I was looking all over for you."

Zilla sniffs disdainfully at the surroundings, which are clearly not up to her standards:

"If I'd known you wanted tea and dim sum, I could have found you a better class place than this."

Embarrassed, Pinkie makes a gesture of apology to Shasha and the women. Zilla grabs Pinkie's hand and pulls her through the door. Back on the street. Zilla brushes off Pinkie's suggestion that they look for the boys. She locks arms with Pinkie to be sure they don't get separated again:

"I just remembered I have to get to the City of Paris before they close."

"First Hong Kong and now Paris?"

"It's a department store, silly! We passed it before, just off the square."

Before long they're standing in front of a massive building with an imposing entrance. When they enter the huge rotunda, Pinkie stares up several stories to a spectacular gold and white stained glass skylight that fills the entire ceiling. Once more Hunnybird is in a quandary. Since he can't follow Pinkie indoors, he circles back to find BB. As he flies away, Zilla calls out to Pinkie:

"Hurry up! They'll be closing soon. I need these outfits for the weekend."

While she waits for Zilla to pay for her alterations, Pinkie admires the rich fabrics of the dresses and suits in the women's department. Zilla leads her to a counter filled with sample fragrances. While Pinkie is examining the imported labels, Zilla sneaks a crystal atomizer bottle from her purse and sets it on the counter.

"Pinkie, try this one. You'll love it! It's my favorite. I save it for special occasions."

Zilla lifts the bottle to Pinkie's face and quickly squeezes the purple bulb. A light mist bathes Pinkie's cheeks and neck. Inhaling deeply, she suddenly sways. Zilla grabs hold of her elbow to steady her:

"Pinkie! Are you okay? We should leave. You seem a little unsteady."

"You're right. It's been a long day. I'm feeling a bit tired all of a sudden."

"Can you walk to my car? It's across the street in the underground garage."

"Sure. I mean, okay... I think..."

When they reach the car, Pinkie gratefully sinks into the passenger seat, rests her head back on the soft leather, and closes her eyes.

CHAPTER FIFTY-EIGHT

Smoke Screen

Meanwhile Aeron and BB are off in the opposite direction passing families enjoying the warm evening. After a few blocks Aeron pulls BB into a side alley with a distinctive wavy pavement:

"This is old San Francisco. Jackson Square. The earthquake destroyed Chinatown and most of this place. But these buildings were spared. Check out the cool hitching posts. There weren't any cars. Just horses."

"And cable cars too?"

"Yeah, those old things too. Good riddance!"

They circle around and pause at the corner. Aeron drops his voice in hushed suspense:

"We're now in the heart of what was once the most decadent place in San Francisco. Maybe on the whole West Coast!"

He waves his arms around and announces dramatically:

"Welcome to the Barbary Coast! Anything you want... that you *shouldn't* have."

He gives BB a sly wink as he spins his story:

"Gold miners and sailors could find any pleasure they desired here. The police gave this place a wide berth, so it was every man for himself."

BB doesn't share Aeron's enthusiasm. Plus he's at a loss picturing this world his friend is so enamored with:

"That's great, Aeron."

"Okay. I get it. No imagination. But I can take care of that."

From his jacket pocket he produces a most unusual combination of glasses and goggles.

"Here! Try these on for size."

When BB puts them on, the street suddenly changes into a scene from the early 1900s. It's the Barbary Coast in all of its notorious glory!

"Whoa! What's going on?"

He quickly pulls off the strange eyeware and stares at Aeron, not believing what he's just seen. Aeron chuckles and nods:

"Quite a sight, huh? Go ahead. Put them back on and we'll take a walk."

BB flips the strange spectacles up and down, changing eras from 1963 to what appears to be around the turn of the twentieth century. Aeron urges him to keep them on:

"So what do you see? Look up at the balconies!"

BB sees scantily clad women leaning out. He actually hears them calling:

"Come on up, Honey. We'll show you a good time!"

BB is spellbound by this jaw-dropping step back into history. Saloons line both sides of the street. Drunken sailors ejected through the swinging doors brush his arm. He can smell the sour beer odor wafting from the bar. Aeron encourages him to keep the glasses on, vicariously enjoying BB's experience. BB willingly suspends his grasp on reality and gives in to the moment. What's there to lose? After all, he'll never be in this place again. Aeron shouts in BB's ear:

"I'll bet you've never seen anything like this before. Just think. All of the fun with none of the consequences. When life gets a little dull, I come down here, don my glasses and throw caution to the wind for a good time."

Fiddle, banjo, and piano music erupt from the next open door. It's like he's stepped into a movie, except it's all so real. He has his doubts, though:

"But don't they notice my glasses? And my clothes?"

"That's the beauty of it. You look just like one of them. No glasses either. Come on. Let's try your luck. Ever play poker?"

BB admits he's played with his high school buddies, but never for big money. Aeron is glad he's not a novice:

"Perfect! Here take this. It should get you into a game real quick."

Aeron removes his ring and hands it to BB. Since he first shook Aeron's hand, BB's been admiring the black onyx stone circled with diamonds. He pushes through the saloon doors and spots a card game in the back. He's making a beeline for the table when someone grabs his arm:

"What's your hurry, sweet darlin'?"

He turns to the husky, honey-coated voice and then steps back. It's obvious this dance hall madam was hoping her heavy makeup would conceal the pock marks in her sallow skin. Black eyeliner rims her vacant, yellow tinged eyes. She smiles seductively revealing gaps between decayed teeth and wraps her feathered boa around his neck to pull him in for a kiss. BB pushes away from her fetid breath and points to the back of the room:

"I'd like to get into that game over there."

With a broken fingernail she traces the inside of his ear:

"Well that will take a pretty rich stake. What d'ya have in mind?"

Her eyes light up when he shows her Aeron's ring:

"I think I can arrange something."

They thread their way through the tables to the corner. It's a rough looking bunch except for the gentleman holding court, his back to the wall. BB admires his brocade vest, trim black waistcoat, and ascot tie secured with a pearl stickpin. He studies BB from under the brim of a black hat. BB's lady friend introduces him to the gamblers:

"Boys, here's someone who'd like to share his wealth with you."

She laughs at BB's alarmed look. The man in the hat motions to an empty chair:

"Take a seat, young fella. Let's see what you're made of."

As BB sits down, the woman casually drapes her arms around him from behind and slips a card into his shirt pocket. The poker game begins. When he checks his cards, he can't believe his luck. He asks for one card and places his bet. With a full house, aces over kings, he'll get Aeron's ring back for sure! BB holds his breath as one by one the others reveal their hands. BB triumphantly lays down his cards and rakes in his winnings. The man across the table slams his hand down on BB's fingers:

"Hold on there. Nobody's that lucky right off the bat. You cheated!"

In his sudden fear, BB's voice rises a full octave:

"No sir! I swear! I just got dealt the right cards."

The man reaches out with his free hand to pull the card from BB's pocket. An ace!

"How many of *these* you got hidden? I know a cheater when I see one!"

"But... but..."

BB knocks over his chair as he backs away. The gambler rises and leans in:

"You know what we do with low life cheaters around here?"

The man draws his gun and points it at BB's head. Expecting certain death, BB covers his face and grasps the mysterious glasses. There's a puff of smoke and an expanding black spot, the bullet whizzing toward him as he rips off the glasses. Once more he's safe on the sidewalk of 1963, obviously shaken:

"I think that's enough Barbary Coast for me."

Just then Hunnybird arrives but keeps out of sight in the opening of a downspout. Aeron pries the magical eyewear from BB's trembling hands and tucks them away. He pulls out a couple of cigars, lights them both, and hands one to BB:

"Go on, just puff on it. It won't hurt you if you don't inhale."

BB takes a small drag on the cigar and coughs on the acrid smoke. A few puffs later he's getting the hang of it. Aeron blows smoke rings like an expert. One ring floats over to the drainpipe where Hunnybird is quickly overcome by the fumes and falls sleep. Another perfect circle splits and slides right up BB's nostrils. Suddenly he's not so steady on his feet. Aeron steers him down the street, holding him close with his hand firmly grasping BB's arm.

"Aeron? Where are we? Did all that just happen?"

"You're okay, BB. Just keep walking. You could use some fresh air."

"Yeah, fresh air. You're right."

Back at Union Square, Aeron leads a still groggy BB into the underground lot. He shoves BB into a convertible, hops over the door into his seat, and revs up the engine. Two rows over he spots Zilla in her car ready to take off. Pinkie is beside her, out cold. A nod and thumbs up, they celebrate their mission accomplished. Zilla leads the way to Highway 101. Aeron checks his passenger who, in spite of his stupor, is clutching his backpack as if his life depended on it. Leaving the city they follow the shoreline down the peninsula where the glow from the setting sun shimmers on the bay. A short hour later their headlights flash on a welcome sign:

San Jose
Elevation 82 Feet
Population 204,196

On the city's outskirts, the two cars approach a sprawling, castle-like mansion. Towers and pinnacles rise like sentries into the night. Windowpane eyes peer from gables and turrets. A gate is open, their arrival expected. The sweeping driveway curves to where a tall young man stands at an open side door urging them to hurry. It's Van Detta!

CHAPTER FIFTY-NINE

Smoke and Mirrors

"It's about time you got here. Hurry! Get those two in the house. Thank goodness everyone's gone for the day. It wasn't easy avoiding the staff. Every time I thought I'd discovered a hiding place, I'd open a door and hit a wall... literally!"

Aeron and Zilla half guide, half drag BB and Pinkie over the threshold and drop them in a dark, wood-paneled room. Van Detta waves Aeron and Zilla back out the door and lets it close. The lock's solid click signals there is no reentry. Van Detta looks at Aeron:

"So you've got the backpack, right?"

"Er... um... actually no."

"What? You've been with him all afternoon and no backpack?"

"I got you the kid, didn't I? Besides, he keeps it so close it's like part of his body."

Zilla joins in to defend Aeron:

"After all, *you* didn't notice the backpack when we threw them into the house. We've done our job delivering those two."

Van Detta is furious. He isn't ready to let it go:

"This is going on your record. The Abyss won't be giving you Elite Agent status after this blunder. But we've still won. That backpack won't do them any good in there. By the time The Abyss finishes with them, they'll be begging to hand it over and join us. Pinkie had better wise up or she'll be in endless limbo. And BB won't ever see his family again. He's obviously The Bond's golden boy. If we turn *him*, we have it all!"

Zilla hops in her car, and Aeron reluctantly offers Van Detta a lift. Inside the mansion the effects of the cigar and perfume are wearing off. BB mumbles a series of questions as he staggers to his feet in the dark:

"Where am I? Aeron? Are you here?"

"BB? It's me. Pinkie."

BB shuffles toward her voice. Relieved, the two of them hug each other. Suddenly a security light outside a window flashes on and bathes their surroundings.

"BB, how did we get here? Is this really their mother's house?"

"It sure doesn't look like the place they were describing. Aeron said it was a luxurious estate. Where is he anyway?"

"How should I know? The last thing I remember is getting into Zilla's car. I was pretty out of it. I can't believe I was *that* tired."

"Yeah. I didn't feel so good after puffing on one of Aeron's cigars."

"Cigars! What were you two doing after we left the restaurant?"

"Oh, nothing much. I'll tell you later."

"What's wrong with *now*? I was really mad at the way you acted back there. You were so rude! I couldn't wait to get away from you."

"Never mind. Let's get out of here and decide what to do next."

BB tries the nearest door, but it won't budge. The knob keeps turning uselessly in his hand. Pinkie opens another door... into a wall. They climb a stairway, hoping for an exit. However, the steps abruptly end at the ceiling! Back down the stairs, they see the glow of an old oil lantern on a nearby credenza. Pinkie's quavering voice unnerves BB:

"I don't remember seeing that."

He shoves down his fear, bravely strides to the lantern, and grasps its wire handle:

"Come on. Let's hope there's enough oil to keep this burning for awhile."

BB leads the way down a hallway that twists and turns in a never-ending maze. Pinkie grabs his arm:

"I smell chicken soup. Someone's cooking."

They follow the aroma into a kitchen. Hot steam rises from an invisible pot on the old, cast-iron stove. BB sees an even more disarming sight:

"Pinkie, is there someone down that hall... in the fog?"

She watches the misty figure dissolve. A cold draft slithers down the back of their necks. Footsteps echo from the floor above. Hand in hand they tiptoe to the next room and turn to see their reflection in a mirror. A Native American warrior in full headdress stands behind them. Screaming wildly, they wheel around, expecting to confront him. No one is there. This last fright propels them aimlessly up and down endless stairs, through doorways that lead to more and more rooms. After trying doors that refuse to open, they finally discover an open window that looks promising. They step through onto the top of a long stairway. But when they get to the bottom another flight leads right back to where they started. They slide to the floor against the hallway wall to catch their breath and contemplate their next move.

"This is ridiculous, BB. We're getting nowhere."

"I'm sorry. We wouldn't be in this mess if we'd stayed together back in San Francisco. I shouldn't have acted that way."

"It's okay. We both let ourselves get distracted. Besides, I'm the one who left you. It's my fault too."

In the quiet of their thoughts, a scraping noise comes from the other side of a door they hadn't noticed before. The knob turns on its own. The door swings open. Their lantern reveals yet another stairway, this one leading to the basement.

CHAPTER SIXTY

Escape to Nowhere

Bravely they venture below where they encounter yet another labyrinth of cave-like rooms and hallways. Everywhere debris and thick dust bear witness to years of neglect and abandonment. They follow the scraping sound to the far corner of the basement. A workman in white coveralls is pushing a wheelbarrow. He stoops to pick up a shovel. The grating sound resumes as he scoops up rubble from the basement floor and dumps it in the wheelbarrow. Pinkie whispers to BB:

"If he works here, he must know where the exits are."

"Excuse me, sir. We seem to be lost. Can you help us please?"

The man jumps at the sound of BB's voice:

"Who's there? Come out of the shadow where I can see you!"

The two intruders slowly emerge, holding the lantern so he can see their faces. His stern tone softens when he realizes they pose no threat. An amiable smile beneath his mustache and the twinkle in his eyes put them immediately at ease:

"How did you two youngsters get in here? Or did you stay after the last tour? I don't get to chat with most visitors."

Pinkie offers a vague explanation:

"Actually we got separated from our friends and lost our way. Maybe you can show us how to get out of this place?"

"Looking for a little excitement late at night, eh? Every so often curious folks try to figure out the secrets of this house. Well, I know every inch of it, all one hundred and sixty rooms. It's time for my break. Let's go upstairs where it's not so dusty."

He leads the way back up the steps:

"There's lots of numbers around here. Oh, not actual numbers. But count the panes in the windows and the panels in the rooms. Go ahead, young lady!"

"Thirteen"

"Exactly! There's the number seven too. And eleven and four. Her favorite numbers."

BB wonders if he's talking about Aeron and Zilla's mother:

"Her? Who's *her*?"

"Mrs. Sarah Winchester of course. She was my boss and the architect of this amazing house. She kept us busy, always working. Sometimes during the night too. Never satisfied. Never finished. But we didn't mind. She was a generous woman. Paid us double the wages most folks were earning around here."

BB and Pinkie take turns asking questions:

"So she was wealthy?"

"Sure! Ever heard of the Winchester rifle? She inherited everything from her late husband. Lots of money in those guns."

"She spent the whole fortune on this place?"

"This and things like orphanages and hospitals. She was a smart lady and talented. Sometimes she let the neighbor kids come in to play her piano and have ice cream."

"She must have been really popular around here."

"Not really. She lost her husband and baby girl, so she wore black and kept a dark veil over her face. People made up all sorts of stories about her and her house."

They continue following him through the maze-like building. Despite his assurances that he knows his way around, BB and Pinkie figure he's just as baffled as they are.

"I was sure this turn was the way out. Maybe if we go back the other way... or not..."

The poor befuddled man scratches his head in total confusion. After another round of endless switchbacks, hallways, and strange stairways, Pinkie finally calls a halt:

"We really appreciate your help and your great stories, but I think we'll just keep looking on our own. One of these doors has to be the exit."

Reconciled to the fact they are totally lost, the fellow gives in:

"I should get back to my work anyway. Don't want to disappoint Mrs. Winchester."

BB extends his hand for a farewell shake, but his fingers pass right through the man's gloved hand. With a smile and a nod, their guide dissolves into vaporous dust that swirls down through the floor.

CHAPTER SIXTY-ONE

House of Cards

"That's it, BB! Time we got out of here. Now!"

BB stares at the vacant space trying to convince himself he wasn't hallucinating. Then once more on their own, they run through hallways, up and down stairs, into rooms within rooms, and down endless networks of halls that twist and turn into dead ends. They try to concentrate on where they've been and where they think they're going, but their exit plan appears doomed. Just as they've given up all hope, they discover a door in an outside wall. BB eagerly tries the knob. He pushes against the door that easily gives way. Pinkie grabs the backpack and pulls him back just before he lurches out into empty space. They peer down the two-story drop to the sidewalk below, their hearts pounding loud enough to wake the dead.

At that moment, a deafening bell echoes throughout the mysterious mansion tolling the midnight hour. BB and Pinkie cover their ears and press down their rising panic. The final toll fades away, replaced by beautiful piano notes. Unable to resist, they follow the sound to a room they've never seen in all of their wanderings. A young woman is seated at a grand piano, thoroughly lost in the strains of her own music. As the lovely piece ends, she whirls around on the piano stool and greets them as if she's been waiting for their arrival:

"Ah, my young initiates! So glad you could join me. I hope you've been enjoying your tour of my masterpiece. Isn't she wonderful?"

Her bright smile contrasts with the long sleeved, high-necked, black mourning dress she wears. Curls framing her lovely face and a bit of white lace peeking above her collar soften her appearance. Gentle eyes with their perfectly arched brows and long lashes enhance her beauty. BB and Pinkie stare in disbelief at this latest, unexpected manifestation. The woman extends a gracious welcome:

"Please. Come. Let's see what we can discover."

They warily take a seat at a small table set with three chairs and a deck of playing cards. The young woman begins to lay out the cards as she speaks.

"Notice the wonderful aspect of a deck of 52 cards. 4 suits, 13 cards in each suit. Both perfect numbers. If you add 5 + 2 it equals 7, another perfect number. Even 1 + 3 equals 4; however, 13 in itself is a glorious number. It's also my favorite! Did you notice these numbers in your wanderings here at Winchester house? Yes? But you don't know about the secret of those numbers, do you?"

She produces a chart of numbers and letters and begins to use it to analyze names:

1	2	3	4	5	6	7	8	9
A	B	C	D	E	F	G	H	I
J	K	L	M	N	O	P	Q	R
S	T	U	V	W	X	Y	Z	

"This, my dears, is called the Pythagorean 1-9 Table. Brilliant men and women have been using it for years. Knowledge is the ultimate goal in life, you know. Knowledge of nature, the universe, everything. In my precious numbers is a hidden wisdom that leads to enlightenment and salvation. Just as the universe is an organism, living and breathing and growing, we are doing the same. Don't you see?"

BB and Pinkie don't really "see" but they nod to be agreeable. She continues:

"And numbers are a reflection of this. They have no beginning or end. They are constantly evolving. Watch! I'll show you! What's your name, young man?"

"BB"

"That's a strange name. But 2+2 equals 4. Good enough!"

"Actually it stands for Heybert B."

She claps her hands with this new challenge:

"If we add up all of those letters... H=8, E=5, Y=7, B=2, E=5, R=9, T=2, and B=2. Wonderful! 40! And 4+0 equals..."

Pinkie shouts out:

"Four!"

Pinkie leans in, growing more and more fascinated with the numbers and letters.

"There's more. We can add H and E to get 13, Y, B, and E to get 14, and R, T, and B to get 13 again. Now take the 13 and add 1+3=4, 14 and add 1+4=5, and then 13 adding 1+3=4. Finally add 4+5+4 and...."

"Thirteen! Look BB your name is magical!"

BB grows increasingly impressed with this name he's always dismissed:

"I didn't know a name could mean so much."

"Now let's see about your last name."

"It's Bradford. Heybert B Bradford."

"So let's take four letters at a time: B=2, R=9, A=1 and D=4. Add them together and we get 16. 1+6=7! And the last four letters: F=6, O=6, R=9 and D=4. They total 25. 2+5=7 again! You have a very special name, young man."

With a sigh, she leans back in her chair and gazes to the far wall as if reliving a dream:

"Before I came to California, I had a wonderful life in Connecticut. I spoke five languages and was close friends with several notable people at Yale University. My marriage to William brought me his name with its wonderful numbers. When he died, his fortune enabled me to build this monument to my genius. I was *somebody*! And now they say I'm crazy, obsessed with ghosts. Not true! I just love my numbers."

BB and Pinkie realize she's the owner, Sarah Winchester. Pinkie offers her approval:

"They *are* lovely numbers."

Sarah changes the subject, totally incensed:

"How *dare* they sell all my furniture. Even my grand piano!"

BB looks directly at the piano she'd just played:

"But isn't that..."

"But I get even!"

Her fiendishly joyous laugh sends shivers down their backs:

"Lights go on and off. Strange sounds echo in the halls. Handles turn on doors. I taunt the tour guides who make up ridiculous stories. I also invite special, non-paying guests to visit."

She laughs again. BB and Pinkie exchange a quick look, remembering the phantoms and unexplained events they had experienced. Her mood turns:

"Our little daughter died soon after she was born. A few years later my husband passed on and I was all alone. I couldn't sleep. And the guilt! All those people who died from those guns! That's where my money came from. I had to keep from going crazy. I needed a project. I thought if I kept building I might keep death from my door. But it didn't happen. I needed someone to continue my work, my legacy!"

She sighs and waits. And then she stares intently into their faces:

"It's been forty years since they opened the house to the public. I knew this would be the year. I've been watching since February for someone to arrive. An incarnation of myself. Someone to carry on the numbers so I won't be forgotten. It could be you!"

She points to BB.

"Or you!"

She points to Pinkie and then returns to her chart:

"What's your name?"

Pinkie freezes and BB blurts out:

"Her name's Pinkie."

"Let's see... Yes! P = 7, I = 9, N = 5, K = 2, and Y = 7. 7+ 9 = 16 1+6=7! 5+2=7, and Y=7! Three perfect 7s! Together, both of you will be able to continue my work!"

They don't have the heart to tell her she's spelling Pinkie's name wrong. But then she grows more and more erratic in her pronouncements:

"Just like my numbers, now *I* will go on forever once you resume construction. I knew death would come. My own body betrayed me."

She dons a black veil to cover her face, slips on black lace gloves, and rises to face them. BB and Pinkie are glad the table provides a temporary buffer. They jump up from their chairs and inch backward. Sarah's agitation swells to a fevered pitch:

"It wasn't fair! I had it all planned out – the numbers, my husband, my daughter – everything was perfect! It's still not fair! They're turning against me! Turning my beautiful, mystic life into an object of ridicule! They don't understand my perfect numbers – my beautiful numbers. They're everything to me! The children I couldn't have. My 'perfect ones' – especially my 13! I tried to explain. I tried to fit in. I invited the little children to my house. I wanted them to like me. And I kept hoping for a little girl who might look like my lost daughter. Oh my Annie!"

She leans forward, resting her hands on the table and bending her head. Her deep moans at the remembrance of her child pull at the hearts of BB and Pinkie. But then she becomes increasingly wild and unstable. Her voice takes on a quavering, ancient sound. The menacing madness grows:

"When my baby Annie died, everything turned inside out. The man next to me at night, coughing his insides out. The blood on his pillow. And then he died and I changed forever! I guess I *am* crazy! Sarah the crazy woman! I *must* be! Am I, though? Or is it this house?"

She stops to catch her breath and then sags with the weight of her sorrow:

"I had it all. Beauty, brains, personality. Everyone who was anyone loved me. I was the 'Belle of New Haven.' And now look at me..."

They are tempted to reach out to comfort her. But then she resumes her litany of woe:

"All is gone.... All is lost... Except my numbers. I still have my numbers! But now even they are turning against me. Demanding more and more. Always more money to keep the never-ending project going. But how else would I ever make sense of life? Understand the universe?"

As she advances toward them, they keep retreating:

"And now it's up to *you*! *You* are the answer to my immortality. *You* must stay to keep it going. Don't let it stop!"

Her demands intensify their growing alarm. Will they too become eternal residents of this house of lunacy? Escape is their only salvation! They try every door in the room, but none yields. They're trapped in a madhouse with this deranged woman.

CHAPTER SIXTY-TWO

Let's Make a Deal

"What are we going to do BB?"

"I don't know! I'd do anything to find a way out of here!"

Another voice joins the trio:

"Did you say *anything*?"

From every corner of the room holograms appear, smiling their taunts:

"If you'd only listened to me you could have avoided all of this. But you can still have it all… fame, money, friends."

It's Janus Wintergreen! And then they see the faces of others: Aeron, Zilla and finally Van Detta. Pinkie is especially distressed with this last apparition:

"It *is* you! Why are you doing this? Why did you abandon me?"

BB is thoroughly confused:

"What's Reggie doing here?"

But Pinkie doesn't hear. She's totally focused on her former partner:

"I thought I'd never see you again. I wasn't sure it was you before, but…"

Van Detta laughs at her confusion:

"What did you *think* happened to me? I found another direction. My name is guaranteed to live forever. Meanwhile I have all the right connections, all the advantages. You should've come with me. Then none of this would have happened. But your friend can still return to his family. And you, Pinkie, can be released from this time trap. We'll be a team again. Just like the old days."

BB is totally blindsided by this revelation of a life Pinkie has never shared. He can tell she's weakening. And then Van Detta discloses his other goal:

"Come on, Pinkie. Enough! Tell him to give Sarah the backpack, and it'll be all over."

They realize their situation is hopeless. Van Detta's demands seem so reasonable to BB:

"So it's all about the backpack? That's a pretty easy exchange if it gets us out of this nightmare. Pinkie, think about us... our future. Our lives could be so much easier."

Van Detta continues his soothing enticement:

"Just hand it over to her and everything will be fine."

Pinkie sighs and looks to BB:

"I *am* tired of always being on the alert, wondering where I'll end up next. I'm ready if you are... I guess..."

Impatient for their decision, Sarah slowly creeps toward BB and Pinkie, extending her hands, reaching out to her captives. BB starts to remove the backpack. Just then a swirling wind envelops Sarah and lifts her veil. Her beauty has mutated into a hoary, rheumy-eyed hag. Her gloves disintegrate like black confetti and float to the floor revealing gnarled, claw-like hands. Too stunned to move, BB and Pinkie are transfixed by this desperate, toothless creature. Her twisted fingers reach out closer and closer:

"It's my part of the bargain. Give it to me! I'll pass it to them, and all will be forgiven."

The holograms and Sarah close in on them. Van Detta's demands grow more insistent:

"Tell him to hand it over to her, Pinkie. You wouldn't even know what to do with all of that power!"

Unnerved by this turn of events, BB and Pinkie slowly step back. Behind them a door creaks open. They run through the doorway and down the hall, more doors mysteriously opening in their path. Sarah and the rest are close behind, shouting warnings and threats. Finally the main entrance swings wide to an undulating vaporous wall. Van Detta's mocking voice rises above the raucous yammering:

"That will only make things worse. But go ahead if you don't believe us."

Pinkie and BB, desperate for a decision, weigh their choices. They look back at the holograms and Sarah drawing closer and realize their destinies are entwined:

"At least we'll have each other."

The die is cast. Hand in hand they leap through the mist and disappear. Sarah wails in distress at her loss. But the others laugh, delighted and congratulating each other:

"They'll never find their way back now!"

"They're completely lost to the past, totally useless to The Bond."

"We've won!"

But then brilliant light flows through the crystals of an interior window, creating a rainbow that dances on the mist. Overcome by the dazzling brightness, the holograms scatter like cockroaches, spiral backward, and disappear. Sarah melts into the floor. Their ghoulish laughter fades into silence. From the hush of the deserted hallway flows a powerful, assuring voice:

"When you are weak, then I am strong. I will never forsake you."

The scene in the hourglass at Headquarters goes black. The steady trickle of sand continues unabated.

CHAPTER SIXTY-THREE

Portal to Panic

BB and Pinkie inch forward through the swirling fog, fearful they'll lose their bearings and return to that house of horrors. When the mist dissolves, they are standing on the cobblestone pavement of an unfamiliar city. Their clothes, totally out of style for the era they have entered, are a startling sight to those they meet. They push their watch buttons and are instantly changed into outfits suited to the early 1900s. Pinkie straightens her skirt and blouse and tucks a stray curl behind her ear. BB adjusts his coat and cap and hoists the backpack higher on his shoulder. Even it has changed into a much less conspicuous leather satchel. The only light in the early morning hours comes from the saloons lining the street. Dawn casts its glow in the eastern sky. Above the rooftops Pinkie spots the Cheshire cat grin of the disappearing moon:

"BB! It's almost gone! That means the sand is running out too!"

But BB is scanning the taverns remembering a recent episode. A dancehall madam calls from a nearby doorway:

"Well look who's back to try his luck! There's a poker game still going on in the back room. I'm sure they wouldn't mind a late arrival joining them."

BB's worst fear has come true. He had barely escaped this trap before. And now he has Pinkie's safety to think about too:

"Sorry. Not tonight... today... or any day! Come on Pinkie!"

BB hurries her away from the woman who calls after them:

"No need to rush off, darlin'. It's still dark enough to have some fun."

Her laugh echoes off the brick buildings and assaults his conscience.

"Who *is* she, BB? And why does she think she knows you?"

"Never mind. It's too hard to explain."

They dodge drunken men and women lunging from saloons and tumbling into the street. In every alcove and entryway someone sleeps off the night's overindulgence in cheap liquor. Off-key strains from a honkytonk piano add to the sleazy atmosphere streaming from every alley and doorway.

"But *have* you been here before? Tell me the truth, BB!"

"It's called the Barbary Coast. It's in San Francisco."

"Does this have anything to do with that time we got separated?"

She stops to wait for his response. Not a leaf stirs. The wind holds its breath. BB looks to the cloudless dawn sky. How can he explain? But before he can answer, the earth shrugs. The city jerks awake. A low rumbling noise gradually swells like an approaching train in a tunnel. Finally it erupts from the depths of the earth, throwing the scene into utter terror. Chaos and fear swirl around BB and Pinkie. The ground jolts and shakes. Screams pierce the air. Bricks, stone facades, and chimneys crash down adding to the rubble that already exists in this hedonistic corner of the city.

The undulating pavement slams BB and Pinkie to the ground. Cobblestones dance like popcorn in a hot kettle. Jolt, sway, rattle. Jolt, sway, rattle. A giant grinding machine, the earth rumbles down deep. BANG! Terrified, they watch a brick hotel lurch forward, slide from its foundation and crumble down over the street. Crushed and buried beneath are guests sleeping off the excesses of the night before. The ground liquefies under the rows of saloons, flop houses, and brothels. The entire district collapses and caves in on itself. Panic drives desperate people into the street. In their haste some throw a wrap over nightclothes. Others are half dressed or completely naked. One barefoot man in a nightshirt brandishes his silver topped cane at the invisible foe.

Above the pitch and roll, throbbing timbers creak and crack. Glass windows crash and smash, adding to the rubble in the street. Chimney bricks begin to fall, thumping down the slopes of roofs and raining down on the wretched people below. A line of wood frame buildings sways briefly and lays flat. The agonizing cries and desperate calls from those perishing below rise hopelessly. No one comes to their rescue. It is pointless in the face of the wanton wreckage that constantly grows. A woman falls to the ground senseless. Blood oozes from the massive head wound that snuffed out her life. The dust of destruction fills the air and hovers over the jumble of wreckage in the street. The shaking is endless. The earth seems bent on leveling all of man's creation. There is no escaping the creaking, the grinding, the rasping breath of destruction.

After what seems like an eternity, the rippling shock waves settle, and BB and Pinkie regain their footing. Half-dressed, barefoot residents wander out of rooming houses. They stand absolutely silent in the middle of the street, wondering where to turn for safety and wringing their hands in dread. One mother stands at the door of their house frantically crying out for her child.

"I'm right here, Mother!"

She tearfully embraces the little boy who's been right by her side the whole time.

More tremors unlock the crowd's hysteria. Grown men blubber like babies.

Others run about without purpose or kneel down to pray silently, looking to the sky and hoping Someone is listening. At that very moment a wild-eyed horse careens around a corner, dragging a broken carriage. Pinkie's screams warn BB. They scramble from the path of the panic-stricken creature to watch it race headlong up a mound of bricks and broken timbers. Finally the carriage breaks away. The horse clambers over the barrier and gallops down the street out of sight.

"That poor thing! Oh, BB, what are we going to do? What *can* we do?"

BB surveys the carnage and destruction:

"Why are we here? What's going to happen to us? Is this my punishment for all the wrong choices I've made?"

Pinkie's own thoughts crowd in as she looks at the terrible scene:

"Is The Bond even in this place, or has it brought us to the edge of this pit to destroy us? Maybe we've been abandoned completely to The Abyss."

Pinkie's confidence is wavering, and BB shakes off any thoughts of intervening help. They resolve to rely on their own wits and judgment to stay alive.

"Come on, Pinkie. We need to get out of here."

As they head down the street, shouts grow louder. Already avarice rears its ugly face. In this early hour of developing tragedy many choose to take advantage of people's misery. The cloud of The Abyss mixed with the dust rising from the collapsed buildings covers the robbing and looting of homes and businesses. BB and Pinkie hurry past broken windows and gangs plundering the shops and stores. No one is there to stop them. Crowds rush from saloon to saloon, carrying away bottles of liquor and guzzling wine. Several collapse to the pavement in a drunken stupor. The morning sun floods the scene, casting long shadows to the west. The Abyss mocks these hopeful rays as it hovers over the panicked city, ready to unleash its self-serving, reckless spirit of despair and misery. BB scans the horizon to the south where the prologue to the impending firestorm makes its appearance.

"Look over there, Pinkie! Is that smoke from a chimney?"

"There's smoke rising from all over. It's spiraling too high for just a chimney fire."

Everyone stands completely silent. No whistles shriek. No bells clang. Just a strange unearthly stillness. All turn their anxious faces to the growing columns of thick black smoke. One man numbly voices his concerns:

"That's the area south of Market Street. I've got family living over there."

"Come on, Pinkie. We've got to keep moving."

"Moving where? Where are we going?"

Before he can answer, they are interrupted by shouts and urgings of a bandy-legged hulk of a man leading a dusty nag through the jumble of debris. Over the uneven path the horse rocks and rolls a wagon piled high with garbage. Perched on the buckboard seat is a modestly dressed businessman with a thick, dark mustache. They turn their attention back to the driver who's dressed in drab work clothes, his pants held up by a rope belt. He pushes his slouch hat back with calloused, blackened fingers poking through the tips of greasy canvas gloves. A wheel jams in the rubble. The driver tries in vain to move a chunk of concrete. The horse strains to pull the wagon free. No one stops to help. Why would anyone bother to haul garbage at a time like this?

CHAPTER SIXTY-FOUR

All that Glitters

BB shouts out to the man leading the wagon:

"Hey, mister! Why don't you and your friend just leave all this garbage and save yourselves... and your horse?"

The man looks around to see if anyone can hear him. He lowers his voice to be safe:

"There's more than garbage in this wagon. There's a huge amount of gold and silver, plus almost $100,000 underneath."

BB and Pinkie give him a disgusted look and step away:

"So you robbed a bank? Like those other guys we saw stealing things!"

"No, no! I'm doing this for my friend. He's the one sitting up there on the wagon seat. I'll introduce you! This is Mr. Amadeo Giannini. He owns the Bank of Italy."

Pinkie and BB acknowledge the gentleman, who tips his hat. Pinkie wants to hear more before they buy into this strange story:

"But why are you hauling away the money? Isn't the vault safe enough from looters?"

Giannini speaks up to explain:

"When I saw the fires, I didn't want to take the chance they'd reach my bank."

BB isn't convinced:

"I thought bank vaults were fireproof."

"They are. But I wouldn't be able to get to it for at least three weeks. Even after the vault cools down, you can't open it up for another week or more. Any paper money or bonds will spontaneously combust. That's why I called on Giobatta."

The driver makes a humble bow:

"The Cepollina family is grateful for the opportunity to help you!"

"Don't worry, Giobatta. I'll take care of your family after this is over. Your son will have a good job at the bank."

Pinkie still can't believe there isn't more to this supposed do-gooder:

"You'll probably make a killing after all of this settles down, loaning money to the wealthy and charging a big, fat interest rate."

The wagon driver indignantly addresses the two young people:

"Why do you say that? You don't know Mr. Giannini like I do. He cares about his city and people like me and him who came to this country to start a new life."

"Calm down, Giobatta! I'm sure they didn't mean to insult us."

He smiles down at BB and Pinkie:

"I'd really appreciate it if you could help us move the wagon. We've got to get this 'garbage' to my home in San Mateo before the streets and roads are blocked. As soon as it's safe, I'll be back to set up a bank. Right in the middle of the street if necessary! I'll give a loan to *anyone* who's willing to start rebuilding the city."

Admitting they judged him unfairly, they help push the stone block away from the wheel. Giannini urges the horse forward with a gentle slap of the reins. Giobatta decides to lead the horse until they're in the clear. BB calls after them:

"Good luck to you, Mr. Giannini. Hope you keep that garbage safe!"

Just then six rough looking fellows emerge from the shadow of a crumbled wall. One of them steps in front of the horse with a swaggering stance:

"Hey, boys. Did you hear what the kid said? This is the one and only Mr. Giannini. He's president of that bank down the street."

The others join their leader to stop the progress of the wagon. Pinkie and BB stand to the side, unsure of how to help. Giobatta makes a courageous stand to shield his friend:

"You heard wrong. We need to get this garbage out of the city so it won't attract rats."

The gang leader pulls out a pistol and circles around to get a better view of Giannini:

"Naw. We heard his name. We'll just take Mr. Giannini off your hands. I'm sure the bank will be more than happy to get him back safe and sound. If they're willing to pay the going rate, that is."

Pinkie whispers to BB:

"We've got to do something fast. They're going to kidnap him. Who knows what they'll do to him if they don't get their ransom money!"

BB suddenly remembers one of the riddles:

"What is worthless to life, yet is sought by millions?"

He slowly slides the satchel from his shoulder. Without taking his eyes from the unfolding drama, he searches inside until his hand grasps what he's seeking. He calls out to the threatening band of lowlifes:

"You don't want to go to all that trouble, do you? You've got to find a place to keep him and then contact someone from the bank. Look around! How are you going to do that in the middle of all this?"

He quickly pulls out what he knows will catch their attention. The huge gold nugget! He holds it high over his head:

"Wouldn't you rather have something *now*? Something you don't have to work so hard to get?"

Their eyes glow with greed. They see a quick path to riches and are drawn to the glittering lump of gold. BB hurls the nugget far down the street toward the saloons where it disappears into a pile of broken bricks and timber. The six roughnecks desperately shove each other aside to be first to reach the treasure. BB grabs the horse's halter to pull it forward. Pinkie calls to Giannini and Giobatta who are too stunned for the moment to move:

"Let's get going! It won't take them long to find that hunk of gold!"

Giobatta shakes off his temporary inertia and takes charge once more:

"You kids better get out of here before they come back. I've got this. Don't you worry, Mr. Giannini! I'm not goin' to let you down again!"

BB and Pinkie watch as the two men and their precious cargo disappear into the dust and tangle of fallen telephone lines. They duck behind a collapsed wall and watch the six hooligans scrambling and fighting to reach their glittering treasure. At last the gang gives up and wanders back, looking for any sign of their lost ransom opportunity. When their leader sees the growing fires in the distance, he has one more idea:

"I'm bettin' no one's guarding the U.S. Mint down the street. It's the biggest prize in the city if we get there first. There's millions and millions just waiting for someone with brains to grab it! And that's us! Let's go!"

They hurry toward the Mint, not realizing the fires are closing in on it from another direction. BB and Pinkie step out from hiding, hail a passing soldier on horseback, and pass on the robbers' plans. BB calls after the officer who gallops away:

"They've got guns too!"

CHAPTER SIXTY-FIVE

Close Calls and Sacrifice

Pinkie and BB carefully negotiate the narrow open path, avoiding the sidewalks where the walls and roofs of nearby buildings are barely holding together. Suddenly an aftershock that rivals the initial earthquake terrorizes the city again. They fall to the ground and cover their heads, hoping by some miracle they will be spared. Under their bodies the pavement pulsates like the heart of some monstrous, angry beast. Tremors follow one after another. A building dances a lively jig, jumping up and down and then swaying precariously. The street ripples and undulates like waves on the ocean. Power lines snap and sputter. Telephone poles splinter, their tops strung together like a sagging clothesline. A plate glass store window, jarred from its wooden frame, bounces several feet down the sidewalk and leans unbroken against the building. Church bells sway, ringing out their mournful alarm.

Frightened residents once more rush screeching into the street. Crying children cling to frantic mothers wearing bathrobes and coats that conceal their nightgowns. Then as BB and Pinkie watch in horror, a huge cornice breaks from the top of a building and crashes to the sidewalk, crushing a man like a bug. Finally all is at rest. But the air still shivers with echoes of the latest unearthly clamor. One man kneels in the middle of the street silently mouthing his requests to the Almighty for safety or perhaps a prayer of thanks for deliverance. Broken water mains gush fountains that fill the gutters and then reduce to a trickle. As they resume their cautious trek, BB keeps a lookout for danger overhead.

"Watch out, BB!"

Only a few feet away, the ends of a downed power line writhe and hiss snakelike, eager to inflict their electric venom on a careless passerby.

"Thanks, Pinkie! That was close. We need to be extra careful from now on."

"What's all of that mangled metal?"

They pick their way through the rubble to the intersection where steel rails and cable car slots twist and turn in all directions. BB checks the name etched into the wall of a nearby building: California. He directs her eyes to where the street makes its climb.

"This is so sad, Pinkie! There was a straight line all the way up to Nob

Hill. Now it looks like someone picked up the end and whipped it in every direction."

"No wonder there weren't any cable cars in San Francisco when we were there. The lines were all destroyed."

"That can't be right. I *know* they survived. I rode them myself."

Pinkie shades her eyes and peers down the broken line in the opposite direction. Against the morning sunlight she spots the silhouette of a child wandering alone.

"There's a kid over there! I think it's a little girl. Maybe she's lost!"

They clamber over ridges and depressions in the pavement to reach a young girl dragging a doll by one arm along the dusty street. Tears streak her sweet face. She sobs inconsolably. Pinkie kneels beside her:

"What's wrong, Sweetie? Are you lost? Where are your parents?"

BB shakes his head and whispers to Pinkie:

"Careful! She may be the only one of her family left alive. Who knows what she's just seen happen to her parents?"

Pinkie takes another approach:

"Why are you crying? Is there something we can help you with?"

The little girl wails her tale of woe, catching her breath between sobs:

"Look at the tracks! My wonderful cable cars are gone! I'll never ride them again!"

"Don't worry. I'm sure everything will be fine."

"How can you say that? They were my heart. I'll never be happy again!"

They follow her to a crevice deep enough to swallow a full-grown man. In the darkness below they see the twisted rails. Deeper yet, the split narrows toward the inner earth. At that moment another aftershock rumbles through and knocks them off balance. The little girl screams and tumbles into the jagged gap. BB grabs the doll she's gripping in her hand, his body hanging over the edge. Pinkie pulls on his legs to keep him from falling in. The child's terror-stricken face steels BB to the task at hand:

"I want you to reach up with your other hand and grab the doll. Good girl. Now I'm going to pull on your doll until you and I can hold hands."

"Don't hurt my dolly!"

"I won't. I promise."

BB is amazed at his own composed voice, the calm confident words he needs if he's going to succeed in saving this little girl. He carefully works his fingers down the length of the doll until they touch the child's hand. With one more tug he grasps her arm.

"Don't let my dolly fall! Please don't let her fall!"

"I won't. But I need you to help me now. Put the doll's dress between your teeth and bite down hard. Don't talk and don't yell. Now give me your other hand."

BB inches backward relying on Pinkie's strength to drag him away from the edge. As soon as his body is clear, she runs to the crevice and pulls the child to safety. The three of them collapse in a heap of exhaustion and relief. Pinkie looks over at BB and then down at the little girl, her doll drooped next to her:

"BB! She's not moving!"

BB lifts the child from the pavement and firmly shakes her limp body:

"Don't die on me now! Not after all we just did!"

Pinkie searches the backpack for the flask:

"Maybe she just needs some water. All that crying and everything she's been through. It must have drained everything from her little body."

BB trickles a few drops of water onto her lips. He bathes her forehead and neck with a handful of the restorative liquid. Small moans gradually grow louder and stronger. Finally her eyelids flutter open. BB brings her to a sitting position and puts the canteen to her lips. She swallows big gulps of water, wipes her mouth on her sleeve, and in a few moments hops to her feet. Fully recovered, the precocious little girl announces brightly:

"Thank you for saving me and my dolly. I should probably get back to my parents."

"Your *parents*? Where *are* your parents?"

"We left our house early this morning after that really scary earthquake. Papa and Mama gathered as much as we could carry, and we walked to the ferry. We have friends across the bay. Anyway, so many people were crowding and pushing, trying to get to the ferry. I lost my family and just went along with the others."

She adds dramatic urgency to her story, ending with a forlorn sigh:

"*Then* I heard them talking about the cable cars, and I just *had* to see if it was true. I couldn't believe they were all ruined! But they were right."

BB and Pinkie waste no time hustling their young charge to the ferry. In the distance the terminal tower stands perfectly straight, a beacon of hope in the midst of despair. They scramble up and over piles of bricks, around fallen poles, and carefully cross deep crevices bridged by narrow boards. Finally they join the desperate crowds surging toward the great ferry building. Above the hubbub they hear a frantic, distressed cry:

"Friedel! Friedel Fischer! Where are you child?"

"Here I am, Papa! I'm here!"

"Ahhh... *Liebchen!*"

The poor man barely contains his emotions as he scoops up his little daughter in his arms. His voice trembles with relief:

"Mother and I were so worried when we couldn't find you! Where have you been?"

"I got lost."

"And who are these fine young people?"

"They helped me find my way back. They've been very nice. But Papa! My cable cars are all ruined! I saw the tracks! And I don't know where the cars could be!"

"Those things can be repaired, I'm sure. And someone is watching over the cars. Don't fret so. Let's get you to your mama. She's been waiting and waiting with the luggage. You had us all so worried!"

He urges Pinkie and BB to come along. Mrs. Fischer greets Friedel with a huge, tearful embrace and then proceeds to scold her for her habit of wandering:

"First it's the house waving back and forth! And then the china crashing to the floor! I thought we were all going to be crushed in our beds under our roof! We were blessed to survive. *Danke Gott!* And then *you* decide to go exploring!"

"Now, Mama. Be happy she's back safe. She's promised to stay close from now on."

Friedel solemnly nods and checks to see if BB and Pinkie are going to add anything to her story. They give her a wink and smile. BB offers to help the family with their suitcases. Pinkie and Friedel's mother each take a handle of the trunk she's been sitting on. Friedel clutches her precious doll. The wide walk funnels into the waiting room with its high, glass-paneled ceiling. They join the crush of refugees, all hoping for a chance to cross on the ferry. With each return of a boat from the far shore, the crowd presses forward. Mr. Fischer weaves through the sea of people to the ticket office. He returns with passage for the family plus two extra tickets:

"I secured a place for you both to cross over with us to Oakland. It's the least I can do to thank you for bringing our Friedel back to us."

At first they accept the tickets. But then they notice a woman with a baby in her arms and a young boy in tow. She has salvaged nothing but the clothes they're wearing. They are at the mercy of anyone who might show them some promise of escape. BB hands Pinkie his ticket, and she walks over to the desperate trio. The young mother's tearful, heartfelt gratitude pours out as she grasps Pinkie's hands. The Fischers are dumbfounded at their generosity. The father protests:

"There may not be another ferry for hours! Or maybe not at all!"

Pinkie answers for them both:

"We'll take our chances here. We're in a better position than most to be resourceful. And who knows? Maybe we can be of some help too."

"Pinkie and I really appreciate your offer. Friedel, I hope your cable cars will be safe."

The little girl's face brightens with the possibility:

"Oh, I hope so too! I'll be sure to take care of them when I come back! I will be back!"

Friedel's father smiles:

"What can I say? My little girl has a lot of passion!"

BB and Pinkie linger long enough to see Friedel's family and the woman and her children safely aboard the next ferry. And then they turn to face the city. Already the smoke is thickening. To the south, flames lick the sky as far as the eye can see.

CHAPTER SIXTY-SIX

Precarious Refuge

"BB, I don't like the looks of all that smoke."

"I know. It seems like there's another fire erupting everywhere we look."

A man walking near them gives BB the explanation:

"There's a bunch of broken gas lines. Power lines are down, and they set off some of the fires. Collapsed chimneys are firetraps too. When women light their stoves to cook breakfast… Boom! Everything explodes and the house catches fire!"

"What about the fire department? Can't they put them out?"

"The earthquake lifted up the water mains and snapped them in two. The firemen can't fight fires without water. You two better keep moving so you don't get trapped!"

The group continues its slow, ponderous trek up Market Street. The pavement humps up in permanent waves of ridges. Cable car tracks bend and twist grotesquely. Staring down into the rubble and dark emptiness of a deep crevice, BB and Pinkie shiver, remembering their recent brush with death. And then someone shouts:

"City Hall! Look at the dome!"

In the distance, the dome of the monumental building stands precariously atop the naked steel structure that had once housed a beautiful rotunda. Their attention shifts to the north as more explosions erupt in the Barbary Coast and warehouse district. They look again to the south past the City Hall skeleton where smoke and flames engulf the crowded residential areas. The dizzying scene unnerves the crowd. Far down the street, a wall of billowing gray advances toward them. Separate fires are converging into a maelstrom of flames that blocks their path of escape.

People from all directions converge onto their street, adding to the throng. Ambulances, fire engines, and horse-drawn wagons mingle with the pedestrian traffic. Foot soldiers and policemen on horseback add their shouts to the growing pandemonium. A few souls go against the tide, heading for the ferry terminal. An authoritative voice shouts to them:

"I don't know where you think you're going. A *very* reliable source said the ferry's stopped running. There's no escape across the bay. You'd better follow us."

Resigned to their loss, the refugees turn grimly to join the rest.

"BB, we can't keep going up this street. It leads right into the fire area."

"I know! And I'm really getting hungry."

Just then a man leaps onto a pile of bricks and calls out:

"They're serving breakfast in Union Square! Free to anyone who needs food! The St. Francis Hotel didn't have much damage from the earthquake, so they opened up their kitchen. They're serving meals on tables right out in the square!"

Pinkie and BB join the stream of people turning onto the street that angles right. After two more blocks of crumbled pavement and downed poles, the huge square opens to a familiar sight: the massive white obelisk and bronze statue reaching to the sky. Hungry people crowd the plaza looking for a seat at the table of generosity. Across the square the elegant St. Francis Hotel appears intact despite the earthquake. Pillars of smoke and fire are blocks away. In this island of safety, the future seems hopeful.

Pinkie and BB join the motley assortment of diners. Wealthy bankers and businessmen rub elbows with deliverymen and shopkeepers. Humble housewives and shop girls in threadbare coats shyly chat with society women in their elegant hats and capes. All are eager for a meal that may be their last for the remainder of that day or longer. Servers bring out platters piled high with scrambled eggs and sausage. Others pour coffee into cups held by grateful outstretched hands. Just as BB and Pinkie are ready to sit down, a robust man, obviously in charge, recruits them:

"Hey, you two kids! I need a couple of strong, willing volunteers!"

BB and Pinkie can hear their stomachs rumbling, but BB quickly accepts the challenge:

"Sure! Just tell us what you need."

"Clear off when people leave so we can set up for the next group. But right now I need you to help bring out food from the kitchen. Tell them Ernie sent you."

Inside the hotel people dressed in everything from nightgowns to evening clothes are milling about in the lobby.

"Wow, Pinkie! I wasn't expecting it to be so calm in here after what's happened."

A nearby hotel page eagerly sets them straight:

"Don't let them fool you. During and right after the earthquake guests were dodging the falling ceilings, screaming and running in every direction. The elevators were out of order, so everyone was crowding and shoving and falling down the marble stairs trying to get out to the square. Mr. Woods, the manager, tried to calm them down, but he looked pretty ridiculous wearing his bathrobe."

"We're supposed to help serve the food. Which way to the kitchen?"

He points them to the back of the first floor. They hurry to the restaurant crowded with a high-class clientele. In one corner, a refined young man, a fur coat thrown over his pajamas, sits alone. On the floor next to him is a picture of President Theodore Roosevelt. He finishes his meal, daintily dabs the corners of his mouth with a white cloth napkin, and lights up a cigarette, obviously not ready to give up his seat.

"What are you kids doing?"

BB and Pinkie turn to face a gruff man directing the servers.

"Sorry. Ernie sent us to help bring out the food."

"Well get going. We've got orders to keep cooking until we run out of food. Tell Victor to keep those eggs and sausages coming."

After several trips bringing breakfast to the thankful people, BB and Pinkie feel a firm grasp on their shoulders. Ernie smiles down at them:

"You two have been a huge help. I haven't seen you take a break. Sit down and enjoy some of this food before it's all gone."

They take a seat near the hotel entrance and tuck into their meal. Eggs, sausage, and bread never tasted so good. An old man on crutches sits down next to BB:

"It's my birthday today!"

Pinkie brightens up at this new topic:

"A most happy birthday to you!"

"Last night I was worth thirty thousand dollars. Quite a tidy sum! Today I was going to celebrate with my friends. I had five bottles of wine and all the makings of a fine birthday dinner. But here I am. No dinner except this handout. And all I own in this world are these crutches."

"We're so sorry."

"What's to be sorry about? Every one of these people has a tale of woe. But we're alive, aren't we? Praise God for that! Happy birthday to me!"

They toast the old gentleman, their spirits briefly lifted. But their respite from sorrow is interrupted by loud wailings. BB and Pinkie look over to see the wealthy young man from the dining room clutching Roosevelt's picture. Collapsing to the ground, he weeps uncontrollably, pouring out his fears in a mixture of Italian and English:

"*Mio Dio!* What is to become of me? I should never have left *mia Italia*! I will *never* come back to this city again! 'Ell of a place! 'Ell of a place!"

People at nearby tables stop to watch this theatrical outburst. The young man pulls himself to his feet and addresses his valet:

"Did you get all of my trunks? And my portraits?"

The weary servant, seated on a steamer trunk, quickly springs up:

"Absolutely sir! All fifty-four trunks safely brought over from the Palace Hotel. And your fifty portraits too! I saw to it myself."

"Very well."

"Here is your hotel room key. The manager wanted you to have it as a memento."

"Why would I want to be reminded of this horrible city? You keep it!"

Refusing to have his anger placated, he gestures with a sweep of his arm to the various diners in the square who are staring at him:

"Why do I have to endure the insult of being with this mass of unfortunates?"

BB and Pinkie can't believe his rude behavior. The crowd, however, ignores the outburst, brushes off the insolence as so much soot and calmly returns to their meal. The square is quickly becoming a depository of various suitcases and household items the fleeing citizens have managed to escape with. Clearly people assume they are setting up camp here. One late arrival directs his wife and young children to where Pinkie and BB are eating. While he gets them settled, he makes the mistake of placing his bag on top of the ill-mannered gentleman's trunk. The angry voice booms forth:

"What are you doing? Get that filthy thing off my luggage!"

BB jumps to rescue the unfortunate soul from further verbal assault:

"I'm sure he meant no harm to your trunk, sir. Here, I'll move it."

BB helps the grateful man reassemble his family and belongings a safe distance from the aggrieved individual. Pinkie stops Ernie on his way to the kitchen to ask if he has any information about this person they've been observing.

"Why yes! He's the great Enrico Caruso!"

She gives him a blank look.

"You know. The opera singer! After his performance last night, he was staying at the Palace Hotel where all the wealthy and famous people usually go. Most of them ended up here this morning for breakfast, though. He's a pretty colorful character!"

"Colorful isn't the word I would choose."

BB returns to Pinkie's side:

"Look above those buildings. Those pillars of smoke in the distance. When I was serving people over on the far side of the square, I could see more and more smoke to the south too. What if we're trapped here?"

"Don't worry, BB. Look at all the personal belongings piling up in the square. The Red Cross is setting up tents, and people are settling in. We should be fine."

They circle the square's perimeter hoping for updated information. As they pass a doorway leading into a makeshift hospital, a loud command stops them in their tracks:

"Make way! Coming through!"

Two men on either end of a stretcher climb the two steps into the hall. Pinkie looks down into the face of an injured firefighter. BB asks one of the stretcher-bearers what had happened. He quietly whispers back:

"Hit by a falling wall fighting a fire. His back's broken. Not much hope."

The stricken man's eyes look straight into Pinkie's, his ashen face signaling death awaits him. BB gently draws her away from the dreadful sight.

"Oh, BB! Such a handsome young man. What a horrible way to die!"

In the distance is a loud explosion. One of the men calls back over his shoulder:

"They're blowing up buildings with gunpowder. And dynamite too! I wouldn't stick around here much longer. Those fires can change direction any time. Better head up the hill. Safer there."

A small group has gathered up their meager belongings and is moving up Powell Avenue. BB and Pinkie decide to join them before panic overtakes the crowd. As they leave the square, an official-looking military man climbs the base of the monument.

"Attention! Attention! A proclamation by the Mayor of San Francisco:

The Federal Troops, the members of the Regular Police Force, and all Special Police Officers have been authorized by me to KILL any and all persons found engaged in Looting or in the Commission of Any Other Crime.

I have directed all the Gas and Electric Lighting Companies not to turn on Gas or Electricity until I order them to do so. You may therefore expect the city to remain in darkness for an indefinite time.

I request all citizens to remain at home from darkness until daylight every night until order is restored.

I WARN all Citizens of the danger of fire from Damaged or Destroyed Chimneys, Broken or Leaking Gas Pipes or Fixtures, or any like cause.

Signed by E. E. Schmitz, Mayor

Dated this day, April 18, 1906"

"BB, we have no home. These people don't either. What's he expecting us all to do?"

"I don't know, but we can't stay here. Come on!"

CHAPTER SIXTY-SEVEN

Convergence of the Masses

BB and Pinkie link up with the assorted refugees fleeing the destruction and fires. At each intersection more join until the street is jammed with people and their salvaged treasures. No one speaks except for a few words of encouragement. They save their energy for the climb to safety. Hatless, coatless mothers and fathers cheer on their children trudging up the long hill, each carrying a portion of their family's worldly goods. A young girl has tied bundles to the ends of a broom handle like a street peddler. Husbands and wives pair up to push and pull heavy trunks. The rattling of tiny castors on hundreds of trunks being dragged across sidewalks and pavements is a sound that will be etched in people's memories for years.

It is amazing what people treasure: phonographs with their huge flaring horns; a new broom and a large black hat with ostrich plumes; a bird cage containing four kittens; a pot of calla lilies; banjos and soup tureens. Many have escaped with only the clothes on their backs. Others haul more practical items using any means available: children's wagons, sleds, wheelbarrows, and baby carriages, one with a single wheel. Some have fashioned human harnesses from bed sheets and ropes to pull carts and chests. One man has nailed a pair of roller skates to the bottom of his steamer trunk. Young mothers carry babies in their arms. It all resembles a giant, broken anthill with thousands of escaping determined ants each carrying an oversized burden.

Surprisingly there are few if any tears on the faces of stone. Complaints and weeping are pointless. They are not alone in their troubles, and there is no one to turn to for help. All have one common goal: follow the streets least obstructed by the earthquake wreckage and in a direction away from the growing fires. The street they're on is usually a thoroughfare of cable cars, taxis and pedestrians. But now it's covered with fallen stones and bricks, wooden signs, and the ruins of walls. Great pillars from stately buildings straddle the street. The pavement is a rollercoaster of rises and falls. Broken water mains have collapsed into sinkholes. Twisted tracks and leaning poles draped with half-melted wires impede the slow crawl up the hill. Looking down a side street, Pinkie and BB watch exhausted families on their hands and knees clamber over piles of fallen bricks and rubble to join the weary parade.

The ongoing tremors and aftershocks bring down walls and buildings as if they are made of cards. One hotel, its front wall torn away, resembles the cutaway version of a child's dollhouse. Houses lean together hoping to avoid total collapse. More and more refugees, men and women, children and babies, old people barely able to walk, some on the backs of family or even strangers, all join the flow of desperation.

Following the crowd to a major intersection, Pinkie and BB face a wall of people streaming from the Embarcadero areas to the east. Their tide of desperation jams its way into this already congested escape route that's dotted on both sides with showcases of the wealthy. The merging columns of people choke the avenue, all heading up the even steeper hill. Adding to the chaos, ambulances and commandeered motorcars carrying the injured steadily part the flood of pedestrians. BB and Pinkie find themselves trudging slowly next to an open transport of wounded. A bandaged, bleeding man weakly smiles up at them:

"That earthquake really made a mess of my house down there past Market Street. The chimney fell through the roof and hit me and my wife. She didn't make it."

Pinkie reaches over to touch his arm:

"Oh, I'm so sorry!"

"That's okay, young lady. I'm not the only one who's lost loved ones today. I thought I was a goner too, but some fellas pulled me out from under the bricks, laid me out close to the street and moved on."

"How did you get all the way up here?"

"Some soldiers came by my house with army stretchers. They said all of the hospitals were wrecked so they took me to the Mechanics Building. The doctors and nurses were great, but the place wasn't exactly safe. I heard them whispering that the fires were coming pretty fast."

"Weren't you scared?"

"Sure! We were *all* scared. Who wouldn't be? But everyone moved quickly and didn't panic. That kept the patients calm. I was one of the last ones they got out. I saw a flame above me and called to a couple of firemen. They dropped their stretcher and climbed up some scaffolding to beat it out with their coats. The next place they moved us to wasn't safe from the fires either."

"Where are they taking you now?"

"Not sure. Guess I'll just have to wait and see."

The makeshift ambulance lurches forward through a brief opening in the human pack. The man lifts one arm in a weary farewell. His calm, accepting spirit inspires BB and Pinkie to look for ways to help as many as possible in these tragic circumstances.

At the next corner a huge, wooden, castle-like building with a turreted tower rises to three or more stories. BB blurts out:

"Whoa! What's that?"

A man walking next to him answers:

"That's the Hopkins mansion. The whole bunch of those railroad tycoons built big homes for their wives up here on the hill. The Stanford place was just back there. They're sure proud of all their money and want everyone to notice. I've made lots of deliveries there from my butcher shop back down the hill."

He points to the clouds of smoke where the fires are most certainly consuming his store. Pinkie gazes at what must have been a magnificent vista of the bay:

"They certainly have nice views from up here. Or at least the view used to be nice."

"Wait 'til you see the other two up the street. The Huntington mansion and then the granddaddy of them all... the Crocker place. That one's really something!"

Above the tense conversations and quiet urgings of the refugees, dynamite blasts announce the destruction is pressing closer. The man turns back to help his wife who calls to him in an unfamiliar dialect. New languages readily mix together in this convergence of San Francisco residents. Chinese, Italian, Polish and other tongues testify to the colorful immigrant neighborhoods being vacated below. Most striking though are the grim-faced, silent soldiers with fixed bayonets and belts full of cartridges standing guard over broken storefront windows. The goods inside are tempting to the passersby, but they dare not take even one small item.

Suddenly a gunshot rings out from the block ahead. As the crowd presses forward, parents shield their young children from the sight. Slumped in the doorway of a mercantile lies a dead man. A hastily written sign placed on his chest announces his crime: LOOTER! Glancing at the nearby soldier, BB grimly comments to Pinkie:

"I guess they're not kidding. Shoot to kill."

"But BB. It does seem a little extreme."

"Look around at all of these people. You don't see many policemen, do you? Without these soldiers, who knows what would happen."

A woman next to them overhears their conversation:

"I know. It happened in my neighborhood. Thugs and bullies pushed people around and grabbed everything they could. It was total chaos. Then the US cavalry arrived at full gallop. You should've seen those looters scatter! We all cheered!"

"Is your family okay? Did anyone get hurt?"

"Just a twisted ankle stumbling over the bricks and broken glass in the street. My husband and three kids are with me. My family in Sausalito must be so worried watching all the smoke. Telephones and telegraph are out. I sent them a letter with a neighbor who was hoping to catch a ferry."

Another dynamite blast, this time closer, jars everyone's nerves. From a side street a terrified, riderless horse bolts into the crowd. Three able bodied men grab the flailing reins and send the horse back in the direction it came from. The trapped animal, eyes bulging and whinnying in fear, dashes headlong into piles of fallen buildings.

"Pinkie, I never thought of the animals, especially horses."

"And imagine all the pets! Some are bringing theirs along, but that's not all of them."

As if on cue, a group of moaning, whining dogs drags by, searching for their masters. Their dripping jaws and lolling tongues testify to long miles of wandering. One little cocker spaniel carrying a huge beef bone slouches down to rest. She lays her paw over her treasure as a signal to thieves. Pinkie reaches down with a comforting pat.

"Don't, Pinkie! It might bite!"

But the little dog just looks up with her brown eyes, longing for the touch of a kind human. Pinkie smiles and strokes the tawny head.

"Come on, Pinkie. We've got to keep moving."

A loud horn honks behind them. Once again the crowd of refugees scatters. A large, black sedan with a huge silver hood ornament shouts the wealthy status of its owner. But this prosperous driver, for the time being on equal footing with his fellow citizens, is doing his part in the relief work. Through the window, Pinkie and BB catch sight of bodies, some hanging onto life and others with a sheet pulled over their lifeless faces. Together the dead and near dead are keeping their next appointment with destiny.

CHAPTER SIXTY-EIGHT

Rubbing Elbows with the Rich

The two-block steep climb they've just covered seems like miles. But now the terrain flattens out. The weary fugitives collapse to the curbs and sidewalks. Bankers sit next to shopkeepers. Well-dressed matrons close their eyes and lean against walls while barmaids and housewives with children huddle close by. New arrivals search for a place to collect their thoughts and renew their strength. BB and Pinkie squeeze into a narrow opening on the curb and watch the pitiful parade. With no place to rest, the surging crowd from below continues past the growing gallery of their fellow citizens.

A dignified Chinese couple cradles a lacquered treasure box between them. Trunks, many now missing wheels, slow the progress of the fleeing people. Sofas with casters are loaded down with belongings. A pair of bicycles with boards stretched between them is piled high with groceries, bedding, clothes, kitchen pots and utensils. Strain shows on every face.Two mothers have tied their tiny babies in slings on their backs. The elderly and invalids are carefully carried on mattresses. Some have nothing, just themselves and perhaps a family member, lucky to have escaped the inferno below.

"Would you two mind standing there next to that lamp post?"

BB and Pinkie turn their heads to see if the request is directed at them.

"Yes. You two!"

A curly-haired, middle-aged man on a nearby lawn holds a large, cumbersome camera. He speaks to them again in a slight German accent:

"I would like a picture of you against the crowd moving up the street."

BB isn't so sure this is a good idea. Who knows what the picture could be used for? But Pinkie seems agreeable, so he goes along. She leans back against the lamp post and BB rests his hand near her head. Just as the man opens the shutter, a large family stops in front of the camera. The woman loudly complains to her husband:

"Do you have any idea where we're all going to sleep tonight?"

"Look around, my dear. Do *any* of these people look like they have a reservation for a room? We're all in the same boat. I'm sure we'll find a safe place. Maybe in a park."

The family moves on, but the photographer is no longer interested in his subject. He's heard a shout from the owner of the house behind him:

"Arnold? Arnold Genthe? Is that *you*? For heaven's sake! What are you doing in the middle of this crazy mess? Come on up and have a drink!"

The hospitable man on the porch seems oblivious to the approaching fire danger. Genthe gathers his camera equipment and starts walking to the house. Just then an aftershock hits. The weary crowd cries out. The homeowner's wife runs outside:

"I told you we should have left!"

And then she spots Genthe:

"Arnold! How wonderful to see you! Come up on the portico and sit awhile."

BB and Pinkie can't believe this scene that contrasts so starkly to the distress behind them. It's as if the lives of these people haven't been disrupted at all. Genthe realizes that it's his fault Pinkie and BB have lost their place on the curb:

"You don't mind a couple of extras, do you? They were posing for me and then the whole opportunity fell apart."

BB and Pinkie gladly take a seat on the expansive porch as their hostess returns with a pitcher and glasses:

"Thank goodness Cook made some fresh lemonade before leaving yesterday. So what have you and your camera been up to lately, Arnold?"

"I was down in Chinatown yesterday getting photos of the buildings and people. The children were especially cooperative. I got lots of pictures of them in their traditional costumes and pigtails. By the way, I haven't heard any good reports coming from that area today. I'd be surprised if anything is left standing after the fires down there. Anyway, I grabbed my camera and extra film after that early morning shakedown. I want to capture in real time what's happening. The freestanding walls fascinate me. Sometimes the empty windows frame a broken structure in the distance. I got a great photo looking down toward the bay. But then I decided to check out the scene up here on Nob Hill where you millionaires live."

Another jolt rocks the house, but their hostess and Genthe seem no more alarmed than if a bird had flown by. He raises his glass to her and they all join in a toast:

"To quote a line from Horace, 'And even if the whole world should collapse, he will stand fearless among the falling ruins.'"

"To Horace. And to our great city!"

"To San Francisco!"

Three simultaneous dynamite blasts break up the party and silence their cheers. They hurry to the street and look east to where the inferno is consuming the city like a prairie fire devouring dry grass. Continuous explosions send up towers of smoke that reflect the flames. A voice in the crowd laments the destruction below and the fate of those trapped under the rubble:

"There go some of our finest hotels. The poor souls under the collapsed floors never had a chance."

A few blocks away, a lone soldier on horseback emerges *from the enormous pillars of smoke and urges the masses to move on. A furry creature scurries past rubbing against Pinkie's leg. Expecting another dog, she looks down and screams:*

"A rat!"

The crowd jumps to its feet, grabbing children and belongings, and hurries up the street. Her terrified eyes follow the vermin as it squeezes under a pile of bricks:

"BB! That rat was as big as a cat!"

A soldier with rifle and bayonet shouts orders to keep moving. Genthe encourages his reluctant friends to lock up and move on before there's an official confrontation. Soldiers, rats, dynamite, and fire. There's no other option. It's time to leave.

CHAPTER SIXTY-NINE

Stubbornness, Generosity and Resilience

Hoping beyond hope that their flight will soon end, they pass the Huntington mansion with its columned front entry and elaborate cornices. In the next block BB and Pinkie take a moment to stare up at the massive Crocker residence, its huge central tower reaching five stories. The earthquake has left both homes unscathed. As the people watch the clouds of smoke in the distance, the presence of such formidable palaces gives them a bit of promise for their future.

In front of one collapsed house, the owners calmly sit on chairs they've rescued from the parlor. They seem not at all alarmed by the unfolding crisis. A horse-drawn wagon is parked in front of another stately home just a few doors beyond. An elderly woman sits inside the doorway, arms crossed, refusing to budge. Her son pleads with her:

"Mother, we've been discussing this all day. I have a comfortable ride for you, so you don't have to walk. I've already loaded up the things you insisted we take."

"Then take them. I'm not leaving. This is my home and I don't want any of these undesirables out there helping themselves to my things."

The son throws up his hands in surrender to this wall of denial. Two policemen who have been moving the crowds along turn to face the defiant woman just as an armed soldier arrives:

"What's the problem here? You know the orders. Move her!"

Without a word the two officers enter the house, pick up the chair and the complaining matron, and set her firmly into the waiting wagon. Her son hops in, grabs the reins, and urges the horse slowly up the avenue.

Coming to the next block, BB and Pinkie are surprised to see a small crowd gathering in front of an open store. Disregarding the official orders, the shop owner is handing out his complete stock of bread, flour, cheese, tea, coffee, hams, and canned goods.

"Take what you can carry. Leave some for others. No need to see this going to waste. I'm sure nothing will be here by tomorrow, so take whatever you think you can use."

There's no escaping the approaching disaster. The tremendous thundering of the fire, the crashing of walls and buildings, and the continuing explosions pound into their ears. Tongues of fire dance above buildings just a few blocks away. Showers of red-hot cinders fly through the air and land on doomed roofs. The wind brings the firestorm closer and closer. With a hungry roar, the blazing red sea rolls toward them. The voracious flames will soon consume not only this storefront but also every one of these palatial homes, these displays of wealth and prosperity.

"Can someone help my wife? Please! Is there a doctor? Or a nurse?"

A frantic young man weaves through the crowd, shouting out his pleas:

"My wife's having a baby. Right now! Over on that porch! I need help!"

Obviously doctors and nurses aren't available since they are all taking care of the injured at the various field hospitals. Sympathetic women, however, step forward:

"Sadie's given birth to eight kids. She'll know what to do."

Sadie knows there isn't any water or a way to boil it either. She asks for clean blankets or sheets. Amazingly the people no longer think of their own welfare and donate whatever they can. There's a new life about to enter the world! Just then another woman comes forward, pushing and shouting her way through the circle of onlookers:

"Step back everyone. The woman needs air *and* some privacy."

She addresses the frantic father:

"Calm down, sir. This isn't helping your wife at all."

She arranges a donated sheet over the young woman's lower body. Kneeling down, she gently pats the fearful girl's trembling hand and smiles encouragingly with her Scottish lilt:

"Don't you worry, lass. Everything's going to be fine. I'm a midwife. I've delivered hundreds of babies and never lost one."

The formidable woman looks at the father:

"I wouldn't suggest you hold your wife's hand unless you want a crushing grip each time she has a contraction. If you want to help, hold up her back and keep her head forward when I ask her to push."

She calls out to the crowd:

"I need a knife and some thread or string. As clean as you can find. And something to wrap the wee one in when it's born."

In a reassuring voice she returns her focus to the mother:

"Now let's have a look. Oh my! I can already see Baby's head. Now just relax a bit. Don't push until I tell you."

BB and Pinkie keep a polite distance but are close enough to hear the drama unfolding. As the waves of contractions come one after another, the calm assurances from the midwife capture everyone's attention:

"Breathe in and now out. That's it. Small panting breaths. Aren't you the brave one? Good girl. There you go now."

What seems forever but is just a matter of minutes, the struggle is over. A lusty cry fills the air. The midwife announces:

"You have a strong, healthy boy! Well done!"

Those nearby congratulate the beaming father and applaud the bravery of this new mother. Everyone is grateful for the outcome and also for the diversion from the day's misery. It is a reminder to all that life continues even in the most trying times. While the midwife attends to the necessary tasks to complete the birth, the exhausted mother cradles her newborn son. She murmurs to her husband who appeals to the crowd:

"She's terribly thirsty. Does anyone have some water?"

Of all things, this is the request that is least likely to be fulfilled. The pointless call goes out to those nearby. Pinkie whispers in BB's ear and nods to the backpack:

"BB, we have water!"

They step forward with the Indian woman's flask:

"This is all we have, but you're welcome to it."

Someone rummages through a sack of dishes and produces a clean cup. BB pours a generous amount and hands it to the father. The mother gulps the water as if it were nectar from the gods. BB pours another, and this time she carefully savors every drop.

"Excuse me, sir."

BB looks down at a forlorn child tugging at his coat, a tin cup in hand:

"I haven't had anything to drink since this morning."

BB fills the child's cup. Quietly, one after another, people step forward with cups, glasses, small dishes, anything that will hold a few swallows. BB keeps pouring, and people keep coming. No one pushes. Each waits patiently for their turn. The water keeps flowing from the small flask. Finally an old gentleman pauses when BB fills his cup. Instead of moving on, he gives the water to BB:

"Young fella, I've been watching you and your friend here. You must be just as thirsty as the rest of us. You drink first, and then give some to her too. I insist!"

Only after they accept the returned gift of sustenance does the man take his own cupful. The water line ends abruptly when a soldier shouts:

"Can't stay any longer. The fire's upon us! Move on!"

The fire fiend's hot breath grows ever closer, the hungry, angry flames eating their way up the avenue, consuming everything in its path. The maw of the fire swallows building after building. Soldiers form ranks between the crowd and the approaching flames and march forward. Someone makes room in a cart for the new mother and baby. The grateful husband walks proudly along, keeping a watchful eye on his new family.

Just then a ragged band of firefighters emerges choking and strangling from the smoke. Exhaustion etches their faces. One staggers forward. BB catches him from falling, and Pinkie quickly hands him the flask. The fireman gratefully swallows several gulps and passes it to his bone-weary comrades. Pinkie and BB watch the container handed down the line. They know it's pointless to try to recover it, and they're glad to have provided relief to these heroic fighters.

"BB, do you remember what the Indian woman told us back on that island? 'This is the source of our tribe's life. It will make you wise.' Do you feel wise?"

"I'm not sure. I know I feel *different*. I keep thinking of this morning when we helped Mr. Giannini and got Friedel back to her family. The day kept giving us opportunities to see what people needed. But this water. It never gave out. I don't get it."

CHAPTER SEVENTY

Desperate Measures

Dynamite explosions, one after another and sometimes simultaneously, unsettle the refugees and rattle their nerves. The shouts of fleeing residents and the clanging bells of racing fire wagons create an indescribable clamor. Looking back to the city the sight is beyond belief. A firestorm leaps from block to block. The flames burst forth from buildings on both sides of the avenue, shaking hands in the middle of the street to congratulate each other on the destruction completed. Devilish tongues of fire fork out through open window frames. Explosions blaze more than two hundred feet into the air. There is no way to stop this demon's wild march up the hill.

Pinkie and BB witness the pain and hardship but also the courage and heroism all around. Firemen who have been on duty all day calmly encourage the people forward even though they are on the verge of collapse themselves. In spite of their exhaustion they will themselves to stay focused on saving as many lives as possible. Running on pure adrenaline these brave men suppress fears for their own safety. A couple of soot-faced men walking near BB and Pinkie offer their personal stories on the day's events:

"South of Market where I live, the fires erupted all over from the broken gas lines. Around ten o'clock I looked up Mission Street. It was like looking into an open furnace. All of a sudden the heat created a cyclone. The air rushed from every side and sucked upward like a vacuum. I thought I was a goner! I dropped down and crawled until I could stand up again. When I looked back, the fire was roaring and rolling up the street. To my left was a wall of flames down a side street."

Not to be outdone, the other gentleman adds his tale of woe:

"Me and my buddies were leaving our neighborhood with the rest of the folks. Walls and buildings crumbled all over the place. Then that second big one hit! We watched a rooming house four stories tall collapse on itself like a one of those concertinas."

He pauses for effect, slapping his hands together one on top of the other.

"We could hear the people trapped in there. A bunch of us tried to lift the heavy timbers off the heap. Even the women grabbed bricks and anything else they could pull loose and kept tossing them to the street."

"You got the people out, didn't you?"

"Sorry, little lady. The fire was coming up the street and we had to save ourselves."

Overwhelmed by this story of hopeless tragedy, Pinkie whispers to BB:

"I can't imagine what they've all witnessed. How do they keep going?"

Staring bleakly down the street, she's encouraged by something she spies ahead:.

"BB, look! It's the cable cars. I wish Friedel was here. She'd be so happy to see them!"

The weary, bedraggled people trudge past the useless cars that someone has moved from the storage sheds hoping for a miracle to save them. Two blocks later, the street rises to scale another of San Francisco's many hills. This latest physical and mental hurdle takes its toll. Exhausted and flushed, the people press upward. Small children struggle with their bundles, tears streaming down their hot, red faces. Wagon and cart drivers whip their horses onward. The poor beasts strain under their loads. Their long tongues hang from their mouths signaling near collapse.

All day, for miles and miles, the people have been carrying their possessions and treasures, but now they begin to lighten their load. All sorts of household and personal goods are flung to the side. The last to go are the trunks. Desperate to save them after enduring so many miles to reach this far, most drag them a few feet and then stop to rest. They drape themselves over the huge chests for a brief respite and then return to the struggle. Finally, heartbroken, the owners abandon them, knowing they will never reach safety with them in tow. Thousands of those treasured trunks will soon be sacrificed to the flames. Just ahead a commotion halts the line of people. Some step out to help. Others keep moving along. A woman calls out to BB and Pinkie:

"Go and help those firemen! There's people buried under there! You can hear them!"

A fireman calls out orders:

"If everyone helps move those bricks, maybe we can get to them."

Several others join in. As faint groans rise from deep in the pile, no one speaks. They all concentrate their energy on maintaining a frantic pace. But when the firemen are called away, the rest, including Pinkie and BB, stop to look at one another. One man speaks the wrenching truth that everyone has been thinking but no one has uttered:

"If we had a hundred strong men working, it would take more than a day to reach them. Poor devils. We can't stay here much longer. It's hopeless."

As if to confirm the fate of the entombed victims, two soldiers force the rescuers to move on. The fire is still blocks away but threatening. Higher and higher the flames lick the sky. Cinders and ash swirl in the air. Two US cavalrymen on horseback, their silhouettes in stark relief against a wall of flames, calmly watch the insatiable fire devouring the homes below Nob Hill. More and more buildings explode in the backfire blasts, the only hope to save the wealthy hilltop. Wherever the firefighters make successful stands, the flames flank on either side and circle around to the rear. Each hard-won victory is lost to the fierce, vicious blast furnace that crackles like musket fire. The picket line of soldiers presses the people forward. Upward and onward they march. All at once a tremendous explosion tears into the scene and rocks BB and Pinkie sideways. Billows of black smoke descend on them creating an impenetrable darkness.

"Pinkie! Where are you?"

The thunderous rumble of a collapsing building answers back.

CHAPTER SEVENTY-ONE

Who's in Charge?

"Pinkie! Pinkie! Can you hear me?"

"Don't leave me now, Pinkie! I need you! Please don't die!"

He peers into the black cloud and hears a cough and confused cry. Pinkie staggers from the swirl of dust. BB runs to embrace her:

"Pinkie! Thank goodness! Are you okay?"

"I think so. My ears are still ringing and I'm a bit unsteady."

An officer arrives on the scene demanding an explanation:

"Who's responsible for that detonation? I said to *wait* for my orders!"

A soldier steps forward holding two wild-eyed, dirty-faced youngsters by the collar:

"These two were running from the building right before it went up."

The officer is in no mood to coddle a couple of kids looking for trouble:

"What's your story? And it'd better be a good one!"

"We didn't mean nothing. Honest! A couple of dynamite sticks fell off a wagon. We just wanted to see what would happen if we lit one."

"What did you *think* would happen? Fireworks? I ought to throw you two in the brig. But I can't be bothered. You're lucky no one was hurt! Get outa here! NOW!"

The furious, red-faced officer stalks away and then whirls back:

"Did you say you set off *one*? Where's the other one? Tell me! NOW!"

One of the boys slowly lifts his shirt and pulls out the other dynamite stick he'd shoved in his belt. The officer grabs it and tosses it to the soldier:

"See this gets to General Funston over on Van Ness."

He shouts at the boys one last time:

"I'd better not see you around here again! Git!"

The two culprits scramble over the rubble and back down the street, foolishly defying the fire. BB and Pinkie put their arms around each other for support as they walk past the last of the cable cars and reach Van Ness. This is the firebreak everyone is hoping for, convinced it's impossible for the fire to leap across the broad avenue. Crowds of people are camped out on the far side. Exhausted after their race from the fire, many are asleep on bedding strewn on the sidewalk. BB and Pinkie take a seat on the curb, clearing their heads after their narrow escape.

A fire truck pulls up nearby. The men skillfully unload the hoses, link them together, and dip the end into a nearby cistern. They stretch the hose across the street and down California. Pressure swells the canvas as the firemen pray there will be enough to save at least one structure from the approaching flames. As everyone pauses to watch this hint of hope, a speeding car swerves to pass a horse-drawn carriage. The driver, heedless of the fire hose in his path, caring only for his own escape from the fires, bumps and rolls across the overworked hose, bursting the line and showering the street with the precious water. Never looking back, he disappears around a corner.

"Captain Sewell! Do you want us to go after him?"

Sewell's exasperation flows from a body that's been on duty all day. All the efforts of his well-trained firemen have been futile against this massive fire. His anger has been directed at the firestorm up until this moment:

"Forget him. He's long gone by now. Those were the best hoses we had! Pull out that section and do your best to reconnect the good ones."

BB and Pinkie overhear two fire fighters working on the hose:

"Sewell's okay. But I sure wish Chief Sullivan was here. He'd have a better idea about beating this fire."

"Didn't you hear? He was sleeping over at Company Number 3 in his apartment. The dome from the hotel next door fell right on his bedroom!"

"Is he all right?"

"He's over at the Presidio hospital. Pretty broken up. They don't think he'll make it."

"No wonder nobody seems to know what to do. All day I've been running around getting people out from under fallen buildings and trying to put out fires."

"I heard they saved the waterfront, at least the docks and warehouses on the piers. The Ferry Building too. Pumped water right outa the bay!"

"Yeah, but did you hear what happened in Chinatown? They blew up a drugstore with black powder. The explosion threw a flaming mattress across the street into a wooden building. Set the whole neighborhood on fire!"

"That's crazy! What were they thinking?"

"Trying to create a firebreak, I guess. Thank goodness they switched to dynamite. Some guy named Funston's supposed to have a plan."

"I hope *someone* has an idea 'cause it doesn't seem like we're making any headway. Looks like the whole city's going to burn. I don't know what's going to happen to all these people. Or us too!"

Just then a truck pulls up and an imposing uniformed man steps out. His double rows of brass buttons and the insignia on his military cap announce his authority. His bearded chin bounces up and down as he shouts out orders:

"Hook that hose up! It's imperative that we get water down to those areas!"

One fireman pokes the other with his elbow:

"Speak of the devil. It's old Funston himself!"

Just then a reporter steps forward and identifies himself:

"General Funston! I'm from *The Chronicle*. I know you're busy, but I'd like a few comments from you about the progress of today's fire battle. If it's okay, I'll just tag along while you work."

The general clasps his hands behind his back and begins to pace up and down the avenue. BB and Pinkie follow close by to hear the interview. Funston humors the reporter with brief answers to questions and elaborates when his emotions rise up.

"Where were you when the earthquake hit?"

"At my house. I climbed to the highest point on Nob Hill to look down at the city. Already several columns of smoke were rising from different areas. I hurried down California where fires even then were burning out of control."

"Why did you get involved?"

"It seemed like no one was taking charge. The police and fire department weren't going to control the people or the fire by themselves. They needed help."

"I heard the city is under martial law. Who ordered it?"

"The mayor made a declaration to keep order. I stepped in to enforce it."

"Have you received any further word from the mayor?"

"I've got my orders."

"Who exactly is in charge?"

"That would be *me*, of course."

"Do you also have charge over the firemen?"

"Considering they were leaderless... you heard about Sullivan? Terrible tragedy! The firemen needed a plan, so I gave it to them."

The general's voice rises with passion:

"They deserve the highest praise. Fighting with determination. Every battalion working tirelessly to conquer this devil of an enemy!"

"And your own men? How have they risen to the occasion?"

"Their bravery and daring are remarkable, risking their very lives to protect and save the population. They look for ways to help and don't wait around for orders."

"Is there anyone in particular you'd like to mention for the story? My readers like it when they can make a personal connection."

"Certainly! Men like Kugat and Jansen. One of my expert dynamiters, J. Curtin, set up a field hospital and organized the staff. Now *there's* a real hero! There's another young Marine Private around here somewhere. Burton's his name. Never seen anyone so cool and focused dealing with dynamite. I'm keeping him close for the next part of my plan."

"What plan is that?"

"Some think this street's wide enough to stop the fires. Just look at all these people hanging out here!"

"So you don't think it's going to stop here?"

"Sure it will! But not without some help. I'm organizing my crews to set dynamite on the side closest to the city. We're going to blow up everything in both directions along this line. We'll have a huge trench the whole length of the street."

BB and Pinkie can't believe what they're hearing. They look with alarm at the row of magnificent houses facing the street. The reporter continues:

"What happens if people refuse to leave their homes?"

General Funston doesn't miss a beat:

"They'll be shot, of course."

With that, the reporter folds his notebook and leaves. The general moves on.

"BB, he's serious!"

"I know! Look at all of these homes. They look really expensive."

"And who knows what's inside."

In contrast to the luxury on the far side of Van Ness is the growing collection of ordinary and extraordinary items and personal effects lining the sidewalk. BB and Pinkie walk by the usual trunks and suitcases, but also chairs, kitchen tables, and even an upright piano. The blank stares, signs of apathy or more likely shock, are alarming. An emotionally charged conversation draws their attention to a mansion on the next corner:

"Father, there's no reason to try to go to the office. There's nothing you can do! The building is still there, but the firemen told me it's completely gutted."

The elderly gentleman is not to be consoled:

"First my beautiful building! And now they want to destroy my home. The earthquake was bad enough. Why can't they just leave us alone? Your mother and I can't take much more."

"It'll be okay, Father. You and Mother can come stay with us. We're further to the west, and I've been assured by the authorities that the fire will never reach there."

"How are you so calm, John? We're losing everything we've worked for!"

"Actually I'm done with this place, especially now that our house down in the city is gone. I've been wanting to move the family to San Diego for some time now. I've started making investments down there already."

"What? How can you leave us now? The family needs you here to carry on!"

"No, Father. I've made up my mind. This earthquake and fire convinced me. When I build down there, and I *will* be building, I'll make sure any structure is as safe as possible from earthquakes and fires."

BB and Pinkie stare at each other, wondering who this person is. Just then a soldier arrives and addresses the older man:

"I'm sorry, Mr. Spreckels. It's time you and your wife evacuate. It'll be dark soon and you need to secure shelter. It looks like your son here is willing to help. I'll be back in a few minutes with my final orders."

The older gentleman calls into the house:

"Anna! Come on! Don't wait for the trumpet to blow! John will take us to his home."

A stately grand dame steps onto the porch in her finest. If she's going to parade down the street, she wants to look her best. But there is no need to walk the seven blocks. The very wealthy always seem to manage conveyance even in these uncertain times. Her son has secured a light carriage. He squeezes in between his elderly parents, takes the reins, and directs the horse up Clay. BB eagerly turns to Pinkie:

"That's the famous John Spreckels! San Diego wouldn't be the same without him!"

Their excitement at this encounter is interrupted by a rush of people following the disappearing carriage. Conflicting stories abound:

"Louise said the ferries are still running! Let's try to go down to the harbor."

"That's not what I heard! There's no escape unless we keep moving west."

"How is *that* an escape? Off the cliff at Land's End?"

"I don't believe anyone who says there are ferries. I'm too tired anyway to go all the way back to the bay."

"We've lost everything anyway. What's the difference if we keep going?"

"Maybe we can find a place for the night and move to the Presidio in the morning."

"It's only a couple of blocks to the park."

Men, women, and children grab their few salvaged possessions and drag themselves up yet another hill. BB and Pinkie witness moments of kindness in the trail of wretched souls. Willing, tender hands reach out to assist the blind, the lame, and the elderly. Behind them General Funston orders a battalion of armed regulars from Fort Mason to stand guard the length of Van Ness. Everyone must be off the streets by 8:30 or be shot! There's no other option but to join the flow to Lafayette Park.

CHAPTER SEVENTY-TWO

First Night in the Park

The park is already filling up with refugees too tired to go any farther that day. A few lucky families secure tents donated by the military. Others spread blankets and settle children down for the night. Some create shelters with sheets and broken lumber from nearby collapsed buildings. Pinkie and BB spot a place beneath a tall shade tree with a view to the city. Soldiers patrol the area assuring the destitute people they are safe. One man pulls out a book and reads by the light from the fires below. A baby wails. An ambulance clangs. Occasional carts and wagons roll by. Otherwise all is quiet. BB and Pinkie hug their knees and look out to the panorama of destruction where hundreds are crushed beneath the fallen buildings. They shudder thinking of the dying being consumed by the hungry flames. Mesmerized by the unfolding catastrophe, they don't notice a scruffy man cautiously approaching:

"Mind if I sit a spell with you? I don't see any of my mates in this park."

BB pats the ground and the fellow slumps down. A heavy odor of smoke clings to his disheveled outfit:

"I thought I'd have a safe place for the night down at Union Square."

"We were down there earlier this morning helping out with the food."

"Yeah? The army set up tents and food lines later, and people were hunkering down for the night. Hey, I've got some extra bread. You look like you could use it."

He pulls out a baguette and hands it to Pinkie. She ignores his grubby hands and gratefully accepts. She passes half to BB as the man continues:

"Around 8:00 things looked pretty good. The worst was the police wagons dropping off bodies in the square. If someone was sleeping on the grass, they'd just roll over to make room for the dead. Didn't seem to bother some, but it gave me the creeps. Then this huge boom came from the south. I complained to a soldier about dynamiting buildings when people were trying to sleep. He said it sounded more like a gas explosion. You'd think by now people would know you can't light stoves!"

"How far away was it?"

"Not sure. Maybe a block or two? But you could already see the flames reaching into the sky! So much for a quiet night! People packed up and cleared out. There was a whole mountain of trunks, but there wasn't enough time to move them. I skedaddled out of there as fast as I could. Saw people moving up the hill, so I joined them."

"Do you live around here?"

"*Here?* Do I look like some swell? Nah. Got a place in a rooming house downtown. Well, I *used* to have a place. Not sure what I'll do now. You can see how the fire climbed right up to Nob Hill. It's like some creature that can't get enough of its fill."

Even this far from the fire, Pinkie can hear its hungry roar. Her voice trembles:

"Do you think we're safe here?"

"Don't worry your pretty little head. You saw that street we crossed? We're fine!"

"But what about them?"

Pinkie points to the inferno below where the walls of fire merge into one huge bonfire. Flames engulf the entire city center from north to south.

"If they got to the liquor before they closed down the bars, they were probably too drunk to get out of the way. The fire just ate 'em up, wretched souls!"

Tears fill Pinkie's eyes. She looks at BB who's also shoving down his emotions. He's remembering the dance hall woman who, just a few hours ago, was so self-assured in her depravity. To emphasize their peril, a tremendous aftershock rocks the park. Buildings nearby that had withstood the earlier onslaught are too weak to stand and crumble into ruin. The little courage people had is wrung right out of their hearts.

"Pinkie, we'd better get some rest. Who knows what we'll face in the morning."

They lean back against the wide tree trunk and sleep the sleep of warriors gearing up for battle. Below in the burning and smoke, darkness hides the reigning chaos. The Abyss is still in business. Most neighborhoods are deserted, but elsewhere vandals and looters run wild. Despite the mayor's orders, there isn't enough manpower to cover every block, every situation, every crime. BB's head droops until it rests on Pinkie's head. She's too exhausted to notice. Adversity is binding them together in unexpected ways that will change their lives forever.

CHAPTER SEVENTY-THREE

Interlude with Fame

"Bakers wanted! Bakers wanted! Union telegraphers wanted!"

The early morning cries wake BB and Pinkie from a sound sleep. These two requests keep ringing through the otherwise silent dawn. People need bread. The world must learn of San Francisco's dire straits. And then a bugle sounds. Sentries pacing and officers galloping by on their horses declare to all: Military occupation. Martial law.

"Pinkie, I hoped I'd wake up and this would've been just a nightmare."

BB helps Pinkie to her feet. Down in the city the dynamiting resumes. Shattered walls and wrecked buildings erupt in orange flames. Vast mauve and pink tinted smoke plumes rise to the heavens. A blood-red sun briefly breaks through the smoke-shrouded morning sky and then disappears, hidden for the remainder of the hot, dusty day. The wind shifts and blows toward the park. Ashes and smoke sting their eyes. The earth shakes and trembles. A huge explosion bursts far to the left and starts another fire. Propelled by gale force wind it tears through a neighborhood. BB and Pinkie stand motionless for several minutes, mesmerized by their view to the mayhem below.

"BB, I don't hear any more blasts. Maybe they changed their mind or gave up!"

"Come on. Let's go back to Van Ness. The fire hasn't reached there yet."

As they leave the park to cross the street, an army wagon rumbles by with supplies from across the bay. People welcome the packages of food. Makeshift brick cookstoves appear in the middle of the street. Against the tide of refugees, BB and Pinkie press their way to Van Ness where they encounter an endless line of soldiers. There are no explosions. Just the ongoing dull rumble and thunder of the furnace below. They walk south until they reach the cable cars still parked down California Street.

"BB! Pinkie! Over here! I want you to meet a friend."

Sitting on the steps of a partially collapsed house is Arnold Genthe, the photographer from the day before. With him are two people whose appearance seems out of place. Their clothes are almost spotless and their hair is neatly styled and combed. Neither displays any distress. In fact they seem eager to experience the day's next adventure.

"This is Jack London and his wife Charmian. Maybe you've heard of his recent book, *Call of the Wild.*"

BB can't believe his ears. Of course he knows the book! He studied it in his sophomore English class. The handsome man with wavy dark hair and piercing gaze stands up and brings his wife to her feet. Her gentle eyes and soft, full, smiling mouth put them at ease. Pinkie and BB are immediately welcomed into the intimate circle.

"When Jack felt and heard the earthquake, he knew it was a story he didn't want to miss. They finally got across the bay just before dawn."

Jack continues with their story:

"We saw the smoke from the fire yesterday, forty miles away at our ranch. It reached hundreds of feet into the sky. Charmian is always up for an adventure and insisted on coming with me. This morning we caught a ride in Sausalito on a supply boat going to Fort Mason and then walked up to a friend's house on Nob Hill."

Pinkie can't believe what she's hearing. Why would they actually choose *to immerse themselves in this tragedy? Charmian invites them to sit down:*

"We were able to gather a few supplies from the boat plus the food we brought with us. I'm so glad we can share our bounty."

BB and Pinkie gratefully accept the meal, not knowing if another will come that day. Jack, the consummate storyteller, continues:

"So I am sitting on the steps of my friend's Nob Hill mansion. The sun's coming up and people are on the move: Chinese, Italians, Negroes, Japanese. The whole world was passing in front of us. Right Charmian?"

"Oh, yes! The grand palaces of San Francisco were all around us. But to the east and south, huge walls of fire were coming right toward us. I don't mind a little excitement, but I couldn't seem to impress on Jack the urgency of our plight."

"Now, Charmian, you know I'll always keep you safe! I was amazed at how quickly our friend was able to come to terms with the inevitable! He spoke of the loss of his fortunes in such a cheerful way. The house behind him that was doomed. His wife's priceless china. The oriental rug and grand piano in his sitting room."

"I couldn't wait any longer for Jack to get us out of there. Down the street we saw a massive wooden mansion catching fire. Soldiers kept moving closer, pushing people along. Explosions and crashing walls and raging flames were closing in on us."

"I got you out safely, my dear. No worries. Anyway, was I ever glad to meet up with Arnold. And now we have two more friends!"

If truth be told, BB and Pinkie are glad for this diversion from the misery around them. The little group distracts each other with stories of their earthquake escapades. Jack keeps his notebook open, recording descriptions of the endless supply of colorful characters milling about or interesting tidbits from their conversations. Charmian continues to offer Pinkie and BB food from her provisions. Though they know it may be a while before they have this many choices again, they are careful not to abuse her generosity. Hours slip by unnoticed. Just as Jack London is about to regale them with another story of his adventures in the wild, a bugle blows and a soldier shouts:

"Time for everyone to move back from this area. The fires are coming fast. Dynamiting will resume immediately. General Funston's orders."

They stand up to view the growing threat from below. Although the winds from the bay have died down, the fire itself creates its own whirlwind. Strong updrafts carry chunks of burning embers high into the sky. They spread in all directions to ignite new fires. The extreme heat causes buildings to spontaneously combust. The battle for San Francisco takes an ominous turn. London attaches himself to one of the soldiers, hoping to garner more information:

"What's the plan? I thought this street was wide enough to stop the fire."

"We did too. But south of here it's tried to jump the divide."

"So how wide does General Funston think it needs to be?"

"We'll dynamite every structure over one story high on the east side of Van Ness."

"How far toward the city will you go?"

"One hundred feet."

"A hundred feet! Isn't that a little drastic?"

"The street's over a hundred feet wide. We need to double that to stop the fire. Funston's sure this'll do it."

"I hope he's right."

"He'd better be. Or the rest of the city'll be gone."

Armed soldiers begin escorting stubborn owners from their magnificent homes. Some prod the reluctant residents with their fixed bayonets. Several of the occupants huddle on their porches refusing to budge as the trumpet announces the destruction of their homes. Only the threat of being shot convinces them their defiance is pointless. The earsplitting dynamite explosions begin. Farther down the avenue, thunderous rows of cannon shoot gunpowder through the windows of the buildings. Beautiful mansions erupt and then crumble to the ground sending great clouds of smoke skyward. Soldiers set fire to the buildings below to meet the hungry flames marching from the city, undeterred by man's efforts to halt them. BB and Pinkie cover their faces from the showers of ash and draw away from the group to discuss their options. Just in front of them on the far side of the avenue, the line of doomed cable cars patiently waits.

"BB, They're not going to make it. Nobody seems interested in moving them."

"I know. I was hoping Friedel would have good news when this is over."

"We need to find a new location for tonight. You saw all those people flooding into the park this morning. I'm sure our spot's been taken."

"I'd like to get farther from this firebreak in case the General's wrong."

"We need a more permanent location. Who knows how long we'll be camping out?"

They exchange goodbyes with Genthe and the Londons, who are eager to experience the next round of firefighting up close. BB and Pinkie wish them well and join the stream of people climbing up California.

CHAPTER SEVENTY-FOUR

Saving Mother

Within a few short blocks the path west flattens out. Everyone is grateful for this relief from the continual climb up and down the hills. BB and Pinkie keep pace with the more able-bodied travelers and listen to the rumors.

"The Presidio is offering food and shelter. I'm hoping there's still room for us all. Seems like the whole city's on the move!"

"I heard it's already filled up. Someone said the fires are sweeping the North Shore and moving that direction. I'm staying up here."

As they cross the next avenue a huge group breaks off to the right toward the Presidio. Pinkie and BB decide the path forward is a safer option. A man from the breakaway group calls back to the ones continuing west:

"Good luck to you! Keep going and the fires'll chase you like a pack of lemmings right off the cliffs at Lands End!"

His taunting laughter rings in their ears as they continue west. They grow more and more worried they've made a wrong choice. Their apprehension grows until they meet a large group coming from the direction of the Presidio. Unsure of their next move, everyone halts. A cavalryman rides up to address the crowd:

"Listen up! The Major is sending you to Golden Gate Park. Plenty of room for everyone. The army is handing out provisions, so you all will be safe."

Relieved that the decision has been made for them, the combined group of exiles turns to the path of hope. Pinkie taps the arm of a Chinese gentleman walking next to her:

"Why are you way up here? Didn't you get to the Presidio in time?"

"We heard they weren't accepting Chinese. No food for us. We turned away from the bay and walked up here instead."

"That can't be right! Why would you be refused?"

"Because we are Chinese. That is all the reason they need."

Pinkie looks around at the calm, accepting faces of his group. Women and children in beautiful green, gold, and dark pink silk jackets and pants pad along on embroidered shoes stained by the miles of walking through debris. Teenage girls take charge of their younger siblings, often carrying babies slung on their backs. Old grannies hobble along under the watchful care of their sons. Each family group has its own pearl-inlaid chest carried between two poles.

"BB, they're just as desperate as everyone else. Why turn them away?"

A band of Italians joins them from a side street adding to the kaleidoscope of costumes and tongues. Men strain under their load of rescued possessions. Women carry baskets of personal treasures on their heads. As they cross Geary, a careless lad runs headlong into an older woman who is inching her way into the wall of people. BB catches the bucket she's carrying just before its contents spill onto the street, certain to be trampled under foot. She cries out in a heavy French accent:

"*Mon Dieu!* You saved me! My family's future is in this bucket. You saved Mother!"

Pinkie and BB curiously peer under the cloth, expecting to see money or a collection of jewels. Instead they find a lump of dough.

"Yesterday morning our bakery burned down after the earthquake. My daughter Lucie and I saved Mother before we escaped up Broadway."

"We still don't understand what he saved."

"*Vraiment!* This is the Mother! The dough starter for our bread! My husband Isidore got it from the gold miners over fifty years ago. Our bread is special because each loaf contains the same wild yeast."

"You mean the bread you make is fifty years old?"

"You could say that! But we make our bread fresh each morning. We were doing just that when the shaking began."

"How did you get all the way up here?"

"Lucie and I saw Chinatown burning and knew we couldn't get to the ferry. The fire was closing in from every direction. The only place that wasn't full of smoke was toward Van Ness, so we climbed up the hill. We slept in a park. I think it was named for some Frenchman."

"Lafayette? We were there too!"

"This morning they were calling for bakers. I told my daughter we had to find a new location for our bakery. We walked along Geary looking for a building. But the day dragged on and we weren't having any luck. We passed cemeteries where people were camping out. Not for me! Lucie went ahead to Golden Gate Park to find us a place for the night."

"Did you ever find a new building for your bakery?"

"*Mais oui!* Just back there. A strong brick building, right on a corner. Excellent location for business!"

"So did you buy it?"

"Not yet. My money's in the Bank of Italy. I hope it's safe!"

Pinkie and BB give each other a confident smile.

"Oh, we think it is!"

"Mr. Giannini is really good about helping out regular working people like us with loans. When this is over, I'll speak with him."

"So how do you know the building is yours?"

"We shook hands! The owner and I did. After this earthquake and fires, he's taking his family away from San Francisco. But I know my bread needs to be baked here where the salty fog kisses it. I can hear my Isidore: 'Louise, *ma cherie.* You must stay! You must keep going!' If he was here he would tell you *merci beaucoup* for keeping Mama dough healthy so she can make lots of babies!"

She gives them both a generous hug. BB and Pinkie share a cheery laugh with this optimistic woman who adds such joy to their trek. In the midst of tragedy she is looking to the future of her business, her life, and her city as well. But a few blocks later at the edge of the park, they meet up once more with the ultimate pessimist.

CHAPTER SEVENTY-FIVE

Safe for Now

"What do you mean you can't take us? I am NOT going to spend another night in this disgusting park in this godforsaken city!"

"I'm sorry sir, but I'm with the water company. I can't stop what I'm doing. People are depending on me."

The indignant man gestures to his companion who brings over a large satchel. Opening the bag, the man pulls out a stack of bank notes:

"How much do you want? Name your price!"

"It's not the money. It's the responsibility I have."

In a huff, the surly man announces to the nearby crowd:

"Can ANYONE get me to the Ocean View train station? I *must* get to New York!"

One man recognizes this ill-tempered gentleman and confronts him:

"Wait a minute! Aren't you the same guy down in Union Square yesterday? Caruso, isn't it? You were blubbering something awful."

The famous singer straightens up and sticks out his chest:

"Nothing of the sort! I was simply commenting on how much I missed my country."

"Well, we've all had enough of your *comments*. And your complaints! And your cowardice! You showed the white feather to the whole world. There was a whole bunch of 'em stickin' to your back!"

This last accusation draws laughter and derision from the gathered crowd. They turn away from the sputtering Caruso who continues to rant. Only his companion is affected in the slightest by his torrent of invective. Pinkie and BB are glad they can dismiss this churlish character and focus on someone more agreeable. They turn back to Louise:

"Did your daughter say where she would be? This is a really big place."

"Let me see. It was a strange combination of words. A meadow I think."

Nightfall is fast approaching. BB spots a policeman to ask directions.

"The only meadow I know of is Speedway Meadow."

Louise perks up:

"That's the one! It doesn't sound very relaxing does it?"

The policeman assures them:

"It's a big place over there to the right. Plenty of room. Lots of families are already there. You should be safe."

Pinkie is still concerned about the approaching fires:

"Any news about the firebreak at Van Ness? It was pretty chaotic when we left there."

"General Funston has things under control. You shouldn't have to move again once you're settled in."

The relative safety of Golden Gate Park welcomes the exhausted people who stake out temporary residence on the vast lawns or under shrubs and trees. Huddled together, many are already sound asleep. In the glow from the fires in the city, BB and Pinkie join Louise in shouting her daughter's name. At last a voice returns their calls:

"Mama! You made it! I was so worried. You took so long to get here."

"Lucie, *ma cherie*. You know your mama. I needed to find our building this very day. I wouldn't have slept a wink tonight otherwise. Let me introduce our new friends."

They settle in under a huge overhanging bush. Nearby an older gentleman sits with his wife who is wrapped in a fur coat against the cold April wind. A man and his three young children huddle together under a blanket. The youngest clutches her soot-streaked doll. When Pinkie asks about his wife, he hesitates, choking on raw emotions:

"We were lucky to escape our home. The second story collapsed into our bedroom, crushing my wife. We didn't have time to retrieve her body because the fires were so close. I grabbed the three little ones and as many clothes as we could carry."

Pinkie turns from this sorrowful scene to notice a dignified Spanish woman with only a blanket to cover her. A cooking pot and a few clothes lie at her feet. It has surely been more than a day since her long black hair has seen a comb. Her future is uncertain. Yet she sits and gazes into the night's intense glare, a serene smile radiating from her face.

As Pinkie and BB drift off to sleep, the wind gradually turns the fire a new direction. Those who now call Golden Gate Park home are unaware of the spectacle unfolding near their sanctuary. The fire advances rapidly, especially when it reaches any wooden structures. From the Mission District to Nob Hill and then on to Van Ness, thousands of dwellings, both humble and palatial, surrender to the voracious appetite of the flames. The furnace thunders its victory. Finally at midnight it fractures the line of defense and leaps across Van Ness.

CHAPTER SEVENTY-SIX

Everyone Has a Story

Everywhere firefighters shout to each other as the flames and glowing cinders sail over the firebreak. The great divide everyone trusted to break the back of the fire proves vulnerable after all. Armed only with wet blankets and rugs, the firemen beat down the errant blazes until by morning's first light all is once again secured. Had they failed, there was nothing to stop the fires from racing to the cliffs beyond.

Totally unaware of the danger that had threatened during the night, the park yawns awake to another day of uncertainty. Numbed by the shock of the last two days, people have grown accustomed to their new way of life, calmly indifferent to the fact that they've lost everything. Families line up for the day's food allowance. Mothers hold out containers for their ration from the huge cans of milk. Pinkie and BB enjoy a humble but sustaining breakfast with Louise and her daughter.

The most precious commodity is drinking water, carefully rationed as so many drops of liquid gold. BB and Pinkie join the slow moving line inching forward. Standing patiently with cups in hand is the full spectrum of San Francisco citizens: men, women, and children, rich and poor, with no regard to nationality, age, or social standing. All require this basic necessity of life, drawn from the city's few artesian wells. All display courtesy and kindness as they wait for their share. As BB and Pinkie reach their turn, a man in an expensive long frock coat strides to the front, demanding to be served:

"Quick! Just one cupful for my wife! She's almost fainting with thirst!"

"Yes, but that cupful belongs to someone else."

The man in charge calmly but fiercely stands his ground and points to the end of the long line that stretches into the distance. He then greets Pinkie and BB with a smile and fills their cups.

Restored by their meal and water, they explore the park's structures, many severely damaged by the earthquake and aftershocks. The band shell sinks in the middle, cracks running through the pillars and stone work. Everything is a mass of brick and glass and stone. The only survivor is the glass dome of the conservatory, almost every pane amazingly preserved. A band of young boys climbs through the wreckage. One lad with a smudged face and cheeky grin speaks up:

"Me and my pals got together a couple of days ago when our folks were getting us safe from the fires. We wanted to see what was happening. All the firemen and soldiers and policemen! Isn't it exciting?"

BB smiles as he remembers his curiosity at their age and his itch to explore. Pinkie is more concerned about their welfare:

"But what about your parents? Are they okay? Where are they now?"

"In the park. We can look around as long as we don't cause any problems."

One of his pals runs up swiping his arm across his runny nose:

"My mama really got in trouble. She was warming up milk for Virginia, my baby sister. She lit a little Sterno, thinking no one would see it. Then BAM! BAM! BAM! BAM!"

Pinkie draws back imagining a gas explosion:

"Was she hurt?"

"Nah. It was a policeman banging on our door yelling: 'Madam, put out the light and if you do that again I'll have to shoot you!' Mama started to yell back, but Papa put out the flame and told her to be quiet."

The gang of ragamuffins runs off. BB and Pinkie wander through the displaced people idling away the day throughout the park, enjoying the mild weather and the relief from imminent danger. They overhear stories and rumors from those who are reliving the recent days:

"My brother Sam had just fallen asleep after his night shift when that big one hit. He swore at some unknown fellow to stop rocking his bed!"

"The first night we saw people sleeping propped up in doorways or against hydrants or just lying on the curbs. We found a little park to sleep in but all around us the flames sputtered and crackled like a giant bonfire. Soldiers came and moved us on. We hardly slept at all moving from one place to the next all night long."

"You think that was bad? In the middle of the night the fires kept pushing us farther and farther until we got to Fort Mason. No food. No water. And right next to us was a pile of dead bodies starting to stink. We could see the flames jumping from one building to another, closer and closer. That's when our group decided to tramp up the hill to this park. I finally slept. All day yesterday and last night too."

"I was downtown in the burnt out areas yesterday. Wanted to see if my shop had survived. I could feel the hot street stones right through my shoes!

Vigilantes were roaming the streets. Looters were picking through what was left of Chinatown."

"Does anyone know what happened to the Mint?"

"I heard thieves got away with over three hundred million dollars."

"Naw. That couldn't have happened. That place is too secure. Probably just burned down like everything else around there."

"I think they saved the paintings in the museum up on Nob Hill."

"Someone said the Cliff House fell in the ocean."

BB and Pinkie continue toward Van Ness where they last saw their friend Arnold Genthe. From the next corner an armed soldier shouts to BB:

"You there! You look like a strong enough fellow. I've got a work crew that needs some help. Your friend can wait for you over there out of the way."

A group of able-bodied men of various ages is clearing rubble that blocks the street. BB joins in, eager to do his part. Pinkie feels silly just standing around, so she starts picking up and tossing scattered bricks. After almost two hours with no break, one of the men stands up to stretch his back. A soldier shouts to him to get back to work. The man angrily answers back:

"How much longer do you expect us to keep this up? I've got things to do. I can't be here all day and night just because you say so."

The soldier simply brandishes his rifle with its gleaming bayonet:

"Quit cher bellyaching! I haven't slept in three days. And neither have any of the firemen, policemen or other soldiers. Or the doctors and nurses either! I don't need to hear complaints from the likes of you!"

BB puts his head down and keeps working as the daylight gives way to dark. He steals a sidelong glance at Pinkie who gives him an alarmed look. Just how long will *they be here? A poke in the ribs quickly brings him back to his task. The young man who jabbed him nods and then nudges BB closer to the edge of the workers. Gradually they fall behind with Pinkie casually shadowing their movements. When the soldiers take a moment to chat among themselves, the three of them make a break around the corner. They hear shouts to stop, but they pray they're out of range of the rifles and keep running. The young man leads them straight ahead through a grove of trees. They climb up higher and higher, finally reaching a meadow. The entire expanse of the city spreads out before them. Gasping for breath the man finally speaks:*

"I hope you don't mind me dragging you along. I've been clearing that street since morning with no break. Those soldiers work guys like us 'til we drop in our tracks. Didn't want to see that happening to you two, especially your girlfriend."

"Oh, she's not my..."

But the man isn't listening. The terrifying sight holds him in spellbound fascination. The view is at once both horrific and majestic. There is nothing between them and the bay except the giant crater of a churning volcano. The entire city is one solid mass of fire. Huge buildings shoot flames high to the heavens. Only when the demon fire's hunger is satiated, when it's had its fill of misery, will it stop.

"I was on my way here when I got dragged into that work crew. I'd heard rumors that my neighborhood was gone. I had to see for myself."

"Can you see your house?"

Their eyes follow where his finger points.

"Right over there. My family's lived there our whole lives. Four generations under one roof. They're all over at the park. Got my grandma out safely and my parents. My wife and kids are okay with this camping out thing, but it's hard sleeping on the ground for the older folks."

Despite the reality of the terrible spectacle, they can't tear their eyes from its lurid fascination. The painful agony throbs in his voice:

"There it goes! All our dreams gone!"

The tears he's been holding back flood down his cheeks. The horrendous sight holds his gaze for several heart wrenching moments before he speaks again:

"When all else falls away, what do you have left? Who you really are!"

BB has heard these words before. Now they sink deep into his heart. Powerful booming explosions resound in the night. The three of them sit on the grassy dome and ride out yet another tremor, experiencing man's frailty in the face of nature's power. The smoky pall overhead accompanies the silence reserved for a graveyard. Again the man speaks:

"I can't believe I'm watching this. I can hardly tell where the buildings were. It's one big glowing bed of burning embers. When will it end?"

BB pulls Pinkie to her feet. She softly encourages their new friend:

"I'm sure your family is wondering what's happened to you. Don't you think it's time we got back to the park?"

"Right. You're right! Come on! My wife must be really worried! Let's go!"

They stumble down the hill and back onto the streets, being careful to avoid the work party. They join a new group trudging to the park who are too worn out to talk. Soon the man is greeted by a very relieved family. BB and Pinkie make their way through the masses, wondering what the future holds for all of these people and their city.

CHAPTER SEVENTY-SEVEN

The Blanket

The dazed resignation on the faces of the newest arrivals testifies to the physical and emotional burden they carry on their shoulders. Weary and hungry they sink to the ground. Others generously share their food from the earlier canteen line with these desperate survivors. Army tents now pop up here and there. There are a few mattresses, a true luxury, salvaged from abandoned homes. Most people are scattered out in the open over the hillsides and grass with only a blanket to protect them from the night air. Some don't have even that. Louise beckons for them to join her and her daughter for another night of an uncertain future:

"Over here! We're over here! How was your day? I was praying nothing had happened to you two."

Louise is quick to pick up on BB's melancholy mood:

"What's wrong?"

"These three days have been like a bad dream. I can't explain it. There's just a feeling of emptiness that's filling me up deep inside."

"You need a project to show you there's hope. Because there is!"

BB is listening to the music of languages around him, trying to identify the various tongues, when a woman's loud voice calls out:

"I'm looking for baby clothes. Anyone have anything they can spare? I'll even take a coat or some clean rags. A blanket maybe?"

The woman stops to explain her need to Louise and the rest:

"You wouldn't believe how many babies have been born in the last couple of days. Right here in the park. One woman just had triplets! We have nothing to wrap the poor things in until we can find some proper clothes. The mothers are desperate."

Louise gives BB a look he can't ignore. Maybe this is the project that will take his mind off his own sorrow and give him purpose. He reaches into the backpack and pulls out his wallet:

"How much do you need?"

With hand on hip, the woman shoots back a derisive answer:

"Money? You want to give me *money*? What am I supposed to do with that? Do you see any stores around here? The army took over all the food and supplies so people wouldn't hoard or try to make a buck."

When she moves on BB meekly stuffs the wallet back into the pack. His fingers brush against the small blanket Carole had given them. As he draws it out, it grows and expands.

"Wait! Come back! I've got a blanket you can use!"

The woman hurries back, and then her smile fades:

"It's way too big for these tiny babies. Besides I need several."

Pinkie is sure this blanket is another sign they are supposed to help. Carefully she examines one of the edges until she discovers a notch. Grasping both sides, she tears off a section and hands it to the woman:

"Will this work?"

"It's perfect for swaddling a newborn! How many more are there?"

There are notches all along the border. As Pinkie rips off pieces and hands them to the woman, the blanket never gets smaller. Finally, loaded down with a bundle of baby wrappings, the woman leaves. A young mother steps forward with two small children.

"Would there be enough of your blanket for us? We had to leave so suddenly I couldn't think of everything we might need."

BB takes the blanket and runs his hand down the edge. The notch is much farther down this time. He tears away a new section large enough for the woman and her children to cuddle under. The youngest tugs at his mother:

"Mama, let's go home now."

"Hush, dear."

"But I want to go home!"

"We haven't a home anymore, dear one."

The mother and her children step carefully between families settled in for the night until they find an open spot.

"Now lie down and let Mama cover you up with this wonderful blanket."

As the little family begins what they hope are a restful few hours, two frantic parents rush into the small gathering:

"We can't find our boy! He wandered off hours ago and we've been looking and looking. He's just disappeared!"

The mother cries out to a policeman who has stepped up to help:

"He probably went exploring for bugs like he always does."

"There are so many children here, madam. Sir, what does your son look like?"

"He's only four years old. He fell against our garden wall during the second earthquake. His face is a mess. Maybe even a broken nose!"

"He's not a strong child. He's always getting sick."

The policeman tries to calm the mother and offer hope to the desperate parents:

"We'll pass the word around. See if anyone has noticed."

"He'll be too shy to ask anyone for help."

"What's his name?"

"Ansel."

"And your names?"

"Adams."

"Well, Mr. and Mrs. Adams, you stay right here. No sense having you wandering around too. If we find him…"

The officer looks at her alarmed face:

"I'm sorry. *When* we find him, we want to get him to you right away."

The parents find a spot nearby to sit and wait. Offers of bread and tea surround them.

Meanwhile word travels quickly that there might be a blanket if anyone needs one. Wealthy and poor, old and young, they line up. Pinkie and BB take turns ripping off pieces, each notch location measuring the exact size needed for whoever is in front of them. Miraculously the blanket keeps giving.

"I don't suppose you'd have one for me."

BB looks up into the face of the dance hall woman he's met twice before. She stands proudly, yet her eyes beg for mercy. It would be so easy for him to remember only her devious ways and her mockery. Yet he's witnessed the misery felt by all of San Francisco, including this woman who was so arrogant not long ago. His generous smile disarms her:

"Sure. Is it just yourself or do you need two blankets?"

"I... I... no. I mean yes. It's just me."

Her shoulders sag. No longer confident in her self-reliance, she waits for the handout. BB carefully folds her blanket and gently offers the gift. She slowly walks away but can't resist a last look back. BB waves and nods his head. Yes, he remembers her. And yes, he forgives her. Pinkie has been busy talking to the next man in line. However, she catches a glimpse of the woman's face when she glances back at BB:

"Isn't that the woman from the Barbary Coast?"

BB views this last encounter with an understanding he's never felt before:

"Maybe. Then again, I don't think she's the same woman."

Just then a cry pierces the darkness:

"We found the boy!"

The officer's shout turns the distraught parents' hope into joy. And then the heartbroken mother catches sight of the lifeless body in the arms of the policeman:

"Ansel! My baby!"

"He's cold as ice. Found him under a bush at the edge of the clearing. If it weren't for a little dog sniffing around and barking, I don't think we'd have even noticed him."

The parents plead to those around:

"We need a warm blanket. Can anyone spare an extra blanket?"

BB shouts above the crowd:

"Bring him over here!"

Pinkie locates the next notch and with BB's help pulls off a huge section. The parents quickly bundle their boy in the warm blanket. His father holds him close willing his own body heat into his son. The desperate man quietly weeps. His tears drop silently onto the boy's cheek. Barely perceptible, color begins to spread across Ansel's bruised and battered face. His blue lips turn a pale pink. Finally, as he begins to stir, the mother and father utter a cry of relief. Before long they are smothering love on their precious only child who they came so close to losing. Their solemn faces turn to pure delight as the young boy slowly regains awareness of his surroundings. He shyly snugs into his father's shoulder as the sympathetic onlookers break out in cheers and clapping. But more people are waiting for their own portion of the everlasting cover. A burly man steps up and jerks it away from BB's grasp:

"Here! Let me have that! You're too slow!"

He rips off a piece for himself and passes it down the line. Watching the extraordinary blanket disappear into the night, Pinkie and BB remember the third riddle:

"What can give yet never grows smaller?"

BB and Pinkie have their own blankets, thanks to the two bakers and their generosity. One more night sleeping rough in Golden Gate Park. The name mocks so many dashed dreams of those who have lost their homes and are facing the reality that all of their material wealth is completely destroyed. And then in the wee hours of the morning a horseman gallops through the park shouting:

"The fire is under control!"

Jubilation erupts and then finally settles down as it begins to rain. The steady drizzle becomes a torrential downpour that soaks bedding and clothes and turns the ground into a soggy, muddy shambles. The combined odor of wet clothing and unwashed bodies fills the night air. The cold wind from the ocean adds to the misery of the dismal scene. As long as the rain continues, the only choice is to hunker down under any available covering. BB and Pinkie huddle together, soaked to the skin. With the rising sun, the rain lets up. If the fires are over, the work of renewal has just begun.

Between brief showers, people try to kindle fires to dispel the chill. Small teepee-shaped fire starters spring up everywhere. But they soon sputter out because the wood is so wet. As BB looks around he pulls out the smooth, blackened piece of wood:

"I know what these fires need. Remember what Carol told us: 'The Colonel said it has the power to regenerate.' And we had that great fire in that old island castle."

"You're right! She said we might need it on our journey. It must be now!"

Pinkie takes out the pocketknife and box of wooden matches from their emergency kit. They slog through the meadow, ignoring their shoes filling with water, intent only on helping folks get their fires going. Pinkie slices a generous sliver from the redwood. BB lights it and tosses it confidently into the wet campfire wood. Immediately a roaring fire blazes up. They leave the dumbstruck family and move on to the next group.

"How do you do that, mister?"

BB looks down at one of the boys from the day before. He winks and whispers:

"It's a mystery!"

Pinkie grabs BB's arm and hurries him along:

"Why did you tell him that?"

"What should I say? A lady said it had the power to regenerate? Same thing, isn't it?"

Pinkie doesn't have a good answer. The two of them continue with their mission to light up this part of the park and give people relief. Finally BB scans the area:

"I think we're done, Pinkie."

He checks the piece of blackened wood, still its original size, and shoves it in his pocket. From the distance a message relays from one group to the next until it reaches them:

"Fire's out! Fire's out!"

BB wants to join the celebrations, but he feels a pull back to the city. Pinkie agrees it's time to move on. Setting their faces to the east, they zigzag their way back to Van Ness to see with their own eyes the results of the fire battle. The fire is gone, but the aftermath is heartbreaking.

CHAPTER SEVENTY-EIGHT

The View to Annihilation

"Oh, BB! It's so sad! They're all lost!"

All along California Street are burned-out hulks of the famous cable cars. The fire-charred hand brakes and cable grips stand straight up, never to be grasped again. BB and Pinkie walk past one scorched wreck after another:

"I hope little Friedel never sees this, BB. She would lose all hope."

They pass blackened areas still smoldering in spite of the deluge of the night before. The acrid smell of wet ash and charred wood fills their noses and lingers on their clothes. A wilderness of ruins spreads out in every direction. Coming to the heart of Nob Hill, they spot a silhouette against the city sky. It's their friend Arnold Genthe with his ever-present camera:

"BB! Pinkie! I'm so glad to see you both are no worse for wear."

"Hello, Mr. Genthe! Good to see you too!"

Genthe sweeps his arm to the city:

"There she is in all of her desolation. Thousands of blocks gone. Three days of fires on top of an earthquake didn't spare much. But what pictures! Look over there!"

Pinkie and BB don't share his enthusiasm. All they see is utter ruin. Fallen electric trolley poles. Tangled wires. Girders warped by the blast furnace of the previous days. Windows melted like butter are now hardened into pools of glass. Remnants of brick chimneys stand guard over the scorched wasteland. A few lonely naked steel towers overlook what had been the heart of the city's wealth and power but is now a sea of ashes. As they watch, a precarious wall finally topples and sends up a cloud of ash. Hundreds of bodies lie beneath the sea of desolation never to be claimed, never to be counted. The once great city of industry and world commerce is nothing but a memory. It's hard not to feel depressed. But Genthe is determined to rise above the despair:

"I'm glad I'm here to record San Francisco's turning point. I know many are leaving, vowing never to return. They feel the city is done, never to rise again. Their fears rule their future.

But there are those who can see beyond the confusion and doom. They are the ones I observed living their lives in whatever way they could in spite of the unheard-of conditions we were all experiencing.

We seem to be in a world apart from everything else. All our values have been reimagined. This has hit both rich and poor. And right now money doesn't seem to matter. Only human life."

BB can't help but think of Caruso and his angry words. The earthquake that spared no one, the mad dash to escape the fires, the camps of displaced families looking for comfort. All those stories are now seared into his memory like the fire itself. And then he remembers Louise and Lucie and all the brave people who watched out for the safety of others. Genthe continues to muse on human nature:

"Wouldn't it be wonderful if life could always be this way... caring only for each other... everything shared?"

He sighs and surveys the destroyed mansions around them:

"Not sure if we'll see those palaces of the rich rising from the dust heap. But I can't imagine San Francisco without the Crocker, Stanford, Huntington and Hopkins names living on in some way."

"We never asked about your home. Is everything okay?"

"Hardly, my dear Pinkie. My studio and home are both casualties of the quake and fire. But that's okay. I saved what's most important."

He pats his camera and bag.

"I'll set up shop again on the far side of Van Ness. I want to see the new city, the one I know will be rebuilt. I want to contribute in my own small way. To record this moment in time that will one day be the past."

Genthe leads them to a survivor of the holocaust that swept through Nob Hill. Where a massive mansion once stood, only a marble columned entrance remains. Genthe sets up his camera and aims it through the opening to the skeleton of City Hall's dome:

"This was once the palatial residence of the Towne family. The widow of the man who built this is quite the civic minded woman."

When he sees the classic, scrolled columns, BB makes a suggestion:

"Wouldn't it be great if this could be saved? After all, the earthquake and fire didn't destroy it. It's like a door from the past to the future."

"Wonderful idea! A monument to the spirit of San Francisco! I'm sure Caroline would agree. I'll have a chat with her!"

He isn't happy, however, with what he sees through his lens:

"This is a great shot, but I'm not satisfied with the lighting. I'll come back in a couple of weeks to capture it in the full moonlight."

BB takes Pinkie's arm and draws her into the entrance frame. From there the entire cityscape unfolds. A sliver of moon hangs in the cloudless sky. From far below the clang clang of a cable car drifts up to BB:

"Mr. Genthe! Do you hear that? It's already happening!"

But when they turn around he's gone. And so is the street. A churning mist invites them into a whirling vortex.

"Come on, Pinkie. I think we're done here."

The moon's faint smile confirms their decision. With a final look to 1906 San Francisco, they join hands and enter the white-gray tunnel.

Back at Headquarters the scene in the hourglass comes to life once more. Relieved and encouraged that all is well, The Council gathers around to watch what unfolds.

CHAPTER SEVENTY-NINE

Old Friends and Acquaintances

As they step through misty fingers, BB recognizes the wavy brick-paved walkway and hitching posts with their distinctive horse heads. The buildings are reminiscent of his 1906 virtual visit, but the sounds and raucous revelry are gone. A familiar chirp interrupts their confusion. Pinkie is thrilled to see their little friend:

"Hunnybird! I'm so glad you're here! I thought we'd lost you when we..."

Hunnybird isn't having any of it. He lets loose a tirade of chirps and chatter. Pinkie listens and nods in agreement:

"You're right. Okay! Okay! We shouldn't have split up. It wasn't fair to you. We promise to stay together now. Right BB?"

But BB is watching the cars passing on the street at the end of the alley:

"Pinkie, we must be in 1963 again!"

"Hunnybird just pointed out our clothes need an update. Better fix that before we get going."

Once they press their watch buttons they're back in style. Pinkie's wearing the same outfit BB remembers from when he first saw her in Escondido. He's in his Hollywood party clothes including the blue jacket and backpack. From the back pocket of his pants the secret signal goes out from Wintergreen's card.

"I'm so glad we're away from all of that misery, BB. I just hope we've done enough to set us free from this year."

"Don't forget I still have to figure out a way to get home to my family."

Hunnybird's insistent chirps guide them to the next corner. Pinkie peers down the street:

"This looks like the area where we met up with Mr. Giannini and his load of supposed garbage."

Hunnybird flies ahead to a massive, eight-story building with a granite façade. He flutters around the entrance to get their attention and then perches on the ledge above. They enter an elegant lobby sparkling with white marble and gold leaf. They gaze up at the coffered ceiling with its creative recessed panels. Heavy mahogany tables and rich carpets create a welcoming atmosphere. The marble counters and bronze teller cages announce the building's purpose. It's a bank, and a prosperous one at that. On the far wall a large oil painting with a familiar face commands the room.

"BB, is that who I think it is?"

As they draw closer, he reads from the brass plate on the bottom of the gold frame:

"Amadeo Pietro Giannini 1870-1949 Founder of Bank of Italy and the Bank of America Banker to the Common Man"

Pinkie stands back to take in the kind face of the man they saw so long ago perched on the seat of an old garbage wagon:

"It looks like he succeeded in helping rebuild San Francisco."

A voice behind them startles her:

"Is there something I can help you with? Open an account perhaps?"

"No thank you. We just wanted to say hello to an old friend."

BB and Pinkie hurry off, leaving the manager clearly confused by this last remark. Hunnybird flies off down the street and crosses to the other side.

"He's got more to show us, Pinkie. Come on!"

This time Hunnybird lands on an awning over the window of a bookstore. They stop to look through the open door. Peering down the store's main aisle they catch their breath at the sight of a huge black and white mural. Massive mountains frame the distinctive view of Yosemite Valley.

"BB, it's almost as if we were there again. What an incredible photo!"

"I *know* I've seen this before."

"That's what I just said."

"No. The picture. It's famous!"

Hunnybird flutters in front of the storefront window and pecks on the glass. The display features books of photos by the same photographer. The focal point is the newest release: Ansel Adams The Eloquent Light. *They stare at the name and then each other, both remembering the face of that frail little boy bathed in his father's tears.*

Just then a familiar clang clang reaches BB's ears:

"Pinkie! I hear a trolley! They're back!"

BB pulls her down the street toward the sound. They're just in time to board a westbound trolley on the California Line. Hunnybird settles into BB's pocket and peaks out at the passing scenes. Before long the hills rise in front of them where new structures replace those annihilated by the firestorm. Safe and comfortable in their cable car seats, they relive that long struggle to the top of Nob Hill where palatial homes of the rich once stood. A park now occupies one corner while a massive cathedral stands in the block just beyond.

A few short blocks later the trolley line ends at Van Ness, ironically the same place where the hulks of burned out cars once proclaimed San Francisco's demise. The grip operator moves to the other end of the car. The conductor announces they are heading back to the harbor. BB and Pinkie wonder what their next move should be. Hunnybird is out of ideas and disappears deeper into BB's pocket. BB makes the decision and steps to the pavement. Barely noticeable, a mist rises from the street. He reaches back to help Pinkie down the steps. As she joins him, they disappear in a swirl of white.

CHAPTER EIGHTY

Uncertain Conclusion

When the haze clears they face a mirrored dream, the placid waters of a small lake.

"Oh, BB! How beautiful!"

BB looks up and around at the familiar portal he thought they'd left behind. The row of stone eagle heads stare straight ahead, their eyes never blinking these many years. The six distinctive columns with their scrolled tops frame the downward steps to the lake.

"Pinkie, we're here again!"

"What do you mean? Where's here?"

"On the porch. Where we were standing looking out at the burning city."

"How's that possible? The sky's clear blue. And we're in some kind of park."

Hunnybird pokes his head out, eager to enjoy this break from the city scene. But he immediately raises an alarm when he spots two ravens across the pond. As they take flight and disappear, BB stiffens:

"It's been a while since we've seen those freaky birds, but you can bet they're up to no good. Let's get out of here!"

They take off to the right on the dirt path to the main road. Two menacing figures march determinedly toward them. BB and Pinkie run back past the portal. Another pair of threatening men plus the ravens stop them in their tracks. Trapped in this pincer of danger they retreat to the portal. The wall of mist begins to swirl, calling them into a funnel of clouds.

"We could be back on the trolley. I don't know. But we can't stay here."

BB makes sure Hunnybird is safely in his pocket. Pinkie grabs his hand and together they step into the unknown. When the agents arrive at the portal, all they see is foliage and a steep grassy slope.

"Where'd they go? Check up that hill! Look in those trees!"

Their boss speaks into a walkie talkie:

"We almost had 'em but they disappeared. We've checked everywhere."

A voice answers back:

"We've lost the signal again. But we guessed right about that stone portal from the fire ruins. The ravens have been keeping an eye on it, and today we struck gold! This place must be significant or they wouldn't have returned. We've got to keep them out of the park until the moon goes dark. By the way, the backpack doesn't have the things they collected. They gave everything away! They'll have to stay in 1963 and start over. And we can take our time getting the statue and those crystals. And time to turn the boy. It's what we've been waiting for. Plus we'll still have Pinkie right where we want her in an endless cycle. Unless she finally gives in and submits to us."

"Can we take a break? It doesn't look like they're coming back."

"We've got the ravens for reconnaissance and the signal will start up again whenever they come back from wherever they've gone. But The Bond doesn't give up easily. Now's not the time to let down our guard. We've lost a lot of ground in this city since 1906, but we can get it back. I'm sending a cohort of agents to help you watch all entrances to the park. If those two try to return, they'll be easily spotted."

When the fog clears, BB and Pinkie are on a hill overlooking San Francisco. But it's the 1906 city, a cauldron of fire! Hunnybird peaks out and then quickly cowers deeper down.

"BB! No! We're back in time again. I can't take this anymore!"

BB recognizes the same meadow where they stood with the demoralized man. They are destined to relive the agonizing hours they know are still to come:

"Why is The Bond doing this? Why can't we just end it?"

Dismay and panic overwhelm them. They embrace, holding each other up physically and emotionally, as once more the tragedy of 1906 unfolds.

"Look, BB! Over there to the left!"

A giant scroll moves across the panorama, consuming the flames and darkness as it unfurls. As they watch, the city transforms into a vibrant, modern metropolis, a city rebuilt, a city reborn. Houses, buildings, and a familiar white cylinder tower replace what was once a wasteland. Pinkie and BB are seeing first hand the answer to despair. Together the determined people dedicated their strength, their labor, their resources to once again create a jewel of a city.

"Look at all those buildings, Pinkie! Everything is clean and new again."

Pinkie suddenly pulls him behind a tree:

"Hunnybird, stay out of sight! They can see us too, BB! Remember? I saw that island in the bay. The one with the searchlight that spotted us on the tower."

BB peeks around the tree but doesn't see a light source. They take a few tentative steps forward. Then throwing all caution aside, they hold their breath and stand in full view, daring anyone who might be watching. Hunnybird pops up from his hiding place and takes a defiant stand on BB's shoulder. Nothing happens! All three breathe out a sigh of relief.

"Things have changed, Pinkie. There isn't such a darkness about this city anymore."

"What about those ravens and those guys at the lake? Not everything's changed."

"I didn't forget. But we're stronger now. We're together. We've accomplished so much. With The Bond's help of course. I'm just not as afraid of the future anymore."

"We can't be careless though. This isn't over yet."

A cool, western wind sweeps the tops of the trees into a slow waltz. Swirls of fog crawl up coastal canyons and roll into the bay. BB spots a sliver of white in the afternoon sky:

"Pinkie! The moon! It's almost gone! What are we supposed to do?"

"I'm not sure. I never got this far before. Oh, BB! I don't want to miss this chance! I don't want to be stuck in 1963 forever!"

A melody drifts from the west. Pinkie's distress turns to determination:

"The carousel! Come on, BB. We've got to get back to that park."

"Are you kidding? We barely escaped and now you want to go back?"

"I know. But The Bond told me when we hear that tune the quest is completed. It's over! We've got to go back."

Hunnybird chirps excitedly. He leads them on a shortcut through the groves until they're on a street familiar to BB:

"This is the same street we took to the park last night. Or was it last year, or decade, or century, or whatever? Who cares? As long as we don't run into those men."

The music grows louder with each block they cover. Before crossing to the park entrance they check around the corner. Up the street two men from the portal are casually munching handfuls of popcorn. The melody continues calling.

"We need a distraction, Pinkie."

"How about Hunnybird? He can annoy them a little and maybe get them to chase him."

Before Hunnybird can nix that idea, a flock of seagulls, their old friends, descends on the men and their popcorn bags. Waving their arms and crouching from the sharp beaks, the henchmen are too consumed by their own self-preservation to notice two teenagers crossing the street and slipping into the park. BB and Pinkie are following the music when a throaty crackle freezes them in their tracks and sends a chill down their spines. Perched high above, the ravens have spotted them.

"BB! We can't outrun them. It won't be long before we're surrounded by agents."

"What agents?"

"Are you still so naïve? Haven't you learned anything? This isn't about taking a trip through time, meeting up with people and having some adventures. This is serious. The Abyss is real. It wants us."

"But we can't give up now, Pinkie! We'll figure something out."

Out of habit he jams his hands into his back pockets so he can think clearly. His fingers touch a small, rumpled card. He draws it out and stares at the familiar lettering:

"No wonder they always seem to know where to find us. It's Wintergreen's card!"

"Why didn't I think of that before? Get rid of it, BB!"

While BB hesitates, unsure of what to do, Hunnybird swoops down and snatches the card. He flies north and deposits it on top of a tower of the Golden Gate Bridge. He races back to announce his accomplishment. Pinkie laughs at his ingenious solution:

"Let's see them track us now! But we still have those two to deal with!"

With a final crackle of victory, the ravens take flight to deliver the report. However, a loud screech announces the arrival of their defender. With its sharp, powerful talons the huge eagle rips and slashes, coming away with several feathers in its grasp and a bloody clump of flesh in its beak. Strong wings batter the pair of sentries and send them plummeting to the earth. With the eagle circling above, the ravens cower on the ground.

"Hurry up, BB. We're safe for now!"

Running down the park road they glimpse the pillars and blue dome of the carousel through the trees. Music pulls them to the colorful animals behind the glass panels.

"BB, I *know* we're supposed to be here. Come on! Let's take a ride!"

Racing through the entrance and onto the carousel platform, they have a variety of fanciful creatures to choose from. A zebra, an ostrich, a rooster and a chicken. A lion, giraffe, tiger, stork, and even a giant frog. A cat and a goat with huge curly horns. Their paint could use a touch up, and the landscape panels are fading beyond recognition. Even so, the music lifts their hearts.

Pinkie can hardly contain her excitement. She disappears behind BB in search of her perfect ride. Just as the carousel begins to move, he hops on a cream-colored stallion with a flowing tail. The animals pump up and down, slowly gathering speed. BB grips the pole, leans back and closes his eyes, lost in the pure joy of escape. After the first circle, he searches ahead and behind hoping to spot Pinkie. But she's not on the ride! She's watching from the platform with Hunnybird on her shoulder. She smiles wistfully and waves. BB calls to her:

"Come on! Hop on before it gets going too fast!"

As the carousel speeds up, Pinkie starts running alongside. Hunnybird flutters to stay close, chirping a message only Pinkie understands.

"I can't, BB. They won't let me."

"Who? What's stopping you? Come with me!"

"The Bond says no."

"Why trust them? How do you know they even care about you?"

"I *have* learned to trust The Bond. I hope you'll learn to trust them too."

"I thought you wanted to get out of 1963?"

"I do! But I guess we didn't finish the quest. We gave everything away."

Pinkie can't keep up. She stops to wait for BB to circle around one more time. Tears well up, but she bravely brushes them away before he sees:

"So long, BB. I hope we meet again."

BB calls over his shoulder as he passes once more:

"That's not fair! Why can't we both go?"

When he comes around the next time, she's gone and so is Hunnybird. His heart breaking, BB lifts his face and cries out:

"I've lost her! I've let her down! Again! It's all my fault!"

BB has no idea what he's supposed to do and he has no one to talk things over with. He panics at the thought of being alone. His heart pounds faster and faster. And then he remembers something Pinkie once told him: "Faith cannot be questioned, only lived."

"Well then let's finish this!"

The carousel picks up speed. The music spins out of control into a single, high-pitched whine. Overhead the dome dissolves. The surrounding glass walls explode into tiny bits and pieces that swirl and float upward. His body follows the spinning shards into the sky. At home on his shelf the last grain of sand falls and the hourglass shuts down.

Back in Bond Headquarters, the team is assembled to celebrate this victory over The Abyss.

Director: "Mission accomplished! Good job everyone!"

Striker: "I'm still not sure what we've accomplished, but it's good to see Pinkie released."

Lady Grace: "I was really worried when we found out they lost everything they'd collected. It was all so confusing. I was sure it was all over for them."

Agent Allen: "I thought they were just supposed to collect the artifacts and we could bring them in."

The Director leans forward, bracing himself on his forearms and clasped hands:

"The Bond was watching what they *did* with those artifacts, those gifts they were given. Would they be so focused on hanging onto them and miss out on opportunities to help others? It wasn't until the last one was gone that The Bond allowed us to bring them back."

A fluttering of yellow lands on his desk.

"And you too, Hunnybird! Welcome home!"

Hunnybird flies to each of the Council members enjoying their approval and praise.

Director: "This was the first of many lessons BB needs to learn if he's going to be that strong, positive influence his generation needs. He's starting to learn how what he does can affect people and also how they can have an impact on him."

Lady Grace: "But how will he know? How will he find out they were successful?"

Director: "Don't worry. He'll get the message. And he'll realize he's been changed. That was the real quest. Pinkie needed a partner to move on, and he needed to be brought on board."

Lady Grace: "I really like BB in spite of his flaws. And I think Pinkie trusts him more now. But I'm worried about the way those two were so easily split up by The Abyss. They're both so young!"

Agent Allen: "I still wonder if he's the right choice. You know how quickly we lost that last one. Plus The Abyss still seems to be one step ahead of us in spite of all we do to help. Even with the hourglass and the wall to remind us of The Bond's strength, sometimes it's hard to not lose hope."

Striker: "Why can't we know more about these quests. I don't like being in the dark!"

Director: "No one but The Bond can see down that path. If you can't trust The Bond, you won't be of any help."

Lady Grace: "So now that he's back home, what's next?"

Director: "This mission has just begun. Pinkie is back with the team and The Bond plans to keep BB's Friday nights busy all summer long."

Striker: "But what about Pinkie? Why can't we bring her in?"

The Director shifts to a serious tone as he stands and paces the room:

"We can't be absolutely sure of those two yet. The pull of The Abyss is still strong, even with Pinkie. The fewer people who know the location of our headquarters and The Bond's source, the better. I've been watching the perimeter of the city. The darkness and fiery red fury are gone for now. The churning clouds have rolled back."

He halts and pivots to address the others:

"But this was just the first battle. The Abyss will be gathering its strength. Everyone be on your guard!"

CHAPTER EIGHTY-ONE

Endings and Beginnings

BB turns over and hugs his pillow. His senses stir before his body fully awakens.

"Hmmmm... Bacon. I smell bacon."

And then there's a familiar tapping at his window. His eyes fly open.

"Hunnybird!"

He flings off the covers and leaps to the window. But it's only a pesky finch conversing with its reflection. BB's shoulders droop. He turns around and spots a backpack. But it's just his regular school one. Nothing inside. Except a wallet! But no. It's the one he got for his last birthday. Empty as usual. The hourglass is right where he left it. He reads the inscription: "Time and history and the future are in your hands."

"Well that about sums up the past two weeks. Weeks! Oh no! How do I explain to my parents where I've been? They must have been worried about me. Maybe even sent out a search party!"

Before he can come up with an answer, his mom calls from downstairs:

"Heybert! Time to get up! I have a special breakfast for your first day of work."

"Work? I have a job? That's right. I do *have a job!"*

BB checks his appearance in the bathroom mirror. He adjusts his slept-in clothes and splashes water on his face. Shoving his hands into his front pockets to straighten them out, he feels something familiar. He pulls out a small, slightly blackened chunk of redwood. Gently rubbing his finger over it, BB recalls how its power impacted so many lives. He hurries to his dresser and opens the bottom drawer. It's been years since he's thought of that special bag. Spreading the drawstrings he peers down at the cherry blossoms, still as fresh as that day they floated onto his head. Carefully he drops in the wooden fragment and returns his treasure trove to its secret spot.

His dad and brother are already at the breakfast table when BB comes down the stairs. His mom cheerfully greets him:

"I hope you got a good night's sleep. I made scrambled eggs and bacon. And

I tried a new recipe. Cinnamon rolls! I hope you like them."

BB's mind flashes back to the last time he ate in this house. The exact same breakfast. Pinkie and her aunt and uncle sitting around the table. But now it's his own family. His dad concentrates on his plate of food. Johnathan keeps giving him nervous looks. It's as if they're waiting for an explosion.

"An explosion! That's right. I did explode the last time we were together. I'll just pretend it didn't happen. Just like I'll pretend the last weeks didn't happen. Maybe they really didn't. I'm not sure of anything right now."

He sits in his regular place and munches on some bacon and a sweet roll. Still no comment from his dad. Thankfully his mom keeps up the breakfast banter:

"You look nice this morning, Heybert."

"Thanks, Mom."

"I'm sorry about your summer plans."

His dad looks up and gives a firm pronouncement:

"It's time the boy learns life doesn't always go the way you want it to."

In his mind BB is in total agreement:

"You've got that right!"

And then his thoughts begin to swirl:

"Has it been only one night? REALLY? Was it all some crazy dream?"

His mom continues her gentle comments:

"I'm sure you'll do well at the job interview."

"Job interview?"

His dad looks up accusingly and firmly sets down his fork:

"Don't tell me you're not going!"

"Sure I am! Right! What time was it again? Eight o'clock?"

He checks his watch. His old watch with the scratched face.

"I'd better get going. Don't want to be late."

BB shoves down some eggs and jumps up from the table. He gives his mouth a quick swipe with his napkin and bolts out the door. His parents stare after him dumbfounded.

"That's certainly a change from last night. Maybe my talk finally got through to him."

BB has plenty of time before he meets with Mr. Carlson, so he decides to stroll through the downtown. His thoughts tumble together:

"Maybe this job won't be so bad. Wish we had some places to hang out like they used to. Wonder what my friends are doing. Senior year should be a good time. I might mix things up a little. Try something different."

BB arrives at the grocery store and asks to see the store manager. The checkout woman gives him a wink and a smile:

"He's standing right next to you!"

BB had ignored the "bag boy" working at the end of the counter. He looks up into the kind face of a tall, slender gentleman wearing a store apron.

"Hello, Mr. Carlson. I'm Heybert Bradford. My friends call me BB."

"Nice to meet you, BB. But you can call me Jack like everyone else around here. Especially now that you're joining the team."

"I *am?* I mean, yes sir! But I thought today was just an interview."

"Come on back to the office and let's chat a bit."

BB follows Mr. Carlson to a small, cluttered office. Obviously this manager doesn't spend his days sitting behind a desk.

"Your dad assured me you were ready for this job. We're always looking for eager workers who are ready to help people."

BB silently thanks his father for focusing on only his good qualities. He does know how to work hard and be helpful when he wants to.

"There's no fancy title to the job. You'll be helping out wherever we need you… sweeping, helping shoppers find items, bagging groceries."

"Sounds good, Mr. Carlson. When do you want me to start?"

"I'll pay you for a five-day week, Monday through Friday. You young folks need your summer weekends for some fun."

"That's great! Do I need to sign anything?"

"I'll take care of the paperwork Monday morning. Your handshake will do for now."

Mr. Carlson comes around the desk and extends his hand. BB remembers to give him a firm grip like his dad taught him. Mr. Carlson puts his other hand over BB's. He looks straight into the boy's eyes, a flicker of recognition crossing his face. When he finally lets go, he holds up a finger as if remembering something important:

"Just a minute. I have something else for you. Call it a signing bonus."

He rummages through a pile in the corner and brings out an old cardboard box. On the cover BB spots a name: "Don Clothier"

"This box is full of all sorts of crazy things. A grocery man, beloved in the community, started putting it together back in 1963. When he retired he gave it to a friend in the grocery business who passed it to several others until it came to me. There were no directions except that we would receive a signal if we ever met a young man who was needed. No one has met that boy after all these years. Until now."

"Me? You think it's me?"

"No. I *know* it's you. No more questions. No more information. For now."

Mr. Carlson opens the box and takes out a small cable car, painted in detail, including its route and an advertisement: "I stop at the St. Francis"

BB accepts the curious gift and then remembers his manners:

"Thank you, sir."

He turns to leave and then pauses to call back over his shoulder:

"See you Monday morning!"

Back home BB rushes up to his room, carefully places the miniature car on the shelf, and lightly dusts his hourglass. He lies back on his bed, arms crossed behind his head, staring at his two treasures, thinking about all that has happened. How his life has been turned upside down. How he *has changed.*

He hears a soft "Ding Ding" and sits up straight. This cable car must be more than just some old souvenir. He picks it up again and moves to the window for a better look. Slowly he turns it over and squints at the engraved lettering on the underside. With the tip of his finger he rubs off some of the tarnish:

"Your friend, Friedel S. Klussmann"

His eyes grow wide. His hand trembles when he sees the familiar first name. On the shelf behind him the little hourglass glows briefly, eagerly awaiting the next call from The Bond.

REAL PEOPLE IN HISTORY
(Where first mentioned)

Chapter 1
David Hickey
George Washington

Chapter 2
Abraham Lincoln

Chapter 4
John Foster Dulles
Ronald Reagan

Chapter 6
Thomas Jefferson

Chapter 8
James Smithson (Smithsonian Institution)
Benjamin Franklin

Chapter 15
James Taylor

Chapter 20
The Escondido locations and proprietors are true to 1963
Buddy Holly and the Crickets
Frankie Valli
Elvis Presley

Chapter 21
Martha and the Vandellas
The Drifters

Chapter 22
The Chantays
John Spreckels

Chapter 23
The Chiffons

Chapter 24
Mrs. Mendoza
Larry Lawrence
Marilyn Monroe

Billy Wilder
Charles Lindberg
Thomas Edison
Babe Ruth
Charlie Chaplin

Chapter 25
Al Capone

Chapter 31
Marlon Brando

Chapter 32
George Stanley

Chapter 33
Svend Petersen

Chapter 34
Elizabeth Taylor
Cary Grant

Chapter 35
Paul Newman
John Wayne
John Tartaglia
Joanne Woodward
Jack Lemmon

Chapter 36
Shirley MacLaine
William Randolph Hearst

Chapter 41
Philip K. Wrigley

Chapter 43
Colonel James Boydston Armstrong
Lizzie Armstrong Jones
John Muir

Chapter 45
John Augustus Sutter

Chapter 46
Acknowledgement and thank you to the Washoe Native American Tribe who provided the legends related to Lake Tahoe

Chapter 48
George Hearst

Phoebe Hearst
Julia Morgan
Millicent Hearst
Marion Davies

Chapter 49
Winston Churchill
Charles Lindbergh

Chapter 51
Nunzio Alioto

Chapter 52
Steven Giraudo

Chapter 56
Edsel Ford Fung

Chapter 60
Sarah Lockwood Winchester

Chapter 61
William Wirt Winchester
Annie Pardee Winchester

Chapter 64
Amadeo Giannini
Giobatta Cepollina

Chapter 65
Friedel Fischer Klussmann

Chapter 66
James Woods
Theodore Roosevelt
Victor Hirtzler
Enrico Caruso
Eugene Edward Schmitz

Chapter 67
Mark Hopkins
Leland Stanford
Collis Potter Huntington
Charles Crocker

Chapter 68
Arnold Genthe
Horace (Quintus Horatius Flaccus)

Chapter 71

General Frederick Funston
Captain D. R. Sewell, Engine Company No. 9
Chief Dennis T. Sullivan
P. Kugat, Gunner's Mate 1st Class, Perry
O. Jansen, Chief Boatswain's Mate, Preble
J. Curtin, Chief Electrician, Pike (submarine)
Adolph Claus J. Spreckels
Anna Christina Mangels Spreckels
Marquis de Lafayette

Chapter 72
Jack London
Charmian London

Chapter 74
Louise Marie Boudin
Lucie Boudin
Isadore Boudin

Chapter 77
Ansel Adams

Chapter 78
Caroline Towne

Chapter 81
Don Clothier

ACKNOWLEDGEMENTS

A big thank you to my beta readers and others who read early versions of my manuscript: Amy Concannon, Dave Hotstream, Debbie Graff, Ian Graff, Karina Graff, Will Peters, Rachel Seierstad, Carrie Anne Vogelsang, and Noah Vogelsang.

Thank you to Gene Bonk, who conducted countless eighth grade trips to Washington, D. C., while a teacher. Your details of what encompasses such an undertaking with middle schoolers added authenticity to the opening chapters.

Thank you to Claire Sargenti for your brilliant inspiration involving the hourglass.

Thank you to Judy Shaw Ricci and Bob Shaw for your memories of Escondido 1963 during your high school years.

Thank you to Dave Hotstream for the wonderful original artwork for the book cover.

And finally a thank you to Lee Zabinsky's eighth grade class at Grace Lutheran School in Escondido for your responses to my early manuscript attempts. Your feedback was spot on and extremely valuable to the creation of this final book. Your enthusiastic encouragement inspired me to continue writing this first novel.